BOLD COUNSEL

TIM VICARY

The third novel in the series 'The Trials of Sarah Newby'

White Owl Publications 2013

First published as an ebook by White Owl Publications Ltd 2011

Copyright Tim Vicary 2011

ISBN 13: 978-1482343649

ISBN 10: 1482343649

This book is copyright under the Berne Convention
No reproduction without permission
All rights reserved.

The right of Tim Vicary to be identified as the author of this work has been asserted in accordance with sections 77 and 78 of the copyright Designs and Patents Act 1988

This is a work of pure fiction. Although most of the places in the book exist, any resemblance to real people or events is purely coincidental.

Bold Counsel

Tim Vicary

The third novel in the series 'The Trials of Sarah Newby'

Other books by Tim Vicary

Historical novels

Cat and Mouse
The Monmouth Summer
Nobody's Slave
The Blood Upon the Rose

Legal thrillers

A Game of Proof
A Fatal Verdict

Website: http://www.timvicary.com
Blog: http://timvicary.wordpress.com

1. Fox

THE YOUNG fox's ribs showed through its coat; its belly clung to its backbone. In the starlight before dawn, it was stalking young rabbits. Its eyes blazed bright in its skull as a couple of baby rabbits hopped cautiously out of their burrow, stood on their hind legs to sniff the breeze, and cocked their ears for danger. The fox's jaws drooled, grinning with anticipation.

But his swift, lunging run sent the rabbits scurrying back underground, his teeth snapping uselessly behind them. The brief effort exhausted him. Outside the burrow, he gasped for breath. If he didn't eat today, he would die.

Frantically, he dug down into the burrow, seeking food and shelter. A place to eat, or a place to die. He scrabbled deeper into the earth, with the energy of desperation. His paws grew sore, his nose and eyes were covered with soil.

But the digging intrigued him; another smell, not rabbit, entered his nostrils. A rare, unusual smell. Finally, to his intense delight, he unearthed it; something hard, crunchy and bone-like. He seized the bones in his teeth, and tugged.

They tasted of ancient, rotten meat. But they were hard to loosen. He braced his forepaws against the rock and tugged, growling through his teeth. It was like a game he had played as a cub, with kills his mother brought home. The strong got the best bones, the weak got the rest. But here it was just him and the rock.

At last, almost frantic with exhaustion, he wrenched the bones free and dragged them outside. Dawn was just breaking, a thin lemon glow in the east. Disappointingly, there were only a few tiny scraps of meat between the bones, as hard as old leather. He chewed disconsolately for a while; then, as the sun rose higher, he fell asleep.

He was woken by a draught of air round his nose. He opened his eyes as a crow, wings spread wide, snatched the bones with its beak. Enraged, the young fox leapt up and lunged. But the crow flicked its wings and floated lightly out of reach. Just a yard away, two - cool orange eyes taunted him to follow. When he did, the crow flew ten, twenty yards further, to the edge of his territory.

The fox knew there was no point rushing after birds; they saw you coming, and flew away. Still, he'd nearly caught a pheasant once by stalking it - belly to the ground, nose hidden in the grass, inching one foot forward at a time, waiting for just that moment when the bird felt safe, and looked down to peck at something. *That* was how to get them, by creeping close enough first.

He tried it now. He crept after the crow until he saw where it had landed. On the road, outside his territory. Probably it felt safe there; it could see all around. But the long grass hid the fox's approach. And the crow was too keen on the bones. It pecked at them industriously, seeking the tiny, leathery scraps of meat between the joints.

The fox crouched in the grass, wound tense like a catapult. The crow pecked, then glanced up - not at the fox, but at something behind it. The young fox sprang. A huge growl filled its throat, with rage at the theft.

Then several things happened at once.

The crow dropped the bones and flew up, its wings flapping wildly in alarm.

The fox snatched the bones with its teeth.

And the car, which came roaring round the corner, its driver enjoying the emptiness of the early morning road, swerved wildly as the bird's black wings flashed across the windscreen.

The fox looked to its right, just in time to see death, in the form of a Michelin tyre, coming towards it at sixty miles an hour.

The driver felt a soft thump and braked, slowing enough to see the crushed body of a young fox on the road behind him, but not stopping to get out or see what it held between its jaws.

The bones of a human hand.

2. Family Troubles

THE MOTORCYCLE headlamp sliced the dusk, creating a clear cone of light down the country lane. The rider, crouched behind the headlamp in her black helmet and leathers, felt no urge to twist the grip and surge ahead down the empty road. On this autumn evening she was unusually aware of the gathering darkness all around, the hint of rain, the chill in the air that meant winter was coming. She had never felt entirely at home in the country, and out here now, alone in the dark, she regretted the lights of the city, the demands of her work, the bustle of people all around.

Fallen leaves had blown across the road at the next bend. She slowed the bike to a crawl. If I skid and fall off here, she thought, I could lie for hours before anyone comes. Even longer, if I was waiting for anyone who cared.

It will be all right at home, she told herself, shrugging off the thought. But when she reached her house, in the quiet lane outside the village, no lights were on, as she'd hoped. No children at home, of course - her son Simon lived in town, her daughter Emily was at university. But Bob might have been here, at least. After all, teachers finished at four, didn't they? Not six or seven in the evening as she often did, preparing for court in the morning.

But her husband's school was in Harrogate, not York. He'd been late home more evenings recently than she could count. Sarah Newby wheeled her bike into the garage, and sighed. Bob had tried to persuade her to sell this house and move to Harrogate with him, but she had refused. Stubbornly, grimly, supported by their daughter Emily who loved this house more than Sarah and saw it as her home. But Emily, as Bob pointed out, was hardly ever at home and likely to be living here less and less. Whereas he faced a long daily commute along the A59, one of the most choked roads in the region.

And I work all over the north of England, Sarah thought. Harrogate would have suited me, just as well as York. So why did I refuse?

The answer had little to do with logic. It was a feeling. For the past two years, nothing had seemed right between Sarah and her husband. It had started with that terrible trial of her son, Simon, whom she had defended when Bob believed him guilty of murder. That had opened a rift between them, across which they'd tried to throw flimsy, aerial bridges which often broke down. Then Bob had had an affair with his secretary, which made matters worse. It ended, but Sarah's respect for him was shaken. And so, when he'd wanted to move house ...

She'd just wanted to keep things the same, that was it.

Only nothing stays the same; time changes everything. Children grow up and leave, old priorities fade into new, relationships not constantly rebuilt are washed away like sandcastles by the sea. Even memories alter; what was once vital in the past seems distant, ancient history, a petty storm in the blood, half-remembered.

Sarah shrugged off her gloom and marched determinedly into the house, switching on lights, shrugging off her leathers, shaking out her hair, and putting on jeans and a sweater. The heating was on, at least - she was warm and comfortable. A Mozart string quartet CD filled the air with colour and life. She popped a Thai steamed dinner in the microwave, poured herself a glass of whisky, sat back in a reclining armchair, and ...

Her mobile rang.

It was her daughter, Emily. She was at Cambridge, studying environmental science. Six weeks ago Sarah and Bob had ferried her mountains of teenage kit down there in the Volvo, and settled her into her room at Sidney Sussex College. Since then Sarah had rung Emily most days, sometimes sharing excited, breathless accounts of her new friends and exploits, sometimes getting an embarrassed brush-off when it was not really a suitable time. Tonight, unusually, Emily had rung her. What she wanted to talk about was her boyfriend, Larry.

Larry was three years older than Emily, a post-graduate at Birmingham university. He was a slim, intense young man with a ponytail and wispy beard. He had two main interests in life: saving the planet, and making love to Emily. Often he managed to combine the two, taking Emily away for long weekends to protest at road developments, promote re-cycling or save wetlands for endangered species of birds, but since Emily had moved to Cambridge, this had become more difficult. Neither had much money, transport was difficult, and both found themselves thrown together in groups of vibrant young people where the other was not present.

'I'm scared I might lose him, Mum,' Emily said. 'I want to transfer to Birmingham.'

'What? Emily, don't be silly - you've only just started at Cambridge.'

'Yes, well that's just it. Maybe it's best to move now - before it's too late.'

'Emily, you can't do this. For heavens' sake, think of all the effort you put into getting into Cambridge in the first place. And Larry supported you, didn't he? He was there when you went for the interviews?'

'Yes, but he was applying to do postgraduate studies here as well. If he'd got in, it would have been so much easier.'

'Life's never easy, love, but you can't throw away an opportunity like this. Not even for ...' She checked herself. She'd been going to say *not even for a man,* but clearly that would be the wrong thing to say. Sarah was quite fond of Larry - the boy was good company, and had a certain sexual magnetism to which she, a mother in her late thirties, was not immune - but her ambition for her daughter overrode any concerns for him. Emily, three years ago, had been no more than an average, not particularly bright GCSE student; the way in which she had blossomed since had delighted her mother. Much of that success had been inspired by the confidence her relationship with Larry had given her, so to ditch him was scarcely an option. Still, to think of leaving Cambridge after only six weeks was even worse.

'What's brought this on, darling?'

'Well, he was going to come here on Saturday but he can't, he's got a seminar paper to write, and ...'

For the next half hour Sarah listened to Emily's troubles, and tried to pilot a way through them. By the end she had persuaded her not to seek a transfer. After all Larry *was* coming to visit, just a couple of days later than promised; the course in Cambridge seemed well taught; and Emily was making new friends. But what comforted Emily most of all was Sarah's promise to visit her next week; she had a case in the Court of Appeal in London and would break her journey on the way home.

Sarah smiled as she clicked off the phone. The girl's homesick, she thought, she needs her mother. It was a comforting role, somewhat novel for her. All too often during Emily's teenage years Sarah had been too buried in her work to listen to her daughter's problems. Well, it's never too late to change. She went in search of the steamed Thai dinner, now languishing stone cold in the microwave.

Bob came home while she was eating it. He seemed preoccupied, grunting a brief hullo as he entered the kitchen. He was a tall, skinny man with a close-trimmed beard that was turning grey. His head teacher's suit looked rumpled from hours of travel, and there were marks of orange board marker on one of the sleeves. He ran his hand through his hair as he opened a cupboard.

'Out of coffee again. I mentioned that yesterday.'

'You drink too much of that stuff anyway. It's bad for your heart.'

'My heart's fine.' He shut the cupboard, took a bottle of beer from the fridge, and surveyed the meal she was eating from the plastic carton. 'Anything for me?'

'Look in the freezer. There's a few instant meals, pizzas and things.'

He found a chicken curry, pierced a couple of holes in the cellophane wrapper, and put it in the microwave.

'Welcome home, Bob.'

'What?' Sarah looked up from the file she was reading as she ate. It was the transcript of a murder trial that had taken place 18 years ago - the case that she was taking to London later that week. It was a complicated, interesting case - the first she had presented in the Court of Criminal Appeal. If she succeeded it would be a giant step in her career. She gazed at Bob blankly.

'Nothing. I was just welcoming myself home, since no one else seems interested.' He poured the beer into a glass, and studied the froth with exaggerated care.

'I've had a hard day too, you know.'

'Really? Nothing new there, then.' The microwave pinged and he searched a drawer for a pair of scissors. Then he lifted the plastic curry container out and cut away the cellophane. He swore as steam scalded his fingers and put his hand under the cold tap to soothe it. Then he tipped the curry out of its plastic container onto a cold plate and sat at the kitchen table to eat it. After a few mouthfuls he put the fork down. 'I sometimes wonder what it would be like, you know, to come home to a proper meal, hot from the oven, not bloody plastic like this. Someone to smile at you even ...'

Sarah pushed the papers away, looked up, forced a smile. 'I'm sorry, Bob. How was your day?'

'Pretty good, actually, till I got stuck on that road again. They're digging it up at Green Hammerton. For four weeks, the sign says. That'll add an hour to my day, if not more. If we'd moved when I said ...'

'We've been through that, Bob. A dozen times.'

'And I drive on that road every day.'

She sighed, studying him carefully. His face was pale, the lines on his forehead clear as they often were when he was tired. But there was something else too, beneath the weariness. Something that scared her slightly. 'Bob, do we have to quarrel now?'

It was a rhetorical question, but he affected to consider it as a real one. He lifted a forkful of curry, studied it carefully, then put it down. 'Yes, I think perhaps we do.'

'What? Come on, Bob, we're both tired.'

'Tired of each other, is that what you mean?'

She stared at him, shocked. 'No. Of course I don't mean that.'

'Don't you? Are you sure?' Their eyes met across the table, searching. His face, so familiar from twenty years of marriage, seemed subtly changed. He took a long drink of beer, then put the glass firmly down on the table. 'That's exactly what I mean, Sarah. I'm tired of ...' He waved his arm around the kitchen, whose fittings they had ordered together when they moved into the house, their first really luxurious home. Years ago, it seemed now. ' ... all this.'

'What do you mean?' Tired of the house was bad enough, but she had heard that before. For a moment she had thought he meant tired of *her*.

'I'm tired of this house, I'm tired of the way we live, and ... I want something better.'

His eyes had a look she had never seen in them before. As though she was - not his wife, but someone else.

'Better than me, you mean?' Sarah had never been afraid of confronting monsters. Most of them ran away, if you stared them down.

Not this time.

'Yes. Not to put too fine a point on it, that's exactly what I mean. Better than you.'

It was such a shocking cruel statement from husband to wife that she couldn't quite believe she'd heard it at first. She stared at him, stunned. His face had assumed an expression she had seldom seen, but which fitted him perfectly, without effort. It was the face of a head teacher dealing with a difficult pupil, someone caught bringing drugs into school, perhaps. A bubble of laughter rose in her mind - did he see her as a naughty pupil, a schoolgirl who'd farted in assembly? She bit her lip to keep down the hysteria.

'Better than *me*, you said?'

'I mean it, Sarah. I think - we've changed.'

'You said you want someone *better than me?*' Her hysteria was changing to anger.

'Someone who cooks meals for me, who has time for me, who talks to me when I get home from work, who doesn't spend all day keeping druggies and lowlifes and murderers out of jail, yes! Someone who understands that running a large school isn't some sort of rest cure but something difficult and challenging and worth doing well. Yes, I need someone like that.'

'And I don't do those things?'

'You know perfectly well you don't. Look at this, for example!' He got up, scooped the curry into the bin, and dumped the plate in the sink. 'Why do we eat this crap? Why don't we have something decent for a change?'

'You could go to Tesco if you want. They're open all night. Get something different.'

'*I* could go to Tesco! Not you?'

'I've got work to do. Anyway, I'm happy with this.' She indicated her food with her fork. 'Bob, what do you mean, *someone better?*'

She stared at him coolly, fear trickling down her spine. Fear, and a sort of misery she had hoped she'd never feel again. She'd felt it last year when Bob had taken up with his secretary, an ambitious young woman half his age who'd led him on for months before dumping him for someone younger. Sarah's misery and humiliation had felt like a disease, a sort of rust inside her, as though her energy and confidence were being corroded from within. Sometimes she had felt like collapsing in despair, sometimes like exploding with anger.

'Bob, are you having an affair?'

The pause before he spoke was an answer in itself. He strode to the window, then turned back to face her.

'It's not an affair exactly. That sounds so cheap ...'

'So you *are!*'

'It's more than that, Sarah. Let me explain...'

'Explain? I don't want your explanations, Bob! You're cheating on me - again! That's it, isn't it? All this crap about meals and home cooking and having a little wife to darn your socks and listen to your troubles - you're having an affair! Who is it this time? Another school secretary?'

'We haven't had sex yet, exactly, so it's not really an affair. It's ... different.'

'Don't patronise me, Bob Newby. Who is it this time?'

The pain she felt was sudden and intense. Her fury did something to her chest that made it hard to breathe. She could cope with that, she knew, she always did. But the pain was a wound that had struck deep. It would never go away. It would be there for ever.

'She ... was a supply teacher at my school. She has a couple of young kids. Their father left her. I ... she's had a tough time. She needs my support.'

'Her name, Bob.'

'Sonya. She knows I'm talking to you, I promised her I would. Look, the point is, Sarah, I'm sorry, I haven't started this very well, but I've had this on my mind for days, weeks even. I mean ...'

'How long has this been going on?'

'Since ... the start of this term, more or less. I mean, we've known each other for longer, but ...'

'So when we took Emily down to Cambridge, you were thinking about *her*, were you? This - what's her name? - *Sonya*. That's who you rang from the restaurant.'

'Yes, maybe, but - look, Sarah, the point is, I'm being honest with you, trying to face facts. And the really important fact is that we've changed, you and I. It started with Simon's case and it hasn't got better since. You know it as well as I do. We're not the same people we once were.'

'Nobody is, Bob. People change, they get older. They don't all go off and have affairs, for Christ's sake! With secretaries and supply teachers!'

'It's not like you to be a snob, Sarah. Just because Sonya's a single parent. After all ...' He didn't need to remind Sarah of what she'd been like when they first met. A sixteen year old girl weeping on her desk in his evening class because her mother had insisted she put up her baby for adoption. A baby whose teenage father had left after nearly breaking her arm and giving her a black eye. A school dropout with no future, whose parents despised her. Sarah's next step, had the lanky, idealistic young teacher not fallen in love with her, might have been to snatch her baby from the clutches of the Social Services and the adoption agency, and try to support him by earning money on the street corners of Leeds. Instead of which, here she was, with a successful career at the Bar, a luxury home in a country village by the river, two grown up children, her daughter a student at Cambridge ...

And a husband who wanted *someone better.*

'It's not just an affair, it's something more. Look, Sarah, we've grown apart, that's all. It's not so strange, it's normal these days. Simon and Emily are grown up, they don't need us like they did. We had what we had, Sarah, and it was good - twenty years is a long time to stay married, more than most people manage. But that doesn't mean we should cling to the husk of a relationship when that's all it is. Something whose time has passed.'

'A husk? That's what you call our marriage now - a husk?'

'It's just a way of describing it. The shell of a seed that has flowered and grown ...'

'I know what a husk is, Bob.'

They stared at each other, speechless for a moment. Sarah was oddly aware of the humming of the freezer in the silence. Keeping the ready meals cold.

'And you feel something ... *better* ... for this Sonya, is that it?'

'Better in the sense of more real, more alive, yes.'

'Not a husk.'

'No. I'm sorry, Sarah.'

'Don't!' Her voice was sharp, like a whipcrack. *'Don't* apologize to me, Bob! Not now, not ever! Don't you dare demean us both like that.' She drew a deep breath. The tears were there, not far behind, but something - shock or rage or both - was blocking them. The one thing she'd always been able to control was her voice. Speaking slowly, she relied on it now.

'You came home tonight to tell me this, did you? Not that you wanted a decent meal but that you wanted to leave me. Is that what you're saying?'

He nodded slowly.

'To live with this woman Sonya. You really mean that?'

He nodded again.

'It know it's painful, Sarah, but it may be for the best. You know things haven't really been right between us for a couple of years now. You can't deny it, surely. You don't want me, you want someone from the world you live in - some lawyer, policeman, someone like that. If we divorce, you could marry again. It's not too late. Think of it as a difficult decision that has to be made. In a year from now it may look different.'

'You're not just leaving then, you want a divorce?'

'It seems the best way. Then we'll both be free.'

The hypocrisy of this suddenly overwhelmed her. He was setting her free so he could go to this Sonya of his, with her home cooked meals and understanding! While she could do what? Live alone, look for someone else. For a second she felt an impulse to throw something at him - a plate, a cup, a saucepan - or rush upstairs and shred all his clothes with scissors, throw paint over his Volvo. But the essence of Sarah's character, the one thing that had brought her success, was ferocious determination and titanium self-control. She might not be physically strong, but there was little that could break her. And much as she hated to admit it, part of her - the cool analytical brain she relied on in court - saw some truth in Bob's words. She didn't really love him as she once had - she tolerated him like an old skirt or jacket too comfortable to throw away, but which, when examined critically in the mirror, was no longer fashionable or a even particularly good fit.

But it was one thing to throw away a jacket, quite another when the jacket rejected you. With a huge effort she controlled her rage and spoke. Her voice was husky with tears that must come - *but not yet! Not until he's gone and can't see me.*

'If that's how you see it, Bob, then I think you should go. *Now*, tonight, straight away. Go to this Sonya of yours and tell her I sent you.'

He looked shocked. Whatever response he'd expected, this wasn't the one.

'Only promise me one thing, Bob, will you - for all the years we've had together. When she throws you out, as she probably will one day, don't come crawling back to me. Don't demean yourself like that.'

3. Jason Barnes

'SO YOU threw him out, just like that?'

The solicitor, Lucy Parsons, settled back in her seat opposite Sarah Newby, as their train pulled out of York station. A comfortable, round woman with a vast fund of Yorkshire shrewdness, Lucy had spotted the signs of strain when Sarah arrived at the station. Her skin looked pale and lined, the bounce was gone from her normal brisk stride. She'd explained as the train came in, heaving her bag into the first class carriage with a defiant shrug.

'Bob's having an affair. I told him to leave.'

Lucy gazed at her friend with concern. She was one of Sarah's closest friends and colleagues. She had been the first to entrust her with a steady stream of cases without which a young barrister becomes simply a highly qualified member of the unemployed. When they first met, Sarah had just completed her pupillage. As an 'elderly' novice in her mid thirties, she was exactly the type whom many solicitors avoided. But Lucy had seen something in the clear hazel eyes and determined face that others had missed. *This one's like me*, she'd thought. *She deserves a chance, at least.*

So she'd sent her a few cases and her trust had been amply repaid. Lucy's clients began to experience an unexpected run of success. Sarah's sharp eye for detail and incisive courtroom manner left lying witnesses exposed and badly prepared counsel humiliated. The two women - Lucy short, cheery, and circular, Sarah slender, smart and brisk - began to appear regularly around the courts in York, Leeds and the North-East. Their cases became more challenging, their successes more satisfying. Two years ago their relationship had been tested in the fire of Sarah's controversial defence of her own son, a case which Lucy feared might end her friend's career for good, in a blaze of tabloid publicity and professional disapproval. But they had come out stronger than ever.

Since then they had prospered. Lucy was now a partner in a firm of solicitors in Leeds, and thus able to send a stream of increasingly complex - and lucrative - criminal cases Sarah's way. Hence now, these first class seats, an extravagance they would once have shunned. The comparative comfort made it easier for them to spread out their papers in relative privacy.

But Lucy had no intention of starting work without hearing the full story of Sarah's quarrel with Bob. Sarah gazed out of the window for a while, as the train picked up speed. Then she turned back to Lucy. Her smile was strained, she wore more makeup around the eyes than usual. The sharp lift of her chin, though, was as defiant as ever.

'Well, yes. I told him to get out, and leave me to mourn in peace. Which he did, somewhat to my surprise. Perhaps it's me, I look fiercer than I feel.'

Sarah attempted an ironic, self-deprecating smile. It worked quite well for a second. Then an unwanted, renegade tear trickled out of the corner of her eye. She stared out of the window, and fumbled for a tissue in her bag.

'And this happened when?'

'Monday. Two days ago.'

'And you haven't heard from him since?'

'He sent me a *text* - for Christ's sake - to say he'd be seeing a lawyer about the divorce, and when could he come round for his clothes?'

'Did you answer?'

'I sent him one word - *Wednesday*. Today, while we're in London. Anything left when I get back is going to Oxfam. Every last sock.'

'I'd have done that already. Or cut off the sleeves and shredded his Y-fronts.'

A faint smile crossed Sarah's face. 'I was tempted, Lucy, believe me. But I've had enough publicity. I didn't want to end up in the *News of the World*. Again.'

Their eyes met, remembering the press pack that had pursued them up the steps of York's Crown Court every day of her son's trial. Sarah shook her head slowly.

'I'd no idea of the depths of rage it would rouse. My hands shake when I think of him. It's the betrayal, Lucy. After all these years. The callous self-centred betrayal.'

Her voice, usually so controlled, shook slightly. She attempted another smile.

'So I'm a free woman, for the first time in my life. Or about to be. Kids gone, no pets, now no husband either. It's a new experience. I'll have to learn to enjoy it.'

It was true, Lucy realised. Sarah had left school at fifteen to have a baby, been married and divorced within a year. She'd married Bob and had her second child, Emily, the year after that. While her contemporaries had been finding their independence, Sarah had been battling with the relentless details of motherhood - nappies, ear infections, vaccinations – and simultaneously struggling to catch up with the studies she had missed - GCSEs, A levels, university, finally the Bar exams and Inns of Court School that had qualified her, in her early thirties, as a barrister.

Supported all the way by her faithful husband Bob.

'Were there no signs?' Lucy asked.

'Well, yes, looking back, of course there were signs. For a start, when he believed Simon was guilty, remember? That was hard.'

Simon was Sarah's son by her first husband, Kevin - a randy little gamecock of a lad who had got her pregnant, married her, and lived with her for a year before punching her in the face and running off with an older woman. Bob had tried to be a good stepfather to the boy, but had had little success. Simon hated school and teachers. When he dropped out of school to work on building sites, Bob washed his hands of him. Since Simon's friends were thugs and petty criminals, Bob was shocked but not surprised when his girlfriend was found dead and the lad was charged with her murder. While Sarah had fiercely defended her son, Bob had urged her to stand back and let the law take its course.

'We never really recovered from that,' Sarah said ruefully. 'It's not the sort of thing you can easily forgive or forget. And then of course, there was his affair with that wretched Stephanie. I should have slung him out then, looking back on it. Only he looked so hurt and pathetic when she dumped him. I thought he'd learned his lesson. And after all, I wasn't entirely free of blame.'

'Terry Bateson, you mean?' Lucy raised an eyebrow quizzically. She had often wondered about Sarah and the handsome, widowed detective. There was a certain chemistry between them; maybe Bob had seen that too.

'Mm. There was a moment ... but if I'd let it go further, who knows where we'd be now? My reputation in the trashcan, I suppose, for starters.'

Lucy smiled. Despite the shocks Sarah had endured in her life, her attitudes could be surprisingly conventional. But she had learned early how harshly the world could condemn.

'That was then, this is now. He's a widower, Sarah. Needs someone to look after him.'

'With two little girls who'll soon be teenagers. You think I'm looking for that sort of burden? Anyway, I don't need a man, Lucy, do I? Look at all the trouble they cause. This is our time, the women's century - you read about it in all the papers. It's men who find loneliness difficult, not women. Look here, I read it yesterday.'

She pulled a newspaper clipping from her briefcase and thrust it across the table. It looked odd, Lucy thought. Sarah usually kept her papers clean and neat; this was folded and crumpled, as though it had got wet and been dried.

'See? I'm bang up to date.' She smiled brightly and stared out of the window while Lucy read quickly. Men, the feminist writer suggested, were surplus to female requirements. Happiness meant independence and freedom. 'The trouble is,' she continued as Lucy looked up. 'It may take a while to get used to. But then, there's always work to keep me going.'

'Yes. Including this,' Lucy said, looking at the bundle of papers on the table between them. 'The appeal of Jason Barnes.'

For the next two hours they worked diligently through the case they were travelling to London to present. It was an exciting opportunity - their first case before the Court of Criminal Appeal. It had come to Lucy out of age and desperation. Jason Barnes had been convicted of murder 18 years ago, and his original appeal had been dismissed. Despite that, Barnes had stubbornly persisted in maintaining his innocence, making it impossible for him to be released on parole. His original legal team had retired, holding out little hope of success. And so the case had come to Lucy, the newest partner in her firm, no one else expressing any interest.

Jason Barnes had been convicted of the murder of a girl called Brenda Stokes, a student at York university. Brenda had been 20, Jason a year older. It was an unusual case because Brenda's body had never been never found. But she was last seen driving away from a party in a car with Jason. Jason had been quite drunk and aggressive at the party, and Brenda had a reputation for being promiscuous.

When Brenda's flatmate reported her missing the police interviewed Jason, who claimed he'd dropped her off near her lodgings in Bishopthorpe. They saw some scratches on his face which he said were caused by a fight with a cat. They asked whose car he'd been driving. 'My mate's,' he said. 'He lent it to me for the night.' He gave the name of a friend who'd initially lied to support him. The police had examined the friend's car and found nothing suspicious.

But unfortunately for Jason, he'd knocked over a motorbike in the university car park as he left the party. When the owner saw him, he'd laughed and given him the finger. The furious owner had noted the car's number and told the police. It matched, not the car Jason said he'd been driving, but a stolen car which had been found torched near Jason's house in Leeds, that same night.

So Jason was interviewed again. This time he changed his story. Okay, he admitted, he had nicked the car and torched it. And his face had been scratched by Brenda, not a cat. After the party he'd driven Brenda to Landing Lane, a quiet place by the river Ouse, and asked her to have sex with him (not an unreasonable request given her reputation) When she refused, a row had erupted. She'd scratched his face, stormed out of the car and flounced off into the night. That was the last he'd seen of her, he claimed.

But the police found a torch, stained with blood, in the bushes beside the river where he claimed to have left her. This was before the days of DNA but it matched Brenda's blood group. The owner of the stolen car recognised the torch. He kept it in the glove pocket, he said, for emergencies. In the blood on the torch was Jason's fingerprint. As a result he was charged with her murder.

Despite a massive police search, Brenda's body was never found. This, clearly, weakened the police case. But then, while Jason was on remand, his cellmate, Brian Winnick, made a statement. Jason had boasted to him about killing Brenda, he said. He'd hit her over the head with the torch because she'd refused to have sex with him. When he'd realised she was dead he'd thrown her body in the river and watched it float away. After that he'd driven home to Leeds and torched the car to hide the bloodstains. Jason denied all this, but Brian Winnick stood by his statement in court. This, together with the murder weapon - the bloodstained torch - and Jason's lies about the stolen car, convinced the jury of his guilt. He was sentenced to life imprisonment. His first appeal failed and, because of his continued protestations of innocence, he'd never been eligible for parole.

The basis of this new appeal that Sarah was travelling to London to present was the evidence of a solicitor, Raymond Crosse, who had visited Brian Winnick in hospital last year, shortly before he died. Mr Crosse claimed that Brian Winnick told him that his evidence against Jason Barnes was a lie. He had made it all up, he said, so that the police would let him off a serious charge of drug dealing. He had seen nothing wrong with this at the time but now he wanted to put things right before he died.

'Tell me about this witness,' Sarah said. 'Raymond Crosse. What's he like?'

'Middle-aged criminal solicitor. Bald, baggy suit, worn down by the job. Talks to ten different liars every day.' Lucy shrugged. 'Don't we all?'

'Will he impress the judges?'

'Should do. He seems honest. I think he believes what he's saying, why wouldn't he? It's whether Winnick was telling the truth, that's the question.'

Sarah grimaced. 'It would help if this man Crosse had got Winnick to sign this statement, on oath, before he died. What was he thinking of, for heaven's sake?'

'Expecting his client to live, I suppose. They often do.'

'Yes, well this one didn't.' Sarah studied the papers. 'What about this other witness, Amanda Carr? What's she like?'

'Perfectly decent, reliable. Married, two kids. Senior nurse at York District. Just a trainee back then, of course.'

'Likely to make a good impression in court?'

'If she's called. Your first problem is to get them to consider her evidence at all. Since it was dismissed in the original appeal.'

'Oh, I think I we've got a fair chance of that. Rules on disclosure have tightened up a lot since then. But whether they let her take the stand, that's another matter. You can't put much reliance on anyone's memory after 18 years. It's her statement at the time that matters most. And the fact that the police suppressed it. Or lost it, as they claim.'

The two women re-read the statement carefully. On the night when she disappeared, Brenda Stokes had been wearing a school blazer, white blouse, and a short black miniskirt. Amusing and provocative, no doubt, on a well-developed nineteen year old. She had left the party with Jason apparently drunk and happy, in the stolen car. At four a.m. that morning, Amanda Carr had been driving home from a different party at Naburn Maternity Hospital when she had passed a young woman with long dark hair, wearing a schoolgirl outfit, walking towards her on a country road.

'So if it *was* Brenda that she saw, she was still alive at four. Two miles away from where Jason claims she left him by the river at - when?'

'Half one, he says. And a man taking his dog for a walk saw the remains of the car just outside Leeds at five thirty. It was already burnt out - a black shell.'

'So if Brenda was still alive and running away from him at four, that would give Jason just an hour and half to catch her, kill her, dispose of her body, drive to Leeds and torch the car. Less, because the car wasn't even smoking when the dog walker saw it. It's not possible.'

'Which is why the police didn't believe her,' Lucy said. 'After all, she only saw her for a second, and can't describe her face.'

'Hm,' Sarah mused. 'Long dark hair, schoolgirl clothes. They'll claim she's a fantasist, made it all up after she read the story in the newspaper. I'd say the same, in their shoes. But still ... what if it *was* Brenda she saw on Naburn Lane at four a.m., and Jason didn't kill her, what happened? Where did she go?'

Lucy shrugged. 'If we knew that ...'

'We'd know everything. But we're not detectives, Mrs Watson, just lawyers.' Sarah gave a wry grin. 'What about this bloodstained torch. With his fingerprint in her blood. Remind me, Lucy, how does our client explain that?'

Lucy sighed. 'Because, according to his story, when he asked her for sex ...'

'Suggested was the word he used ...'

'Okay, *suggested* they might have sex, she attacked him. Ripped his face with her nails. So, in self-defence of course, he lightly punched her on the nose. Like you do. And her nose unfortunately bled on his hands. Whereupon she got out of the car and flounced off into the night. Never to be seen again.'

'And the torch. With his bloodstained fingerprint?'

'He found it in the car and got out to look for her. Wandered round saying he was sorry and offering her a lift. Only she'd disappeared. So he chucked it in the bushes and drove off.'

A waiter appeared, pushing a trolley. Sarah took a black coffee, poured elegantly from a china pot. Lucy had a cappuccino and croissant. As the waiter left she buttered it enthusiastically, spreading flakes of hot croissant over the papers between them.

'Well, the main thing is the false confession.'

'Yes. If I get that into court we stand a chance. Otherwise we're sunk. Amanda Carr is incidental to that, really. And the other thing, of course, is this detective - what's his name? Baxter. The one who led the investigation.'

'Yes, nasty piece of work. I've made notes on him.'

They fell silent again, sipping coffee and studying the details of the confession their client was alleged to have made to Brian Winnick while on remand. Winnick had been a drug dealer who occasionally supplemented his income by informing to the police. Jason's original defence team had tried hard to get Winnick's evidence excluded, on the grounds that the man had been told what to say. The investigating officer, Robert Baxter, had denied this strongly.

'It stinks,' Sarah said. 'It's a classic police ploy when they can't get enough evidence. The judge should have thrown it out on the spot. Trouble is, once a decision has been made, it's not easy to overturn it. Judges are like everyone else; they protect their learned friends. Especially from northern fishwives like us.'

She and Lucy spent the rest of the journey re-reading the transcripts of the original trial and first appeal, as well as the statements of Raymond Crosse and Amanda Carr. Sarah's first struggle would be to get this evidence into court at all. Even if she managed that, she still had a mountain to climb. Approaching London, two hours later, both she and Lucy felt daunted. They saw, more clearly than before, why none of the senior partners in Lucy's firm had taken the case on.

Travelling in a taxi to Pentonville, Sarah asked what their client was like. Lucy wrinkled her nose in distaste.

'Average lowlife thug. Hates the world for what it's done to him. Hates women because he never sees any. Apart from that he's quite nice.'

Sarah laughed - her first that day. 'So tempting you make him sound! And we've travelled all this way to see him.'

'Don't expect much intelligent conversation. He'll be undressing you with his eyes the moment you walk into the room. Me, he didn't bother.'

Lucy's prediction proved accurate. Jason was a short man in a black sleeveless teeshirt. The muscles of his arms and upper body bulged in a way that suggested long hours in the prison gym. He was light on his feet, and his hair was cut short, close to his scalp. His face was set in a bitter, cold sneer and, as Lucy had predicted, his eyes focussed first on Sarah's blouse, and then travelled lower.

'Where's the brief?' he asked, without glancing at Lucy.

'This is your barrister, Mrs Newby,' Lucy said, emphasising the *Mrs*. 'She's come to meet you before the hearing tomorrow.'

'You a QC?' he asked, his eyes travelling up to Sarah's face for the first time.

'Not yet,' she answered coolly. 'In a few years maybe.'

'Christ.' He shifted the gum in his mouth, and glared at Lucy. 'Not even a QC!'

'Mrs Newby's a very competent lawyer,' said Lucy firmly. 'She's fully up to speed on your case. More competent than many QCs, in my opinion. That's why I chose her.'

Jason studied Lucy, considering. 'She'd better be,' he said at last. He turned to Sarah. 'This matters to me, you know, it's important. I've been banged up for 18 years for something I didn't do. Get that detail, did you?'

'Of course. The fact that you could have gained parole by admitting your guilt is something the judges will have to take into account. It's not the main point, but it's not insignificant.'

'So what *is* the main point then, darling? In your professional opinion.' Once again the eyes focussed involuntarily on her blouse.

Sarah sighed, and began to go through the details she had been studying on the train. At each stage she asked for his comments, to see if they tallied. It was not her job, of course, to sit in judgement on him, but she was encouraged to see that his story had a certain coherence. It was plausible, at least, and his stubborn refusal to accept parole showed his commitment to it. There were a few prisoners, she knew, who actually feared the outside world, and preferred life inside, but this man showed no signs of being one of them. At the end of their discussion she smiled.

'Well, Mr Barnes, that's our case. I won't pretend that it's watertight, but we have a chance, and I'll do the best I can.'

His eyes met hers, as they had done more frequently as the discussion progressed, an involuntary acknowledgment that she had a brain as well as breasts. For a second, anxiety replaced the bitter lust in his eyes.

'Yeah, well make sure you do, darling, all right? I want my life back again.'

'The world has changed a bit since you were young,' Sarah said sympathetically. 'If we win, you may need some help settling down.'

It was kindly meant, but the comment fell on polluted ground. His face assumed a mocking leer which, she imagined, was uncannily like the expression Brenda Stokes might have seen on the face of her murderer.

'What's up, darlin', hubby run off, has he?' If the eyes had undressed her before, they were stripping her now. Sarah felt an angry flush warming her cheeks. Was her pain so obvious? Jason shifted the gum in his mouth, and laughed. 'Nah, I'm not that desperate. You just get me out. I'll sort out the totty on me own.'

'Charmer, isn't he?' said Lucy, as the prison gates closed behind them. 'Huge benefit to society, if we do manage to get him out.'

Sarah searched the street for the taxi they had ordered. 'Maybe Bob was right,' she said. 'I'd have been better off as a schoolteacher. Got more respect, at least.'

As they walked towards the taxi, a group of schoolchildren surged towards them, swearing at a teacher who was failing to control them.

'Or maybe not,' said Lucy, watching. 'After all, we've only got one delinquent client, not thirty. And he's still locked up. So far, at least.'

4. Fingers of Death

'STOP THE car! Gary, he's doing it!'

'Just hold on, you little bugger! There's services in three miles.'

'He can't wait! Mum, the seat's wet!'

'For God's sake, Gary, stop here!'

'Shit. OK, get the little pisser out. You take him, Shar.'

The car, a blue Ford Orion with a rusting front wing and a yellow passenger door that Gary had promised to respray three months ago, screeched to a halt on the hard shoulder, taking another millimetre of rubber off the suspect front tyres. Sharon dumped her joint in the ashtray and lurched out onto the tarmac. She wrenched open the rear door and dragged her youngest, the dribbling Wayne, out onto the road, yanking his tracksuit bottoms down to his knees. They were already soaked with warm urine. A chorus of curses about the damp seat came from his two brothers. Then, before Sharon or Gary could stop them, the boys were out of the car and exploring the hard shoulder by themselves. A 40 ton wagon swerved violently as it passed them, the trucker leaning on his horn as the Orion shuddered in its wake.

'Oi! Declan! Sean! Get back here, you little bastards!'

By the time Gary hauled himself out of the car the kids were away, on some stupid mission of their own. Gary cursed - they were Sharon's kids, not his, and paid him no more respect than his heavy hand, erratically applied, could enforce. No doubt they hoped he would leave their lives soon, just as their own fathers had left Sharon before him.

Another wagon thundered past, its driver's eyes widening with shock at the boys an inch from his wheels. Fall under it, why don't you, Gary thought. As far as he cared they could run under a truck anytime they chose, but he guessed Sharon would see it differently. And since she was the best shag in years, and the kid in her belly was, in all probability, his, he felt a dreary sense of duty to her kids. After all, this was supposed to be a family holiday, a celebration of seven months of him and Sharon shacking up together, and it would be a poor start to lose two kids before they even reached the beach. So he lumbered after the boys, swearing, as they sprinted away around the bend.

Gary was no runner, and the weight of his gut held him back. He had stopped the car on a slip road, of all places, so the traffic came towards him around a tight bend, only seeing the Orion at the last moment. Several swerved dramatically, leaning on their horns or raising fingers as they zoomed into the distance. Gary glanced over his shoulder and saw Sharon holding out the half naked Wayne, pissing like a cherub plumbed into the mains. Then he looked ahead, to see where the boys were heading.

They had totally disappeared.

'Shite!' Was this a place to play hide and seek? He'd crack their stupid heads together when he caught them, Sharon or no Sharon. 'Come back here, you little fuckers! If you don't, I'll ...'

He lumbered on, further round the corner, until Sharon was out of sight. Still no sign. To his right, on the inside of the bend, was a wilderness area, just grass and bushes, not even much litter to show human habitation. A bird, a hawk or something, hovered motionless overhead. Gary swore. If the boys had gone in there he'd never find them. He turned to walk back.

'Sod it, we'll go without you. Stay here and see how you like it!'

A small stone hit him on the back of the leg. He turned to see Declan and Sean grinning at him from behind a bush. Declan was waving something through the leaves - something brown that wobbled and shook.

'Little bastards. Get back in the car!'

'Look at this, Gary. See what we've found.'

Reluctantly, he went over to look. Coming closer, he saw that Declan was holding some sort of animal - a dog perhaps. No, with that colour it must be a fox. It was in a foul state - its chest and stomach were crushed and its guts hung out like long unfinished sausages. But the head was undamaged and its lips were drawn back, teeth bared in a snarl, as though it had seen its death approaching.

'Watch it, Gary, he'll rip out your throat!'

Declan lunged for him with the jaws but Gary smacked him aside with the back of his hand. 'Where the fuck d'you find that?'

'Down there on the road.'

'Wicked, innit?'

'Can we keep it, Gar - take it in the car?'

'What, that? No way. Piss off - it stinks.'

'Careful, Gar, he'll hear you. Bite off your balls.'

'Yeah, right! She won't want you then, will she, Gary? Chuck you out in the street!'

Sean minced around Gary just out of reach, clutching his crotch and leering at him. 'Ooooh Sharon, can't do it no more!' he mocked, in a high, squeaky voice. 'Fox got me knackers!' Despite himself, Gary laughed. It was the sort of joke he might make himself.

'Chuck that thing, you little pissers, and get back in the car. Before I beat you so hard yours'll never come down.'

'Be nice to foxy, Gar - he's a killer you know. Look what he had in his mouth.'

'What?'

Until now Sean had held one hand behind him. Now he produced it, shockingly. To Gary's horror Sean didn't just have one right hand, but two. A second hand inside the first, bony, skeletal. Long thin fingers of bone jiggled in front of his face. Gary took an involuntary step back, almost into the path of a wagon whose horn, deep-throated, howled its indignation into the distance.

'What the fuck have you got there?'

'Hand, Gary. Fingers of death. All that's left of the last bloke who swore at this fox. So keep your gob clean.'

'Where did you find it?'

'In foxy's mouth, of course. What did I tell you?'

'That's why we're keeping them both.'

'Be a sport, Gar. It's good for a laugh. Think about Wayne.'

'Wayne, yeah. Wayne'll love 'em. He needs toys on this trip.'

Weakening, Gary saw the fun of it. He'd been like them, a few years ago. 'Your Mum, Declan, is not going to want a dead fox in the car.'

Head on one side, Declan conceded the force of this point. 'But she don't have to know, do she? Not till the car's started.'

'A few more puffs on her joint, she'll be too zonked to care.'

'Until suddenly, foxy has a little nibble at her ear ...'

'And the fingers, too - don't forget the fingers ...'

'She'll be that scared, she'll stick her head straight out through the roof.'

'Then she can keep a look out for the filth. And foxy can watch out the window.'

Despite himself, Gary was drawn into the wickedness of it. 'All right, stuff it under your coat. But if it starts to stink, it's going out. I can't drive and puke at the same time.'

5. Hotel Bedroom Blues

THE HOTEL bed was comfortable enough, but Sarah did not sleep well. An intermittent groan from the central heating didn't help. It sounded like a lovesick rhinoceros trapped in the cellar, trying to mate with the boiler. Good luck to it, Sarah thought wryly, it's happier than me. She lay on her back on the crisp newly laundered sheets and gazed at an orange glow on the ceiling from the streetlamp outside.

What's Bob doing now, she wondered, tormenting herself. I hope he's collected his clothes, the bastard. I don't want to see those when I go home. To an empty house, half of the wardrobe bare. Memories gone too - his touch, his smell, the way he reached for me in the night. It used to annoy me sometimes, but now ...

What's he doing now? Reaching out for his - what's her name? *Sonya*. Sarah had never met Sonya, she couldn't put a face to her, but suddenly, unbidden, into her mind came an image, vivid as day, of Bob copulating with this unknown faceless woman. It was so clear and sharp that she swung her legs over the side of the bed and sat up, staring into the darkness of the room. The pain was visible. It was as if a hologram had appeared and she could *see* them doing it right there in front of her. Bob kissing and fondling this woman as he did to her, groaning as he came to his climax, only louder and sooner than he did with her, because she was *new* - new and different and thrilling for him, no doubt, the treacherous shit. The woman's image was clear too - she had a younger fitter body than Sarah, with long fair hair and a face - she peered closer to see the face, but somehow it was always obscured, behind the woman's hair or Bob's arms or his head - *show me your face, damn you, bitch!* I've seen all the rest!

But her mind put no face to the vision. And slowly, as she realised it was a vision projected by her mind, not something that was really, actually there, she began to experiment, allow her mind to play with it. The woman's body became larger and slacker, the thighs dimpled and fat, the breasts sagging, the hair short and grey and permed. But still no face. It was a sort of revenge, to imagine Bob caressing such a faceless monster. But it did little to take away the pain.

She switched on the light, poured herself an overpriced whisky from the minibar, and sat hunched on the bed, nursing the drink. *I shall have to cope with this pain*, she thought, *or it'll drive me mad*. It was a physical pain, a shortness of breath, as if her heart had been bruised. She imagined doing wild things to ease it - scream, commit murder, pour petrol over Bob and set him on fire, run out into the street howling and throw herself into the Thames. Anything to fight back, ease the pain.

But Sarah did none of those things. *I'm not like that*, she told herself firmly. *I can take it, I'm in control. That's who I am, I cannot, I will not let my mind slide into this chaos, this cauldron of boiling emotion. Not even to fight this pain, which is the worst thing anyone's ever done to me, worse than when Kevin punched me in the face and left, worse than when my mother tried to put Simon up for adoption, worse than when I thought Emily was dead, worse than when Simon stood in the dock charged with murder.*

Is it really worse than those things? It feels unbearable now but how did I feel then? Those things were hammer blows to the heart and I survived them all. Somehow. I can't remember how.

Yes, I can. It was work.

Work is what defines me, work is what gives me control, work has always saved me from poverty and despair and chaos. Work is what keeps me sane.

I've come to London to work. Tomorrow I appear in the Court of Criminal Appeal for the very first time. I'm not as well prepared as I should be. The bundle of papers are over there on the desk. I should look at them now.

She stayed hunched on her bed, nursing her whisky. Slowly, the agony faded to a pain that was just seriously bad. The vision of Bob and the woman shrank in her mind to a tiny bubble, a pinhead - gone! She sat, thinking of nothing at all. Then she glanced at her watch.

3.30 a.m.

I met a client in prison today. What was his name?

She couldn't even remember that.

Slowly, as if she'd just run a marathon, she dragged her stiff legs off the bed and crept to the desk. Jason Barnes was the name of her client. If he lost his appeal tomorrow he'd stay in prison for many more years. That would hurt too.

She turned the pages, began to read and make notes.

6. Court of Criminal Appeal

Entering the Royal Courts of Justice next morning, she felt an unaccustomed flutter of nerves. Sarah was used to appearing in court - she did it every day - but this was something different. In the huge echoing foyer she recognised her opponent, a Welshman, Gareth Jones, QC. She had met him briefly once in the Middle Temple, where his name appeared much further up the list of members than hers. He smiled and held out his hand.

'First time in these exalted chambers, is it now? Don't let the surroundings intimidate you, Mrs Newby - it's all stucco and plaster, you know. Just like their Lordships - no one knows if they're alive or dead, half the time.'

'Oh well, I'll have to try and wake them up a little then.' Sarah smiled politely and shook his hand, determined not to let his good manners intimidate her.

A little behind Gareth Jones stood two men in suits. She recognised one; the other, a burly man in his sixties, she did not. Gareth Jones waved an arm in jovial introduction.

'Mrs Newby, this is Detective Superintendent Robert Baxter, retired, who led the original prosecution. And his colleague, Detective Chief Inspector Will Churchill, who is keeping an eye on the case for North Yorkshire police.'

'Gentlemen.' Sarah nodded politely. Will Churchill returned the nod, but Sarah was not deceived. Ancient enmities lurked behind their eyes. Sarah loathed the man for his attempt, two years ago, to prosecute her son Simon for murder; it was not something she could forgive or forget. Churchill, in turn, resented the humiliation she had inflicted on his department in court. He faced her with a look of blank contempt.

The older man was no better. A powerfully built man, he had a florid, pock-marked face that suggested much of his retirement was spent with a bottle. His small eyes narrowed as he fixed her with a hostile intimidating glare. Sarah studied him coolly. She was used to this sort of thing at the start of a trial. She normally encountered it from relatives of criminals whom she prosecuted, but occasionally, as today, it came from the police

'Jason Barnes is an evil bastard who deserves to be locked away for life,' Robert Baxter said without preamble. 'Just you remember that, young woman, when you go into court today.'

'I'll bear it in mind,' said Sarah, surprised and faintly amused. She seldom encountered open aggression from police in court these days. PACE, sensitivity training, and political correctness had ended most of that. But clearly Baxter was one of the old school - no nonsense, arrest the bad guys, and beat the crap out of them or anyone else who got in the way. Maybe she could use that against him if he appeared on the witness stand.

She introduced Lucy, and then went to see her client, who was about to be escorted into the dock by a security guard. Sarah was pleased to see him in a smart suit and tie, at least. She assumed that the scowl on his face was caused by nervousness more than aggression - it was an expression common to many clients in the moments before trial.

'Right then,' he said. 'I hope you know your stuff, missus.'

'So do I,' she said easily. 'We'll look foolish if I don't, won't we?'

'Yeah, but it don't matter so much to you, does it?'

'It matters to my reputation. So don't worry, Jason, I'll be doing my best.'

'Yeah, well, if you do manage to win, I'll take you up west for a meal, get to know each other better. How about that, darlin'?'

'I'll look forward to it,' said Sarah, with a bright professional smile, thinking *in your dreams, buddy*. Still, it was best to keep her client's spirits up so that he went into court looking optimistic. A surly defeatist stare would arouse no sympathy in the stony hearts of the judges.

Sarah and Gareth Jones rose to their feet in the courtroom as the three judges processed solemnly to their ancient leather covered thrones. Their Lordships bowed and sat down, raised high behind a wooden bar intended to give them authority, and also protection from any defendant who might choose to dispute their judgement with a carving knife. Sarah remained on her feet, ready to present her case. Butterflies fluttered beneath her breastbone, but her voice, as usual, was calm, controlled, and, she hoped, persuasive.

'My Lords, as you will have read from my submission, my client has two major, and three minor grounds for appeal. The major grounds being firstly, the total unreliability of his alleged confession, and secondly, the evidence of the witness, Amanda Carr, which was never disclosed to the defence in the original trial.'

She looked up. Three lined faces - two men and a woman - watched her attentively from beneath their white wigs. She saw the fingers of one of them fluttering over the bundle of papers in front of him. I hope he's read it, she thought. Though probably not from three thirty to five in the morning, as I did. She hoped adrenalin would clear the sleep from her mind.

'My first point, my Lords, is the unreliability of the evidence of Brian Winnick. My Lords, in the original trial Brian Winnick gave evidence that Mr Barnes had confessed to murdering Brenda Stokes while they were both remanded in custody in the same cell. That evidence was of crucial importance in Jason Barnes' conviction. The trial judge, His Honour Paul Murphy, made this crystal clear in his remarks to the jury. *'If you believe Mr Winnick, then you must convict,'* he told them. *'If you doubt him, you should acquit.'*

'My Lords, Mr Winnick has recently died of lung cancer. But two days before his death he was visited in hospital by his solicitor, Raymond Crosse. He told Mr Crosse that his evidence at Jason Barnes' trial - and in several other trials - was a lie. Mr Winnick was a criminal, but also a paid police informer. He told these lies, Mr Crosse says, in the hope of leniency and reward from the police. Mr Winnick had become a Christian and wished to atone for the lies he had told, he said. Mr Crosse agreed to return to hospital and take a formal statement under oath, at Mr Winnick's bedside. But before he was able to do so, Mr Winnick died. My Lords, Raymond Crosse is here in court today, and is prepared to give evidence to this effect.'

She paused. This was the first, key point. If Raymond Crosse's evidence was admitted in court, Jason Barnes' appeal had a chance. If not, not.

The senior judge nodded, then glanced towards Sarah's opponent. 'What do you have to say about that, Mr Jones?'

Gareth Jones rose to his feet beside Sarah. His voice, she noted with dismay, sounded even more mellifluous in here than it had outside. How do they learn this in Wales, she wondered. Do two year olds sing for their supper?

'My Lords, I feel this is stretching matters too far. Mr Crosse's evidence is surely hearsay, so it must be inadmissible. There was no mystery about Mr Winnick's status as an informer; it was plain from the outset. The defence made great play with this fact. The learned judge emphasized it too. The jury reached their verdict only after having seen both Jason Barnes and Brian Winnick give evidence in person, on the stand. They were able to judge each man's character for themselves. Now my learned friend seeks to call, not Mr Winnick, but Raymond Crosse. Mr Crosse was not called at the original trial. He has no first hand knowledge of the facts. He did not take a statement from Mr Winnick under oath and there is no witness to corroborate what he says.'

The senior judge nodded. 'Mrs Newby?'

'My Lords, Mr Crosse wrote notes of his conversation with Mr Winnick shortly after he visited him in hospital. These notes were typed up as a formal statement for Mr Winnick to sign before witnesses on his next visit. Unfortunately Mr Crosse did not realise how close Mr Winnick was to death or he would have returned sooner. I submit that under section 23 of the Criminal Justice Act 1988 this evidence is firsthand hearsay and should be allowed.

'My Lords, it is true that the jury in Jason Barnes' trial were aware that Brian Winnick was a police informer. What they did *not* know was that he was a drug dealer whose charge of intent to sell cocaine was reduced to possession only, three weeks *after* Jason Barnes' trial was over. My Lords, Mr Winnick specifically told Mr Crosse that the police, led by er ...' Sarah pretended to consult her file, but she already knew the answer. '... Detective Superintendent Robert Baxter, promised to reduce the charges against him if he gave evidence against Jason Barnes in court. Which he did, resulting in Mr Barnes' conviction.'

She paused, and glanced to her left, where the two detectives sat glaring at her from their seats. Will Churchill looked dapper and smooth; Robert Baxter, beside him, was built like a rugby prop forward.

'My Lords, if Brian Winnick was still alive I would of course have put him on the stand to test his evidence directly. But since that is not possible, I submit that the only way to get at the truth now is to admit the evidence of Mr Crosse. And since Mr Winnick was a principal witness - in fact, perhaps *the* principal witness for the prosecution - at the trial of Jason Barnes, it seems to me that the interests of justice require that this evidence be heard at this appeal.'

She saw eyebrows rise as she spoke, and realised that she was running a risk in lecturing the judges on what was, and what was not, justice. But Sarah had always held the view that there was no sense pussy-footing round in court. If something needed to be said, then it was her job to say it, as forcefully and persuasively as possible, and hope for the required effect. After all, why else did the hood of her gown fold into a neat little pocket at the back? It was there to collect the fee from the grateful client, for arguing his case better than he could hope to do himself.

'Finally, My Lords, I refer you to the statement of the prison chaplain, who is also present in court. He can testify to the state of mind of Mr Winnick in the weeks before his death, and confirm that he spoke of lies which he had told in the past.'

During her last speech she had been aware of a certain amount of whispering from her left, where Gareth Jones was leaning over his shoulder to talk to the two detectives. As she sat down, Gareth Jones got to his feet.

'My Lords, before you decide on the admissibility of this evidence, it may be helpful to hear from the man who my learned friend appears to suspect of misconduct, Detective Superintendent Robert Baxter. He is present here in court.'

The three judges bent their heads together, conferring. The senior judge looked up, a wintry smile on his face. 'Very well, Mr Jones, we will hear Mr Baxter.'

7. School Project

PREDICTABLY, THE fox had not stayed in the car for long. Sharon felt its jaws nibbling her ear just as Gary started the car, and after a brief outburst of hysteria it was dumped a few yards down the road. Sharon's howls of rage were well worth it as far as the boys were concerned, and the resultant quarrel between Sharon and Gary even more so.

'You think that's funny, do you? Letting them bring a fucking corpse into the car?'

'Their idea, not mine. Anyhow, we could have skinned it, made a whatdoyoucallit - fox scarf thing for you to wear.'

'Skin you more like. Keep all your brains in your bollocks, you do.'

Somehow, in the fuss about the fox, the hand stayed in the car, and when they reached the coast Sean smuggled it beneath his pillow. Over the following week he became quite attached to it. He kept it in a bucket with sea creatures, using its long bony fingers to battle crabs' claws. Several times Sharon told him to throw the horrid thing away, but he brought it back to Leeds, stuffed in his tracksuit pocket where he could feel it whenever he wanted. He liked the way the fingers moved in the same way as his own, and wondered if the owner could have cracked the knuckles as he could crack his. He slipped it under the pillow at night where it crunched under his ear.

Half-term over, they went back to school, and his teacher, Ms Sheranski, predictably asked them to write about their holidays. Julie Sheranksi was a probationer, still young and enthusiastic, with little hope of keeping order except through her innocent, encouraging smile. Sean and his classmates fell in love with her and ragged her unmercifully. He put the hand on the table and waited for her reaction. She'd greeted his earlier specimens - a squashed toad, a tropical spider he'd found in a packet of bananas - with a cheerful welcome which had somewhat deflated him. This time, however, he was not disappointed. There was no disguising the appalled, disbelieving shock which drained the blood from Julie Sheranski's face as she surveyed the skeletal fingers on her pupil's desk.

'Where - what's this?'

'It's my hand, miss. I found it on holiday.'

'But - for heaven's sake - where?'

'In a fox's gob.' He launched into an elaborate tale of how he and Declan had been attacked in their caravan by a fox at night. With superhuman courage they had fought it off, chased it back its lair, and found this, the sole physical remains of its last victim who had paid the ultimate price.

'But Sean, this is an adult hand. A fox couldn't kill a grown person.'

Sean's eyes narrowed. 'It was a big fox, miss. Huge. Jaws like Dracula.'

'I'm ... I'm sorry. I'm going to have to show this to the head.'

'Hey, no, miss, you can't have that. It's my hand. I found it.'

'It's a human hand, Sean. It came from a dead person.' Shuddering slightly, she picked it up.

'Yeah, well, he don't need it no more, does he? Give it here - it's mine.'

'Yeah, miss, you can't just take things. We got rights.'

'Stealing, that is. There's laws about that.'

'This hand's going to the head. Sean, you'd better come too. Mr Hudson will want to hear your story for himself.'

8. Cross Examination

AS ROBERT Baxter took the stand Sarah reflected that he was, indeed, a powerfully built man. In his late sixties, he was over six foot, with broad shoulders and a boxer's flattened nose. The only sign of weakness was a slight tremor in the liver-spotted hand that held the Bible as he took the oath - but that might have been anger rather than age. He would have looked a formidable interrogator in his younger days, she thought, to a young tearaway like Jason Barnes - five foot ten on tiptoe and only nineteen years old at the time of his arrest.

Gareth Jones took him smoothly and efficiently through the relevant points. Yes, he had led the investigation into the murder of Brenda Stokes. Yes, he knew that Brian Winnick was a police informer. Yes, it was true that Brian Winnick was a drug dealer who had been sentenced three weeks after Jason Barnes. No, it was quite wrong to suggest that any pressure had been put on Brian Winnick to manufacture evidence.

Gareth Jones sat down, and Sarah rose to her feet.

'Inspector Baxter, when Brian Winnick was held in custody with Jason Barnes, what was he charged with?'

'Possession of Class A drugs with intent to sell.'

'What was the quantity of those drugs, do you recall?'

'Four ounces of cocaine, I believe.'

'A significant amount, then?'

'Significant, but not unusual. He argued that it was for his own personal use, but we didn't believe him. However, we reduced the charges later, before it went to court.'

'Yes, quite. Why did you do that?'

'For two reasons, really. Partly because we didn't think we had enough evidence to get a conviction for supply. And secondly because he'd been helpful to the police.'

'By acting as a witness against Jason Barnes, you mean?'

'That and other matters. His evidence against Barnes was important, of course. It was a very serious case.'

'Indeed. When he eventually came to court, what sentence did he receive?'

'Three months.'

'But he'd already been in custody for that time, so he was immediately released?'

'That's right, yes.'

'So this reduction in sentence was in part, a reward for his evidence against Jason Barnes.'

'In part, yes.'

'I see. Inspector Baxter, how did it come about that Brian Winnick was placed in the same cell on remand as Jason Barnes?'

'I've no idea. That was a matter for the prison authorities.'

'You had no influence over it?'

'No.'

'Really? You're quite sure?'

'Perfectly sure, yes.'

'Inspector, could I direct your attention to paragraph 4 of Brian Winnick's statement in the original trial. Would you read it out for us, please?'

Robert Baxter fumbled for a pair of reading glasses in his breast pocket, and began to read. *'"When I was on remand I was placed in a cell with a man called Jason Barnes. He told me he was charged with the murder of a girl called Brenda Stokes. He said he'd met her at a party and driven her away in a car that he'd stolen. He said when she wouldn't have sex with him he got angry and killed her with a torch he found in the car. He told me he dumped her body in the river so the police would never find it."'*

'You took that statement from Mr Winnick yourself, did you, in Wakefield prison?'

'I did, yes.'

'Thank you. Could you tell us, please, how long after the arrest of Jason Barnes this statement was made?'

'About six months, I believe. It was roughly seven months after Brenda Stokes disappeared.'

'So you had already conducted extensive searches for the body by that time?'

'We had indeed, ma'am, yes.'

'Where did you look?'

Robert Baxter sighed. 'We used police divers to search the river Ouse all the way from York to Selby, fifteen miles or more. We used motorboats and helicopters to search further downstream, all the way to the Humber estuary. We searched the riverbank, too, and many areas in the surrounding countryside. It was a very difficult, tedious, and expensive process, as you can imagine. But unfortunately we did not find a body.'

'Why did you search the river Ouse in particular?'

'Because, under questioning, Jason Barnes told us he had driven Brenda to a secluded spot called Landing Lane near the river. When we searched the surrounding area we found a bloodstained torch with his fingerprint on it. A torch which came from the stolen car.'

'Were you certain it was her blood, at the time?'

'As certain as we could be, ma'am. We didn't have the benefit of DNA in those days, but it matched her blood group. Since then, DNA tests have revealed that the blood does indeed bear a close family resemblance to that of her mother.'

'So you assumed from this that Brenda Stokes had been murdered, and the killer had thrown her body in the river?'

'That seemed highly likely, yes.'

'And you assumed that Jason Barnes was her killer?'

'I was sure of it, ma'am. All the evidence pointed that way.'

'Nonetheless, your case was rather thin, Inspector, wasn't it? One fingerprint, and some blood on a torch. Which Mr Barnes explained quite plausibly by saying that he and Miss Stokes had a violent argument, during which he got blood on his hands from her nosebleed. Then when she ran off into the night he searched for her with the torch.'

'I didn't believe that tale for a minute.'

'But you were worried that the jury might believe him, weren't you, Mr Baxter? Without a body, you couldn't even prove for certain that Brenda Stokes had been killed, let alone dumped in the river, could you? It was only an assumption on your part.'

Robert Baxter sighed. 'You must remember there was an inquest, which returned an open verdict. The coroner accepted that it was possible she had been murdered, and her body washed out to sea. That was the basis on which we proceeded to trial.'

'Nonetheless, you were desperate for more evidence, Inspector Baxter, weren't you? Without this alleged confession, you would never have obtained a conviction.'

The old policeman shook his head forcefully. 'I disagree. We already had a lot of other evidence against Jason Barnes. He was the last person seen with Brenda. We had the torch, and the lies he told about the car. He admitted himself that he had quarrelled with her and attempted to have sex with her against her will. He also had a string of convictions for theft and violence, including violence against women.'

'None of which you could lay before the jury, of course.'

'No, but all the same ...' Baxter shrugged.

'He was a useful suspect, wasn't he?' Sarah sneered.

It was an unwise comment, she realised, as soon as she made it. Robert Baxter drew himself up to his full height, and turned, with great dignity, towards the judges. 'He was the *obvious* suspect, Mr Lords. All the evidence pointed clearly in his direction. The jury recognised this in their verdict.'

'Let's return to this alleged confession, shall we?' Sarah said, trying to recover. 'You must have been hugely relieved when it confirmed all your previous assumptions.'

'I was pleased, naturally.'

'Were you surprised?'

'Not really, no.' A wary look crossed Robert Baxter's face, as if he guessed what was coming. But Sarah was not ready, yet, to make the obvious accusation.

'Presumably you confronted Jason Barnes with it, before the case came to trial?'

'We did, ma'am, yes.'

'And what did he say?'

'He denied it. He refused to admit that he'd confessed to Brian Winnick at all.'

'Is that all? Did he say nothing else?'

The question had a gratifying effect on the burly policeman. Baxter's ruddy face darkened noticeably, and his massive hands gripped the lectern as though they would tear it in two.

'He said if *had* killed her, he wouldn't have dumped the body in the river. He would have dumped it in a slurry pit.'

'And what was your response to that?'

'I questioned him about it forcefully. I asked him if he was saying he really had dumped the body in a slurry pit. He laughed in my face and denied it. Nonetheless ...'

Baxter paused, his face dark, scowling across the court at Jason Barnes. A little imp in Sarah's mind longed to turn round and see the expression on her client's face, but she resisted the temptation.

'... since he occasionally worked as a tractor driver on farms, I felt duty bound to investigate this suggestion. We drained a number of slurry pits ...' Baxter gritted his teeth. '... without result.'

'I see.' Sarah imagined the burly inspector towering over Jason Barnes, steaming with fury after yet another unsuccessful search of a slurry pit. She felt a twinge of pity for her unlovely client. The interrogations, she felt, would have been dramatic.

'Was it as a result of these interrogations that you were accused of assault?'

'What?' Baxter's eyes turned to her in shock.

'My client lodged an official complaint against you,' she said sweetly. 'Don't you remember? He claimed you handcuffed him to a boiling hot radiator and left him there, sitting on the floor, for four hours until he was forced to defecate in his trousers.'

'That's a lie.' Baxter drew a deep breath, trying to control himself. 'There was a full investigation which exonerated me. It was impossible, anyway, because he was interviewed in prison, not in a police station. The prison officers would have noticed.'

'Whereas in a police station it would have been all right?'

'No, of course not. I didn't mean that at all.' Baxter's eyes met hers, with a glare that suggested that he would happily handcuff her to a boiling radiator if he could, and leave her there all night. She looked down, quietly leafing through her notes.

'My client's suggestion, you see, Inspector, is that there was collusion between yourself and the officers in Wakefield prison. You were left alone with Mr Barnes for a considerable period of time.'

'That's not true either. The prison logs totally refute it.'

'So there was no collusion here, or in the placing of Brian Winnick in Jason Barnes's cell?'

'None at all.'

'It just happened, did it?'

'So it seems.'

Baxter's shrug, Sarah thought, was satisfyingly complacent. She glanced up at the bench, where the female judge was studying Robert Baxter with distaste, as if she had just sucked on a lemon.

'Inspector Baxter, how well did you know Brian Winnick? Before this happened, I mean.'

'Winnick?' Baxter shrugged. 'He was a well-known villain. I'd arrested him a number of times, I suppose.'

'For what offences?'

'Drug-dealing, mostly. Burglary, theft.'

'He was a habitual criminal, then? Someone you knew quite well?'

'You could say that, yes.'

'He was a police informer, too, wasn't he? Even before this case?'

'Yes, he was, a very good one. Over a period of five years he fed us information which led to the conviction of many individuals, several of them major players in the drugs trade. All the information he gave us over that period was later corroborated by other sources, or by what we found when we made arrests. I never knew him lie to us.'

'And yet he himself was a convicted drug dealer, wasn't he?'

Robert Baxter sighed again. It was a convincing act, clearly intended to indicate how the wealth of his experience in the real world qualified him to understand criminal activities far better than this jumped-up lady barrister. He turned away from her to address his remarks directly to the three judges.

'He was, yes, my lords. By definition, an informer is only useful if he is himself part of the criminal world. So as I am sure *your lordships* realise, almost all police informers have a criminal record and are involved in criminal activities. If they were honest innocent citizens, they would be no use to us.'

'Indeed.' Sarah noted the wry smiles of acknowledgement from the judges. A point to him, she thought. But she hadn't finished with this man yet. Carefully, she fished a sheet of paper out of her bundle and smoothed it on the lectern in front of her. It was an interesting result of Lucy Parson's detailed researches. She addressed the retired detective in her most polite, disarming tone.

'Detective Superintendent Baxter, when you went to Wakefield Prison to interview Brian Winnick, what was the purpose of your visit?'

A brief frown of hesitation crossed Baxter's brow. 'To interview him about a crime I was investigating, of course.'

'The drug-dealing charge, you mean?' Sarah smiled lightly, watching Baxter's eyes. But the man wasn't stupid. He knew, just as she did, that if Winnick was being held on remand for drug-dealing, he had already been charged. So it would have been against procedure to interview him further about that offence. There must have been another reason.

'No, not that case. It was for a different crime.'

What Baxter's asking himself, Sarah thought, *is whether I know what that crime was. Oh yes, I do, sunshine. Lucy Parsons has found out.*

'What crime was that?'

'It was, er ...' Baxter hesitated '... nothing to do with this case.'

'Really?' Sarah smiled sweetly. 'It was a rape case, wasn't it?'

Baxter glanced towards the judges. 'Do I have to answer that, my lords?'

The senior judge looked at Sarah. 'Is this relevant, Mrs Newby?'

Oh yes it bloody well is, Sarah thought. *Especially now he's given the game away by looking flustered. But will the court allow it, that's the question?* As calmly as she could, she said: 'I believe it is highly relevant, my lords. If you allow me just a few questions I believe the relevance will become abundantly clear.'

'Very well, Mrs Newby. Just as long as we don't go down too many side alleys.'

'I am grateful to your lordships. If you could answer the question, Inspector Baxter?'

'It was a rape case, yes,' Baxter replied, rather sullenly.

'Mr Winnick was suspected of rape, was he? In addition to the drug-dealing charge?'

'He was, yes.'

'And that was the reason you went there to interview him? Not to talk about drug-dealing, or about Jason Barnes, but about an accusation of rape?'

'Yes.'

'I see.' Sarah studied him coolly. Her fish, she hoped, was almost hooked. 'So how did the subject of Jason Barnes come up?'

'I beg your pardon?'

'Well, Inspector, you say you didn't know Mr Winnick was even in the same prison as Jason Barnes, let alone in the same cell. And you went there to interview Brian Winnick about rape, a very serious charge. How did you end up talking about Jason Barnes instead?'

Baxter flushed. His liver-spotted hands tightened on the front of the witness stand. 'Well, it ... he mentioned it, I suppose, because it was such a dramatic thing. I mean, his cellmate had confessed to murder.'

'Was this before, or after, you discussed the accusation of rape?'

Baxter paused, thinking. *Working out how to get out of the trap*, Sarah thought. *But there's no exit. The doors are shut at both ends.*

'I don't remember. It was a long time ago.'

'Oh come now, Mr Baxter. This was an important moment - a big surprise. A breakthrough in a murder investigation. And you're saying you don't remember?'

Baxter glared at her. 'Of course I remember it. I just don't remember exactly when it came up, that's all.'

'But you spent a lot of time on it when it did come up? You took this statement? That must have taken some time.'

'Of course, yes.'

'Did you have time to discuss the rape accusation, too? That was an important matter, as well.'

'Of course we discussed it.'

'And what was the result of that charge?'

'It was later withdrawn.'

'Oh? Why was that?'

'The complainant withdrew the accusation.'

'I see.' Sarah paused. The atmosphere in the court had changed - everyone was suddenly listening and watching with greater intensity than before. Every tone of voice, every nuance of the witness's body language, mattered now. Sarah had still not made the obvious accusation - that Baxter had gone to the prison with the deliberate intention of blackmailing Brian Winnick into giving false evidence against Jason Barnes. But the implication was clear to everyone in court.

'You mean, the woman changed her mind and said she wasn't raped after all?'

'In effect, yes.'

'And you were leading that investigation, were you, Inspector?'

'I was, yes.'

'You spoke to this young woman, did you?'

Here it comes, Sarah thought. She felt the adrenalin surging through her. These were the moments of drama she lived for in court. Lucy's suspicions were right. Ever since she'd seen Robert Baxter outside court this morning, she'd felt sure of her ground. He hesitated now, shuffling slightly in the witness stand. There was a faint tremor in his liver-spotted right hand.

'I ... may have done, yes.'

'May have done, or did?'

'I believe I spoke to her once, yes.'

'And was it very shortly after you spoke to her that she withdrew this charge?'

'Mrs Newby ...' The senior judge was leaning forward. *Damn*, Sarah thought, *they're not going to allow it*. She turned away from the witness towards the bench.

'My Lords, I believe the relevance of these questions is now clear. I seek to establish that my client has been affected by a conspiracy to affect the course of justice. It is my contention that the significance of this alleged confession in Jason Barnes' trial should be wholly discounted on the grounds that his integrity as a witness was compromised by his role as police informer. As Inspector Baxter has testified, he was so valuable to the police that they were prepared to go to almost any lengths to protect him, including, it appears, putting pressure on a rape victim to withdraw her charge. My client believes that this was done to reward Brian Winnick for supplying the police with a false confession.'

Long before she had finished speaking, Gareth Jones was on his feet beside her. 'My Lords, I must protest ...'

The senior judge waved him to silence. 'No need, Mr Jones. Mrs Newby, this is a serious accusation. Do you have any evidence to back it up?'

'Only this, my Lords. A week after she withdrew her accusation, the young woman, Julia Smith, committed suicide. She left this note, saying the police had let her down.'

She produced four photocopies of a small, handwritten suicide note and passed them to the bench and Gareth Jones. The senior judge turned towards Robert Baxter and read it out.

Sorry Mum, I can't take it no more. No one believes me, not even the police. They're all men together, aren't they? He's free now, and they're following me in their cars, just like that Inspector said they would. It's better like this, honest.

Julie

The court was silent for a moment. Then the judge asked Baxter: 'Have you seen this before, Detective Superintendent?'

'It was read out at the inquest, my lords. Medical evidence was offered that the young woman was suffering from a paranoid disorder. The verdict was that she took her own life while of unsound mind. The coroner expressly cleared the police of all misconduct. *As Mrs Newby should know!'*

The last words were hissed directly at Sarah, with a venom quite uncommon in a police witness. The big man's hands shook violently as he spoke.

The judge turned to Sarah, frowning. 'Is that true, Mrs Newby?'

'I have a copy of the coroner's remarks here, my lord.' She fished the papers out from her bundle. 'His actual words were: *"although it is clear that Miss Smith harboured a deep sense of resentment against her alleged attacker and the police who investigated her complaint, it is impossible for this court to say whether her resentment was a product of her paranoid mental state or was grounded in fact. It is the strong desire of this and every law-abiding community that the police should investigate each crime impartially, and there has been no conclusive evidence produced before this court to suggest that in Miss Smith's case, this was not done."'* I submit, my lords, that the warning in the second sentence, combined with the use of the word *conclusive,* imply that there were, in fact, some doubts in the coroner's own mind.'

The judges studied her thoughtfully for a moment. Beside her, Gareth Jones spoke up.

'My Lords, whilst I commend my learned colleague for her ingenuity, I believe we are straying very far from the remit of this court, which is to determine the safety or otherwise of the conviction of Jason Barnes. We are not here to cast unsubstantiated aspersions on the reputation of a retired - and I may add, much decorated - Detective Superintendent.'

'No we bloody well aren't.' The words, shocking in their

vindictiveness, came in a low growl from Robert Baxter. All eyes suddenly turned to where he stood, red-faced with anger. His liver-spotted hands gripped the sides of the lectern, and his powerful shoulders hunched as if at any moment he might rip the thing apart and advance on the object of his fury, the slim lady barrister who stood facing him coolly.

Sarah may have looked cool, but she was trembling from her wig to her heels. This is it, she thought, this is the moment when they see that man for what he is. This is old style policing, the big men who got to the top by crushing everyone in their way. We all hoped it was only criminals who suffered, and often it was, but it could also be young girls who stood up to them and accused their precious informants of rape. Or it could be young thugs like my client, who probably did murder Brenda Stokes - only no one could find the body or bully him into admitting it, so what do they do? Smuggle their precious informant into his cell and get him to manufacture an entirely false confession in return for immunity from all other crimes. That's what's happened here, isn't it?

Perhaps.

Certainly Robert Baxter's display of fury was damaging him. Belatedly, he realised how his outburst had drawn all eyes his way. He drew a deep breath, and loosened his grip on the witness stand.

The lady judge spoke for the first time. 'I hope that wasn't meant as a threat, Superintendent Baxter?'

Baxter drew a second deep breath. 'No, ma'am, of course not. But it comes a little hard at my age, to be wrongly accused of things that were settled so long ago in the past.'

'Indeed, my lords,' Gareth Jones cut in mellifluously. 'Superintendent Baxter is well past retirement age after an extremely distinguished career. His health is not what it was. He should certainly not be treated as if he were on trial here.'

'Quite.' The senior judge glanced at the clock. 'Eleven fifteen. I think perhaps this would be the ideal moment for a short recess. Shall we resume in fifteen minutes?'

When the judges had retired Robert Baxter marched past Sarah without a word. Beside her, Gareth Jones turned to her with a wry smile.

'For a first timer, you certainly set the place alight, don't you, Mrs Newby? Are your cases always like this?'

Sarah was feeling slightly sick as the adrenalin ebbed away. *I've got to stop doing this,* she thought, *I'll make myself ill.* With an effort, she summoned up what she hoped was an appropriate grin.

'Oh no,' she said. 'Sometimes it's really dramatic.'

9. Afternoon in Court

AS THE day wore on Sarah began to feel better. Last night's emotional turmoil was forgotten - her energies were wholly focussed on the battle in court. Part of it was pure fear. It would be easy to be humiliated in such august company. Gareth Jones was an eloquent, experienced advocate. His arguments were detailed and precise, sending the lawyers and judges on scavenger hunts through learned tomes, and technical discussions which the senior judge in particular clearly enjoyed. Sarah was no more than an average legal scholar, and more than once she felt a sense of rising panic as she floundered to keep up. Nevertheless, she won the first round. Shortly after lunch, the judges agreed to hear Mr Crosse, Brian Winnick's solicitor.

Mr Crosse was a drab, earnest solicitor in his mid fifties. He wore a dark suit, rimless glasses, and the regimental tie of the Royal Engineers, which he had served in as a young man. Sarah led him through a series of questions to establish his credibility; he was chairman of his local parish council, and a senior partner in a firm of criminal solicitors. He had known Brian Winnick for ten years, and represented him in court several times. He had last seen him in St James's hospital in Leeds.

'Was he very ill when you saw him?' Sarah asked.

'He was, yes. He had difficulty breathing, and was hooked up to an oxygen cylinder.'

'What was the nature of his illness?'

'He had lung cancer. It was terminal. The doctors had told him he had just a few weeks to live.'

'What was his state of mind at the time?'

'He was quite lucid. Perfectly clear in his head, no doubt about that. But he was in a serious frame of mind, as you'd expect. That's what he'd asked to see me about. He wanted to make a statement about all the lies he'd told in the past.'

'And what was his motive for this?'

'Remorse, I think. He'd just been received into the Catholic church. There was a priest at his bedside shortly before I arrived.'

This comment seemed to impress the judges. They asked a number of questions, to ensure that the priest had had no hand in the actual phrasing of the statement. Then Sarah led him through the details of what Brian Winnick had said, and the notes Mr Crosse had made of their conversation.

'He told me that the evidence he gave in the trial of Jason Barnes was a lie. Mr Barnes did not tell him he had murdered Brenda Stokes. Mr Winnick made that up, and lied about it to the police, he said.'

'Did he tell you why he'd done that?'

'To get a reduced sentence, he said. He was charged with drug dealing, and hoped the police would drop those charges if he helped them convict Jason Barnes.'

'Did he say which police officer promised to do that?'

'That ... he didn't say.' Mr Crosse hesitated, glancing nervously across the court at the two detectives who sat glowering at him. 'I don't think he mentioned names.'

'Very well.' Sarah moved swiftly on, but when she had finished and Gareth Jones rose to cross-examine, he returned immediately to this point.

'You're an experienced solicitor, Mr Crosse. You understand the importance of getting a statement as clear as it can possibly be. So why didn't you ask your client? Which officer was it who made him such a promise?'

'I suppose ... I was too surprised by the nature of the details he was telling me. And then, he was very weak. I didn't want to put him under too much strain.'

'It was difficult for him to speak, was it?'

'Yes. There were long pauses. At times he closed his eyes and seemed to sleep.'

'I see.' Gareth Jones paused. 'Mr Crosse, you've told this court you believed Mr Winnick was of sound mind, even though he was dying and needed oxygen. Did you get medical evidence from a doctor to support this belief?'

'I ... no, I didn't. I did consider it but there was no one around at the time. The doctors were all very busy.'

'I see. As a layman, Mr Crosse, do you accept that when a dying person has difficulty breathing, their brain may become starved of oxygen? In which case their grasp on reality may be somewhat limited?'

'I don't know. I'm not medically qualified.'

'Quite. So your opinion, that Mr Winnick was of sound mind and telling the truth, rather than indulging in a fantasy, is just an opinion, isn't it? You have no medical basis for saying that?'

'No medical basis, no. Just thirty years professional experience of interviewing clients.'

'Many of whom lie, no doubt.'

'Of course. I believe Mr Winnick was telling the truth.'

'But you didn't administer an oath?'

'No. I intended to do that when I returned, with the statement typed up for him to sign. Unfortunately he died before that was possible.'

It was an incisive performance, inflicting maximum damage on Sarah's principal witness. As they adjourned for lunch, she wondered if she might have more time in Cambridge with Emily than she had anticipated.

As court resumed after lunch, the senior judge looked down at the barristers.

'Very well, we have heard Mr Crosse, and have come to a decision. This court is prepared to consider the notes of his conversation with Brian Winnick in the appeal. But before we hear argument on what weight to attach to it, do you have any other evidence you wish us to consider?'

Hugely relieved, Sarah rose to her feet once again. The first hurdle had been cleared. She might be only a junior barrister from the north east, but she had won a point, at least, in the Court of Criminal Appeal. She addressed the judges, half-aware as she did so of a background of bitter whispering from the two detectives.

'Yes, my Lords. The second major point of Mr Barnes's appeal concerns the evidence of Amanda Carr. As your Lordships will know, Ms Carr was a student nurse at Naburn Maternity Hospital at the time of the original trial. As soon as she read about the case in the local press, she went voluntarily to the police to make a statement. She had seen a young woman answering Brenda Stokes' description on the road outside the hospital at four a.m. that night, she said. This evidence was available to Superintendent Baxter...' She glanced coolly at the elderly detective. '...

but was never used in trial or disclosed to the defence. My Lords, I submit that this was a serious abuse of process. Had the defence been aware of this evidence, they could not have failed to use it to establish reasonable doubt. My Lords, Ms Carr has been troubled by this matter ever since. Her memory of that night remains clear, and she is here in court today.'

The judges turned to her opponent. Gareth Jones rose swiftly.

'My Lords, I strongly oppose my learned friend's submission. Your Lordships will be aware, as she is, that this matter was raised at a previous court of appeal. On that occasion their Lordships concluded that it was *not* possible to say that it would have created reasonable doubt in the minds of the jury, as Mrs Newby contends. In view of this prior judgement, My Lords, I submit that it is unnecessary to consider this evidence once again.'

Sarah had expected this. She had read the details of the previous appeal at four o'clock that morning. As he sat down, she rose to her feet.

'My Lords, my learned colleague omits a crucial point of their Lordships' previous judgement. Let me refer you to paragraph 12. What their Lordships actually said was that they were not convinced that Ms Carr's evidence *on its own* would have been sufficient to create reasonable doubt in the minds of the jury. My Lords, those three words *on its own* are crucial. My client's appeal today does not rely on Ms Carr's evidence alone. We seek to combine it with the statement of Brian Winnick, as well as three minor points which I also intend to lay before your Lordships. It is my client's contention that these five points *taken together* are more than sufficient to persuade you that he has, for the past eighteen years, suffered a serious miscarriage of justice.'

The judges took several minutes to consider. Then, to Sarah's relief, the senior judge said: 'Very well, Mrs Newby. We are prepared to hear from Amanda Carr.'

Amanda Carr was a small round cheery woman in her early forties. Her evidence was brief, clear, and helpful. Eighteen years ago she'd been a student nurse at Naburn Maternity Hospital outside York. Driving home from a hospital party she'd passed a young woman wandering along a country road. The young woman had been wearing a schoolgirl outfit, but looked too old to be a schoolgirl, so Amanda assumed it was fancy dress. It was only a few days later, when she read of the disappearance of Brenda Stokes, that she went to the police and made a statement. But to her surprise, she was never called to give evidence.

Gareth Jones stood to cross-examine her. His manner, as Sarah had expected, was very polite, gentle, and charming.

'Mrs Carr, this is very public-spirited of you. This matter still troubles you today, does it?'

'Yes, it does. If only I'd stopped to offer that girl a lift, she might still be alive today.'

'Naturally, a very troubling thought. You're assuming, of course, that it was Brenda Stokes who you saw.'

'Yes, of course. I'd never met the girl in my life. But the person I saw matched the description in the newspapers. Almost exactly.'

'Yes, I see. Did you think of stopping to offer her a lift?'

'No. I wish I had now, but it just didn't enter my head.'

'You were coming home from a party at the hospital, were you?'

'Yes, that's right.'

'About four in the morning, you say?'

'About that time, yes. It was quarter past four when I got home. I remember that; my mother was waiting up, and she made a big fuss about that.'

Gareth Jones smiled. 'I'm a lawyer, as you see, but I went to a few parties with nurses when I was younger. Pretty lively affairs, as I recall. Were yours like that?'

'We had a lot of fun, yes.'

'Quite a lot to drink?'

'Yes, probably.'

'Mrs Carr, I'm not here to be awkward or score petty points. We're here to find the truth, all of us. But, purely in the interests of truth, would it be fair to say that when you were driving home from that party eighteen years ago, you might possibly have had rather more to drink than you or I would consider safe to drive on today?'

Amanda considered the point seriously. 'Was I drunk, you mean?'

The old rogue, he's charmed her, Sarah thought. Cunning move.

'Well, yes. I mean, don't worry, nobody's accusing you of drink driving or anything like that. Things were different then, after all. And we've all been young once.'

'Yes, well, it's possible, I suppose. But I wouldn't say drunk. I could still drive the car ok. I must have done, I got home.'

'Yes, but my point is, when we're drunk, you know, our perceptions aren't as clear as when we're sober. We make mistakes. And you only saw this girl for a few seconds, didn't you, in your headlights? So what I'm suggesting, you see, is perhaps you did see someone, and thought nothing of it. Then a few days later when you read this description in the paper, your mind played a trick on you, and you imagined the person you saw looked like Brenda Stokes. Whereas it wasn't really her at all.'

Amanda frowned. 'Well, I never said it was Brenda, did I? But did I see a girl in a schoolgirl outfit? Yes. Did she have long dark hair, as it said in the newspapers? Yes, I think so. I can see her now in my mind's eye. I wasn't that drunk, Mr Jones.'

Gareth Jones bowed to her slightly, and sat down.

Sarah's success in persuading the judges to consider Amanda Carr's evidence began to fade almost as soon as she left the stand. The next hour was taken up with argument about how much significance should be attached to that evidence. And here, Sarah frequently found herself worsted by her opponent. Gareth Jones was not a QC for nothing, and he was determined to run rings round her if he could.

Amanda's evidence, Gareth Jones argued, was worth very little. As experienced High Court judges, their Lordships could not fail to know how notoriously unreliable identification evidence was. Witnesses frequently picked out the wrong people in identification parades, even when they had seen their assailant face to face, which Mrs Carr had not done. Given all these doubts, it was hard to see what difference her evidence could have made to the jury. Even if the girl on the road had been Brenda, it was still possible that Jason had killed her after Amanda saw her.

Sarah opposed this point vigorously, using a map to illustrate the distance from the point where Amanda had seen the girl, to the point where Jason said she had left him by the river on Landing Lane. 'My Lords, there is no dispute about the time when Amanda Carr got home. It was after four a.m. – her mother berated her for it. So if the girl she saw *was* Brenda Stokes, she was still alive at four in the morning. Which means that my client would simply not have had time to murder Brenda, dispose of her body, and then drive to Leeds and torch the car so that it was completely burnt out before 5.20 a.m. It's not practicable. In any case it conflicts with the version presented in court, which is that my client murdered Brenda Stokes soon after 2 a.m., and dumped her body in the river.

'But what if my client's story is true? They had a violent quarrel at Landing Lane, after which she fled into the night. She ran off, bleeding and terrified, to hide from him in the undergrowth. He searched for her with the torch, but eventually gave up and drove back to Leeds. Then, when it was quiet, she may have ventured out, and made her way south along the footpath by the river, to a field opposite Naburn Lane, where the old Maternity Hospital used to be. Which is exactly where Amanda Carr saw a young woman, dressed as a schoolgirl, wandering along the road at 4 a.m. that morning.'

Sarah looked up, at the three learned faces watching her thoughtfully. 'My Lords, I do not say this definitely happened; I cannot be sure. But I do say that it is a version entirely consistent with the evidence. It fits my client's story; it also explains the evidence of Amanda Carr. The only evidence it conflicts with is Jason Barnes's alleged confession to Brian Winnick, which Mr Crosse has told us is a lie.

'And that, My Lords, explains quite clearly why Amanda's statement was such an embarrassment to the police, and why they failed to follow it up, or disclose it to the prosecution. It ruins their version of events. It gives my client a watertight alibi, which was never presented to the jury. Quite simply, it proves his innocence.'

Gareth Jones rose to his feet beside her. 'My Lords, I am reminded of games I used to play as a child. We balanced one playing card on top of another, to build a castle as high as we could. But sadly, it always collapsed in the end. The foundations were simply not there.'

Sarah turned on him coldly. 'That, it seems to me, is more apt as a description of the prosecution case than the defence. My client has spent 18 years in prison for a conviction in which there was no body, no real forensic evidence, and a fake confession.'

'My Lords,' Gareth Jones persisted, 'as I have already stated, the evidence of Amanda Carr is flimsy in the extreme. She has no idea who she saw, she was drunk, it was dark - need I go on?'

The senior judge raised his hand. 'No, Mr Jones, you need not. We take a short recess, and hear further arguments later.'

'Keep it up, eh, darlin',' Jason muttered grimly. 'Grab that Welsh bastard by the nuts and squeeze. They sing lovely, I've heard.'

Sarah grinned. 'Not allowed under judge's rules, I'm afraid. I'd get a red card.'

'Worth it, though, eh?' His face clouded with anxiety. 'Are we going to win?'

'We have a chance,' Sarah said. 'No more.' She left the dock and returned to her place as the judges returned. The senior judge looked down.

'We have considered counsel's submissions and agree that the evidence of Amanda Carr can be considered together with the statement of Brian Winnick. How heavy these weigh in the scales of justice, however, has yet to be decided. Now, are counsel prepared to submit final arguments?'

'My Lords, yes.' Sarah drew a deep breath, and drew a fresh sheet of notes from the bundles in front of her. Several of these were hand-written on hotel notepaper - how well had her mind been functioning at four a.m. this morning? The terrible vision flashed into her mind, of Bob making love to the faceless Sonya, and her heart lurched wildly. She almost forgot where she was, then saw the judges watching patiently. *Forget Bob*, she thought. *Come on, girl, concentrate, now!*

Sarah had three further points to add to the evidence of Mr Crosse and Amanda Carr. First, she emphasized the absence of a body. There were very few cases in which someone had been convicted of murder when the body had not been found. In the original trial, Jason's defence had suggested that Brenda might be still alive. Sarah accepted that she was probably dead, but that did not mean Jason had killed her. If Amanda's evidence, suppressed in the original trial, was accepted, then someone else might have done it.

'She may have been murdered by a malevolent stranger; she may have been kidnapped and imprisoned by a sexual sadist; or she may simply have met with a terrible accident which was covered up. My client does not know, and neither - in the absence of her body - do the police.

'What we can say, however, is that if she did try to walk home, she presented the perfect target for whatever evil-minded man she happened to meet. A nineteen year old girl, provocatively attired in school uniform, including a miniskirt and tight-fitting blouse, wandering alone down a country lane in the middle of the night. This girl was in danger, my Lords, from anyone who met her.'

Sarah's second point was the bloodstained torch. Yes, it had blood on it which recent DNA testing had proved to be similar to that of Brenda's mother. No one could be certain it was Brenda's, because her body had not been found to take samples from. But even if it was Brenda's blood, with Jason's fingerprint in it, that did not prove he had killed her. He admitted he had assaulted her, and she had had a nose bleed. That was how her blood got on his hands. And from his hands, it got onto the torch – not the other way round. In the original trial, the torch had been presented to the jury as the murder weapon. But there was no dent on the torch, and even though it had been minutely re-examined with the most modern forensic techniques, not even the most microscopic trace of Brenda's hair or skin had been found anywhere on it.

'Surely this only proves one thing, my Lords,' she said earnestly. 'That torch did not kill her. It was not the murder weapon, as the jury were told in the original trial. Neither the blood nor the fingerprint are sufficient to establish that. The evidence of the torch supports my client's story, not that of the prosecution.'

She searched their faces for sympathy, but found none. Only solemn, thoughtful attention. Grimly, she ploughed on.

'I would like to make one further point. My client has been in prison for eighteen years, far longer than the normal tariff for such a crime. He could have been released long ago, if he had agreed to admit his guilt. Yet he has consistently maintained his innocence. "I did not kill Brenda Stokes," he says. That is what he said when he was arrested, that is what he said at his original trial, and that is what he says to your Lordships today. This consistency, I suggest, is a further point in his favour.

'I therefore respectfully submit that the right course for your Lordships is to overturn this verdict, and set this man free.'

Sarah bowed, and sat down. That's it, she thought. Unless they have any questions, or Gareth Jones says something totally outrageous. I'm done. She watched her opponent rise and smooth his gown. He looks a nice man, she thought. Maybe I'll meet him later in the Middle Temple. We could have a drink together. It's very attractive, that Welsh accent. Pleasant manners too.

Gareth Jones dealt first with the absence of the body. It had been a difficult feature of the case, he agreed, from the beginning. The original defence had claimed that Brenda Stokes was still alive. Now it seemed

Mrs Newby wished to change this story. A hint of derision entered his voice.

'Brenda Stokes is dead, she says, but it was not her client who killed her. Well, my Lords, what are we to say to this? Here we have Jason Barnes, a man with several prior convictions for violence, who was the last person to see Brenda alive. This man drives her to a remote riverside car park with the intention of having sex with her. He admits that when she refused, they had a violent quarrel, which left her blood on his hands. After which she vanished without trace.

'And what do we have on the other hand, my Lords? Nothing at all. Just ghosts, my Lords - shadowy figures with no substance and no name, brought forward by Mrs Newby to confuse the issue. Sexual sadists, kidnappers, malevolent strangers - people of whose existence there is no evidence whatsoever. Need I say more? The police conducted an extensive investigation and came up with only one credible suspect - Jason Barnes, the man who was convicted eighteen years ago, after a thorough examination of the evidence.'

The evidence of Amanda Carr, he said, had been rejected at an earlier appeal. 'And having seen Mrs Carr, your lordships may well understand why. Her evidence is unreliable. She admits she had been drinking. She caught a brief, fleeting glimpse of a girl in her headlights - no more. And it was only months afterwards - when photos of Brenda Stokes had been all over the media - that she belatedly decided that the person she had seen matched Brenda's description.'

He then turned to something Sarah had tried to avoid - the evidence of Jason's unlovely character, and his dishonest, criminal behaviour.

'Mr Barnes, we must remember, lied when he was first interviewed. He did not steal a car, he claimed, he drove one belonging to a friend. This proved to be a lie. He now admits he stole a car, which he torched before he went home. Why did he do that, my Lords, except to conceal evidence? Burnt clothes were found inside the car - were they his clothes, perhaps? Burned with the car because they too, like the torch, had Brenda's blood on?

'And so to the torch, which Mrs Newby claims cannot be regarded as the murder weapon. Well, my Lords, I submit that any jury, confronted by a bloodstained torch, with the defendant's fingerprint on it, would find it very hard to acquit. Particularly when it is found hidden in bushes by the river, where, by his own admission, Jason Barnes attempted to rape the young girl he had brought there. A young girl who has not been seen alive since that day. Were the jury misled about this torch? My Lords, I submit that they were not.'

Finally, he turned to Sarah's last point. Jason Barnes had always protested his innocence, he said. Was that a good reason for mercy? No, not in his case. There was another way to look at it entirely.

'For 18 long years, my Lords, this man has refused to admit his guilt. And for all those years, Brenda's mother - now in her seventies, my lords, and too frail to come here today - has had no body to bury. Jason Barnes knows of her grief. She has sent him letters begging him to tell her where her daughter is hidden, so that she may bury her in peace. And what has been his response? Laughter, my Lords. Mockery of the lowest kind. Allow me to read you one letter which Jason Barnes sent to Brenda's mother, in reply to her appeal. It is very short.

'Why don't you jump in a slurry pit yourself, you old cow? Might make you smell better.'

Gareth Jones sat down in the shocked silence. He turned to Sarah with a grim smile.

'That's your client for you,' he said. 'Enjoy.'

10. A Helping Hand

'HE JUST brought it into your classroom?'

'Yes. Said he found it on holiday - somewhere near Filey. Not that I necessarily believe it. The story sounds fantastic to me.'

'But then, so is this hand.' Detective Sergeant Wilson favoured the flustered young schoolteacher with a gentle smile. 'I don't suppose you get many of them in your classroom, do you, Ms - er ...'

'Sheranski. Do you think ... it *is* real, isn't it?'

'Looks real enough to me, certainly. But the pathologist will know.'

DS Wilson contemplated the hand in its plastic evidence bag. There were some greenish strands between the bones which might be dried seaweed. If so, they would support the Filey story. But the first thing, clearly, was to interview the boy who had brought the hand to school.

The school in which Julie Sheranski was battling through her probationary year was well known to the police, and Sean Tory proved to be a typical nine-year-old delinquent in the making. His mother had a printout two pages long on the police computer, and seemed to have worn out as many social workers as boyfriends. Gary James, her latest choice, was currently resting from paid employment but had a string of offences including theft, handling and GBH.

So when DS Wilson interviewed the lad in the presence of Ms Sheranski, he was not surprised to get less than willing co-operation. Sean's sole concern was to get back his hand. 'It's mine,' he insisted truculently. 'I found it, and she nicked it. What about my rights? You're the filth - you want to arrest her, not me!'

'What I want to know, Sean,' the detective insisted patiently. 'Is exactly *where* you found it.'

'Why?'

'Well, it could be evidence, son, couldn't it? I mean, people don't just go leaving their hands around the countryside when they get tired of them, do they? There could be a crime committed here.'

'And you could help solve it, Sean,' Julie Sheranski put it in optimistically. 'Help the police catch a criminal.'

'Get real, miss. I ain't gonna grass no-one. You're the criminal here! Nicking my hand!'

'Tell us the story, Sean,' DS Wilson prodded patiently. 'It's got to be a good one.'

Reluctantly, Sean consented to elaborate on the story he had told Ms Sheranski earlier that morning. The three boys were left alone in their rented caravan one night while Sharon and Gary went to the pub. Around midnight, they heard a scratching outside, which terrified the two-year-old, Wayne. While Sean's brother Declan comforted the boy, Sean took a breadknife and bravely crept outside. In the darkness he saw a large animal, about the size of a small wolf. It was trying to get into the caravan. Naturally, Sean admitted, he'd been scared, particularly since he remembered a terrible film from the telly where a dingo ran away with a baby in Australia. This holiday place, Filey, DS Wilson should realise, was nothing like Leeds - it was all quiet and lonely and dark - much darker and wilder than anywhere in Australia, for certain. So there was a real threat to young Wayne and himself. But bravely, he challenged the fox, and it ran away. He chased it into the sand dunes for quite a distance - four or five miles, he estimated - until it ran into a hole in the ground. Just outside this hole he found the hand.

'So you picked it up and brought it back to the caravan?'

'Well yeah, course. Otherwise no-one would have believed me.'

'Oh, you showed it to other people, then?'

'Well, yeah. Declan and me mum and him.'

'So they'll confirm this story, will they?'

Sean's steady gaze never wavered. 'Declan will, yeah, 'course. I'll fetch him now, shall I? He's in Mr Purdy's class.'

He was halfway to the door before the detective stopped him. 'No, no, Sean, that's all right. You stay here with Ms Sheranski. I'll find Declan myself, if you don't mind.'

By the end of the afternoon, having interviewed first Declan, then Sharon and finally her boyfriend Gary, DS Wilson had managed to uncover a different and rather more credible version of the story - that the boys had found the hand in the mouth of a dead fox on a slip road near

York. After careful questioning of Gary, aided by the discovery that the Orion's road tax disc related to a completely different car altogether, he managed to establish a location for this slip road. Having done that, and had a pathologist confirm that the bones were genuinely human - not plastic from a medical exhibit - he decided reluctantly to pass the investigation over to the police in York.

So he drove east. It was a pleasant drive, but DS Wilson, like most of his colleagues, had a poor opinion of police forces outside Leeds. It was only a year since a much-resented team from York had screwed up a serious joint drugs investigation, causing stress to all concerned. So when DS Wilson learned that the DI he was to meet had been involved in this same investigation, he saw a childish opportunity for revenge. Carefully, he folded the forefinger and two outside fingers inside the evidence bag back against the palm, leaving the middle finger pointing rigidly upwards. He presented it in York like this, an ingratiating smile on his face.

'Always willing to give our country colleagues a hand,' he said.

A tale that was worth a few pints, when he got home.

11. Judgement Day

COURT ADJOURNED at three, with judgement promised for tomorrow. That gave Sarah and Lucy two hasty hours to explore the West End shops. It was welcome therapy for Sarah. She bought a pair of spike heeled leather boots for herself, and a cashmere sweater for Emily. She was hunting for a Christmas present for her son when the blues returned. It was the corduroy shirts that did it; they were too like those she had bought for Bob last year. He had worn them every weekend until summer. She had been so pleased with the success of her choice, she'd even enjoyed ironing them.

No more. Now another woman would rest her head against those shirts, another woman buy his presents at Christmas. Not me. Well, I wish him joy of her, the swine. Eyes misting with rage, she hurried Lucy to the lingerie section, where she bought a soft silken camisole which the assistant promised would cherish her skin every day that she wore it.

'Just what I need,' she said, with a bright, determined laugh. 'A bit of cherishing. Clothes that make you feel like a star.'

'And don't shrink in the wash,' said Lucy practically. 'Anyway, you *are* a star, honey. That presentation in court today was masterful ...'

'Mistressful, you mean?'

'Whatever. If they don't release Jason after that, they never will.'

'And doesn't he know it. Well, if I did well today, Lucy my love, it was down to your meticulous preparation. Come on, let's call a cab. We've got to look our best before we dine with the mightiest lawyers in the land.'

Sarah had booked them in for dinner at the Middle Temple, her own Inn of Court. She was in London rarely enough for this to be a treat, and Lucy had never been. Two hours later they sat together at one of the long wooden refectory tables in the ancient Elizabethan hall, where Law Lords, judges, and eminent QCs mingled with aspirant pupils eating their required number of dinners. Lucy gazed about her in awe.

'Is this really as old as it looks?'

'Of course.' Sarah was determinedly full of high spirits. 'This is the hall where Shakespeare's *Twelfth Night* was first performed. I was younger then. A poet in a ruff propositioned me.'

Lucy laughed. 'You do look a bit ghostly. Is this where you ate your dinners?'

'I did. And I was called to the utter Bar. By that old gent over there, standing in front of the portrait. He got my name wrong - called me Newlyn. It was deeply moving.'

'Why do they call it the utter Bar?'

'Because we're utterly wrong, most of the time. You should know that, Luce - you've listened to me often enough.'

They had a cheerful evening, talking to a high court judge, an ex-policeman who had become a barrister, a Chinese lady QC, and an earnest undergraduate who was president of the Cambridge Law Society. Sarah wondered at the intensity of the questions he posed. How will Emily cope, she wondered, with young men like this? Oh well, maybe I'll find out tomorrow.

At the hotel Sarah collapsed into bed, exhausted. But two hours later she awoke. The rhinoceros had resumed its mating activities with the boiler. She lay alone in the orange glow from the streetlamp, listening.

Jason Barnes was nothing to her. He could rot in jail or run free; it was all one. She'd done her best; it was out of her hands. But it wasn't just Jason who'd be released tomorrow, if she won. She'd been released herself, by her husband. Only the freedom he'd given her was one she neither wanted nor knew what to do with.

Oh Bob, Bob, why did you do it? Am I too old, too ugly? Too obsessed with work, perhaps? But Sarah had always been a workaholic, he'd known that for years. As a young wife she'd had studied day and night, sometimes sitting at her desk inside the playpen, to shield her books from the sticky hands of toddlers, while they trashed the house outside. Bob had often come home to find her frantically restoring the wreckage, while the food she'd meant for his tea smouldered into a black snack under the grill. He hadn't seemed to mind then - he'd laughed, helped her clean up, and encouraged her studies, proud when she got all A grades, keen for her to go further.

And she *had* gone further - to the utter Bar, to her own place in chambers, a luxurious house in the country, an appeal in the Royal Courts of Justice.

So how did I lose a husband on the way? Just when we'd succeeded, we had everything? What is it? Is it me? Are my legs too fat, my hips too broad suddenly, my face too wrinkled? At three a.m, unable to sleep, Sarah got up to look. She switched on the light and subjected herself to a meticulous examination in front of the full length mirror. Can it really be that? It's true there are lines round my eyes and mouth, my breasts are not as pert as they were, my bottom a little heavier. But not a lot, not really. I can still get into suits I wore ten years ago. Last time I weighed myself I was four pounds less, amazingly, than I was last summer.

And Bob's no athlete, after all, never was - hairy pigeon chest, pot belly, skinny arms, knock knees, a varicose vein on his right calf - what in God's name gives a bony bearded creature like him the right to reject me for my looks?

Is that why he's gone? No, it probably isn't. I'm not a challenge any more, that's what matters to him. I've succeeded. I'm no longer the desperate dropout schoolgirl with a baby to care for, like some Dickensian waif he's rescued from the poorhouse. I've made it. I'm not his project any more.

And so suddenly, he falls out of love. I'm boring, that's what it is, *I'm boring*. Whereas that bitch, whatever her wretched name is - *Sonya* - she's divorced, isn't she, with kids and a part time job - she needs help now. She's his new project, that's her attraction. Not the fact that she's younger than me, not her thighs or her bottom or her hair - Bob needs someone *dependent,* that's what it is. Someone who's grateful to him, who worships him for his generosity.

Which I didn't do. Not often enough, anyway - and not at all recently, since Simon's trial, when I was right, after all, and he was wrong. I thought I was equal - more than equal to him, if the real truth be known. He realised that, and didn't like it.

He *is* a kind, generous man, after all. Up to a point. But now we've reached that point, and he's gone. Left me to stand on my own two feet. All alone. And lonely.

She shivered suddenly, looking at her nude reflection in the mirror. The room was surprisingly cold for a hotel. Perhaps the rhinoceros had killed the boiler in its enthusiasm. Or the management turned down the heating in the middle of the night.

Or perhaps she was shivering from loneliness.

She forced a smile - a determined smile that aped happiness. Her reflection smiled back. She turned to one side, struck a pose, looking over her shoulder, one thigh half raised. Not a bad-looking body, for its age. The stomach was - well, possible to pull in if she tried, the breasts still ... almost as firm as they were. Quite a fair silhouette. She smiled and arched her fingers like a dressmaker's dummy in a shop window. I can do it, this is me, I don't look bad. I should - what did that woman in the shop say? Cherish myself.

She remembered the silk camisole she had bought and put it on, hugging it smoothly to her hips. Oh yes, I need this. If I'm going to be alone I must be kind to myself, make myself happy. If I can. She did a small, hesitant dance around the room, brushed away a sudden, unexpected outburst of tears, and ran a hot bath. That, at least, was working in the middle of the night.

Four hours later, wearing a black trouser suit, smart heels, and silk camisole under her blouse, she entered the court. For once the tension in the atmosphere didn't touch her. Her client's release or continued imprisonment was out of her hands. It was how she handled her own freedom that mattered. She settled quietly in her seat, and waited for the judges to enter.

12. Ten o'Clock News

IT WAS the lead item on the ten o'clock news. But Terry Bateson almost missed it, because of the volcanoes. Terry was neutral about volcanoes, but his eldest daughter Jessica seemed to hate them. He'd got home at six to find her in a foul mood. She refused her food, swore at her younger sister, and sat scowling in front of the telly with the sound turned up. 'She's been like this since I fetched her from school,' Trude said. 'I think it's something to do with geography.'

'Geography?' Terry asked, bemused. 'Don't you mean hormones?'

'No, I mean geography at school. It's something the teacher said.'

Terry Bateson was a Detective Inspector in York CID. He was also a single parent, which didn't go well with the demands of his work. Since his wife, Mary, had been killed by a hit and run driver three years ago, he'd fought hard to find time for his two daughters. Trude, their Norwegian nanny, took care of them in the day, but now it was his turn. Jessica had just started at secondary school, and things were not going too well.

He sat down beside his daughter on the sofa. She ignored him, staring sullenly at the telly. He put an arm round her shoulder. She hunched up, her body a tense little ball of rejection. He tried again, moving closer. She pushed him away, then changed her mind, leaning tight under his arm. They sat like that for a while, watching the Simpsons together. Then the adverts came on and he muted them with the remote.

'Something happen at school?' he asked quietly.

'No,' she muttered shortly.

'Nothing at all?'

'Nothing good.'

'Something bad then?'

'Yes.' They watched a hamburger advert. 'It's Mrs Murton. I hate her.'

'Why?'

'I got a C for last week's homework. She said I didn't try.'

'Really? Fetch your book and show me.'

She hesitated, then got up and stomped upstairs. Two minutes later she came back, an exercise book in her hands. She held it out. 'You won't be angry?'

'No. Let me see.'

They sat together on the sofa and studied the offending pages. There were drawings about mountains and valleys, and a few sentences in Jessica's blue pen. Not very many, Terry could see; not hugely informative. There were a great many more teacher's comments in red ink, scattered here and there. *More information needed. You could say more about this. What about erosion!! Jessica, you could do better. Try harder!!*

The comments hurt, much more than Terry expected. He imagined the teacher's scowl, her disapproving cluck as she scored the words into the page. Attacking my child, he thought. Even if the comments *were* justified.

'What's she like, Mrs Murton?'

'Horrid. Very strict.'

'Is it geography homework tonight?'

Jessica nodded glumly. 'Volcanoes. I hate them.'

'Let's do it together, shall we? Look them up on the computer. And in the encyclopaedia.'

It took time, but in the end Jessica agreed. They sat by the computer, with books spread on the table, researching details about volcanoes. Terry found it interesting, but Jessica didn't. The enthusiasm she'd once had in primary school - for dinosaurs, whales, giant turtles - seemed almost extinct. He worked hard to revive it, praising her drawings, suggesting extra details she could add.

It took an hour before he raised a smile.

At half past nine he read both girls a story in bed. At ten he came down at last. He poured himself a whisky, slumped on the sofa, and switched on the TV.

Just in time to see Sarah Newby.

She was outside the Royal Courts of Justice in London. She stood at the back of the screen, on the left. In the centre of the picture was the circular figure of Lucy Parsons, the solicitor. Lucy wore a black jacket, white silk blouse, and long flowing black skirt. She stood beside a short, muscular man in a dark suit and tie. He had a pale, seamed face and a short prison haircut. Lucy was reading a statement on behalf of her client, while the police held back a crowd of journalists and photographers. Sarah Newby stood quietly at the back. She had a look on her face that Terry knew well. It was the quiet, satisfied smile of victory.

Lucy's statement said: *'Eighteen years ago a young girl mysteriously disappeared, and Jason Barnes was unjustly convicted of her murder. He has always protested his innocence, in the face of immense pressure from the police and prison authorities. Now that innocence has been recognized, and he is free to start a new life again.'*

The crowd jostled her and she paused for a moment. The TV cameras zoomed in on Jason Barnes. There was an odd expression on his face - a grin that was part ecstasy, part sneer, part snarl. As though he was exhilarated, scared and angry all at once. Understandable, Terry thought, in a man wrongly imprisoned for 18 years, but it looked unpleasant all the same.

'My client has asked me to extend his sympathies to the mother of the murdered girl, Brenda Stokes. He hopes that her real killer will one day be brought to justice. But he has no sympathy whatsoever for the police, who took away 18 years of his life, and he hopes there will be an enquiry into their conduct.'

Jason raised a fist in the air as she ended. 'They can rot in hell!' he yelled. Then the bulletin returned to the studio, where the BBC's court correspondent outlined the original case against him, and the reasons for his successful appeal today. Terry's boss, Will Churchill, appeared, speaking for North Yorkshire Police. The case would remain on their files, he said. In due course it would be re-examined. But they had no other suspect at present for the murder of Brenda Stokes. Her family were devastated by the outcome.

Terry had no particular interest in this trial - like Will Churchill, he was too young to have been involved in the original investigation. But it was that sudden, brief glimpse of Sarah Newby that caught his attention. He hadn't expected it; it caught him by surprise. He hadn't met her for weeks. She'd begun to fade from his thoughts; he'd forgotten her. Or so he'd thought.

But that single glimpse of her face - less than a minute in total -

changed everything. He felt it like a pain in his chest. His breath came short, his heart beat faster. The words of Lucy Parsons' statement, the details of the case, washed over him like muzak; he scarcely heard them. It was that slim face at the back of the screen that transfixed him. She had her dark hair pinned back, he noticed, probably to fit under her wig in court. The hairstyle made her forehead look broad. She wore white legal bands around her throat, and some sort of dark robe. She was smiling quietly in triumph, and her hazel eyes watched the media scrum with interest and amusement.

It was a pretty face, but not excessively so. No prettier than dozens of female faces he saw every day. Objectively, he told himself, she bore no comparison to Trude, who sat watching the news with him. She wasn't even in the same league, really. But then Trude was a young healthy Norwegian girl, twenty two years old. Her features were perfect, her body lithe and athletic. She could have been a model if she'd wanted, instead of a nanny. Terry's colleagues at work couldn't believe his luck. They ribbed him about Trude unmercifully, thought up endless excuses to visit his house.

But for Terry, Trude was just a child. Beautiful, yes, but out of his class. He was old enough to be her father, after all - a point quite clear to Trude. There was a glass barrier between himself and girls like her. She saw him as a safe, trustworthy employer; he trusted her to care for his daughters. That was as far as it went.

But then, there was a glass wall between Terry and most women. It had been there since Mary's death. He could *see* that other women were beautiful, *understand* how men found them sexy. He could even imagine going to bed with them, as he had done with many girls as a student. It would be pleasant, exciting, enjoyable.

But it wouldn't *matter*. Not in the way it had mattered for years, with Mary. That was why he'd married her. Because she was different to other women. Because she'd become, quite literally, the other half of himself. The person who understood him more than any other. Who looked back at him as if she were the female face in his mirror.

So when Mary had died - snuffed out in a second by a careless, cruel teenager - he had thought that love for him was over. Sexual love, that is, between himself and a woman of his own age. Love for his children, of course, was different. That was a responsibility he would never lose. His daughters were what remained of Mary; she lived in their eyes. But other women looked like strangers.

Some were beautiful, some were sexy, some witty or amusing; a few were all of those things. One or two had made passes at him, without success. He wished them well, but they did nothing for him. They existed behind a glass screen.

Until he met Sarah Newby.

She was the first woman, since Mary's death, who was truly *there* for him. Who really *mattered*. Who filled his mind with her image when she wasn't there, and made him see no one else when she was. Who made him feel light and happy when she spent time with him. Who made his chest tight and painful when she turned away, or seemed to ignore him.

Which, sadly, she often did.

Because, unfortunately, Sarah Newby came with several serious disadvantages. Firstly, she was married. Terry didn't think it was a very happy marriage. He'd met her husband and despised him; he'd seen husband and wife quarrel in public. But it was a marriage nonetheless, and one Sarah set some store by. She'd made that quite clear in the past, on the one occasion when he'd almost managed to get her into bed.

They'd been at a wedding that day. She had quarrelled with her husband, who stormed out of the hotel and left her. Sarah had got drunk, danced with Terry, and invited him up to her room. But then she'd ruined it all by being sick, and nothing happened. It might have been nerves, or the alcohol, or both; Terry wasn't sure. Next day he'd sent her flowers, hoping for a second chance. She'd thanked him, but explained she'd made a mistake. Her marriage and her career came first. An affair with Terry would wreck them both. That wasn't going to happen. Ever.

That was the second drawback to Sarah Newby. The phrase 'career woman' had been invented for her. Terry didn't know all the details, but he knew she'd had to fight to get her place at the Bar. So hard, that her career had become part of her character. She'd got pregnant at fifteen, and left school with no qualifications, no connections, no hope. And a child to bring up, in the slums of Seacroft, near Leeds. Somehow, with her husband's help, and her own iron determination, she had clawed her way up from that disastrous beginning to this triumph on today's TV News. A victory in the Court of Appeal, in the Royal Courts of Justice in London.

That was Sarah, that's what she did. Terry thought of that smile on her face, the quiet smile of victory. That was what she lived for, what she wanted. It was admirable and terrifying at the same time. Admirable as an achievement; terrifying to a man, like Terry Bateson, who feared he might be in love with her. Because she'd made it quite clear that an affair that might wreck her career was simply not going to happen. Not even with him.

And yet. Terry had also seen her put her career on the line for her son, Simon. When the boy had been accused of murder, she had defended him, knowing that if she lost, her career was over. Who would employ a barrister who had spawned a murderer? She didn't have to do that, she could have backed away. But she'd done it for the love of her son. One thing that mattered to her more than her work.

Terry thought about this now, as he'd often done before. He couldn't help it; with all her faults, the woman fascinated him. And she had faults in plenty. When he'd first met her, her children had been in open rebellion, the daughter running away from home, the son wanted by the police. Part of this, probably, was because she'd been a poor mother. She was never home, she was always working; her career came first. Terry understood, since Mary's death, how difficult it was to get that balance right. But when things went wrong, really wrong, Sarah *was* there for her children. She'd fought for her son like a tigress. It was terrifying, and admirable. Terry had never seen a woman fight like it.

When the news broadcast ended, Trude yawned and went to bed. Terry sat for a while longer with his whisky. The house was quiet, the children sleeping. Jessica's homework lay on the table, ready for the morning. She'd worked hard on it, two full pages of drawings and descriptions, carefully written and coloured in. If she gets a poor grade this time, he told himself, I'll see the teacher. Or better still, send Sarah Newby.

He smiled at the thought. That would put a bomb under the old dragon, all right! He sipped his whisky, feeling the warmth spread in his chest. An image came into his mind, of Sarah Newby in full barrister's gear, chasing Jessica's geography teacher down the long corridors of some gothic girls' boarding school. They took to the air suddenly, like witches in Harry Potter. In midair Sarah whisked the broomstick from under the geography teacher, who fell screaming to earth. Terry grinned to himself. Jessica'd like that, he thought. If only.

Then another image came, of Sarah in this house, sitting opposite him, having fought the good fight for his child. She smiled at him, as Mary had once smiled. Then she got to her feet, stretched out a hand, and said, 'Come to bed?'

You sad old bastard, Terry muttered, shaking his head ruefully. Snowballs will freeze in hell, before that happens.

Still, the chance would be a fine thing.

13. Mother and Daughter

ARRIVING IN Cambridge, Sarah caught a taxi to her daughter's college, Sidney Sussex. Emily met her at the porter's lodge. Sarah hugged her, then stood back to examine this new phenomenon, her undergraduate daughter. She looked blooming, Sarah thought, her cheeks healthy, a sparkle in her eyes, her hair - well, perhaps the hair could do with a little more attention. But then she was a student, not a fashion model. Torn jeans, desert boots, combat jacket. Oddly, she seemed more of a child than Sarah remembered, as if she had shrunk somehow.

Emily led the way around a quadrangle towards her room, Sarah pulling her wheeled suitcase behind. Her heels echoed smartly on the ancient paving stones.

'Mum, what have you got on your feet?'

'What, these?' Sarah extended a leg, proudly displaying her new suede spike heeled boots. 'Do you like them? I bought them yesterday in Harrods.'

'They're ... very ostentatious.'

'Yes, that's why I bought them.' Sarah beamed, suddenly realising why Emily had shrunk. 'They make me taller for one thing. More impressive in court.'

'Great. Now I have a mother on stilts.' Emily ducked through a passageway, shaking her head at the perverse ways of adults. Sarah followed, noting with a grin how everyone they passed - students, dons, even the porters - lived with a dress code far scruffier than in the world of her work.

In Emily's room she strolled to the window and looked out over the walled college gardens. Last time she had been here - with Bob - the trees had been beautiful and green. Now the leaves were falling. Emily lit the gas fire.

'You've made yourself comfortable, I see.'

'Yeah, it's not too bad. Coffee?'

'Please. Just black.' Sarah looked into the small kitchen area and winced. 'I could take you out for dinner, if you like.'

'Yes, okay. Unless you want to eat in college. Meet my friends.' Emily brought two mugs of coffee and they settled either side of the fire in two ancient battered armchairs.

'You're making friends, then?'

'Yeah, quite a few.' Emily peered at her mother through the steam from her coffee. 'Mum, you look tired. Is everything all right?'

Sarah bit her lip. She'd intended to save this till later. But ...

'I stayed in a hotel for the last two nights. I didn't sleep so well.'

'Oh well. Let's hope the one here in Cambridge is better.'

'Yes.' Sarah sipped the coffee. It was bitter, sharp. 'Emily, there *is* something, as a matter of fact.' It was harder to say than she'd expected. 'I've ... had an argument with your father.'

'So? Is that news?'

Emily looked puzzled. Sarah gazed at her, thinking, I don't want to do this, but I have to. It's already too late. An image came into her mind of a film she'd once seen where a developer blew up a beautiful old house to make way for a housing estate. There'd been a moment, like this, just before it happened. The camera lingered on the facade of the ancient, two hundred year old building, calm and peaceful in the sunlight, and then the plunger was pressed. There had been a pause - perhaps a quarter of a second, no more, when the building still stood as it had for centuries, warm red brick against a blue sky, and then it was gone, just a cloud of smoke and a heap of rubble.

'He wants a divorce.'

'What?' The teenage self-confidence in Emily's face suddenly crumpled. There was shock, disbelief, and somewhere behind it, welling up from the depths, anger and insecurity. 'What are you talking about?'

Slowly, carefully, trying to keep her voice and emotions as much under control as she could, Sarah tried to explain. How for months, things had been difficult between her and Bob. How he'd had an affair last year with his secretary, Stephanie, which Sarah had hidden from the children at the time. And how, since he'd moved to his new school in Harrogate, they had drifted apart again.

'So it seems he's met this supply teacher, Sonya's her name. She's a single mum with three small kids. Only it's not just an affair, he says. He wants to ... move on, make a new start, whatever the correct phrase is.'

She fumbled in her handbag for a tissue. To blow her nose; she had no intention of weeping. Emily's response, in any case, contained more anger than sympathy.

'But why? How could this happen?'

'Well, it was a new situation, I suppose. We were both busy with our work, he had his new school, you weren't at home any longer ...'

'Oh, so it's my fault, is it?'

'What? No, of course not, darling, how could this be anything to do with you?'

'Well, you said I wasn't there any more. Mum, is this because you wouldn't let us move to Harrogate? You know how Dad wanted us to.'

'I don't know. Maybe that's part of it, but ...'

'We only stayed in York because of you, Mum, and you're hardly ever home. Perhaps if you'd gone with him, he'd never have met this ... Sonya.'

This wasn't the way Sarah had imagined the conversation. 'Darling, if you remember, you wanted to stay in York because of your friends, you know you did. You insisted.'

'Yes, but I didn't know this was going to happen, did I? Or about this Stephanie woman either. That was much more important and you and Dad kept it to yourselves.'

'We didn't want to bother you with it, darling. You were in the middle of your A levels, how would that have helped?'

'And now I'm here at uni and you're telling me my home has blown apart. How do you think that's going to help me when I'm sitting writing essays? As if that matters anyway, compared to this.'

'It does matter, Emily, of course it does. More than this, in fact. You've got your career to think of.'

'Oh, that's you all over isn't it, Mum? Typical. Work, work, work. That's probably why Dad wants to leave. He wants a woman who doesn't work all the time.'

'Emily, that's not fair.' Sarah could face most demons, but not this one. She got up and turned away from Emily, staring out of the window. A young couple stood on the college lawns, their arms wrapped round each other for warmth, as they gazed indulgently at a child searching for conkers. 'I was like that when your father married me. I've always been like that.'

'Yes, well.' Sarah could hear Emily behind her, but didn't dare turn round. If her daughter rejected her too, what was there left? Only her son, Simon - God knows how he'll take this. Only Simon, and her work.

Work's important, it rescued me from poverty and failure and disgrace, it gave me everything I wanted, it gave me freedom ...

Only this isn't quite the sort of freedom I need.

'Mum, I'm sorry.' Emily's hand was on her shoulder. Tentative, insistent. 'I shouldn't have said that, I wasn't thinking. After all Dad's the one who's cheated, isn't he? You didn't cheat on him.'

'No.' Sarah turned, grateful for the embrace. 'Only with my work, as you say, and that's just me.'

The shock of the news put Emily off the idea of eating in hall with her new friends, so they went in search of a restaurant instead, and ended up in Garden Court Hotel, beside the river. Emily had brushed her hair and put on a skirt and make-up for the occasion. She seemed at once impressed and resentful of the opulent surroundings.

'This is what you get, is it, for all your hard work?' she said, as the waiter lit the candles, and left them with the menu. 'Creepy waiters and high prices.'

'Sssssh,' Sarah said. 'He might hear you.'

'Well, I suppose he knows he's oppressed, without me telling him. All these rich capitalists eating here.'

'Emily! For heaven's sake! You have servants in college, don't you? Bedders or gyps or whatever you call them?'

'Yes, I know, Mum. It's one of the things I don't like about this place. I mean, it's as if we're all being encouraged to think we're better than everyone else.'

'You're not better than everyone else, but you're just as good, that's the point,' Sarah said firmly. 'Think of how I was when I was your age, and how far we've all come ...'

'Oh Mum, not again!'

Sarah drew a deep breath. 'Okay, I'm sorry, you've heard it all before. But look, you're here, and you should make the best of this opportunity. That's all I meant. You haven't ... had any more thoughts about moving to Birmingham, have you?'

'I've *thought* about it,' Emily said. 'But I haven't decided yet. Larry and I are going to talk about it next weekend.'

'I think you should stay,' Sarah insisted. 'Why doesn't Larry transfer to Cambridge instead?'

'It isn't that easy,' Emily said, pulling a face. 'Anyway he's not that keen, he likes it there. The trouble is, it means three years apart, and that's hard. The people here are okay, but - he matters a lot, you know. Especially now, if I haven't got a home to come back to any more.'

The remark hurt, like a child turning its back on her. 'But of course you've got a home to come back to, darling. Don't be silly, you always will have.'

'Yes, but where?' Emily asks. 'It won't be our lovely house by the river, will it? You'll have to sell that, won't you, if you divorce?'

The waiter returned to take their order. Sarah chose blindly, shocked by Emily's practicality. When he'd gone she leaned across the table, taking Emily's hand in her own.

'Look, darling, all this is new. Your father and I - we haven't even discussed what to do with the house yet. I like living there, just as you do. But if I do have to move somewhere else, you'll have a room just the same. You can choose the wallpaper, the furnishings, make it just how you want it. You'll be welcome home any time.'

'But it won't *be* my home any more Mum, will it? That's just the point.' Emily shook her head sadly. 'It'll just be a flat or a little semi where my Mum happens to live, that's all. I won't have any friends or memories there. I'll just come for a few days for a polite visit and then I suppose I'll have to go off and see Dad and that Sonya woman and her wretched kids. I mean, this is the end, Mum, isn't it? Our home's all gone.'

'I may try to keep the house,' Sarah said grimly. 'I could try to buy your father out. After all, he's the one who walked out, not me.'

'Well, that would be better,' Emily said, softening slightly. 'Mum, it's only been a few days. Maybe Dad'll come back. I mean, who is this Sonya person anyway?'

Sarah sighed. This wasn't the sort of conversation she wanted to be having at all. All this is Bob's fault, the bastard, she thought bitterly. 'I've never met her,' she said. 'But she's got three kids and no husband or proper job. Your father - I think he feels he's going to rescue her somehow, just as he did with me all those years ago. Only I ...'

Only I did things for myself, she was about to say, but thought better of it. Emily hated to hear of her struggle for success - she'd suffered too much from its effects.

'Or maybe it's just his mid-life crisis,' she continued ruefully. 'She's younger than me. Perhaps it's just her figure he's interested in.'

Emily smiled. 'Oh come on, Mum, that's crazy. I mean you, for your age, that is - what are you, not fifty yet?'

'Forty, Emily,' Sarah said, appalled. 'It's my fortieth birthday next summer.'

Emily looked abashed. 'Well, whatever - look, Mum, I'm sorry, I mean I wasn't *counting* exactly. What I meant was, you look great, you've kept your figure, much better than most mums, you ride that motorbike ...'

'Which your father hates ...'

'Yeah, well, forget about him. I mean if he's really left now you can do what you want. You might even find someone else, you know - I mean, people do!'

'Even old ladies like me, you mean?'

'Yes, why not? I mean, the papers are full of these adverts, we used to laugh at them at school, but I guess they're serious, really. And then you'd need the house, wouldn't you?'

'What, to keep my lover in?' Sarah smiled, indulging Emily's fantasy. 'He's going to need a lot of space, is he, to keep all the gear for his hobbies? What are you talking about - motorbike gear, gym equipment, a sailing boat in the garage?'

'I don't know, Mum, it depends. But seriously, it could happen.'

'Well, I'll do my best, darling, I promise. But however well preserved I may look, there isn't anyone on the horizon just at the moment. It was your father who ran off with a bimbo, not me.'

'I know that, Mum, but now things are different. You've got to make things happen, give them a chance.'

The waiter poured the wine. Sarah tasted it and nodded her approval.

'There was that policeman, wasn't there?' Emily continued eagerly. 'That tall detective fellow - Bailey - no, Bateson. You fancied him didn't you?'

'Who told you that, young lady?' Sarah looked at her over the wineglass, surprised. *Am I as transparent as all that?* In fact there *had* been a moment last year when ... but never mind, it came to nothing. *So how did Emily know?*

'Oh Mum, it was obvious. I mean of course nothing happened between you - or did it?' She looked anxious. 'That's not why Dad ...'

'*No.* Definitely not.' *But only because I was sick at the wrong moment,* Sarah thought, blushing at the memory.

'Well, good then.' Emily sipped her wine, reassured. 'But now ... I mean, if you really *are* getting divorced, you're still young. I mean, only forty anyway...'

'Not quite dead yet, yes, I see your point. I get the Zimmer frame next year. But darling, I haven't spoken to the man for ages. Anyway he's got two young kids and I'm always at work. I'd be rubbish as anyone's mum.'

'You're *my* mum, aren't you?'

'Yes. Well, so they told me at the hospital. And I know I was always busy when you were young and I'm sorry about that. But you've turned out okay all the same, thank God. Better than okay, in fact.'

'Careful, Mum, don't overdo it.'

'All right, *moderately* okay, then, let's say. So far, at least. And I'm proud of Simon, too, in his way. But as a stepmother, well ... I'm too old. Emily, it's a crazy idea. Forget it.'

'Hm. How does this policeman manage?' Emily persisted, thoughtfully. 'It must be difficult in a job like that. He's a widower, isn't he?'

'Who told you that?'

'Mum, I'm not blind. I do notice things.'

'So it seems.' Sarah sighed. Why not indulge in an agreeable fantasy for a while? It was a sort of therapy, in a way. 'Okay, how does a single detective inspector manage his job and two little girls? I don't know. But I've heard, Emily, that he lives with a stunning Norwegian au pair. So what chance does that leave an old lady like me? None at all, I wouldn't know where to start. Even if I *was* interested, which, as I told you, I'm not.'

'Okay, Mum.' Emily took another draught of wine and leaned forward across the table thoughtfully, her eyes shining in the candlelight. 'This is what you do ...'

14. Slip Road

'HERE, IS it?'

'Yeah, well, somewhere like this. I can't tell to the exact yard, can I?'

'But this is the right slip road? You're sure of that?'

'Sure as I can be. They all look the fucking same, don't they? Don't know how you lads can stand the country, all this grass and weeds and shit. Screws yer 'ead.' Gary caught the grim gaze of the York detective, and decided against taking the thought further. His day was already ruined - dragged out of his bed in Leeds at seven, for a start, before it was even light, and presented with the choice of either going to York *right now, this minute, Gary, get it?* or spending the day down the local nick while the police examined every square inch of his untaxed, uninsured, and probably unroadworthy car to see how many traces of illegal substances they could find in it. 'And we will find them, Gary,' DS Wilson had assured him. 'Whatever you say, we'll find some, I can assure you of that. Quite large amounts, I wouldn't wonder. Enough to keep you away from the lovely Sharon for a long time, which could make her lonely - know what I'm saying?'

Whereas if he could spare the time to help the York police - quite voluntarily, of course, his public duty as a citizen - then the search of the car could be postponed to a later date. Before which he might have found time to tax and insure it, possibly even wash and valet it as well.

Put like that, Gary found himself convinced. So now he stood on this dreary slip road outside York, looking for the place where Sean and Declan had discovered the hand. The two detectives assigned to this task were, in Gary's view, distinctly unfriendly and not very bright. Nonetheless, a good report from them, it seemed, was his best chance of continuing as a permanent occupant of Sharon's bed. So he did his best.

After half an hour they found the fox. Or at least *a* fox - it was impossible to be sure it was the right one. But there it was, on the hard shoulder where, he remembered, Sharon had flung it a second after Sean had wrapped it round her neck, saying it was a fur scarf - there were even skid marks where a truck had braked to avoid the Orion as it swerved erratically during their hysterical argument.

But if it was the right fox it was a lot worse for wear. Cars had flattened it, crows had pecked out its guts and eyes, and dust and insects were ruining the rest. Only the teeth still snarled, bitterly defying death. A detective snapped on latex gloves and gingerly lifted the thing by the gritty remains of its once glorious brush into an evidence bag.

'Make some pathologist's day, that will,' he said morosely.

'At least they get to work indoors,' muttered his companion. He nodded at an ominous dark cloud looming in the west. 'Let's get this finished while we can.'

Gary led them back along the slip road to the point where he thought the boys had originally found the animal. He wished they hadn't, now, but who could foresee the future? If little Wayne's bladder hadn't been about to burst he'd be safe in Leeds now, instead of trudging towards the mother and father of all rainstorms with two miserable coppers ...

'It was here,' he said, picking a spot at random. 'They hid behind that bush and sprang out at me. With the fox, and the hand.'

A wagon roared past, the wind rocking the three men on their feet. 'You let your kids play *here?*' The detective gazed at him in disgust.

'Not mine. Sharon's,' Gary said, as if that explained everything. Which it did, in a way. Even to the detectives, who shrugged and began a desultory search around the bush and the grass near the road.

When that yielded nothing, except a few cigarette packets and coke cans, they glanced at the approaching storm and decided to retreat to the car until it had passed. They sat and ate sandwiches while rain lashed the windscreen and wind rocked the car. Gary, who had brought nothing, was given a crust and a packet of crisps. When the sky finally cleared the detectives put on rubber boots and squelched around in the long grass while Gary stood on the hard shoulder, shivering and bored. An hour's search yielded nothing more significant than some windblown supermarket bags and a few rabbit holes.

'What did you expect?' Gary asked as they drove him back to the railway station. 'A skeleton, hopping about? A bagful of bones?'

'It's not funny, son,' one answered, leaning towards Gary with a face as blank as a killer whale. 'That hand belonged to a person, a human like you and me. It didn't just fall from the sky, as you and your kids - oh, sorry, *Sharon's* kids, are they? - seem to think. It's evidence, so we need to know where the rest of that evidence is - i.e. the body that hand came from. That person may be dead, a victim of an accident, or even murdered for all we know. Did that thought never occur to you, when you were letting your - I mean Sharon's - kids use it like a toy? Never think of taking it to the police, did you?'

He stared at Gary for a moment, waiting for an answer. Then he shook his head.

'No, of course not. Never crossed your mind, did it, Gary old son? Well, not to worry. We know where to find you. So if that body turns up, and it turns out to be someone you knew, well, we may just invite you back to answer a few more questions. That ok with you, Gary, is it?'

15. Michael Parker

SARAH SPENT the following day with Emily, meeting some of her friends, and taking her shopping in town. They seldom agreed on style - Emily despised her mother's weakness for designer labels as a sell-out to capitalism - but they did agree that Cambridge, with an icy east wind blasting across the fens from the North Sea, was one of the coldest places in the world. Sarah bought Emily some fingerless woolly mittens like those the market traders wore, and an Afghan sheepskin coat which the Irish salesman swore he had imported directly from a village in Tora Bora flattened by US marines. Neither of them totally believed him, but the warmth of the fleece around her neck, and the attractive ethnic embroidery, persuaded Emily to give him the benefit of the doubt. It really suited her, too.

'Thanks, Mum,' she said, hands thrust deep into the luxurious pockets as they battled the wind. 'At least we were supporting small traders against monopoly superstores, even if he has kissed the Blarney stone too often.'

'Take it as an early Christmas present,' said Sarah. 'I'll know you're warm now, not dying of some romantic chill as you crouch over your books in the library.'

The mention of study made Emily frown. She had an essay due on Tuesday which she had scarcely begun. So on Sunday morning Sarah worked in her hotel room until midday. Then she met Emily for lunch and caught a train in mid afternoon.

That went quite well, she thought, settling back into her seat and waving as Emily and the platform moved backwards. The train was full; even in first class most seats were taken. She unzipped her boots and was about to put her feet up on the seat opposite when a man came through the sliding doors. He surveyed the carriage for a moment, swaying slightly with the motion of the train. Then he glanced apologetically at Sarah.

'Is this seat taken?'

'No, it's free.' Regretfully, she pulled her feet back under the table, and watched as he slung his bag on the rack and sat down. He was tall, about her own age, clean shaven, with a pleasant lined face and dark hair greying at the temples. He wore a red and yellow anorak which he unzipped as he settled in his seat.

'Not many seats,' he said. 'Parents going home after the weekend, I suppose.'

'Probably.' She gazed out of the window at the darkening fields, then picked up a folder from her briefcase. But she'd read most of it already this morning; she only needed to check a few points. She was aware of the man's eyes watching her. 'Is that what you're doing then, too?'

'Me?' He seemed surprised and pleased that she'd asked him. 'No - well, yes, in a way. I'm sorry, that sounds like a politician. I mean, I don't have a child at the university, if that's what you meant. I've been visiting my daughter - she's at school here, in Cambridge.'

'I see.' It was a safe enough subject, Sarah thought. 'At boarding school, then?'

'No, she's at the Perse - a day girl. She lives with her mother.' The man hesitated, looking embarrassed. 'We're, um, you know, not together any more, you see. Hence my weekend visit.'

'Oh, I'm sorry.' It's happening everywhere, Sarah thought. 'How old is your daughter?'

'Thirteen. It's a difficult age. She's grown a foot in the past six months, cares passionately about her appearance, and her emotions are as stable as a mine field.'

'I remember,' Sarah smiled. 'That was a difficult age with my daughter too. They grow out of it, as the hormones settle down.'

'I'm glad to hear it. Sometimes I wonder if it's all because of me leaving home. But what can you do?' He chewed on his lower lip, as though at some memory which haunted him. 'What about your daughter? How old is she?'

'Nineteen. An undergraduate at the university. Just as you guessed.'

'Settling in well?'

'Well enough.' For the next few minutes Sarah talked about Emily - just the easy bits for public consumption - how well she'd done in the sixth form, the anxieties of the Cambridge interview, the trauma of leaving your daughter in a strange city for the first time, the relief at seeing her make new friends. The man listened courteously, relaxed in his seat, giving her his full attention.

'This is the first time you've visited her then? Since the start of term?'

'Yes. Which shows how well she's managing without us, I suppose.'

Us, she reflected sadly. So little relevance that word had to her now. And how well would Emily manage now, really - now that there was no *us* any more? She studied the man opposite. Were those lines around his mouth caused by the pain of divorce, or some other battering life had given him? Perhaps she could milk him for advice.

'How about your daughter?' she asked. 'Do you always come to her, or does she visit you sometimes?'

'In York, you mean? That's where I live. No. She came once, and didn't like it. I'd made her a nice room - got her a music centre, you know, toys and wallpaper I thought she'd like, but it wasn't any good. She has her social life in Cambridge, and that's what matters to them at that age, isn't it? So it's easier if I just fit in.'

'I see.' Sarah probed gently. 'You're divorced, then?'

'Yes, I'm afraid so.' He smiled - a rather winning smile, Sarah thought, doing interesting things to the lines around his eyes and mouth. 'But there are compensations, I'm glad to say. Freedom, especially.'

'Freedom?' That scarey word again. All her life, Sarah had been part of a family. It was within that family - her own, since she was sixteen - that she had created her own space, the only freedom she knew. Now she was alone.

'Yes, you know - at my time of life, to be free to come and go as you choose, do what you like, whenever you like. With whoever you choose.' He smiled again. He had green eyes, she noticed - an unusual colour in a man. 'It takes a bit of getting used to, but it's worth having when you do. Believe me.'

'Isn't it very lonely?' It was a bald, intimate question to ask a stranger, but Sarah really wanted to know.

'Lonely? Well, sometimes, yes. But then there are so many people in the same boat these days that - well, you get to recognize each other. And seek mutual comfort.'

Belatedly, Sarah saw that the conversation was leading her down an alley where she didn't feel safe. 'I'm sorry,' she said, retracing her steps. 'It's none of my business. What do you do, anyway, in York?'

'Property developer.'

Emily wouldn't like that, Sarah thought. But then the man who sold her the Afghan coat is a capitalist too, of a sort. 'What, you mean you build shopping malls, things like that?'

'I wish. No, strictly small-time, I'm afraid. Most of the time I buy derelict houses and do them up for a profit. I did one housing estate, but it nearly drove me into an early grave. Property rental, as well. That brings in steady cash.'

'Renting to students, you mean?'

'Students, single people, families caught in a chain - anyone who needs it, really.' He studied her for a minute. 'What about you?'

'Me? I'm a barrister.' Sarah smiled faintly, wondering which of the many familiar responses this announcement would elicit. Most people, if they first met her away from court, were surprised; the stereotype of a barrister still seemed to be a middle aged man in a pinstriped suit. Some were intimidated, and backed away; others were embarrassed, as though it were not a nice job to mention in polite society. Others became aggressive, haranguing her with tales of their bad experiences with the law, and the excessive fees they had been charged. A few - the ones she liked - were intrigued or simply curious.

'Really? How interesting! What sort of cases do you do?'

'Criminal, mostly. I've just come from the Court of Appeal.' It was a boast, but so what? She enjoyed saying it, and this man wouldn't realise how much it meant.

'Did you win?'

'Yes.' And before she knew it, she was describing the case, which had appeared in the Sunday papers this morning. He was a good listener, this stranger, and reasonably good looking too. As she talked, she remembered with sly amusement the advice Emily had offered the other night. 'Make the most of yourself, Mum, tell people what you do, and how you got there. It's interesting, and people like that. Bright men will, at least, unless they're intimidated by an intelligent woman, and you don't want that type anyway. You know, your eyes light up when you talk about your work - because you love it, I suppose. And you really look quite pretty at times.'

A compliment of sorts, from a critical daughter. She wondered what she looked like now. The man seemed interested, certainly, those green eyes watching as she talked. But there was something wary, too in his expression - something he disliked about the story. Or was it her? She cut the tale short with a shrug.

'And so that's it. He's free. To begin life again after 18 years, if he can.'

The man looked out of the window - *that's not in Emily's plan, surely?* - and frowned

'But was he really innocent, do you think?'

Sarah sighed. So that was it. He must be one of those people who trust the police implicitly, so anyone who challenges them must be wrong. 'That's not my job to determine. The judges rejected his conviction as unsafe, which is what matters. So he's a free man at last. Great triumph for me. And him. Not so good for the police, of course.'

'Congratulations.' He continued to gaze out of the window, as if the conversation was over. Thanks for the advice, Emily, Sarah thought wryly. But it doesn't seem to work. Better stick to the day job.

With an effort, the man turned back. 'So, where did you stay, in Cambridge?'

Oh well, perhaps he wanted to talk to her in spite of her job, rather than because of it. 'At the Garden Court Hotel. What about you?'

'Oh, at my old college, St John's. I got a grotty room, but it's cheap, and less anonymous than a hotel. Helps me remember my youth.' He smiled again, briefly.

'So you were a student there too?'

'Yes, many years ago. It's where I met my wife. Happy memories, you see. And sad ones too, of course.'

Sarah felt sorry for him. Perhaps that was what he'd been thinking about while she was boasting about her triumph in court. If he'd suffered anything like the pain she'd suffered over the past few nights, he might well still be scarred by it. It occurred to her suddenly that this was the first divorced person she had actually met since that traumatic night with Bob.

'How long have you been divorced?' she asked.

'Three years,' he said sadly. 'In some ways it seems like yesterday. Then when I look at Sandra - that's my daughter - and compare her to the photos of when we were together I see how much I've missed.'

Maybe I'm probing too much, Sarah thought. Especially in a chance encounter with a stranger. She gazed out of the window, remembering her own photo albums at home, and for a while they didn't speak.

'So what about your husband?' he resumed, breaking the silence. 'Does he come to Cambridge sometimes?'

'Bob?' A dry laugh, like a sob, escaped her. 'No, I'm afraid not. He, er ...' She drew a deep breath. 'He came down that first time, to settle Emily in, but ... I'm sorry, you weren't to know, but I ... I came to Cambridge partly to tell my daughter her father's asking for a divorce. So you see I'm joining the club.'

She fumbled for some tissues in her handbag. This is becoming a habit, she told herself grimly. But it's my own fault, for starting to talk about it.

'I'm sorry, I didn't realise.'

'It doesn't matter.' She blew her nose and smiled brightly. 'I'll have to get used to this, I suppose.'

'How did she take it, your daughter?'

'Badly, at first. She thinks we'll have to sell the house and she'll lose her home. But you must remember what it's like. It's new to me, you see.'

'Yes, well, Kate didn't sell the house. I just left, and started again. Your daughter's how old?'

'Nineteen.'

'She'll get over it. Young people do, you know. Youth has terrible resilience. Think back to when you were her age. Did you care, really, about what your parents got up to? I'll bet you were more bound up in your own emotional traumas.'

Sarah laughed. 'You can say that again. But then my life was pretty traumatic.' She looked up as the drinks trolley arrived. He ordered beer, she a small cocktail. Sarah smiled. This was a good way to travel; drinks, pleasant conversation with a good looking man. She leaned back in her seat and relaxed, watching some horses galloping in a field outside the window.

'Go on then,' he said. 'Tell me. What were you like at nineteen? Committed to social justice, I'll bet. Smashed out of your mind on dope and arguing with your parents about capitalist oppression.'

'Hardly.' Sarah smiled reflectively. 'I was wheeling a buggy round a slum in Leeds and going to evening classes.' For the next hour, as the light outside the window gradually faded to dusk, she told him the tale of her catastrophic teenage years. It was therapy for her, in a way. 'So Bob was my white knight, you see. He rescued me from failure. Only now I'm such a success he's lost interest, it seems. So he's found another young mother to save.'

The man listened with sympathy and interest. 'It's a great story,' he said at last. 'I'd no idea. I mean, I often make quick judgements about people but I'd never have guessed any of this.'

'No? What would you have guessed?'

'Oh, you know, working class girl makes good, goes to redbrick university, takes up the law to do what? Make money?'

'That's part of it,' Sarah conceded. 'But I'm lucky to have any work at all. Do you have any idea how many people get to the Bar and no further? About fifty per cent.'

'Good Lord! So what do they do?'

'Go into the City, become teachers, lecturers, backpackers, whatever. What about you? How did you get into property developing?'

'Well, I got my degree, did a postgrad year in business management in York, and then joined a training scheme at Jolyons, a big construction company in East Anglia. As a sort of management trainee. I didn't know anything about construction but I learnt on the job. Then, after five years, I began to see how to make money - you know, how to spot an opportunity, how to put a deal together, how to squeeze out your rivals. So I thought, I'm learning things here, maybe I can put them to my own advantage. There were a couple of ruined cottages in a village where we lived. I bought them for a song and did them up as commuter homes, and it worked. Then I bought a barn and converted that as well. I was on my way.'

'You make it sound easy.'

'It's not, it's a lot of hard work. But working for myself, there was more satisfaction. I paid off our mortgage, got in at the start of the property boom - it went well for a while. Until I lost a wife on the way. And the family home, which cost more.' He grimaced, sipping his beer.

'That was generous,' said Sarah, thinking of Bob and her home by the river. 'Couldn't you have sold up and divided the equity?'

'I could have insisted on that, yes. But Kate, she's a teacher, she doesn't have much money. And I had a couple of deals to keep me going. So I thought what the hell? Bite the bullet, move to York, and start again. Which I did.'

Let's hope Bob does the same, Sarah thought. Fat chance. I should have married a man like this instead. They talked quietly for the rest of the journey. The man showed her plans of his latest projects - a farmhouse and two barns near Scarborough, and a windmill near Pocklington which he was converting into a house. He gave her his card, with the name *Town and Country Properties* on it - and she gave him hers. And as they passed Doncaster and headed towards York, she described one or two of the more interesting cases she'd been involved in.

They'd been talking for nearly two hours, and getting on well. Sarah wondered if the exchange of cards would lead to anything else - a phone call perhaps, a meal together. He seemed confident, pleasant, attractive. Emily would be proud of me, she thought. After all, now she was free ... But she'd been married so long, she had little idea of what to expect. Or how to deal with it, if anything happened.

Then, near York, his mood changed. She'd been describing her successful defence of a robber, when he frowned.

'Don't you sometimes get sick of it, though? When you get some thug off just because the police can't prove it, even though you're almost certain he's guilty? You must hate yourself then. I mean, what about that case in the Court of Appeal? Don't you worry about that man - what's his name? - James Barnes? What if he kills someone else?'

'Jason Barnes. It's a risk, I suppose,' Sarah said, surprised at the intensity of the question. 'But you have to put it out of your mind. After all, he can't really do it *again*, can he? Not after he won his appeal. So far as the law is concerned, he never did it in the first place.'

'Well, let's hope the judges are right, that's all' he said, as they got up to lift down their bags. 'So we can all sleep safely in our beds.'

They parted outside the station, amicably enough. In the taxi on the way home, Sarah thought back on the conversation, curiously. Pleasant enough for most of the journey. Then there'd been that change of mood, this sudden waspishness at the end.

16. Broken Glass

DETECTIVE CHIEF Inspector Will Churchill was a very different man from his retired colleague, Detective Superintendent Robert Baxter. Churchill was young, in his mid thirties, suave, well dressed, and single. His bachelor status was a source of mystery to some, envy to others. Since his arrival in York he had become notorious for the string of nubile young women who seemed to accompany him on adventure holidays. Photographs of these girls, water-skiing, hang-gliding, or windsurfing, succeeded each other with bewildering rapidity on the wall of his office. Each looked attractive and daring, but none seemed to stay with him long. Perhaps it was his technique, the gossips whispered; he wasn't man enough to satisfy them. Or perhaps it was his ambition; he was seeking perfection in women and couldn't be satisfied with less, just as he aimed high in his career and would never be satisfied until he reached the top.

If Baxter had once shared this ambition, it was almost the only thing the two men had in common. It grated with Will Churchill that this big, powerful athlete, a heavily built bruiser who had played prop forward for police rugby teams, had been Detective Superintendent, a rank above his own. To Churchill he looked like a bouncer rather than a detective. Baxter was a family man, a grandfather with a married son in the Royal Artillery. He spoke seldom, only when he had something to say. And when he did, he exuded bitterness and contempt. Jason Barnes' successful appeal disgusted him. He had given his life to the police force, he said, and for what? He'd been betrayed. He held forth at length about this in the train on the way home. It wasn't just the lawyer, Sarah Newby, whom he despised - at least he and Churchill could agree about that - but almost everything, in his opinion, had got worse since he retired. Paperwork, political correctness, gender equality, health and safety, offender profiling - the list went on and on.

'In my day, lad, we knew the villains, and they knew us,' he said, staring reflectively out of the train window with a can of Boddingtons in his hand as the fields flashed past. 'And no one got to the top unless he was fit, strong and had a good record of arrests. None of this bollocks about targets and sensitive management styles. And the streets were a lot safer, believe you me. Now it's them that have rights, and our lot have none.'

'Things have changed, sir, but some have got better,' Churchill said quietly. 'We've got a lot more technology, for a start. Better forensics.'

'That's what I said too, at your age.' Baxter supped his drink gloomily. 'But I don't envy you lot, I tell you straight. You've a harder job than we did. Makes me mad, all that red tape.'

His cross-examination by Sarah Newby had enraged him, and his fury when Jason won his appeal was so great that Churchill had feared he might commit an assault. One can of Boddingtons succeeded another, until his face glowed like a fire bomb.

'That lad's guilty as hell, always was, always will be,' he repeated, in a voice that grew louder as the journey progressed. 'Fancy bitch barrister, getting him off on a technicality - how would she like it, if it was one of her daughters, eh? If she's not too dried up to have any, like she should be doing. And my reputation ruined - thirty years' service, and in my obituary they'll say I got the wrong man. Like fuck I did! Wait till he kills someone else - then they'll see!'

Will Churchill was glad to get him safely off the train and home without incident. But despite the swearing and out-dated prejudices, he felt sorry for the old man. It was a dreadful thing to happen to anyone, to see a case that should have been the pinnacle of his career turn into a millstone round his neck, a label for fools to point scorn at. Particularly when he'd been trashed by a pair of middle-aged women - Sarah Newby and her overweight solicitor sidekick, Lucy Parsons. Churchill knew what that felt like. He'd loathed the sight of them ever since they'd humiliated him in court last year. And now, by proxy, it had happened again. He himself had only been a trainee constable in Essex at the time of the original case, but he'd read about it when he came to York. It had been a big deal at the time. Another murderer locked up, more proof that the police got their man, and justice was served. Now all that was undone. Once again the York CID - his team - would be vilified in the press. Sarah Newby had triumphed, while he, DCI Will Churchill, sat in court and watched.

He didn't like it, and he wanted to put things right.

The one thing Sarah had not expected to find when she got home was Bob's Volvo in the drive. Her hands shook as she paid off the taxi. What did this mean? Had he changed his mind after all? She'd been nervous enough about coming home to an empty house as it was, but this ...

She walked up the drive, dragging her wheeled suitcase behind her. All the lights were on, including the outside light above the garage. The Volvo's tailgate was raised, the back full of boxes and bin liners. As she came nearer, Bob came out of the front door, staggering under the weight of a large cardboard box. He stopped when he saw her.

'What have you got there?'

'It's my wine. From the wine club,' he said defensively. He was wearing an old pullover and corduroy trousers, she noted numbly. His hair was ragged and uncombed, his glasses pushed slightly sideways on his nose.

'I thought I asked you to take all this on Wednesday.' Her voice sounded pale, distant, detached from her body somehow. A body that was trembling with shock.

'Yes, I know, I'm sorry Sarah, but we - I've been busy.'

'*We?* You mean that woman's here too?' She left her suitcase and pushed past him into the house, nearly causing him to stagger and drop the wine. The hall was cluttered with more boxes.

'No, of course not. I'm here on my own.' He dumped the wine in the Volvo and returned to the hall. 'I'd hoped to be gone before you came.'

'It's eight in the evening, Bob. You've had four days.'

'As I said, I've been busy.'

'And I haven't, I suppose.' They stood staring at each other in the hall, across a wasteland of his possessions. She shook her head slowly. This man whom she had loved. 'How long will it take you to clear all this?'

'Five, ten minutes, I suppose. I'm nearly done.'

'Get on with it, then. I don't want to see you.'

She marched into the kitchen, put the kettle on, sat down at the table, put her head in her hands, got up, walked round in a circle, went back to the kitchen door. Bob was lifting a box full of books.

'I just said take your clothes, that's all.'

'I'm taking all my things. Then you'll be shot of me.'

She stood there watching numbly as he took out the books, then more boxes and bags. The last one, she noted, had a photo album on top.

'Stop! You're not taking that!' She snatched it out of the box as he lifted it. He put the box down.

'I am, Sarah. That's mine.'

'It's *ours*, you mean. Photos of all of us.'

'Who do you think took them and put the albums together? Me, Emily and Simon. Not you.'

She opened the album and saw photos of the children making sandcastles on the beach at Filey. Emily looked about five, Simon eight. 'These are my children, Bob!'

'They're mine too - Emily is anyway. And *I* took that photo. You weren't even there, on that holiday. You were at an Open University course!'

'You're not taking these photos!' She put the album on the stairs behind her and snatched another from the box. 'None of them, they're mine! What are you going to do, share them with your fancy woman in Harrogate?'

'No, Sarah, I'm taking them for me.' He picked up another album and opened it at random. 'See, look at this here. Photos of me and Emily. Emily with her friends. Emily and Simon in the park. Me teaching Emily to swim. Where are you in these photos?'

'I must have taken it, mustn't I?' She pointed to the swimming photo. 'You couldn't have taken it, you're in it!'

'No, it was Simon probably - or some lifeguard I handed the camera. You were too busy, Sarah, most of the time. Nearly all the time in fact.'

Sarah was so angry she nearly choked. 'You come here, Bob - you come back here tonight when I told you to be gone by Wednesday - and not content with wrecking our marriage you ransack our house for every little memory of our family! You ...' For once in her life words failed her.

Bob turned the pages of the album, with a look of calm, invincible reasonableness. A look so maddening that, Sarah recalled, it had once driven her son Simon to try to kill him with a poker. He pulled out three photos and passed them to her.

'There you are - there's one of you. And two more. That's all I can find. You keep them, Sarah - I'm taking the rest.' He reached behind her, grabbed the album from the stairs, picked up the box and walked out of the door.

She looked down at the photo. There was Emily, aged about eight, standing proudly in a pink ballet dress, holding her hand. Sarah vaguely remembered the occasion - a play the ballet class had put on. She'd been bored but felt duty bound to go. Her other hand in the photo, she noted with horror, held a book.

Bob came back in. 'That's the lot. I won't trouble you further. There's just this.' He held out an envelope.

'What's that?'

'A letter from my lawyers. I think it's best if we handle this through them, don't you? Less pain in the long run, no doubt.'

'Less pain?'

'Yes. Don't think this doesn't hurt me too. I haven't had much sleep this week - or last week either, come to that. But I'm sure it's the best in the long run. I wouldn't have done it otherwise.'

'Oh, you bastard!' Her body trembled, his image blurred in front of her eyes. 'Get out of here now! Go on, go!' Her hand closed round something and picked it up.

Looking alarmed, Bob retreated, pulling the door to behind him. As he did so, Sarah hurled the potted plant in her hand. It smashed into the door, shattering one of the small glass panes near the top, and spraying the hall with soil, leaves and broken glass. She heard the Volvo start up outside, and opened the door in time to see it turn right onto the road.

She slumped on the doorstep, head in her hands, defeated.

Then she got up and walked into the wreckage of her home.

17. New Recruit

ON TUESDAY morning, just to improve Terry's life further, his daughter Esther refused to go to school. Her throat was burning, her face flushed, she had a temperature. Terry drove Jessica to school while his nanny, Trude, made an appointment with the doctor. As a result he arrived late for work where his desk was already piling up with problems for the week. He was due in court on Friday to give evidence in a complicated drugs case. He'd arrested the villains six months ago - ancient history for a busy Detective Inspector - but he would need each detail fresh in his mind to avoid the traps set by a cunning defence barrister, who had probably read each sentence of his witness statement a dozen times. He'd meant to read the statement last night, but this business with Sarah Newby and now Esther had put it out of his mind. There'd been a spate of street robberies in the last few days, probably a visiting gang from Leeds or Hull, and Terry had organised a team of undercover officers to go out and deal with it. He briefed them now on what to do. While he was speaking to them a report came in about another woman being harassed by a flasher in Bishopthorpe.

Terry sighed. It was an annoying problem that just wouldn't seem to go away. With so much else going on, it was hard to find enough time to devote to it. Four weeks ago, a series of disturbing headlines had begun to appear in the *York Press*. The first had been relatively trivial - *Knicker Theft in Naburn, Ghoul Ogles Keep-Fit Lady* - but the incidents had been upsetting, Terry knew, for the women themselves. In the first, female underwear had been stolen from a washing line in a village just south of York; in the second, a housewife had been doing yoga in her front room when she'd seen a strange man watching her from the end of her garden. A young man, powerfully built, ogling her while he urinated against a tree. At least, that's what she hoped he was doing. When she ran for the phone he hopped over the garden wall onto the cycletrack and disappeared.

The cycletrack - that was the second thing that linked the two incidents. City of York Council prided itself on its environmentally friendly pro-cycling initiatives, so the city and surrounding villages were criss-crossed by an elaborate web of cycletracks. This second incident - in the village of Bishopthorpe, where the Archbishop of York had his palace - occurred in a house that backed onto the same cycletrack that passed through Naburn two miles further south. It was a fine cycletrack: Terry Bateson, in training for the Great North Run, knew it well. It was laid out as a model of the solar system, on a scale of 575,872,239:1. It began with a model of the Sun near York, and then little informative plinths marked where each planet would be along the route. Mercury, Venus and Earth were a few hundred yards apart, then the distances gradually extended to Pluto, in the village of Riccall, ten kilometres away. Terry had taken his daughters there to show them. They had been entranced to learn that on their bikes they were travelling at something like 6 times the speed of light, making them younger at the end of the journey than when they began.

We puzzled over that for hours, Terry remembered. But I'd hesitate to take them there now, with this pervert around. That's what criminals do; limit other people's freedom.

The third incident came a week later - a jogger, a young woman, was accosted by a cyclist who tried to get into conversation with her. At first it seemed innocuous, then he started to ask what she wore under her tights, what colour her underwear was, did it get sweaty ... She escaped into the house of a friend, and called the police, but the young man was gone. Terry had arranged for a photofit to appear in the Press, under the headline *Cycle Pest Strikes Again*. The letters column of the paper had featured urgent calls for the police to protect women, and householders with gardens backing onto cycletracks complained that their property was being devalued.

And now, here was another report. A woman called Sally McFee claimed to have come home from shopping in the afternoon to see a man climbing hurriedly over the fence at the end of her garden and pedalling away along the cycletrack. At first she'd wondered if she was imagining things, because of all the reports in the *Evening Press*, but then she'd found that the French windows, which she'd forgotten to lock, were wide open, and - more disturbing still - someone appeared to have been in her bedroom. Her underwear drawer was open, and the intruder seemed to have taken several pairs of knickers and an expensive necklace which she had worn to a party the previous night.

Terry sighed. Clearly the situation was getting worse. If this was the same man, he was getting bolder and more dangerous. But there were all these other demands on his attention.

He snatched a coffee from the machine, reached his desk, and sat down, wondering whether to refresh his memory about the drugs trial, or investigate this new report. Before he could decide, he saw his boss, Will Churchill, advancing on him across the floor. Coming towards him beside Churchill was a woman Terry had not seen before. She was tall, about five foot ten, with short brown hair and a mannish, confident way of walking. Her face was not ugly exactly, but somehow devoid of any suggestion of femininity. A snub nose, wide mouth, firm chin, cool, assertive grey eyes beneath a line of dark eyebrows. She wore a brown leather jacket and jeans which clung tightly around hips which, to Terry, looked more powerful than appealing.

He wondered what Churchill, whose office was festooned with photos of glamorous waterskiing blondes in wetsuits, was doing with such a woman. He soon found out.

The pair stopped in front of Terry's desk, a sly ingratiating smile on the younger man's face.

'Terence, allow me to present Jane Carter - newly promoted Detective Sergeant and assigned to our team. I want you to look after her and show her the ropes.'

'But - I'm up to my neck!' Terry indicated the mess of papers on his desk.

'Then Jane can give you a hand. She's a smart cookie, Terence - highest arrest profile in Beverley this year! That's why I brought her - thought she might help you with the Bishopthorpe flasher case - see it with a fresh pair of eyes. How's that going anyway?'

'It's getting worse,' Terry said. 'There's been a new report of a burglary, and I'm short-handed. Bill Jones is off sick, I've got a team chasing shoplifters round town, I'm due in court on Friday, and ...'

'Always the same,' Churchill said sympathetically. 'Too many bad guys, not enough saints. I'd help you myself, only I've got a management training course later this week, and a report on a missing hand to look into.

Still, my loss is your gain, eh? Keen young woman to take the weight off your shoulders. Just what you need, Terence - man of your age!'

With a broad wink, Will Churchill stepped back, made as if to slap Jane Carter on her rump, thought better of it, and strode smugly back towards his office. Terry sighed, got to his feet, and held out his hand. 'Ok, well, nice to meet you.'

Her grip was firm, as strong as his own. 'Good to be here.' She glanced at his desk. 'Busy day?'

'Busy week, looks like.' Terry sat down, waved her to a chair, and took a sip of the scalding coffee. It burned his throat. No, please, he thought. Don't let me be coming down with what Esther's got. That would be the last straw. 'Come from Beverley, have you?'

'Yes. It's not as dramatic as he said, but ...'

'I can imagine.' Terry thought of Beverley, a quiet country town on the Yorkshire Wolds, halfway between York and Hull. Now that would be a quiet place to work. No Will Churchill, for a start. 'Lot of cattle rustling, was there? Stolen tractors and lads buggering sheep?'

Jane Carter stiffened. 'Agricultural crime is big business, you know. Some of those syndicates steal to order. By the time the farmer wakes up, his tractor's halfway to Poland and he's lost fifty grand.'

'And you got them back?'

'Some of them, yes.'

Terry looked at her, saw the determination in the woman's face. A young woman, he realised slowly. Probably not thirty yet, and already a detective sergeant. That would take some doing, particularly in rural North Yorkshire. Progress might have led to a few token women being favoured with positive discrimination, but a greater number had probably been held back, or deterred from applying for promotion altogether. This girl didn't look as though she'd received any special favours. For a start, her appearance was against her. If there was a casting couch in Northallerton, he doubted if she'd been laid on it.

'What's all this talk about a flasher near Bishopthorpe?' she asked. 'Sounds quite serious, in its way. Guys like that can cause a lot of fear in the community, if they aren't caught straight away.'

Terry sat back, looking at her thoughtfully. Maybe she could offer some help after all. 'That's true, of course. And another report came in yesterday.' He searched among the papers on his desk. 'Here it is. Why don't I fill you in? Someone stole knickers and a necklace, it seems. From a woman called Sally McFee.'

18. Mother and Son

'YOU WERE aiming for his head, were you?'

'I don't know what I was doing, Simon. It was purely spontaneous. I threw it before I even knew I'd picked it up.'

'Well, it's head height here. You'd have laid him out flat if he hadn't closed the door in time.'

Sarah's son, Simon, stood in the hall with his mother, contemplating her ruined front door with interest. The pane that she'd smashed with the plant pot was small, about head height as Simon said. She'd taped a square of cardboard over it to keep out the wind, but was grateful that he'd come over with his bag of tools to fix it for her. She'd told him the bare bones of why it had happened - Bob's decision to move out, his demand for a divorce - but it had shocked Simon less than Emily, at least on the surface. Despite all the photos Bob had taken with him - of himself playing football, making sandcastles, tobogganing with Simon as a young boy - Simon's teenage years had been one long war of attrition with his stepfather.

As a man, Bob was gawky, clumsy, academic. His attempts to involve himself in boys' games had always been well-meaning failures, distractions from the real business of childhood, which was schoolwork, academic success. Simon's priorities had always been exactly the opposite: he loathed schoolwork, but everything physical or practical he understood immediately. He doesn't inherit that from me, Sarah thought, watching him calmly assess the minor problem of the window; all these traits must have come from his natural father Kevin, the teenage tearaway who had seduced her at the age of fifteen, and given her the most tumultuous, passionate time of her life, before divorcing her 18 months later.

Simon seemed surprised but not hurt by the new situation. He'd given her a hug as soon as he'd arrived - an unusual demonstration of affection for him - and it seemed there was no question whose side he was likely to take in the divorce. 'You're better off without him, Mum,' he said calmly, 'if that's how he behaves. He's probably been cheating on you for years and you didn't know.'

'What, *Bob?* Not for years, surely, Simon, he's not that kind of man,' Sarah said, grateful but a little worried by Simon's suggestion. 'There was that secretary, Stephanie, sometime last year. But there wasn't anyone else, was there, that you know of?'

Simon shook his head. 'He wouldn't have told me anyway, would he, Mum? I'm just guessing. But if he's done it twice, he may have done it more often.'

'I don't want to think about it. That Stephanie was awful - how he could choose a woman like that ...'

'Have you met her, this - what's her name - teacher he's moving in with?'

'Sonya? No. And I don't want to. If I liked her I'd be jealous and if I didn't I'd just be humiliated. I'm humiliated anyway. I hope we never meet.'

'You could do better, Mum,' Simon said thoughtfully, rolling thin sausages of putty carefully into the rebate of the door. 'There's lots of guys out there who'd give their eye teeth to meet a woman like you.'

'Thanks, Simon. A man with no teeth. Just what I need, at my time of life.'

He laughed. 'You know what I mean.' He picked up the pane of glass, pressed it carefully into place, and began to cut a thin wooden strip to go on top of it. Sarah watched, admiring his calm practical confidence.

'Yes, and it's kind of you, but right now I need a fish like a man on a bicycle. No, that's wrong, I mean ...'

Simon put his tools down, amused but slightly offended. 'If that's how you feel, you can fix this door yourself.'

She laughed. 'No, Simon, of course I don't mean you. Please go on, don't stop now. What I mean is, my main priority now is to work out how to live on my own. I'm not used to it. I've never been alone before, not since you were born.'

'When you were what? Sixteen?'

'Yes. And even then I'd run away from home to live with your father. When he left I was lost until Bob came along. I could never have managed on my own.' She sighed, thinking how close she had come to putting

Simon up for adoption, as her mother and the social worker had wanted. She'd never told him that, and now didn't seem to be the time. 'At least I'm a bit older. But it's hard.' She sighed. 'I may have to sell this house, for a start. Either that or take out a massive loan which I can't afford.'

Simon stood back from the door. 'There, that should hold it. I'll come back in a few days when it's dry, to give it a lick of paint.' He began to put his tools away in his toolbox. 'What are you talking about, Mum, sell the house? Why? I thought you liked living here.'

'I do, Simon, you know I do. But for a start, there's only one salary coming in now instead of two. And more importantly, Bob wants his equity. He says so in that letter from his lawyers. Anyway, it's too big for a woman on her own. Look, I can't even shut the front door without smashing it.'

Simon smiled thoughtfully. 'I could move in here for a bit, Mum, if you want.'

'What? No - Simon, that's sweet of you, but you'd hate it.'

Unlike Sarah and Emily, who loved it, Simon had loathed this house from the moment they'd moved in. He'd been sixteen at the time, in the middle of his teenage crisis. The luxurious, detached house, with its beautiful garden, trees, lawns, riverside views and country walks, had epitomised everything he wanted to rebel against. It was too far from town, for a start, where his friends were; and everything about it spoke of affluence, education, middle-class values - all things that Simon, a resentful failure at school, had been desperate to reject.

Bob, and Sarah too, had tried to persuade him to stay on at school, but Simon was having none of it. He was a working class lad like his dad; he wanted to use his hands, not books and paper. So he left home to live in a terraced house in town and work on building sites, where he'd got into the most awful trouble from which Sarah had had to rescue him. But now, surprisingly, here he was, three years later, a calm, confident young man, able to come to her aid when she needed him. Perhaps, she thought hopefully, he was even happy.

'You wouldn't want to live here. You've got Lorraine, haven't you - your own life to lead?' She was touched, but also a little apprehensive. This new relationship with her son might not survive actually sharing her home with him and his new girlfriend.

Simon pulled a crumpled newspaper out of his toolbag - yesterday's

Press. 'Look here, Mum, have you seen this?'

It was a report of a prowler spying on women near the Bishopthorpe cyclepath, and stealing underwear from their gardens.

'You ought to think about that, Mum. Check your locks and alarm. Draw the curtains before you put the lights on.'

'Why? You don't think I'm in any danger, do you? I'm too old, for a start.'

'Mum, don't be silly. Perverts like this ... anyway you're not old. And more to the point, every time this guy attacks, it's some woman who lives alone in a house that backs onto some cycletrack or footpath. And what's out the back of your house? A footpath along the river.'

'Yes, I know Simon, but all this happened the other side of town. Anyway, not all these women were at home, look. One of them was actually walking along the cycle track.'

'Yes, well, you do that too sometimes, don't you, Mum - walk by the river? Not any more, Mum, please, not on your own. Not until this weirdo's caught, at least.'

Sarah looked at him, touched by his concern. 'Okay, Simon, I promise to look after myself. But ...'

Just then the telephone rang. 'Make us some tea, Simon,' she said, going to answer it. 'I'll be with you in a minute.' A few minutes later she joined him in the kitchen, with a quizzical smile on her face. 'Well, there you are. It seems you're a prophet as well as my protector.'

Simon passed her a mug of tea. 'Why? Who was that?'

'A man I met on the train a couple of days ago. A property developer.'

'And?'

Sarah drew a deep breath. 'Well, his name is Michael Parker, and he's about my age, quite good-looking, still has his teeth, and, er - he's divorced, with a daughter at school in Cambridge.'

'So?' Simon stared at her, surprised. 'Why are you telling me this? *Mum?*'

'Well, the thing is, Simon, we got talking, and ... well, he's asked me out for a meal.'

'A date, you mean?'

'Yes. I suppose you could call it that, Simon. I've been asked out on a date.'

19. Peter Barton

WHEN JANE Carter had been posted to York she had hoped, perhaps naively, that her reputation would have gone before her. She was a serious, dedicated policewoman, and her arrest score in Beverley had been second to none. But here, she found herself in the position of the unknown new girl. The team she was posted to did not seem particularly happy - there was friction between the boss, DCI Will Churchill, and his number two, DI Terry Bateson. Churchill seemed glad to be rid of her, and Terry Bateson was little better. He'd driven her to Bishopthorpe on Monday morning, but on the way he'd stopped off at a chemist and then spent fifteen minutes at his own home, leaving her to twiddle her thumbs in the car outside.

The man seemed obsessed with his family, which Jane found hard to relate to. Unmarried as she was, she'd always thought that a career officer - particularly in the CID - had to make a choice. The irregular, unsocial hours worked by criminals demanded a similar commitment by their pursuers, a lifestyle hard to match with a young family. If I ever have children, Jane thought, my husband will have to care for the kids. But she'd never met a man like that. And anyway, Jane asked herself gloomily on the occasional lonely evenings when she thought about it, what sort of man would that be? Hardly the sort to set her blood racing.

But here was Terry Bateson, a detective inspector, no less - and a single parent as well! To Jane it seemed an impossible combination. Her first week in York only confirmed that judgement. The man seemed obsessed with his daughter's asthma attack, only half focussed on the work at hand. And now he'd given her this issue of the flasher on the Bishopthorpe cycletrack.

She had a suspicion that Terry Bateson, being a man, didn't regard this case as very serious, but Jane certainly did. The man had already progressed from stealing knickers from a washing line to stealing them from a bedroom, and from exposing himself in a garden to accosting a jogger on the cycletrack. It looked to her like the early stages of the classic progression of a sex offender, beginning with small offences and then daring himself to try bigger ones. If he wasn't stopped soon, it could become very serious indeed.

The three women who had seen the man came in to make photofits. The results were reasonably similar. All the images of their persecutor had dark, shoulder length hair, thick eyebrows, and - not surprisingly, perhaps, given the women's anxiety - a menacing frown. The image made by the jogger - Melanie Thorpe - looked slightly younger than the other two, but the eyes, mouth and nose were close enough. It increased Jane's belief that she was after a single offender.

Over the next few days she visited shops, pubs and farms, the sewage works and marina at Naburn, and even the imposing riverside palace of the Archbishop of York in Bishopthorpe. She distributed the photofits and asked about any suspicious behaviour towards women. One evening, she even jogged along the cycletrack herself. She wore tightfitting lycra shorts, as Melanie Thorpe had done. But no strange men accosted her. She hadn't expected it, really. She had few illusions about her attractions - or, sadly, lack of them - as far as the male sex were concerned. The only way her face would launch a thousand ships, her younger brother had once cruelly told her, would be if they were full of men fleeing for their lives. So if the pervert was there, he was only one of many whose eyes scanned her briefly, then looked hurriedly away.

The breakthrough came on a Thursday afternoon. A 999 call came in from Bishopthorpe - a girl had been assaulted on the cyclepath. An area car was despatched but within minutes Jane was on her way. She arrived at an address on the south-eastern side of the village, where the cyclepath passed through an estate of small detached houses not far from that of Sally McFee, the woman who had lost knickers and a necklace from her bedroom. A uniformed constable was dealing with an altercation between two men. One, a burly, bald-headed man in his mid thirties, had an armlock on a younger man, who the constable was trying to persuade him to release. A teenage girl was watching, her arms folded, her hair hanging forward over her face.

'You cuff him,' the older man insisted. 'Then I'll let him go.'

'If you don't let him go I'll charge you with assault,' the constable insisted, somewhat feebly, Jane thought.

'Bollocks to that. This is a citizen's arrest. I called you, didn't I? Do you want him to rape more teenage girls? Nasty little pervert, he needs gelding!' He twisted the younger man's arm behind his back, so that he cried out in pain.

'Everyone has rights, sir. Why don't you just release this man, then we can all calm down and I can take a statement.'

Jane strode forward, flashing her warrant card. 'All right, constable, I'll take charge of this. I'm a detective sergeant, sir. Is this your house?' The man nodded. 'Then I suggest you release this man and go inside. The constable will take charge of the man you've arrested and sit with him in his car. That way everyone will be secure and we can take statements from all of you.' She turned to the girl leaning against the wall. 'Are you involved in this, love?'

'Yeah.' The girl looked up. Her face was sullen, defiant, and streaked with tears. 'It's not his fault, though. He's just stupid. And this other one's a brute.'

'Did someone attack you?'

She nodded. 'Yeah, he did. The young one.'

'All right, love, come with me.' As she took the girl's arm a second car arrived with two young constables. She sent them inside to interview the older man, then sat in her car with the girl.

Her story was simple and, from Jane's point of view, quite damning. She had already noticed how similar the young man looked to the photofits. Now this girl, Julie Willis, told a story entirely consistent with the women who'd made them. She was seventeen, she said, a student at the sixth form college. She lived in Bishopthorpe and had been walking home as she did most days. When she was halfway home a cyclist had come up behind her. She had seen the young man on the bike before; he was a kitchen porter in her college, and sometimes wheeled away the trolleys with the dirty plates on them. She'd never spoken to him though, so she was surprised when he got off his bike to walk beside her. But they were only a couple of hundred yards from the village and she wasn't alarmed at first.

'He was trying to chat you up, was he, love?'

'I suppose that was what it was, yeah. He wasn't very good at it, though.' Julie rolled her eyes and grinned, then dabbed at her tears with a tissue.

'What sort of things did he talk about?'

'Just boring crap. The weather, I think, and his bike. It had a lot of gears or something - as if I care! He's proud of it, I suppose - he needs something to be proud of, with a job like that. But then, well, then he changed ...'

'Changed how?'

'Well, he went all weird, you know, talking about things ... you know ...'

'What things, Julie?'

'Well, he asked if I was wearing a thong, for a start, and what colour it was. I mean *hello*? I've just met this guy! And then he says he's worn a thong himself once and it felt great. So I'm like, no way, I'm out of here. Only then ...'

'Yes, what happened then?'

'Well, we've almost reached the houses, in that narrow bit back there. So I'm like, stay cool, Jule, keep walking, just a few more yards and you're safe. Then it happened, just like that. I mean, he drops his bike and grabs me. I tried to get away but he shoves me up against the wall by the shoulders, so I couldn't. And he's saying he loves me and he's loved me for ages and trying to kiss me, you know, it was horrible.'

'So what did you do?'

'Told him to piss off and let me go, what do you think? But he wouldn't. He's got his hands down my bra, so I scream, and that's when this other brute turns up.'

'The older man, you mean, with the bald head? The one in the house?'

'Yeah, him. He must have heard me, I suppose. I mean I know he saved me and that but he's a pig too, isn't he? He was really rough the way he grabbed him - knocked me over too. But I should be grateful, I guess.'

'Do you know the name of this young man?'

'No. I told you, I've never spoken to him before.'

'All right. Wait here a minute, will you, love?' Jane got out and went to the police car, where the uniformed constable was talking to the young man.

'Have you arrested him yet?' she asked.

'Not yet, sarge. I was just taking a state ...'

'All right. What's your name, son?' She turned abruptly to the young man.

'Who, me? Peter,' he said, surprised by the interruption. 'Peter Barton.'

'Right, Peter Barton, I'm arresting you on suspicion of indecent assault. You do not have to say anything but it may harm your defence if you fail to say anything that you later rely on in court. Put the cuffs on him, constable. It seems the man in the house was quite right. I'll fetch one of the others to help you take him in.'

An hour later, she sat opposite Peter Barton and the duty solicitor in an interview room. To her annoyance, the Detective Inspector, Terry Bateson, sat with her. She'd made the mistake of boasting to him about her arrest and he'd insisted on taking part in the interview. 'Give me an idea of how you handle things in Beverley,' he'd said, smiling pleasantly enough. But it felt like another put down all the same. A trivial matter like this, she could handle it perfectly well on her own. But there was no point in making a protest. She was the new girl and he was her senior officer. She repeated the caution and set the tape rolling.

'Right, Peter, you know why you're here, don't you?'

'No. I didn't do owt. That feller grabbed me, twisted me arm. It's him you should arrest, not me!'

Jane studied him. His face was quite red, indignant. Dark shoulder length hair, quite greasy, looked as if it needed a wash, several acne spots on his cheek and chin, dark eyebrows which almost met together as he frowned. He was a big lad, six feet tall, with a powerful physique, but puppyish in the way he moved, as though he had not quite grown into his strength. His first response did not suggest a high powered computer humming behind the dark, sunken eyes. If he really believed he was the victim in this incident, he had a lot to learn.

'You've been arrested on a serious charge of indecent assault. Do you understand what that means, Peter?'

'I never touched her! She was asking for it!'

Jane sighed. The blatant contradiction between the two phrases lay at the root of most male problems, she thought. Denial and projection, the textbooks called it.

'You're talking about Julie Willis, are you? The girl you met on her way home?'

Peter nodded defensively. 'Julie, yeah.' He said the name slowly, almost tasting it, as though it were new to him.

'Know her well, do you?'

'I've seen her about.'

'Where would that be, Peter?'

'At the college, where I work.' The next few questions confirmed that Peter was a kitchen porter at the sixth form college. He'd seen Julie there, while he was clearing away dishes.

'Have you talked to her - before today?'

'Not talked. She smiled at me though. I knew she were watching.'

'She smiled, so you thought she liked you?'

'Yeah, I knew it. You can tell.' A foolish grin lit up his face, like a flash of sunlight through clouds. Jane almost felt sorry for him.

'And so today you decided to talk to her. Tell me about that, Peter, will you? In your own words, from the beginning.'

'Well, I knew she fancied me, like, and so I'd been waiting, you know, for the right time. So then, I was on me way home, and I saw her in front of me, like. So I thought, this is it, go for it now. I rode up to her, got off me bike, and we were chatting like - it were going right well. She were up for it, I could see she were. Only then he came, that bald bugger, and stuck his nose in. You should arrest him, the shite - he hurt me arm!'

'Why do you think he attacked you, Peter?' To Jane's annoyance, Terry Bateson intervened.

'How should I know? Ask him. He were jealous, like as not!'

'What were you doing exactly, when he attacked you?'

Peter flushed. 'We were, you know - snogging, like.'

'You and Julie were kissing, is that what you mean?'

'Like that, yeah. What's it to do with you, any road?'

'Nothing, if Julie was happy about it,' said Jane, resuming the questioning. 'But she says she wasn't, you see.'

'Well, she's lying, in't she? She were up for it, she were!'

'That's not what she says, Peter. She says you grabbed her, and put your hands inside her bra. Did you do that?'

Peter Barton stared down, his face flushed. His big fleshy hands gripped the sides of the table, his knuckles white, as if he would like to rip it from the bolts holding it to the floor.

'She was afraid, Peter. She screamed for help.'

'They all do at first. It means nowt, though.' He lifted his head to stare straight at Jane, the small dark eyes hot with accusation. '*You* know that well enough, don't you?'

As if, Jane thought. Thank God. 'So there've been others, Peter, have there?'

'What?'

'There've been other women apart from Julie. Other girls who've fancied you?'

'May have been. What's it to you?'

'Peter Barton, I have to tell you we've been investigating a series of nuisance incidents reported by women in the Bishopthorpe area over the past few weeks. A woman in Naburn, for example, reported a man stealing underwear from her washing line. Could that be you, perhaps?'

'Me? No.'

'Really? I wonder, Peter. You see, when you were booked in, the custody sergeant went through the pockets of your clothes and wrote down what he found. Do you remember that?'

Silence. Peter looked around the room, as if seeking a way out. Slowly, Jane lifted an evidence bag and put it on the table. 'For the benefit of the tape, I'm showing the witness a pair of female underpants, found in the pocket of his jacket when he was arrested. Do you recognise these, Peter?'

The young man shrugged. 'A girlfriend gave them to me.'

'Really? Why did she do that?'

No answer.

'You didn't steal them from a washing line in Naburn then?'

'You think I'm some sort of pervie, do you? I'm saying nowt.'

'Perhaps you could give us the name of this girlfriend who gave you these, Peter, then we can check it out. If your story's true, she'll say so, won't she?'

'I'm not telling.'

Jane persisted, asking Peter about the jogger, Melanie Thorpe, and the housewife, Sally McFee. But he denied a connection with either of them. The solicitor, in a belated attempt to earn his fee, suggested that his client had had enough. Frustrated, Jane sent Peter back to the cells, and told Terry what she planned to do next.

'I'll apply for a warrant to search his home. If he carries one set of trophy knickers round in his pocket he may have others in his bedroom. We'll show these to Mrs Whitley in Naburn, see if she recognises them. And I'll arrange an identity parade as well, see if Melanie Thorpe or Sally McFee can pick him out. If they do, that's it, we've got him.'

'Even if they don't, you've still got him for assault on young Julie. Do you think her story'll stand up in court?'

'Should do, with the witness who made the citizen's arrest.' Jane allowed herself a brief smile, flushed with success. This was what she enjoyed about police work - action, progress, a result. 'I think you'll find Bishopthorpe's a bit safer for women after tonight.'

'Let's hope so, detective sergeant. You're off the mark, in less than a week. Well done.'

Jane supposed he meant it well, but she couldn't help feeling patronised. You wait, you idle bugger, she thought, as he strode away with that easy, athletic lope. Back to his children, no doubt. While she'd be here until midnight, with all the details left to tie up.

Just you wait, Bateson. I haven't even started here yet.

20. Whose Hand?

WHEN WILL Churchill had first learned about the hand that had been found in the fox's jaws on the slip road, he was intrigued. The initial search by the ring road found nothing, but Churchill wasn't satisfied. He sent the hand to the best forensic pathologist in the area. When the report came back, he read it eagerly. Then he phoned Robert Baxter.

'If you can spare the time, Bob, I've got something here that might interest you. Unless you're too busy gardening, that is.'

At 4.15 that afternoon Will Churchill stood in front of a dozen CID officers in an incident room. Robert Baxter sat at the back, receiving several curious glances from younger officers. On the table in front of Will Churchill was a laptop and a plastic evidence bag containing the hand; his own hand held the forensic report.

Briefly, he explained how the discovery had been made. He pressed a key on the laptop and a photo of the skeletal hand appeared on the screen behind him. He had recently been on a PowerPoint course and learned how to do this. He felt sure this skill would advance his career. He smiled smugly at his assembled team. Bob Baxter scowled at the computer distrustfully.

'A preliminary search failed to find any body parts in the area ...' DCI Churchill paused for a moment, his eyes seeking out two of the younger officers in front of him - not the most diligent pair, in his opinion. '... but the hand was sent for forensic examination and now we have a full report. The findings, in brief, are as follows.'

He pressed another key. The hand disappeared from the screen, to be replaced by the words *Time since death: 10-30 years approx*. DCI Churchill beamed at the words approvingly; it had taken him half an hour to get them exactly the right size, colour, typeface and background. 'This means two things: the hand was not severed as the result of a recent accident, but neither are we dealing with some kind of archaeological remains. As you see, we are investigating an incident which occurred before the majority of us were in our present posts, which is why I have invited Detective Superintendent Robert Baxter, retired, to attend this briefing. You're very welcome, Bob.'

Baxter acknowledged this with a curt nod. DCI Churchill had an uncomfortable feeling that, proud as he was of the language and technological expertise displayed in this presentation, Bob Baxter would have done things more simply.

'Secondly, as we see from this slide...' he pressed the key again and a close-up of a bone appeared on the screen. '... the bones of the wrist are fractured. Detailed forensic examination of the edges of the fracture led the pathologist to conclude two things: firstly, that the original fracture occurred between ten and thirty years ago, but secondly, that one of the bones, the small ulnar here, was not fractured at that time, but was broken more recently, probably, as we see from these marks here ...' he pressed another key. ' ... by the teeth of an animal such as the fox in whose jaws the hand was allegedly found. In other words, lads and lasses ...' he gazed around the room significantly '... the fox didn't just find a hand on its own, it found a hand attached to an arm, and it tore the hand off. In which case, if that arm was still attached to a body, it's our job to find it. At the very least we're looking at an unexplained death here; quite possibly at a murder.'

He pressed the key again. A buzz of excitement spread around the room, leavened, to DCI Churchill's embarrassment, with one or two stifled giggles. Glancing behind him at the words

Unexplained Death
or
Murde
?

tastefully displayed against a green background, he quickly pressed another key and moved on. This time the screen displayed a close-up of two fingernails from the hand.

'As you will see, there are traces of red nail varnish on these fingernails, confirming the pathologist's belief that this is the hand of a young woman. The nail varnish itself has been analysed, and shown to be of a type no longer in use today, but common in the 1980s and 1990s. So, to sum up ...' More headings appeared against the green background, better spelt this time. 'We have here the left hand of a young woman who in all probability died between ten and thirty years ago. Some time around the time of death she suffered a severe fracture of her left wrist. At a later period, probably in the past few weeks, an animal, probably a fox, found the body and gnawed the hand off. Now foxes, lads and lasses, are territorial. They only travel far when they are leaving home, looking for a mate, or being chased by men in red coats. This fox ...' A groan of disgust went around the room as a photo of a flattened, dusty corpse appeared on the screen '... was less than a year old, so it may have picked up the hand on its travels. However, given the time of year, it's also possible that the animal had already left home and established a territory in the rough ground next to the ring road where its body was found. It's not the sort of place, after all, where it's likely to be disturbed, so long as it stays off the tarmac. So ...' At this point DCI Churchill would have liked to round off his presentation with a photograph of the road junction near Copmanthorpe, but he'd had no time to take one. He had, however, scanned in a section of the map. '... this is the area which we are going to search. And I mean a real search, girls and gents, inch by inch, every blade of grass. If that body's out there, we need to find it.'

He switched the computer off. 'Any questions?'

A hand went up. 'Do we have any idea who the body might be, boss?'

DCI Churchill preened himself. 'That's why I've invited Bob Baxter here. He was in charge during the time this female apparently died. And as you all know, there's at least one murder of a young woman dating from that time, whose body has never been found.'

Another hand went up. 'Can't you do a DNA analysis of the hand, boss?'

'We're getting one, of course. But it's taking a little time. Don't worry, if we do establish identity, you'll be the first to know. Now, let's get to it.'

As he moved towards the door a voice murmured behind him softly: 'Yeah. We'll announce it on screen, won't we? With bullet points.'

21. Identity Parade

'SO THERE wasn't anything?' Terry asked.

'No. Porno mags a-plenty, two hunting knives, but no female underwear. And his mum swore she would have known if he had any. She does all his washing, she says. It's true his clothes were quite clean.'

'And she didn't mind the porn mags?'

'Apparently not, no. Seemed to think it was a normal interest for a young lad. Which it is, I suppose, up to a point. Wouldn't surprise me if she'd been on the game herself. It was that sort of place.'

Jane Carter sighed, remembering her futile search of Peter Barton's bedroom. The room had been reasonably tidy, but disturbing nonetheless. The curtains were black, and the light bulb red, throwing the posters of big-breasted fantasy women on the walls into lurid relief. The hunting knives hung neatly beneath a poster of a woman being eaten alive by a monster, half-bird, half lizard. There was a pile of well-thumbed pornographic magazines under the bed, two with an explicit sado-masochistic content.

His mother had seemed angry, but not surprised, that the police had arrested her son. If he'd been molesting girls, she said, that was what all young men did, wasn't it? There was no real harm in the lad. If he'd had a pair of female knickers in his pocket, what did that prove? Probably the police had planted them on him, to make things look worse.

'But they were identical to the ones stolen from Mrs Whitley in Naburn,' Jane said. 'Same size, same design, same everything. She'd just washed them, so there's no DNA trace, but - where else did they come from?'

Next day she arranged an identity parade. A uniformed inspector supervised the parade, but Jane Carter and Terry Bateson came to watch. The first to go was Sally McFee, the yoga-practising housewife. She seemed to have dressed for the occasion. She wore a smart navy blue trouser suit and heels, with an expensive gold crucifix round her neck. Her hair and make-up were immaculate, and a light musky scent floated around her as she walked nervously into the room. As if she's put all her warpaint on to protect her from the grime of real life, Terry thought.

The grime stood behind the one way window. A line of eight young men in various stages of fashionable dishevelment. Four had longish hair, three short, one had his head shaven altogether. It's the fashion, the inspector told the defending solicitor apologetically, you're lucky to find anyone with hair at all nowadays. Each man faced the glass holding a card with a number on it. Peter Barton was number seven, second from the end.

Sally McFee walked slowly along the row twice, as she had been told. She looked long at Peter Barton, then at a shorter boy with curly hair. But she didn't seem satisfied. She walked along the line again before stopping in front of the shorter boy.

'It might be him,' she said. 'None are exactly right but he's the closest.'

The inspector bowed politely and showed her out. He returned with Melanie Thorpe, the jogger who had been pestered about her underwear. She wore jeans, teeshirt, and leather jacket, but seemed more nervous than Sally McFee. She turned her back to the window.

'They can see me,' she said, 'that one's staring at me.'

'It's just an illusion, love,' the inspector assured her. 'He can't see a thing. Wave at them if you like, or stick your tongue out. It won't make any difference.'

Reassured, she walked slowly along the line. She paused in front of Peter Barton, moved on, then came back for a second look. 'Can you ask him to say something, please?'

'What would like him to say?'

'Ask him to say "You look sweaty. Are you hot?". Is that possible?'

'It is.' The inspector spoke into a microphone, and after a moment's awkward pause, Peter Barton spoke the words. They came out surly, reluctant, like a teenager obeying a teacher. But it convinced Melanie Thorpe.

'That's him,' she said. 'That's the cyclist who pestered me.'

'Sure of that, are you?'

'Quite sure.' She smiled in triumph, as though she had passed a test, and turned to Jane Carter. 'Was it you that caught him? Well done. What'll happen to him now?'

'We charge him,' Jane said. 'Then it's up to the court.'

Peter Barton was charged with the theft of a pair of knickers, two cases of assault, one of indecent exposure and one of actual bodily harm - the result of a small bruise on Julie Thompson's left breast. The charge of assault against Melanie Thorpe was justified by her claim that his behaviour had put her in fear of imminent attack, even though he hadn't actually touched her.

Melanie had been shown Peter's bike. It looked like her assailant's, she confirmed. The hunting knives from his bedroom were like the one she had seen on his belt.

'And that's about it,' Jane said to Terry reluctantly. Peter's fingerprints and a DNA sample were taken, and he was released on police bail. 'With luck he'll get probation, which may teach him to behave. But if not, we'll know where to look next time.'

'Good work,' Terry said. 'You may have nipped this in the bud.'

'I wouldn't count on it,' Jane said. 'OK, he may be just a sad harmless moron in search of a girlfriend, but what about those knives in his bedroom? I didn't like that. And the smirk on his face when I asked about those stolen knickers? I bet he's got more hidden somewhere.'

'What if he has? It's hardly the crime of the century.'

'Not yet it isn't, no. But what if he takes it further next time? He needs locking up now. But the courts won't do it, will they?'

22. Body Search

WILL CHURCHILL had detailed thirty officers to search the scrub near the ring road. The announcement did not make him popular; the weather was cold and the opportunity of spending all day crawling on hands and knees through frozen grass, pizza cartons and coke cans did not appeal to everyone. Churchill himself did not have time to supervise the search. He had an important meeting at police HQ in Northallerton, on investigative procedures. 'But I'll be there to kick things off,' he told Terry Bateson breezily. 'Point things in the right direction, motivate the troops. Then I can leave it in your capable hands, Terence, I'm sure. Make sure there aren't too many cock-ups.'

It wasn't the first time, Terry thought gloomily, and it wouldn't be the last. Will Churchill's distaste for routine spadework - which was what this threatened to be - was only matched by his energy in claiming the results of any success that spadework might bring. No doubt he would be boasting to the Chief Constable in Northallerton about his energy in setting up this investigation, even while Terry was knee deep in mud.

But then where would I rather be, Terry asked himself sternly, as the day dawned bright and clear. Out in the fresh air, or in some meeting in an overheated office? That's the difference between Churchill and me. Why he'll reach the top and I won't.

Enthusiasm revived as the party clambered out of their minibus, their breath steaming in the frosty air. They stamped their feet and clapped their gloved hands together for warmth as they gathered for instructions. Will Churchill parked his Porsche on the hard shoulder and bounced out to give his speech.

'Good morning, lads and lasses,' he began, 'and thanks for coming. I know it's cold, but you've got an important task ahead of you today.' He noted the envious glances at his car with satisfaction, before continuing.

'Now, for the benefit of those of you who missed my PowerPoint presentation on Monday,' he grinned. 'A human hand was found in this vicinity a few weeks ago. It was the hand of a young woman, and it was found in the jaws of a fox which was killed on this slip road. So the probability is that the rest of her body, or parts of it, at any rate, are in this area. So that's what we're looking for, team. It may be a whole body, or just a few bones; it could be on the surface, or buried underground. Not a nice task, I know, but a necessary one. DI Bateson will be in charge, and keep in close contact with me as and when necessary. And I've ordered hot bacon sarnies at eleven, so you've that to look forward to. Double for anyone who finds her - if he's still got an appetite, that is. Right then - that's it. Sooner started, sooner done. Chop chop, then, lads! Let's go!'

As the Porsche drove away, the line spread out under Terry's more detailed direction. There were a few murmurs, but most of them were used to Churchill's behaviour and resigned to it. They began to move slowly through the area, quartering each inch of ground. There was a lot of long grass, small trees and bushes. They found surprising amounts of litter, some dog shit, dead birds, the skeleton of a cat, several used needles and a couple of deep frozen condoms, but no body.

Time passed. They were blowing on their hands and glancing eagerly down the road for the promised sandwich van when a young woman constable at the end of the line almost fell into a fox hole.

'Careful there, Lindy,' her friend said, 'you'll end up in Narnia.'

'This is what we're looking for, though, isn't it?' Lindy said, testing her ankle to see if she'd sprained it. 'If the fox was down here, the body might be down here too.'

Terry Bateson agreed, and after refreshing themselves with bacon sarnies and coffee a group were given picks and spades to excavate the foxhole. The earth was hard and frozen on the surface, but soft as they got further down. They were digging just under the bridge linking the A64 to the ring road. A few feet away was the dual carriageway, whose traffic thundered constantly beside them. After half an hour they were three feet down, and had found nothing. Their spades jarred on the concrete foundations of the bridge.

'We'll get nothing here,' one of them said, wiping his sweating brow with a muddy glove. This is just rabbit skulls and shit. Nothing human.'

'Dig a bit deeper,' Terry insisted. 'We need to be sure.'

'You'll dig to bloody Australia if you need to, young man,' a voice growled behind him. The retired superintendent, Robert Baxter, had turned up at ten on Churchill's invitation, and begun treating the operation as if he was in charge. But the old man was right to crack the whip, Terry thought; half of these young constables were treating this as a joke.

Ten minutes later they found it. Not a whole body, not yet - just an arm. Or rather, the bones of an arm. Broken bones, as far as Terry - squatting in the bottom of the hole and brushing away the soil like an archaeologist - could make out. Bones that might possibly have been chewed. But even to a layman, they didn't like those of a fox or a sheep. Too big, too long and straight.

The bones were protruding from concrete. If there was a body there it was buried under the foundations of the bridge, Terry thought. And what is that going to cost to get out? Nonetheless, he turned in triumph to Robert Baxter squatting beside him.

'I think this is it, sir. We've found your missing girl at last.'

23. First Date

SARAH STOOD in front of the mirror in her bedroom. She was wearing the silk camisole she had bought in Cambridge. It suits me, she thought, pulling her stomach in and turning sideways to study the effect. Not that anyone else is going to see it but me. Probably.

Definitely. She frowned sternly at her reflection, which only a moment before had sent her a secret, mischievous smile. Definitely not; not yet anyway. But it was nice, in a way, to entertain even the thought of such mischief. She was going out on a date with a man - Michael Parker, the stranger she had met in the train. It made her feel young and giggly, like - well, like what, exactly? Like a schoolgirl, a teenager, a girl in her twenties? For Sarah, none of these really fitted: she'd scarcely had this experience of dating before. Once briefly, as a schoolgirl, with Kevin, a first date which had swiftly led to the loss of her knickers, her innocence, and her school career in the back of his father's Ford Cortina; and then later, again briefly, with Bob, when she was seventeen and already a mother, with more interest in nappies, colic, social workers, and evening classes than romance. Her desire to marry Bob had been based far more on a longing for a home and security than for sex. Sex, after all, was what had betrayed her so disastrously with Kevin.

Nonetheless, just the thought of Kevin strutting towards her made her feel damp and weak at the knees, as no man had since. Sarah smiled, smoothing her hands down the silk camisole as she remembered their bedroom in that council house in Seacroft. They'd had nothing then, except a baby; just wooden floorboards, a mattress, and a rail to hang their clothes on; yet when baby Simon was asleep, a red candle and their two lustful bodies had made that bare room seem like a cave in the Arabian Nights. Whereas here ...

She sat at the ornate dressing table Bob had bought her four birthdays ago and looked around her bedroom. King-sized bed, woollen carpet, fitted wardrobe, recessed lighting, full-length mirror, en-suite bathroom with power shower and heated towel rail. They'd even discussed whether to install a jacuzzi in the en-suite or a hot tub in the garden. All the luxury she could need.

And no husband. Well, so now I can go out on a date. She glanced at the clock on her side of the bed - the whole bed was hers now - and saw she had twenty minutes before Michael was due to arrive. Time for decisions. It mattered what impression she gave. She laid a skirt and jacket on her bed; it suited her figure, she knew, but ... maybe too formal, for an evening meal? It reminded her too much of case conferences, parents' evenings, interviews with clients. A dress? That would be more feminine, but the ones she liked were light, and the weather was too cold.

She opted for a smart grey trouser suit and a frilly pink blouse over the camisole. Formal, but feminine as well. Her hips were slim enough for the suit and the blouse displayed her cleavage quite well. She leaned forward at the dressing table, studying her face as she did her make-up. Not a bad face, she thought, though hardly a young girl any more. There were little wrinkles around the corners of her eyes and her mouth - wrinkles that would only deepen, she supposed, with age. But her skin was clear, and her bone structure good - one decent thing I inherited from my mother, she thought wryly. She lifted her chin, wondering whether to hide her neck with a scarf, but decided there was no need.

It's a perfectly adequate face, she told herself firmly, brushing her dark hair. Anyway, he had two hours to look at it on the train; if he didn't like what he saw he wouldn't have asked me out on a date.

It was that word - *date* - that kept troubling her. Simon had seemed deeply amused when, somewhat shyly, she'd told him, and she'd been puzzling about it ever since. Well, it *was* a date, wasn't it? A man had asked her out for a meal. The problem was, how to deal with it. She'd been married so long, she hadn't learnt the skills. It wasn't that she hadn't had admirers - there'd been Terry Bateson, for example, the detective whom Emily had teased her about. He'd come closest to Kevin in arousing her desire, and she was almost certain - well, she *was* certain - that he fancied her too. But Terry had always known she was married, and so that night at Savendra's wedding when they had danced and so nearly gone further had been entangled, for her at least, with so much guilt and anger and betrayal that she scarcely knew what she was doing. If they had carried on, their relationship would have had to have been hidden, an explosive, guilty secret which, if it had been discovered, could easily have destroyed both her career and his.

And since nothing came between Sarah and her career, she had backed off. Attractive as Terry Bateson undoubtedly was.

But then, so was this Michael Parker. Tall, handsome, broad-shouldered - she remembered the way his face had crinkled when he smiled on the train. Lines like that were all right in a man - it made him look experienced, mature, worldly wise. He was an adult like her, with no ties. So there was no need for guilt or deceit. Bob's empty closets, the fact that she was alone in this house, were proof enough of that.

She put on her shoes, went downstairs, and checked the locks on the windows and back door. She'd become more careful about that since Simon's warning. After he'd left she'd been washing up in her kitchen when she'd seen a man, a jogger, running along the riverside path in the field at the foot of her garden. The man had stopped at the stile by the willow tree, and stood there for three or four minutes. He'd drunk something from a bottle, but he'd been there quite a while, staring at the backs of the houses. She'd even wondered if he'd noticed *her*, standing at the sink with the light on. It had been an uncomfortable feeling, like a centipede crawling up her neck - the fear that he might guess she was here alone, slept here alone all night ...

The doorbell rang and she started, then relaxed. No need to worry now, of course not - this was her date! She went to the front door and opened it.

The restaurant he had chosen - an expensive Indian one on the quay overlooking the river Ouse - was one Sarah knew and liked. She wondered if any of her colleagues would see her there and what she should say if they did. It doesn't matter, she told herself firmly. I'm not deceiving anyone - I'm free to do what I like. It's Bob who should provide the explanations.

Michael picked her up at 7.30, in a smart new BMW with only 8,000 miles on the clock. The engine purred, the leather seats creaked when she leaned back. He wore chinos, a blue woollen blazer over a light fawn polo-necked jumper, and a camel hair coat. It looked good, Sarah thought, and went with the car, and yet ... it was not quite the sort of looks she was used to. Too casual, too cool perhaps?

Oh stop being fussy, woman, she told herself sternly. Relax and enjoy yourself.

He parked in the Castle car park near the court. It had rained during the day, but the skies had cleared and the temperature fallen. There was a sickle moon and a few bright stars in the sky.

'There'll be frost before morning,' Michael said. 'Fog too, I shouldn't wonder.'

'Don't worry,' she said. 'You'll be warm enough in that car.'

'Yep. That's why I bought it. As a hot water bottle with wheels.'

Sarah laughed. 'A hot water bottle that does 160 miles per hour.'

'Oh no, that's illegal. Only duvets can go that fast.'

They laughed together. Not the greatest jokes in the world, perhaps, but something to break the ice. There *was* an ice-rink too, she saw suddenly, looking to her left - a real floodlit ice rink under the old Norman castle, between the Castle Museum and the law courts. She'd noticed them erecting it the other day when she was in court, but this was the first time she'd seen it in action.

'Come on,' she said, 'I've got to see this. We've got time, haven't we?'

He glanced at his watch. 'I booked for nine, so we've got a while yet. Why not?'

They stood side by side in the crowd, mesmerised like everyone else by the skaters swishing round in front of them. One or two were clearly expert, turning, pirouetting and even dancing arm in arm - but most tottered along uneasily trying to keep their balance. A teenage boy attempted a turn right in front of them. He almost made it, grinning proudly, then staggered backwards, arms flailing, and crashed on his bum.

Michael laughed. 'Have you ever tried that?'

'No, never, have you?'

'Yes, I did a bit when I was young.' He glanced at his watch again. 'Come on, we've got time if we're quick. I'll show you!'

'No! What do you mean? I can't!'

'Nonsense! Give it a try!'

They were standing right next to the entrance, and before she could stop him Michael had paid for the hire of two pairs of skates, and was sitting on a slatted bench taking off his shoes. Sarah stood in front of him holding her skates in her hand.

'Michael, I've never done this before in my life!'

'Don't worry, I'll hold your hand. If you don't mind?' he grinned. 'It's easy really - give it a go and you'll see.'

'Well, all right.' Nervously, not sure whether this was fun or just foolish, she took off her shoes and handed them to the attendant. The skates felt hard and clumsy and she laced them up far too loosely until Michael crouched down and tightened them for her. Well, this is a way of getting to know someone, she thought, as he grinned up from between her knees. 'But what if I break my leg?' she said out loud.

'You'll sue me, I guess. So I'll take care it doesn't happen.'

He helped her to her feet and out onto the ice. Almost immediately her right foot slid out from under her and she clutched his arm to avoid falling. He put his other arm round her until she recovered that foot, then the other slid off in an unlikely direction. Slowly, awkwardly, feeling that she was either drunk or walking on marbles, she tried to move forwards. She clung desperately to Michael; without his arm round her she would have fallen for certain. But it was clear that he knew what he was doing. Somehow - she had no idea how - he not only kept his balance but managed to propel them both forwards, out on the ice with the rest.

'Bend your knees slightly, and push with one foot at a time,' he said in her ear. 'That's it, good! Now the other one. See, you're skating!'

Watching her feet carefully, she managed three steps - she thought it was three - before a teenager turned suddenly in front of her, sending up a crunching spray of ice which distracted Sarah totally. She lost control of both feet and sat down hard on her bottom, dragging Michael down across her legs.

'Ow!' she said. 'That hurt. I told you I couldn't do this!'

'Everyone falls a few times,' he said, laughing. 'Come on - get up and try it again.'

He stood with one skate either side of her and hauled her to her feet, and for the next age - probably a quarter of an hour but it seemed to Sarah like a week - he dragged her around the rink like a rag doll, trying to teach her the basics. Mostly he kept his arm around her, but she managed a few steps on her own, holding tightly to his outstretched hand, and once, before she knew what was happening, he turned her to face him and pushed her gently backwards, holding on to her arms with his. She fell twice more, and when they finished she collapsed, bruised and breathless, onto the bench.

'There! How was that?' he asked grinning, as he unlaced his skates.

'Terrible. I feel like I've been run over by a herd of buffalo - twice!'

His grin faded slightly. 'But wasn't it fun?'

'Yes, of course. It's just not something I'm very good at, quite yet.'

'We'll have another go sometime.' He bent to unlace her boots. 'If you'd like to, that is.'

The cold air and exercise had made her face tingle, as if it were bombarded with thousands of tiny ice crystals. She drew a deep breath. 'Yes, maybe. After I come out of intensive care.'

'I'm sorry. I didn't bully you into it, did I?'

'Well yes, you did rather.'

She frowned down at him and he looked worried, like a little boy who has made a fool of himself. Then she smiled, and relented. 'But it *was* fun, Michael, really. Even if my bottom feels like it's been hit by a pile driver. I enjoyed it, honestly. Thanks.'

'Good. I'm glad. Now we've worked up an appetite, too.'

On the way to the restaurant Sarah's bruises made her limp slightly, and she leaned against him, putting her arm round him for support as she had on the rink. They were laughing together like old friends, recalling the various falls and incidents, when a jogger ran towards them along the quay. As he came nearer he caught Sarah's eye. *Surely I know that man,* she thought. *But how?*

Then, as they came closer, she saw that the jogger recognized her too. He wore tracksuit trousers, long sleeved teeshirt, and woolly hat. *Why is he staring at me?* she wondered. *Is it that man on the riverbank, come out of nowhere to haunt me?* She shivered, and clung to Michael tighter for protection.

'What's the matter?' he asked, looking down at her solicitously. 'Are you hurt?'

'No, it's just ...'

'Hi, Sarah!' The jogger raised his hand, and in the same moment Sarah recognized him. Not a phantom prowler after all, but

Oh God no! Terry Bateson.

'Hi.' She released herself slightly from Michael's grip, and smiled. An awkward, embarrassed smile. 'Out for a run?' Silly question.

'Yes.' He stopped for a moment, breathing deeply and glancing curiously at Michael.

'This is Michael Parker,' Sarah said, with an embarrassed laugh. 'He's been teaching me to skate.'

'I see,' Terry said. 'Sounds fun.'

And then for a moment no one said anything. Michael smiled politely, his arm firmly round Sarah's waist, and Terry just stood, his warm breath steaming in the frosty air. He assessed Michael with a long, steady gaze, then looked back at Sarah, his eyes shaded, inscrutable in the semi darkness.

'Well, have a good evening,' he said, after a moment that seemed to Sarah to last several hours. And then he was gone, padding away lightly into the night.

'Friend of yours, is he?' Michael asked casually after the waiter had shown them to their table in the restaurant. 'The jogger outside, I mean?'

'Yes, well, an acquaintance really. He's a detective - we've worked together a bit.' She buried herself in the menu - this wasn't a conversation she wanted to prolong. Why did it have to be Terry - just there, at that moment, when she was arm in arm with this man? What must he have thought? Presumably he didn't know - how could he? - of her break-up with Bob. So it must have looked like - what? - that she was out with a stranger, a man who was clearly not her husband but whom she was nonetheless happy to wrap her arms round as she walked down the street, a man with whom she might well be having an affair. Damn! Which had been precisely the reason why she had *not* had an affair with Terry last year – to avoid ruining her reputation. So what must he think now? That she was not prepared to commit adultery with him, but she *was* prepared to do so with someone else.

Great. Wonderful. What a slut he must think me. Especially after that time in the hotel bedroom, when I was so sorely, sorely tempted. Oh God, hell and damnation! Why did Terry have to come along just then?

He'd looked embarrassed; as though he'd have liked to stop and talk if Michael hadn't hadn't been there. I don't think he approved of Michael. Well, what's it to do with him? Nothing, of course. If I choose to go out on a date it's my business and no one else's. Certainly not his.

Only she suddenly wished, so strongly that she almost ran out of the restaurant, that she could be out there in the night jogging alongside Terry Bateson, while Michael went into the restaurant to eat by himself.

But she banished the emotion as swiftly as it had come. That's not fair, she told herself firmly. Michael's a perfectly decent man and we were having fun - good fun - until Terry came and ruined it. Grimly, she set herself to recovering her good spirits. She liked Indian food, and the chef's speciality was one of her favourites. By the time they had ordered, and were nibbling on a selection of chapatis, pickles and sauces, the atmosphere between them had revived.

Michael talked briefly about his day at work, visiting a farmhouse and barn conversion near Whitby, and then began to describe his home, a converted windmill on the Wolds.

'It's been my main project for the best part of a year,' he said, 'and it's nowhere near finished. Have you ever been inside a windmill?'

Sarah hadn't, but she prompted him with generous questions, and was rewarded by the obvious enthusiasm shining in his eyes. 'You must come out and see it,' he said. 'I want to convert it to a house, but keep the sails to generate electricity. I've got the planning permission, now it's all a matter of time, energy and craftsmanship.'

'Do you work on it yourself?' she asked.

'No, sadly. Only a few basic things, that I'm sure I can manage. I leave the rest to the experts. My job is to provide the vision, keep them up to the mark, and provide them with cups of tea and money. Lots of money, unfortunately. But I enjoy it, so why not?'

The talk, together with the subtle spices in the curry, revived Sarah's spirits, and by the time the waiter brought the sweets menu she was relaxed and comfortable again. Their table was in a quiet corner close to the bar, and as the waiter left she glanced idly at the small TV behind the barman's head. The ten o'clock news was on, showing pictures of a car bomb in Baghdad. Then the newscaster returned to the screen, and in a sudden lull in the conversation Sarah caught a few words.

'Unusual police discovery ... body near York ... murder ... Jason Barnes.'

'What's that?' She called the barman. 'Excuse me, could you turn that up for a moment? I'd like to hear what they're saying.'

The barman turned up the volume just as the programme switched to a reporter standing under floodlights beside a motorway. Behind him was an area of grass and scrub, with chequered blue and white crime scene tapes fluttering in the breeze.

'Yes, thank you, Natasha,' the reporter was saying. 'Well, this has been a most remarkable discovery. The North Yorkshire police have found some human remains, buried under concrete on a ring road outside York. So far they have only uncovered an arm, but they believe the rest of the body may be there. They were led to search this area after a family stopped on the hard shoulder for a child to relieve himself, and his brother found a human hand in the mouth of a dead fox. Surprisingly enough, the parents allowed the child to take the hand home, and it wasn't until he took it to school that his teacher showed it to the police. Which led to this search here today.'

'A strange story indeed,' the newscaster said. 'So James, does that mean that the arm found today was missing a hand?'

'Yes, Natasha, the police confirmed that a few minutes ago. Chief Inspector Churchill, the man in charge of this search, said it was far too early to establish who these remains belong to, but one possibility they are considering is that they might be those of a young woman called Brenda Stokes, who disappeared in this area 18 years ago. If so, that will give the police quite a problem. You may remember a recent report on this programme about a man called Jason Barnes, who was convicted of Brenda's murder and sentenced to life imprisonment. Well, Jason Barnes always protested his innocence, and last month the Court of Appeal set aside his conviction as unsafe. A decision which, I think it's fair to say, was greeted with dismay by the detectives in the original enquiry. But one of the points made in his appeal, of course, was that no body had ever been found. So if they do manage to excavate this body and it does turn out to be Brenda Stokes, that will raise quite a lot of interesting questions, Natasha.'

'Yes, indeed, James,' the newscaster said. 'Well, we look forward to future developments. Now, the Chancellor of the Exchequer said today ...'

'That's enough, thank you,' Sarah said, as the barman turned the volume down. She stared at Michael, stunned. 'Did you hear all that?'

'Some of it, yes. It was about your case in the Court of Appeal, wasn't it?'

'Yes, Jason Barnes. They may have found the body of the girl.'

Michael looked at her strangely. 'They can't be certain yet, can they?

I mean, after all these years.'

'Not yet, no but ... oh, excuse me.' Sarah's mobile was chirruping in her bag. When she took it out, she saw the call was from Lucy.

'Did you see the TV news?' Lucy asked without preamble.

'Yes. They've found an arm. Maybe Brenda Stokes' body.'

'It doesn't mean that Jason killed her, of course. I mean, how would he have buried her there, under the motorway?'

'God knows. But they're going to want to ask him, aren't they? Especially that retired Inspector Bob Baxter, after what I did to him in court.'

'And DCI Churchill. He's no friend of yours, is he?'

'Not exactly. If it is really is Brenda, Luce, they'll be crawling all over the scene for evidence to link it to Jason. And if they find any ...'

'We'll be back in court with egg all over our faces.'

'Yes. Look, Lucy love, I'm in court for three days. Can you keep an eye on this, check with the police, see what they say? Maybe talk to Jason too, if you can.'

'Will do. Anyway, apart from all this excitement, honey, how are things with you?'

'Oh, not too bad,' Sarah said, aware of Michael listening across the table. 'I can't talk now, I'm out at a restaurant with a - friend.'

'Oh, I see.' The slight hesitation tipped Lucy off. 'A *man* friend, you mean? Sarah? What's he like? A dish?'

'Talk to you later, Lucy. Bye.' She clicked the phone off and looked apologetically at Michael. 'Sorry about that. Work. It's always interfering.'

'Tell me about it. I switched mine off before I came.' He looked distracted, she thought, oddly unhappy. God, I wonder if he heard Lucy's last remark, Sarah thought. Well, what of it? He *is* quite a dish.

But Michael was thinking about the TV newscast. 'That man, Jason something ...'

'Jason Barnes.'

'Yes, the one you defended. Will he be re-arrested now, do you think?'

'Hard to say. It depends what evidence they find. If this *is* Brenda Stokes' body, of course.'

'It will be, I'm sure it will.'

Sarah smiled. 'What are you, psychic? How can you possibly know?'

He looked confused. 'Oh no, of course I can't, really. But it seems quite likely, doesn't it? I mean, there aren't very many murders in York, and this was a particularly horrid one. I remember how shocked everyone was.'

'You remember it?' said Sarah, surprised. 'Why, were you here at the time?'

'Yes, after Cambridge I did a postgraduate year in York. That was the year it happened. Everyone talked about it. And I have to say, most people were glad when Jason was convicted. The evidence seemed pretty strong, I remember. That's why I was surprised when he was released. If he does turn out to be guilty after all, you'll feel pretty bad, won't you?'

Sarah shook her head. 'Not really. I conducted the appeal on the evidence available at the time. The court decided that he'd spent 18 years in prison for something he didn't do. That's a pretty bad miscarriage of justice.'

'Yes, but if he *did* do it and you've got him off, what then? That's a miscarriage of justice too, isn't it? He can't be convicted for the same offence twice.'

'He can now,' Sarah said. 'The government's amended the law of double jeopardy. So if significant new evidence is discovered - from this body, for example - then, yes, he could be tried for the same offence twice.'

'And you'd defend this man, would you?'

Sarah shrugged. 'If I was asked, yes. Why not? That's my job.'

'Hm. Rather you than me.' He frowned, rather disagreeably, Sarah thought. This was an old argument about the ethics of her profession. She didn't want to go through it again, though she would if she had to.

Michael changed the subject, and the evening ended, agreeably enough. But somehow the sparkle had gone from it. He seemed quiet and withdrawn as he drove her home, and the anticipated decisions about whether she should let him kiss her, or ask him in for coffee, didn't materialise. He simply smiled, and asked if she'd like to go out with him again. 'I could show you the windmill, if you like? And go for a walk on the Wolds. We could make a day of it.'

'Yes, I'd like that,' she said, with an attempt at sincerity. 'Give me a ring.'

'All right, I will.' He smiled again, shook her hand, and waited with his headlights illuminating her drive while she walked to her door. She turned and waved as he reversed.

She stood for a moment, watching his tail lights fade into the darkness. What happened there exactly? He seemed so lively earlier, with the skating and the meal. Then his mood changed. Was it my work, interfering again, as it used to do with Bob? Probably. I should have switched my phone off.

But then, perhaps it was me. I didn't really want anything more. Perhaps he noticed.

She smiled as she turned to go in.

At least he shook my hand.

24. Digging Up the Past

TERRY BATESON slept little that night. He usually enjoyed running - the sensation of his limbs moving smoothly and easily, the clean air in his lungs, the glowing warmth of the endorphins flooding through his veins at the end - it all helped to relax him and settle his mind. But not this time. Not after he met Sarah, laughing in the arms of another man.

If it had been her husband it wouldn't have mattered. Terry had met Bob Newby several times, and while he had hardly warmed to the man, he accepted him as a fact of Sarah's life. She had a husband, a rather wimpish school teacher with a beard; well, too bad. Sarah must have been fond of him once, and she valued her marriage above the risks of an affair; she'd made that clear enough in the past.

So what had happened to change her behaviour? Perhaps I misunderstood, Terry thought. Perhaps what she meant before was, she valued her marriage above an affair *with me*. That's how it appears tonight, anyhow. She looked quite happy when I first noticed her, walking towards me. And then when she did see me, what?

He re-ran the painful meeting in his mind. She'd seemed surprised, he seemed to remember, a touch embarrassed.

But no more. Not ashamed or guilty, as she should be.

The shock shattered Terry. He ran on into the night, heedless of where he was going. His stride lengthened, his feet bounced off the footpath, faster and faster. He ran until his legs shook and his lungs were on fire, but it made no difference. *How could she do that?* he asked himself, bent over and gasping on a bridge by the river. Sarah, who had told him her family and career mattered so much. *Who was this man, anyway?* Her brother, perhaps? But she didn't have a brother, surely - and anyway, the way he'd looked at her wasn't brotherly at all. No, it's quite simple, he told himself grimly. She's having an affair.

But not with me.

Well, it's her choice, he thought, jogging home in the dark. Such things happen all the time. So why should I care? She's just not the woman I thought she was, that's all. Not the woman for me.

So why does this hurt so much?

Ever since he'd first met Sarah Newby he'd been attracted to her. He'd worked closely with her on a number of cases - on several of which, particularly the trial of her son, they'd had moments of bitter disagreement - but always, when he looked back on them now, the moments he'd spent with her had been somehow special. Even the arguments had been like that. They mattered to him in a way that arguments with others didn't. He'd replayed them often in his mind.

Not any more.

It wasn't that she was strikingly beautiful - she was slim, moderately pretty, no more. Mary, his wife, had a nicer smile in the photo he kept by his bed; every pin-up in a magazine had a better physique. Nor, he told himself savagely, was Sarah Newby even a particularly nice person. Tonight was just proof of it. She could be sharp, strong-willed, stubborn, aggressive, sarcastic, dismissive and even downright cruel to people who threatened her or got in her way. It was part of what made her so effective in court, and, he guessed bitterly, so difficult to live with. Both of her children, he knew, had had problems. Probably her husband had too.

But to Terry, until now, none of this had mattered. With her he felt something he'd felt for no one but Mary, and Mary was dead. He'd been drawn to Sarah like a moth to a flame - a cruel, heartless flame, he now told himself sternly, which could burn him up without caring. Each time he'd come close to her, she'd turned him away. He should have taken warning from that. She was married, she'd told him, and he'd respected that. An affair between them could wreck her family and both their careers. So over the past few months he'd tried to see less of her, put her out of his thoughts. He'd thought he'd succeeded, until tonight. There she was.

Glowing with happiness, in the arms of another man. Not her husband.

So it was me she rejected. Not the idea of an affair.

These jealous thoughts went on long into the night. Somehow he finished the run, went home, showered, changed, looked in on his sleeping daughters, ate something and talked quietly to Trude, all in a trance like a man who's been wounded and is waiting for the bruise to come out. Then he lay on his bed and listened to the voices arguing in his head.

She's worse than I thought, that woman. She's a total bitch. No she isn't, you're just jealous. She has every right to have an affair, of course she has. Then why didn't she choose me? Because you backed away, you thought it was wrong. No I didn't, it was *her, she told me it was wrong!* Well, maybe things have changed since then. You don't know what's going on in her life. Maybe she just fancies this other guy better. Great, thanks a lot.

Or maybe things have got worse with her husband; they weren't very good before. So why didn't she talk to me about it? I could have offered, well ... comfort. She didn't have a chance to talk to you because you've been avoiding her, you know you have, trying to get her out of your mind. After all she has a life of her own, it's nothing to do with you. It's best to stay out of it, then you won't get hurt.

It would hurt more if I talked to her, would it?

Yes, it would, you know it would. Forget her, Terry, stay away.

It already hurts like hell.

The excavation took a week, even with contractors working night and day, and the inside lane of the dual carriageway had to be coned off, causing huge tailbacks and hassle for the traffic division. A team of archaeologists were recruited, to advise on the best way of extracting the body from the concrete without unnecessary damage to the road. The expense was considerable, but the body was there, just as Will Churchill had hoped. The body which now lay on the pathologist's table in front of them. The body of a young female, with a missing left hand.

Terry Bateson stood with Robert Baxter beside him, both in white coats. Churchill, typically, was away on a management training course. Peter Styles, the young forensic pathologist, was almost puppy-like in his enthusiasm. Clearly he was delighted by this change in his routine.

'Well, it'll all be in my report,' he said, 'but there are a number of significant items which I can show you straight away. In the first place, as you see, this is a young female, late teens or early twenties, no sign of childbirth. The body is significantly decayed - at least ten, possibly twenty years underground. But the soil where she was found was relatively damp, anaerobic, and that and the effect of the concrete, which served as a sort of massive coffin lid, have preserved a small amount of flesh. You will see the greatest decay was around the left arm, the lower part of which I understand has recently been exposed to the air.'

The sight - and even worse, the smell - of dead bodies cut open on the pathologist's table were a rite of passage for most young detectives at some point in their career. Terry Bateson had vomited the first time - many did. Since then he thought he had become hardened to it, but this blackened, shrunken flesh of a corpse that had been many years underground was no easy thing to look at. He thought with alarm of the sausage, eggs and bacon which had started his day, and concentrated firmly on the young man's report.

'There is some difficulty in establishing the cause of death, I'm afraid. That's not because we have no evidence, but too much, oddly enough. You see on the one hand this strip of grey cloth around the neck. You may want to send this for more detailed forensic examination, but I've had a preliminary look under a microscope, and it looks like a scarf. A silk scarf, in fact. And as you will see it's pulled very tight - in fact there are even strips of skin attached to it ...' Terry Bateson swallowed quickly and took a deep breath '... so it seems pretty likely the young woman was strangled. Certainly she would have been unable to breathe with something this tight around her neck.'

'Where's your difficulty, then?' Robert Baxter asked gruffly.

'Well, not in the scarf itself,' the young man answered smoothly. 'But here, do you see? At the back of the skull.' He turned the head sideways. 'Significant injuries here too. The skull is cracked, as if by a fall or blow. Several blows, in fact - you see the impact in several places. This could well have caused brain haemorrhage. She would have been unlikely to survive it alive.'

'So you're saying her head was smashed in, and she was strangled with a silk scarf. Is that right?' Terry Bateson asked carefully.

'Precisely. And there, you see is my problem. You want to know which came first, and unfortunately, in a body of this age ...' The young man shrugged. 'It's almost impossible to say. If I could examine her lungs or airways, but ... they're almost totally shrivelled. As is her brain - the worms have been at that. Are you all right, Inspector?'

'If you have a glass of water,' Terry Bateson, said, cursing himself. The young pathologist filled a glass from a tap at a sink beside which were several skulls and a hand pickled in brine. He handed the glass to Terry. Robert Baxter watched, hands thrust deep into the pockets of his white coat, a wooden scowl of contempt on his face.

'So as I say there appear to be two possible causes of death,' the young man resumed. 'She was either strangled first and then beaten, or beaten first and then strangled. Or maybe damaged her head in a fall. That's as far as I can go. But there are several other points of interest which may help you.'

'Yes?' Terry sipped his water cautiously. 'What are those?'

'Well, first of all this hand, or rather lack of hand. My colleague's report on that says it was chewed off the wrist by a fox, which matches with what we have here. Several marks of the teeth of a mammal. But as the report also points out, the wrist was semi-detached already - the main bone was broken long before your fox arrived.'

'Presumably at the time of death?' Bateson asked.

'I would assume so, yes. Or if not, very near to it. This is a severe injury, a broken wrist. No normal person would walk around with it untreated. But if she'd taken it to hospital, they'd have put it in plaster. There's no sign of such treatment here.'

'And the hand is definitely hers?'

'Yes. A perfect match.'

'Good. That's one thing at least. Anything else?'

'Yes. Two things that may help. Firstly, I've scraped under the fingernails. Of both hands, but the right was more productive than the left. Look here.' He led them to a microscope. 'Mostly mud and soil, of course, but look there! Those might be fragments of skin, do you see? Microscopic, invisible to the naked eye, but they're there all the same. And if I'm right, we may be able to find enough DNA to trace whose skin it is. In which case...'

'We'll know who she scratched!' A smile cracked Robert Baxter's face for the first time. 'Good work, lad. We'll have that lad Jason Barnes yet.'

'If this *is* Brenda Stokes,' Terry warned cautiously.

'Well of course it is,' Baxter said impatiently. 'Her hand, her body - look at these clothes! What are these, lad? Have you been able to establish that?' He pointed at the brown muddy threads of clothing draped here and there around the bones.

'I've had a look at them, yes. They're pretty perished but they look to me like ... well, the remains of a school uniform.'

'Exactly!' Baxter said. 'It's her, without a doubt of it! No need to wait for DNA - check her dental records! They're in the file somewhere - we had them ready, years ago, when we were searching for this body the first time.'

'We'll do that. But then we have to find out who put the body there, and how,' Terry Bateson said cautiously. 'Just because it's Brenda doesn't mean that Jason killed her. After all, how did the killer - whoever he was – get her to the A64? And then bury her under all that concrete?'

'That's for you to find out, son. But when you do, you'll find that it's Jason Barnes,' Baxter answered grimly. 'You mark my words. And then if you've got any gumption about you, you'll put him back inside where he belongs.'

'That won't be easy,' Terry said. 'Not now he's won his appeal. I'm not sure it's legally possible.'

'Even if it isn't, you can publish the evidence in the papers. That'll be enough for me.'

Baxter turned and marched towards the door. Terry was about to follow him when the pathologist said: 'Oh, there's one other thing.'

'Yes, what's that?'

'It'll be in the report, but I may as well tell you now. Those injuries to the skull. They would have left an awful lot of blood - head injuries do. There would have been blood all over the place.'

25. Riverbank

'SO THIS is where it was found?'

'According to the records, yes.'

They'd reached the end of Fulford Main Street, the southern edge of the city. Terry Bateson and his new assistant, Jane Carter, had spent the last few days reading the file on the case of the murder of Brenda Stokes. A key piece of evidence against Jason Barnes had been the bloodstained torch, which had originally been believed to be the murder weapon. Now they had come to see where it had been found. The place, according to Jason, where he had last seen Brenda alive.

Terry turned the car right across the traffic onto an unmade track. There was a metal bar overhead to prevent access by lorries or gypsy caravans. A sign on the right read Landing Lane. The track wound right and left under overhanging trees, and in twenty yards they were in a different world, away from the buzz of people and traffic and housing, in sudden rural solitude. The car bounced in a pothole, a rabbit scurried into the undergrowth.

'Just the place for a spot of nookie,' Jane Carter murmured. 'Or murder, if that's your preference.'

'You're all right with me, love,' Terry said, regretting it instantly, as her plain, earnest gaze met his. 'Anyway, there's a copper on duty, just in case,' he added. Poor girl, she thinks I'm insulting her, he thought desperately. Probably no-one's ever flirted with her in her life.

As they came round a corner they saw a parking place with an old red hatchback in it. Beside the car was a burly man in an old tweed jacket; Detective Superintendent Bob Baxter, retired. As they pulled up beside him, he glanced pointedly at his watch.

'Fifteen minutes I've stood here, young man,' he said, as Terry got out. 'Trying to waste my time, are you?'

Terry sighed. He found it hard to be polite to the old man. Maybe this was why Will Churchill was glad to be away. 'No. Just trying to find the truth, that's all.'

'The truth is that Jason Barnes murdered that young girl,' Baxter growled. 'Just as I always said he did.' He scowled at Terry's blank, non-committal face, then glanced at Jane, hoping for more support. 'And this, in my view, is where he killed her.'

They looked around. It was certainly an appropriate spot. Even now, in the middle of the day, it was quiet here. Just a couple of bluetits peeping to each other in the trees, and the distant swoosh of traffic, like the sound of the sea, from the A64. This major road, Jane worked out, was a short distance away to the south, over a field that rose like a low hill to their left. She saw a horse grazing under some large parkland trees. Straight ahead of them, the track diverged, with a white gate marked Private on the left, and an old rusty one across the track beside it. Both appeared to lead into further wooded seclusion. On the right of the track where they stood was an overgrown hedge, with what looked like a marshy meadow behind it, overgrown with willowherb and nettles. If it was quiet like this now, Jane thought, what must it have been like at three o'clock in the morning, 18 years ago?

'So where did you find it?' Terry asked.

'The torch? Just down here. I'll show you.'

Baxter led them a few yards down the track, through the rusty gate. There was marshy untended ground on either side, and to their left, Jane realised, a glimpse of the river Ouse.

'Just in there.' Baxter pointed to a patch of grass with docks and nettles, the far side of a small ditch on the right hand side. 'Didn't find it straight away, of course. Took three days before he admitted he'd been here, the little shite.'

'And this torch was covered with blood?' Jane asked, peering at the ditch.

'That's right. *Her* blood,' Baxter emphasized firmly. 'We didn't have the benefit of DNA then, of course, just matching blood groups, but that definitely matched hers. Today we know the DNA closely matches her mother's, even if we can't check it against Brenda herself.'

'We'll need to check it against this body,' Terry said. 'Then we'll be absolutely certain.'

'Sure, go ahead.' Baxter shook his head, like a bull bothered by flies.

'But it'll be hers, all right. So as far as I was concerned we had the murder weapon, years ago. A torch covered with *her* blood and *his* fingerprint in it. What more did we want?'

'Hairs, bits of skin,' Terry said quietly. 'To prove he'd hit her with it. Did you look for those?'

'Of course we did,' Baxter said grimly. 'I went to the lab myself. But you've got to remember, that torch had been lying in long wet grass for three days before we found it. And it had rained. So what do you expect?'

'They'd probably have found some trace today, on the torch or in the grass where it was lying,' Terry said. 'But things have changed.'

'We looked all round here for the body,' Baxter said. 'Never found it, of course.'

'It's a fair bit to search.'

'It is that.' Baxter strode on, as though to illustrate the point. In ten or twenty yards they were on the riverbank. The wide slow-moving Ouse flowed quietly in front of them. Willow trees wept over the bank in spots favoured by fishermen. There was a metal picnic table and chairs, and sheep grazing on the far side. A footpath ran north and south along the riverbank; a jogger loped past as they watched.

'Where does this go?' Jane asked.

'North into the city, south under the A64 to the meadows opposite the archbishop's palace,' Terry answered. 'It will have taken some time, to search all this,' he said to Baxter.

'Forty men for a week,' Baxter said. 'Plus divers, of course. We searched the river for five miles downstream; it took ages. And then the little bastard came up with his tale about the slurry pits. We even checked Naburn sewage works.'

'You did that because of what Jason Barnes said when he was arrested?' Jane asked, reminding herself of the details she'd read in the files.

'That's right.' Baxter lit a cigarette and drew on it deeply, watching a brightly painted canal narrow boat chug slowly past on the water. 'We took it seriously at the time, but now we know he was just taking the piss. Buried her under the ring road instead.'

'So the question is, how did she get from here to Copmanthorpe?' Terry said thoughtfully. 'What is it, about four miles?'

'Well, that's obvious, isn't it?' Baxter said irritably. 'He left the party at the uni, drove her down here to get his leg over, and when she turned him down he lost his rag and smacked her over the head with the torch. Then he flung the torch away, dragged her into the car, drove along the A64 to Copmanthorpe where they were building the ring road, and buried her in a ditch hoping she'd be concreted over next day. Which she was. All but her hand, that is.'

'Which didn't turn up for eighteen years,' Jane said. 'Almost the perfect crime.'

'Except,' Baxter pointed out, 'that he boasted about it in jail to Brian Winnick.' He fixed Terry with a grim stare. 'And the jury, who unlike the sodding court of appeal actually saw Winnick cross-examined in front of them, believed him. Just as they *dis*believed Jason Barnes. So why that verdict isn't allowed to stand, I'm at a loss to say.'

Because you bribed Winnick to lie in court, Terry thought. *You dropped the drug-dealing charges against him in return for an invented story that sent a man to prison for 18 years. You didn't have enough evidence to prove your case, so you manufactured some. And now you've been found out.*

But he didn't bother to say it. There was no point. Over the past few days he and Jane Carter had read through the files of the original investigation and the transcript of the appeal in London. He'd seen, with pain and admiration, how Sarah Newby had shredded Baxter's reputation, and left him with a retirement full of bitterness and shame instead of pride and contentment. The conviction of Jason Barnes, in a case where the body had never been found, had quite probably been the highlight of this man's career. Now Barnes walked free, while his captor was reviled.

It was harsh, Terry thought. Thirty years service in protection of the community, trashed in a moment. But Baxter deserved it. If he'd bullied, cut corners and cheated in this case, he'd probably done it before, many times. It was people like him who got the police a bad name.

And Sarah Newby, of all people, had exposed him. But that's what she's like, Terry told himself grimly. Turns people's lives upside down. All well and good, if they deserve it, like Baxter. But what if they don't?

And what if the man's right after all?

'I still think he's guilty,' Bob Baxter said firmly. 'Whatever those judges say, sitting on their arses in court. I knew the lad, I interviewed him, stared into his eyes. Believe me, he's a killer, he did it. And now we've found the body, at last, it's your job to prove it.'

Later that week, Terry had a conference with his boss, DCI Will Churchill. Churchill had just returned from his management training course, brimfull of new ideas. 'We're way behind the times here, Terence, way behind the times,' he announced, bustling into Terry's office and using the version of his name that he knew Terry hated. 'New technology, slicker management, mini systems and micro peer review. That's the way forward!'

One of the advances, Terry noted wryly, appeared to be sartorial. Churchill was wearing a soft new woollen suit, exquisitely tailored to flatter his short, slightly pudgy physique. Underneath it was an expensive shirt with cufflinks and a gaudy silk tie. He noticed Terry looking at it and smoothed it with his fingers proudly.

'Smart, don't you think? We had a few hours in town, and I thought why not? Appearances matter these days, and good clothes last a lifetime. Ought to try it yourself, Terence old lad,' he said, with a pitying glance at Terry's worn, double-breasted suit, which hung loosely on his lean body like an ancient tracksuit. Terry had an uncomfortable feeling that traces of scrambled egg, the result of a collision with Jessica in the kitchen this morning, might be visible on his sleeve. *Maybe that's why Sarah Newby's not interested in me.*

Churchill smiled. 'Just say the word, and I'll mention you to Nigel, my tailor. Only too delighted. Now, how far have you got with this case of the girl under the motorway, eh? Have we got enough evidence to put her killer back behind bars?'

'Jason Barnes, you mean?'

'That's the man. Who else?'

Terry shook his head slowly. 'Hardly. Given the evidence we have so far. Nothing much fits.'

Will Churchill's face darkened. He strolled to the window moodily, lifting the blind to peer out a pair of young female constables crossing the car park. 'Really? Why not?'

'Well sir, you were at the appeal, so you probably know this. Barnes was originally convicted on the grounds that he drove her to Landing Lane by the river, attempted to rape her, bashed her head in with the torch, and then disposed of the body somewhere. Either in the river or a slurry pit.'

'Yes, well we know it wasn't a slurry pit now. It was under the ring road. In a trench just about to be concreted over.'

'Which proves that the evidence of this informer - what was his name, Brian Winnick - was a lie, just as Barnes said it was,' Terry said. 'Robert Baxter suborned him.'

'Yes, well, maybe.' Churchill turned back from the window, frowning. 'Doesn't mean Barnes didn't do it though, does it? Maybe he's the one who buried her.'

'There's no real evidence that it was him, though, is there?' Terry insisted. 'No more than before, anyway. I mean, we can't even say for certain how she died. There are the crush injuries to her skull, which could possibly have been caused by this torch, I suppose. But they could have been caused by anything - a stone, a brick, whatever - and we don't even know for certain it was those injuries that killed her. Maybe she was throttled by that silk scarf, and her skull was damaged later, when he buried her in the trench.'

'Or maybe he throttled her with the scarf and then bashed her skull in with the torch to make sure. I don't see that it matters all that much.' Churchill began to count off points with the fingers of his left hand. 'The real point, Terence, is that Barnes was the last person seen with her, right? He admits they had a quarrel and he tried to rape her. His fingerprint was found in blood on the torch. He set fire to the car afterwards to hide the evidence. He had ample opportunity to get rid of her body in the middle of the night. Copmanthorpe is on the way to Leeds. And he was a nasty little shite with a record of violence. So, he probably did it.'

'Which is exactly what Bob Baxter thought,' Terry said wearily. 'So when he realised he hadn't got quite enough evidence, he asked his tame informer to manufacture some.'

'Maybe, maybe not.' Will Churchill sighed. He didn't like Bob Baxter, but the memory of the man's humiliation in court by Sarah Newby needled him. He'd give a lot to put that bitch in her place. 'But he didn't have the body. We have.'

'Yes, sir, but what does it tell us? We know she was throttled and her skull crushed, but not in which order. We also know her right wrist was broken - how did that happen?' Terry shook his head. 'Questions, but no answers. And to add to that, we have her in four separate locations that night, all quite different.' He pointed to a map on the wall, which he had illustrated with pins. 'Firstly, a student party at Goodricke College on campus, here. She's seen driving away from there with Jason Barnes at about 1.45 a.m. Next thing, Landing Lane in Fulford where the torch was found. It's about five minutes' drive from the party so let's say they arrive about 1.50. How long are they there? We don't know. Anywhere between five minutes and half an hour for a row to develop when she refuses to have sex with him ...'

'More like five minutes, I should think,' Churchill said smartly. He met Terry's eyes and grinned conspiratorially. 'I mean, with kids that age.'

'Maybe.' Terry turned back to the map. 'Anyway, sometime about 4 a.m. a nurse, Amanda Carr, sees a girl in school uniform walking down Naburn Lane, near the old Maternity Hospital. Just here.' Terry pointed to a small flag on the map. 'She only catches a fleeting glimpse of the girl, and when she tells the police later they take no notice.' Terry sighed. 'But what if *was* Brenda she saw? That would mean she was still alive nearly two hours *after* Jason Barnes claims she flounced off into the night. And Jason was in Leeds, torching the car he'd nicked.'

'*If* it was her,' Will Churchill said. 'Bob Baxter never believed it was.'

'Quite,' Terry said contemptuously. 'So he failed to disclose it to the defence.'

'Which was wrong, obviously,' Churchill agreed. 'But standards were different back then. We've improved. You may sneer, but we have. And to be fair to the man, he had his reasons. He was convinced this Amanda - what's her name? Carr - was a fantasist, longing to see her name in print. She may have seen no one, just a shadow in the moonlight, anything. She'd been to a party, she was drunk, should never have been driving in the first place ...'

'Even so ...'

'Baxter should have disclosed it, agreed. But he didn't because he thought the girl was a nutter. Which she probably was - I saw her in the witness box, remember? Our QC made mincemeat of her.'

'Nonetheless, Mrs Newby won the appeal.'

'Quite. On a technicality, in my view.' Will Churchill sucked his teeth, as if he'd tasted something bitter. 'Even if this Amanda woman was telling the truth, how does that help us?'

'Well.' Terry traced a route across the map. 'Brenda lived in Bishopthorpe, so she was probably trying to walk home. She could have crossed the river at Naburn by the old railway bridge. So somewhere between the old Maternity Hospital - where the Designer Outlet is now - and her home, someone must have picked her up and killed her.'

Churchill studied Terry pityingly. 'Who exactly? We know one lad's tried to rape her, but instead of going after him, you're suggesting someone else, some unknown psychopath from Mars maybe, just happened along that road a while later, sees the girl, picks her up, throttles her with a scarf, breaks her wrist, bashes her head in, and buries her in a trench by the ring road near Copmanthorpe? Just like that? Come on, Terence, get a grip. *Why* would anyone do that?'

'Who knows? All I'm saying is, it might have been someone else who killed her. Not Jason.'

'Who?'

'I don't know. I'm just saying it's a possibility we shouldn't dismiss.'

Churchill sighed. 'Look at the map, Terence, and consider the facts. Two right turns from Landing Lane, and Jason could be on that same road himself.'

'Not after 4 a.m., surely,' Terry insisted. 'That would mean he'd hung about for nearly an hour an a half. Why would he do that?'

'Looking for the girl, perhaps. We know he did that, he says so himself. Stumbled around with the torch, that's his story ...'

'After he'd hit her with it?' Terry asked. 'With those cracks in her skull? Surely she'd be unconscious.'

'Which is why, Terence, I don't believe the evidence of this nurse.' Churchill moved nearer, deliberately invading Terry's space, and stared directly into his eyes. 'If you believe her, I grant you, Jason would have been pushed for time. But if what she says is just some drunken fantasy, then everything falls back into place. Jason tried to rape her, and when she fought back he killed her. With the torch, or with the scarf, it doesn't really matter. What matters is he's got a dead girl on his hands, and plenty of time to hide her body. He had time, motive and opportunity. He was actually on the scene, he existed, unlike your wandering psychopath from Mars. And then he lied about dumping her body in a slurry pit, to take the piss out of friend Baxter and put him off the track.'

Terry nodded. 'True. But all that was the original prosecution case. It wasn't strong enough then, which was why our friend Baxter manufactured a false confession, to strengthen it.'

'If it *was* false, yes.' Will Churchill's eyes met Terry's. 'This Winnick was a crackhead, a lowlife, just like Jason Barnes. Maybe young Jason did spin him a tale in prison, telling him everything that happened except where he'd buried the body. Then Winnick told the truth in court, but decided to lie to his lawyer before he died, to get his own back on Baxter. Ever thought of that?'

Churchill grinned, looking pleased with himself. Terry shook his head slowly.

'The Court of Appeal decided otherwise.'

'I know that - I was there! With that fancy knickers Newby woman smirking all over her face.' Churchill paced across the room irritably. 'Well, they didn't have the body, and we do. So now we can find out who really committed this crime, and bring him to justice. And if it turns out to be Jason Barnes after all, I for one will be delighted.'

Terry frowned. 'Even if it is him, sir, we can't prosecute him again, can we? Not twice, for the same crime - that's double jeopardy, surely.'

A grin of pure, superior delight crossed Will Churchill's face. He put a hand on Terry's shoulder. 'That's what I love about you, Terence. Always a step behind the times. Our beloved former Prime Minister altered that - didn't you notice? In cases where there's exceptional new evidence, double jeopardy no longer applies. The first case came up a few months ago; this could be the second.' He strode to the door.

'What I'd like - what I'd really like - is for this department, just once, to be vindicated, and see that Newby woman stand up in court with egg on her face, admitting she's wrong. It would help that poor bastard Bob Baxter, too - show that his life chasing villains wasn't wasted.' He smiled. 'So go out and find the evidence, Terence, why don't you?'

26. Mask and Mirror

THE CALL came in the early afternoon. A woman had made a 999 call from a house on the Bishopthorpe road. An area car was on its way but DI Terry Bateson had asked to be informed immediately of any reported assaults on women, and this sounded like one. Within minutes he had set out. DS Jane Carter sat in the car beside him.

The house was on an estate between the Bishopthorpe Road and the A64. It was a pleasant area - several large Edwardian villas, and plenty of smaller modern detached houses with their own gardens and integral garages. The call had come from one of these. It was at the end of the street near a small area of woodland, lovingly preserved by the Woodland Trust. There were footpaths where local residents walked their dogs and children rode bikes. On the far side of the woods was the Knavesmire, York's racecourse, which was also traversed by footpaths and cycletracks.

The front garden contained a few shrubs, a silver birch tree and a drive just wide enough for an ambulance, which stood there now. A small crowd of people who looked like neighbours stood nearby. Terry and Jane pushed past them and went into the house.

Inside, the paramedics were talking to a white-faced young woman in a dressing gown. She sat with her arms round a two-year-old boy, perched on the edge of the sofa in her living room. Her hair was tousled, her eyes huge and terrified. Her hands trembled as she clung to her child, and her voice shook as she spoke.

'He didn't touch him. He didn't touch you, Davy, did he? It's all right. The nasty man's gone now. You're all right darling, you're safe.'

The boy looked as shocked as his mother. At first it was hard to see his face because it was buried in her chest, his hands clinging tight around her neck. But a female paramedic was talking to him softly, gently touching his arm, and once or twice he looked round swiftly to check who she was, before turning back for comfort to his mother.

'What's happened here?' Terry asked a constable from the area car.

'Burglary, sir, it seems, and attempted rape. We're not too sure of the details yet, but the woman was surprised by a masked intruder in her bedroom. He tried to assault her but she fought back, I believe, and then he was disturbed by a neighbour bringing the child back from playschool. He rode off on a bike in the direction of the Knavesmire. We've got cars out there searching for him now.'

'My God,' Terry said softly. 'No wonder she's shocked. Where's this neighbour?'

The neighbour, Muriel Jarrett, looked as shocked as the mother. She confirmed that she had picked up little Davy with her own daughter as she often did. When she'd brought him into the house she'd heard banging and screaming upstairs. Then a man had run downstairs past her and out of the back door. She hadn't seen his face - it was covered by a mask which scared her rigid. She'd seen him get on a bike and cycle away, through the woods towards the Knavesmire. She'd followed little Davy upstairs to find his mother shaking and trembling on her bed, with her dressing gown loosely pulled round her and a pair of hairdressing scissors in her hand.

Leaving Jane with the victim, Terry went upstairs. In the main bedroom was a pine double bed, with elaborately carved wooden headboard and posts at the foot. The duvet was twisted and rumpled, hanging half off the bed. There was a damp towel on the floor, and an overpowering sweet musky smell. After a moment he realised this was coming from a dark stain on the wallpaper near the door. Under the stain, on the floor, was a smashed perfume spray. The bedroom carpet was littered with several other feminine items - a jar of moisturising cream, a silver-backed hairbrush, a broken vase. A small jewel case lay in the middle of the floor with rings and necklaces spilling out it. There was a pair of running shoes too, one by the bed, one near the door as if it had just been flung there.

The bedroom window looked out across the garden to the woods, where a squirrel was scurrying up a tree. Looking back into the room Terry caught sight of himself in a full length wall mirror. Beside the mirror was a washbasket with a pair of jogging pants hanging over the edge. On the other side was a door leading to an ensuite bathroom whose floor was still wet, as if someone had been taking a shower. The top drawer of the chest of drawers was open, and female underwear spilled over the side.

He was about to leave when he noticed something half-hidden under the rumpled duvet. It looked like a rope of some kind. He pulled the duvet back carefully and saw it was a pink dressing gown cord.

Terry went downstairs to where Jane was talking to the woman. She wore a long loose pink dressing gown, he saw, clutched around her waist where the cord was missing. The paramedics were insisting she go to hospital, and Jane wanted to accompany her. To the crucial question: 'Did he rape you, love?' the woman vehemently shook her head, but she was still so clearly in shock that she could scarcely speak.

'I'd have killed him,' she whispered. 'I'd have killed him if he'd touched my little boy.'

Jane Carter took the female paramedic aside. 'We have a rape suite at the station with a doctor,' she said softly. 'She'll get full medical attention there but also, if she has been assaulted, it's the best place to hear her story and gather evidence. It's completely private and all the doctors are female.'

The paramedic nodded. 'Can she take the child?'

'Of course. We've got female constables trained in this sort of thing. I'll call one now.'

'All right. But we'll stay with her until the doctor arrives.' The paramedic turned back to the woman, who still sat clutching her child, her arms trembling with shock. She held out a blanket. 'Lizzie, my love, we're going to take you to a doctor, all right? She'll check you over and see you're all right. You can bring your son too - have a ride in the ambulance, ok? Look out of our special windows - would you like that, Davy? Just like on TV. And this policewoman's coming with us to keep us all safe.'

Several hours later, DS Jane Carter briefed Terry Bateson on what she had learned at the rape suite. Jane looked tired, but fired with a grim determination that gave her energy. She paced up and down as she spoke.

'The good news first, if there is any in a crime like this. She wasn't raped or badly beaten in any way. Just a few bruises on her neck and arms from the struggle. And the shock, of course. That's what's really going to take time to get over. If she ever does, that is.'

'And the little boy?'

'He wasn't touched as far as we know. His name's Davy, his mum's Lizzie - Elizabeth Bolan. She's a single mum, apparently; Davy's dad left a couple of years ago. Lizzie's an accountant - works from home on her computer, she says. Anyway, this afternoon she'd been for a run on the Knavesmire - despite all the warnings we've issued over the past week - then came back in time for a shower before the neighbour brought her kid back from playschool. They take it in turns, apparently, alternate days. She was drying herself in front of the mirror when she saw a face peering over her shoulder. Not a normal face - something awful. She spun round and saw a man in her bedroom, near the door. He was wearing a sort of thin black anorak with the hood pulled up, and under the hood was a mask - the *Scream!* mask, she says, from that painting by Munch.'

'My God,' Terry said softly. 'No wonder she was shocked.'

'He wasn't just wearing a mask - he was wearing gloves as well. And he had a sort of rope or cord in his hands. She thinks it was her dressing gown cord. He came round the bed towards her, holding it out. She was petrified, poor woman.'

'I'm not surprised. What happened then? He didn't rape her, you say?'

'No. He told her to strip - she was only wearing a towel anyway - and wrapped the cord round her neck. He twisted it tight so she couldn't breathe and held her in front of the mirror like that. His face in the mask leering over her shoulder, hers going red as she struggled for breath. She thought she was going to die. But then he pulled her back towards the bed, and she panicked and started fighting to get away. She clawed at the cord with her hands, and grabbed his mask as well by mistake, pulling it sideways so he couldn't see. She didn't mean to do that, but that's probably what saved her, she thinks.'

'She didn't get a look at his face?'

'No. But he loosened his grip on the cord to try and get the mask straight, so he could see probably, and she wriggled free and started throwing things at him, anything she could lay her hands on, she says - perfume, pictures, whatever. Then she snatched a pair of scissors from her chest of drawers. She held them in front of her and said she'd stab him if he touched her again.'

'Brave woman,' Terry said. 'Did it work?'

'Well, it stopped him for a second, apparently, and she thought she might escape out the door, but he was standing in front of it. Then she realised he had a sort of hunting knife in a sheath at his waist and he was just about to pull it out when she heard the door open and her little boy calling from downstairs. And that scared her more than anything, she says, because she thought he might harm her little Davy. So she screamed at Davy to watch out, and then her neighbour shouted back up the stairs to ask if everything was all right. That's when the intruder took flight and ran. That's the last she saw of him. He went straight downstairs and out of the house. Then the neighbour came upstairs with Davy, she put on her dressing gown, and they rang 999.'

'Poor woman,' Terry said softly. 'How is she now?'

'Traumatized, as you'd expect. The hospital are keeping her in overnight. For observation, they say. Her kid's staying with his granny in Heworth. Lizzie wanted to take him home, but I told her the SOCOs would still be there - tomorrow as well as today probably. And she'll feel safer knowing her mum's looking after him. Anyway she needs to sleep.'

'She's a lucky lady,' Terry said. 'Plucky, too. If she hadn't fought back ... and if the neighbour hadn't turned up just when she did ...'

'She'd have stabbed him, sir. That's what she kept saying, over and over. No doubt in her mind at all. If he went for that knife she'd have stabbed him with those scissors. Not so much for herself, but for her kid.'

'Well, good for her.' Terry grimaced, imagining the scene. 'Maybe that'll help her get over it. To think she fought back, and won.'

'It'll help even more if we catch him.'

'Quite. This looks like attempted murder, with the cord,' Terry said. 'Attempted rape, too, presumably.'

'Well, obviously it looks like it, doesn't it? The way he pulled her back towards the bed. But ... her real fear was that he was going to kill her. She said he was muttering something as he held her in front of the mirror - something about being ugly, she thinks - but with the mask on she couldn't really hear what he was saying. She wasn't focussing on it anyway - she was in a panic, thinking she was going to die.'

'Of course.' Terry pondered for a moment. '*Ugly*, she thinks? That's a strange word to use, in the circumstances. Do you think he meant her, or him?'

'Who knows. The point is, he's a dangerous maniac.'

'And he wasn't just a burglar who thought the house was empty. He broke in, looking for her.'

'Almost certainly. After all, it was the middle of the day - he had no reason to expect the house would be empty. She's a single mum, and works from home. Which he would have known, if he'd done any research.'

'He wouldn't have worn the mask if he'd thought the house was empty. He had the gloves too, and the knife, though thank God he didn't use it. He knew what he wanted, and went there looking for her. At a time when he thought her kid wasn't there.'

Terry nodded in agreement. Both, inevitably, were thinking the same thing. 'And since she was out jogging, he may even have followed her home. On his bike.'

Jane shuddered. 'It's creepy. You know, when I was a girl, I didn't believe there were men like this. Women don't do these things.' She scowled at him accusingly.

'Nor do 99% of men,' Terry replied. 'Come on now, sergeant, we're dealing with a seriously weird individual here. And it looks more than likely it's the same one we've come across before.'

'You think it's Peter Barton, don't you?' Jane asked.

'More than likely,' Terry said. 'There's too many similarities to ignore. Single mother, alone in the house. He came and went on a bike, the house backs onto the Knavesmire where there are cycletracks everywhere. He didn't take any trophies this time, but then he didn't get much chance.'

'It has to be Peter,' Jane said. 'Maybe this time the SOCOs can prove it.'

'Let's hope so,' Terry said. 'In that struggle, he must have left a trace somewhere, however careful he was. I've already been to his work, the young bastard, but he didn't turn up today. No one knows why. So I think we should pay another visit to his mother, don't you? And talk to anyone else who's had anything to do with the nasty little pervert. We've got to find this lad, sergeant, and soon. Before we have another assault on our hands. It could be murder, next time.'

27. Gone to Ground

'HE'S NOT here,' the woman said, peering at them round the half-open door. 'And you're not welcome.'

'We have a search warrant, Mrs Barton.' Terry waved it under her nose.

She studied the document suspiciously, still propping the door half shut. It was the second time in a month that the police had visited her house. 'So? Search for what?'

'Evidence.' Terry put his hand on the door. 'We're investigating a serious arrestable offence and have reason to believe there may be material on these premises relevant to our inquiry. So please let us in.'

'My Pete's done nothing. He wasn't there.'

'Wasn't where?'

'Wherever you say he was. He was home here with me.'

Terry eyed the woman with contempt. He pushed back the door and squeezed past her into the narrow hallway. Her protests came sharp in his ear. 'Just because he's slow, doesn't make him nasty. It's a free country, he can do what he likes.'

'Not if it involves assaulting defenceless women,' Terry said, heading for the stairs. 'Look, Mrs Barton, we're investigating a serious crime here. Not just a naughty boy stealing some knickers, not any more. A woman was nearly raped in her own home. Would you like that to happen to you?'

'Threatening me now, are you?'

'No, just asking you to think. If your son did this he should give himself up, right now. Before something worse happens.'

'Probably asked for it, the slag.'

Terry shook his head in despair. 'No, she didn't. This happened in her own home, to a decent young mother with a child. The man who did this is dangerous and probably sick.'

'Well then, it's not my Peter.'

'No? Then why did he attack those other women?'

'He didn't. You stitched him up.'

'Let's ask him then, shall we? Where is he now?'

'At work, of course. Where else?'

'No he's not. We went there and asked. Hasn't been in for two days.'

'No? Well, he's sick.'

'I'm sorry to hear it. Lying upstairs in bed, is he?'

'No. Sick of you, more like. Pestering him about that girl. You scared him witless!'

Terry turned, halfway up the staircase. 'So he's not here?'

'Look for yourself. Maybe he's under the mattress.'

Terry shrugged and went on up the stairs. If Peter Barton had run away, it was a further indication of guilt. The boy's bedroom was much as Jane Carter had described from her earlier visit. The black curtains, the red light bulb, the posters of big breasted fantasy women were all there, with the hunting knives pinned up beneath them. The curtains were drawn, the windows were closed, there was a stale, unpleasant smell. Two porn mags lay open on an unmade, rumpled bed. Shoes, clothes and cigarette ash were strewn across the floor. Several drawers were open as if clothes had been taken out.

For half an hour they searched diligently. Under the bed, in the drawers, in the pockets of his clothes. They lifted the carpet and looked for loose floorboards. They lifted the mattress and checked inside the pillowcases and duvet cover. They flicked through magazines and picked up clothes from the floor. All the time Mrs Barton hung in the doorway, smoking and jeering at them.

'Put it back neat and tidy, won't you? Take me hours to clear up the mess you make.'

'We'll leave it just as we found it,' said Terry, dropping a grubby teeshirt on the floor. 'Where's he gone, anyway?'

'Told you, I don't know. And if I did I wouldn't tell you.'

Jane climbed on the bed, leaned across to the top of the wardrobe, and let out a whoop of triumph. 'Guv?' she said. 'Look at this.' A plastic facemask dangled from a string in her hand. It was a Dracula figure. Fake blood dripped from fangs, vacant eye sockets leered at Terry grotesquely.

'Is this your son's?' Terry asked.

'Might be. So what?'

'This woman's attacker wore a mask.'

'So? You can buy 'em in the costume shop. People hire 'em for parties.'

'Go to a lot of parties, does he, your son?'

'He's been to a few.'

'Bag it up,' Terry said to Jane. 'What about the knives then? And the survival magazines? Are those normal interests?'

'Normal to some. It gets him out of the house.'

'What about his friends? He must have some.'

'A few. Lads from work, friends from school.'

'Names?'

'Don't remember. Not my business.'

'Oh come on, Mrs Barton! You must know some of your son's friends.'

'They're his friends, not mine. Don't talk to me anyhow.'

'Look, love, he's already skipped bail,' Terry said grimly. 'If he's got nothing to hide, he ought to hand himself in. The longer he stays on the run, the worse all this gets.'

'If I see him, I'll tell him.'

'Does he have a mobile? Can you call him on that?'

'No. He hasn't got one.'

'Must be the only lad in the country who hasn't, then. Mrs Barton, you're lying to protect your son.'

'Can you tell me a better reason for lying? He's a decent lad, I tell you! He didn't do none of these things.'

They went back to Peter Barton's work to interview his colleagues. They were less obstructive than his mother, but little more helpful. He was a loner, they said, with few friends. He did his job, talked little, kept himself to himself. The only person who seemed to know much about him was an underchef called Roger Clark. He was a short, wiry man in his mid thirties. He had a short, military style haircut, a deep barrel chest and muscular arms with a snake's head tattoo on his left bicep. He stared at Terry suspiciously.

'Peter? Yeah, what d'you want with him?'

Terry studied the man thoughtfully. 'People say you're a mate of his.'

'Me?' The man laughed. 'Daft git. I'm not his mate. I took pity on him, that's all.'

'Why pity?'

'Have you met him? Then you'll know.' The man shook his head slowly. 'We get a few like him in the army. They don't last long. Lots of tough ideas, soft as butter underneath. No idea what the real world's about. Say boo too loud and he'll shit his pants.'

'What did you talk about?'

'His magazines, his hobbies. He knew I'd been in the army, we talked about that.'

'His hobbies being what, exactly?'

'Survival. Military stuff, weapons, living rough, that sort of thing. Kid's stuff, really. He had these books about the SAS - he showed me once.'

'You encouraged him, did you?' Terry asked. 'Told him stories of military life?'

'Do me a favour. I was in the catering corps, me, snug and warm in the kitchen. Think I want to crawl around in mud and shit with guys trying to blow your head off? No thanks. But Peter, yeah. That's what he's interested in - or thinks he is. Goes off at weekends, stalking people, spying on them, or so he claims. In the woods, on the moors. Lives rough at night, so he says. Got a hideout somewhere.'

'Do you know where?'

'Sorry, no idea. His big secret, that is. Just grinned when I asked.'

'But he's left home now. His mum won't say where he's gone.'

'Yeah, well.' The man shrugged. 'Gone to ground then, I guess.'

Terry looked out of the window. It was cold, damp, windy. At four thirty it was almost dark. 'You really think he might be living rough? At this time of year?'

'Wouldn't put it past him. If you lot are after him, might be all the motivation he needs. He'd see it as a game. Peter Barton against the world.'

Especially against women, Terry thought. They're the victims in all this. 'What about girls? Does he talk about them?'

'Peter? No, not much. Doubt if he'd know where to start, to be honest with you. Is that his problem, then? That why you're looking for him?'

'He's been pestering women.' Terry gave a few details of the assault on Lizzie Bolan. 'So if it was Peter who did this, we need to find him urgently before he does it again. Or something much worse. You see the point?'

'Sure.' The man shifted his feet uncomfortably. 'But there's not much I know. Like I say, he loved secrets. Made him feel big, I guess. Though if he was doing that to women ...' He shook his head. 'Not something you'd boast about, is it?'

'He never mentioned that to you? About his arrest, I mean?'

'Not a word. Poor sick bugger. I can see him pinching knickers, but that other - you wouldn't think he'd have the guts.'

'It may not be him; until we've found him we don't know. What about his mobile, can you ring him on that?'

'Sorry, no. Don't think he had one. He's not like, talkative, this lad. Probably hasn't got anyone to ring.'

'So where might he be?'

The man studied the ground for a moment, thinking. 'Look, if he's really done these things, I'd help you, 'course I would. Though I can't see it myself. He's all bluff, just a jelly inside.' He shook his head slowly. 'He comes to work, he does his job, hardly speaks to anyone. Only reason he speaks to me is because I feel sorry for him. But where he goes after that, I haven't got a clue. He may have friends I don't know, though I doubt it. Maybe he's got a hideout in the country ... though at this time of year, be bloody cold, wouldn't it? Or a squat somewhere in town. I could see that, him fantasizing about being a spy on the run, that sort of thing. But where, I couldn't tell you.'

Stumped, Terry and Jane drove back to Bishopthorpe Road. The young woman, Lizzie Bolan, had gone to stay with her mother. Blue and white police tape sealed off house and garden. Neighbours walked past along the street, rubbernecking at the white overalled SOCO team who were packing up their equipment for the day. Terry talked to the team leader, Sergeant Dave Tanner.

'Find anything useful?'

'One or two things. The dressing gown cord, obviously, we'll send that for DNA testing. And then, it's possible our lad didn't wear gloves. Or not all the time, as the victim thought. There's strong clear fingerprints - not in the bedroom, but on the garage window sill outside, where he parked his bike.'

'What? How do you know he left the bike out there?'

'It's the obvious place. Between the kitchen door and the garage - there's a little passage along the side of the house. It's out of sight from the street, and that's where the neighbour says he came out when she brought the kid home. He pushed past her just as she was going in.'

Terry already had the description of the man the neighbour had seen. Six foot tall, quite strongly built, in a dark tracksuit, with a *Scream* mask hiding his face. Naturally she'd focussed on the mask; she'd screamed herself. He'd ridden away through the little wood towards the Knavesmire, and the SOCO team had found distinctive mountain bike tyre tracks on the path through the woods. Uniformed officers had been stopping cyclists and dog walkers on the Knavesmire all day, asking if anyone had noticed a man of that description hurrying away. No one had seen a man in a *Scream* mask, but Sergeant Tanner was able to explain why.

He took a plastic evidence bag from the back of his van. Inside it, stained with leafmould and mud, was a plastic *Scream* face mask.

'Olé!' He grinned triumphantly at Terry. 'Seems our lad didn't fancy scaring half the population of York as he cycled away, so he dumped the mask in a ditch in the woods. A little kiddy brought it in this afternoon. So even though it's pretty mucky from the ditch, chances are he's left some DNA inside this somewhere, what with all the heavy breathing that must have been going on.'

'And possibly fingerprints too,' Jane said. 'If you're saying he put his gloves on at the last minute.'

'That's how it looks to me,' Sergeant Tanner agreed. 'He cycles up to the house all quiet and peaceful, obviously not wearing the mask so as not to draw attention to himself, and maybe not wearing latex gloves either because that looks weird too, not normal cycling kit. Then he parks his bike in the little passage beside the garage, steadies himself with a hand on the window sill, leaving three beautiful prints, and then he puts on his mask and gloves and bursts into the house. So yes, if a print on this mask matches those on the window sill, that ties the two together.'

'And if they match Peter Barton's,' Jane said. 'We've got him!'

'Except,' Terry pointed out gloomily. 'We don't know where he is.'

28. On the Edge

SARAH STOOD on the steps of York Crown Court, enjoying the light breeze which ruffled her hair and lifted the skirts of her gown. She had spent most of the day getting an eviction order against a surly youth who had been selling drugs from his council flat, attracting a steady stream of addicts into the building at all hours, playing loud music, and swearing at his neighbours when they complained. It had been a slow, tedious business, but as a civil case it paid Sarah's own rent rather better than crime, so she was happy to take such work when she could.

She walked around the court, filling her lungs with the crisp, cool afternoon air. It was nearly dusk, and just below her was the illuminated skating rink, where a steady flow of skaters swished around a tree decorated with Christmas lights in the middle. Her legs were still sore; there was a yellowing bruise on one buttock where she had fallen heavily. But she had enjoyed it all the same; she wondered if Michael had, and whether she would hear from him again.

Que sera, sera, she told herself, crossing the road under the castle to her chambers. It was fun, and if it leads to anything more, well and good. If not, it still shows that even at my age I can - what does Emily call it? - *pull* a man for one date anyway. Why do they make the language so crude? Ah, well, it's a basic urge - I guess they're honest, that's all.

Swiftly suppressing thoughts of what Bob might be doing with Sonya later that night, she mounted the stairs to her room, and began a stream of phone calls she had to make before the end of the day. The first two were to solicitors for next week's cases, the third to Lucy Sampson about the body found near Copmanthorpe.

'So what did they say, Luce? Have they found anything more?'

'Hard to say. They weren't exactly keen to talk to me, surprise surprise. But they've completed the post mortem and are waiting for some bits of forensic evidence, apparently.'

'What sort of forensic evidence?'

'That they wouldn't tell me. What they did say was that they're 99% sure it's Brenda Stokes, and that she suffered a pretty horrendous assault. Throttled with a silk scarf, skull crushed in several places, and her arm broken at the wrist. I think they wanted me to feel guilty for getting Jason Barnes released.'

'No doubt. But is there any proof he did it?' Sarah asked.

'I kept asking that and they wouldn't say. My guess is they're asking themselves the same question. But if it was Jason he was a busy lad that night, must have been. Not only did he have a huge fight with her - crushing her skull and breaking her arm as well as throttling her with this scarf - but then he somehow managed to bury her under the ring road ...'

'Was it being built at the time of the murder then?'

'Yes, it was. Sorry, I should have said. I checked that too. The dates tally pretty well. The contractors were pouring concrete on that junction the summer Brenda disappeared. The police confirm that too.'

'So what are they saying? Jason crushed her skull, broke her wrist, throttled her with a scarf and then drove her to the ring road to bury her body. All in one evening?'

'That's what they'll say if they still claim it's him. My guess is it's going to be quite hard to prove. I mean, the car was found burnt out in Leeds by when? Five thirty wasn't it?'

'That's right, yes. So he would have had to have done all this before then. Seems unlikely to me. But they won't give up easily. They've got their reputation to salvage, after all. They've got that retired superintendent Baxter in there. I heard him in the background.'

'Charming man,' said Sarah thoughtfully, kicking off her shoes and flexing her cramped toes under her desk. 'What about our even more charming client, Luce? What does he make of all this?'

'Ah, well, there's a mystery,' Lucy answered. 'I rang that cousin Jason went to stay with after the appeal and guess what? He's done a bunk. Left with no forwarding address.'

'Great. When was this?'

'The day after the TV news, when do you think? No one's seen or heard from him since. The police'll take that as a sign of guilt, won't they, for sure.'

'Obviously. But then if you'd been in prison for 18 years, and you thought they were coming after you again, what would you do? Whether you were guilty or not.' Sarah sighed. 'Okay, Lucy love, keep in touch. And thanks for the other thing, too.'

'What's that?'

'You know, the name of the divorce specialist you sent me.' Sarah spoke the words with distaste. 'I'll deal with that in the next few days, probably. Steel myself to give him a ring.'

'He's quite personable, I'm told. Sympathetic bedside manner.'

'He probably needs one. I feel like biting someone's head off every time I think about it. Which is highly unusual for me, as you know.'

Lucy laughed. 'You're a pussycat, Sarah. Soft as silk. Got to rush, I've got a client at the door. Keep in touch.'

'Bye.' Sarah put the phone down and thought, that's it for this week. Just these files to take home and prepare, ring Emily and Simon. And then, well, that's it really. Watch TV, read a book. It's a while since I did that. Maybe call in at Waterstones on the way home, choose something. Something long, light and frothy.

The phone rang. She picked it up.

'Is that Sarah?' A man's voice. 'Michael Parker. Remember me?'

'Oh yes. Yes, of course. Hi - hello.'

'How're you doing?'

'Fine. I'm just finishing up for the week. How about you?'

'Same here. End of the week. I was wondering, erm - you know that development I told you about, the barn conversions out on the moors towards Whitby?'

'Yes.'

'Well, I'm going out there tomorrow and I just wondered if you might, er, like to come along. We could have lunch somewhere, stroll on the beach perhaps, and then on the way back I could show you my windmill. If you're not doing anything else, that is.'

Visiting Waterstones, Sarah thought. Checking the TV schedules. Wondering whether to sell the house. Preparing my files.

Trying not to sound too eager, she said: 'Yes, that would be nice. I'd love to.'

'That's it!' Terry said jubilantly. 'We have a match.'

The fingerprints taken from the window sill on Lizzie Bolan's garage matched Peter Barton's perfectly. Sixteen points of similarity was the required standard; these reached that easily. Looking at the prints side by side on the computer screen, there was no room for doubt.

'So it *was* him,' Jane said, peering over his shoulder.

'Yep. Not much chance of prints from the mask, unfortunately, but they reckon they can get a DNA trace, despite all the gunk from the ditch. So if - when - we catch him we should be able to tie him to that as well. So now the only question is, where is he?'

It was a question that was proving frustratingly hard to answer. The more they probed, the more they found that his workmates' analysis was true - Peter Barton was a loner. If he had any friends, no one knew who they were. They tried his school, but they got the same answer: he'd been a quiet, lonely boy with few social skills and no friends. Girls had shunned him, boys mostly steered clear. A few recalled his interest in military and survival skills, but it hadn't been something he'd wanted to share. He'd joined the voluntary cadet force, but left after one term, not liking the discipline. He'd been a poor student in class, getting only two grade D GCSEs. For a while he'd worked in the school garden, but his interest faded after a row with the master in charge. 'He was big, scarey, even then,' the man told Jane. 'Not someone you'd want to trade punches with. You felt he didn't know his own strength. That's what saved him from bullies, I think. He was a prime target, a slow learner, awkward, not good with words, physically unprepossessing. But you wouldn't want to provoke him. It would be like poking a stick at a bear.'

'How about girls?' Jane asked. 'Did he have any luck with them?'

'I doubt it. I think they avoided him. Probably scared.'

'Were there any incidents, any other trouble he was in?'

'Not that I'm aware of. But it's a long time ago, and we have so many boys.'

'So you've no idea of where he might be hiding now?'

'No, sorry. None.'

The answer was the same whereever they asked. Peter had no friends, no-one knew where he was, or was much interested. He was a person people shunned. There was an air of menace, of unpredictability, which put people off. And it wasn't as though he sought people out or tried to ingratiate himself with them. He seemed to enjoy being alone.

The photofit of Peter was printed in the *Evening Press*, with a story saying that police needed to find him to eliminate him from their enquiries. But no leads came forward.

'You know, it's all very well mocking the lad for his interest in all this survival business,' Jane said a week later. 'But he's doing a good job at the moment. It's eight days since that assault on Lizzie Bolan and no one's seen hide nor hair of the lad.'

'Maybe he's enjoying it,' Terry suggested. 'His big moment's come at last. His photo in the paper, his crime described in detail. And he's laughing, like bin Laden. The man whom no one can trace.'

'He may not be in York at all,' Jane said. 'If I'd done a thing like that, I'd go to London, Birmingham, Glasgow - somewhere I could hide in the crowds.'

Terry shook his head. 'This lad doesn't like crowds. People scare him, I guess cities do too. I doubt he's travelled further than Leeds in his life. No, I reckon he's still local, hiding somewhere he knows. Somewhere he's been preparing for a while. Watching us hunt him. Waiting. For his next opportunity.'

The BMW purred into Sarah's drive at nine the next morning. During the night she'd had a brief fantasy of ringing to offer to take him pillion on her motorbike, but in the end she hadn't dared. She had no spare helmet or leathers, and anyway she wasn't certain she could manage the bike safely with a man's weight behind her. The BMW seemed more inviting on a cold winter's day.

The farm development was more interesting than she'd expected. He showed her photos of the old farmhouse and crumbling stone barns which he'd bought a year ago. They looked like something abandoned after a war. Now, the three half finished dwellings were full of clean new wooden rafters, several ancient oak beams which had been salvaged from other sites, tiled kitchen floors, newly installed Agas, gravel drives and feature ponds. A lot of work had gone into finding old bricks and tiles that exactly matched the originals, and Michael was full of tales of his battles with planners, the Environment Agency, building inspectors, plumbers, electricians and tilers. The houses were half finished, but he had already sold one, and had glossy sales brochures prepared for the others. He gave her one. She glanced at the price and laughed.

'I'd never afford this, Michael. Not in a million years.'

'You never know. You can always dream.'

They ate at a fish and chip restaurant overlooking the sea. He asked what she had been doing since they last met. She described her cases, and he listened sympathetically. Thinking it would interest him, she told him what Lucy had told her about the police deliberations since the discovery of Brenda Stokes' body, and Jason Barnes' disappearance. The police had released a photograph of a fragment of the silk scarf, and Sarah showed it to him in this morning's *Times*. He peered at it and frowned.

'I don't see how that helps,' he said. 'I always thought Barnes was guilty. Let's hope they catch him. It would be terrible if he killed someone else.'

'You're assuming he did it,' Sarah said. 'But the evidence seems to suggest ...'

He lifted a hand. 'I'm sorry. D'you mind if we talk about something else? Such a nice day, and murder, you know - it's not really my thing. Let me show you where my dad taught me to scuba dive. Best beach on the east coast. I've loved this place since I was a kid.'

After lunch they strolled along the beach and then drove back across the Wolds towards Pocklington. Just before the high chalk hills dipped towards the Vale of York, they turned down a narrow country road outside a village. After a couple of miles of twists and turns Michael sighed with satisfaction. 'Here we are,' he said. He turned left through a gate and drove slowly down an unmade road through a small wood of larch trees and birches. The track wound gently downhill for about a quarter of a mile, the car bouncing gently over potholes covered with a carpet of fallen leaves and pine needles. They turned a last corner and Michael stopped the car. He switched off the engine, turned to her, and smiled.

'There. What do you think?'

'It's magnificent.'

Twenty yards in front of them was a circular stone tower. It was about four stories high - at least twice the height of a normal house - and was built on a slight mound, which made it seem even higher. The tower was widest at the bottom, tapering towards the top, and had a number of small windows at different levels. At the height of the first floor a wooden balcony ran right around the tower. Further up, the weathered stone was capped with a small green roof with what looked like a smaller balcony round it. And just below the roof, on the right of the tower looking out over the valley, was a central hub, to which were attached four huge lattice work sails. They looked to Sarah like the blades of an enormous propeller. Opposite them, on the side of the tower nearest the wood, was a smaller vertical propellor set at right angles to the roof.

Her eyes were almost immediately drawn to the view beyond them which made it instantly clear why the windmill had been built in the position where it stood. They were on the western edge of the Wolds. Beyond the mound on which the windmill stood was a soft grassy slope about twenty or thirty yards wide, after which the ground simply disappeared. From where Sarah sat in the car it seemed to swoop away into nothingness - and beyond, far, far below, was a valley of villages and farmland extending to the western horizon, which was barred with rosy clouds behind which the sun was already beginning to sink.

'Would you like a closer look?' Michael asked.

'Yes please.'

They got out of the car and walked over to the tower. As they came closer Sarah saw that the sails, which had seemed so stunning on first appearance, looked rather tatty and in need of attention. But the front door was painted bright red, with a new brass door handle and letter box. A white van was parked nearer to the tower, and as Sarah watched, a man in white overalls took something out of the back and went in through the front door.

'Is this really where you live, then?' she asked.

'It will be, as soon as those guys have finished tiling the bathroom. At the moment I'm living over there.' He pointed to her left, and she saw a cottage that she hadn't noticed before, behind the windmill on the edge of the woods. 'That's the miller's house. Basic, but adequate. I'll modernise that later, when the mill itself is finished.'

'Didn't the miller live in the mill, then?'

'No, none of them did. They couldn't because it was full of machinery. A windmill was a factory, really, for one man. But I'm changing all that. In the teeth of opposition from the conservationists, of course. Let me show you how it's going.'

He opened the door and showed her into a wide semi-circular room. There was a stone floor and the walls were plastered. About two-thirds of the way across it was divided by a plaster wall along which was a sink, oven, hob, worktop and a range of expensive new wooden kitchen units.

At one end of this wall was a door, leading through to the bathroom, where the men were working. The floor where they stood was dusty and littered with cardboard packing, but Sarah could see it was well on the way to becoming a luxury farmhouse style kitchen. There were more kitchen units and a breakfast bar set along the outside wall under a window.

'The fitters had the devil of a job to match these to the round walls,' Michael said. 'But they've done a good job, don't you think?'

'It looks great,' Sarah agreed, running her fingers along a granite worktop. 'But what on earth is all that?'

Just below the ceiling was a large black painted metal wheel, with a number of metal wheels and levers attached to it.

'That's part of the machinery which I've kept, to make it a feature,' Michael said. 'Like wooden beams in a farmhouse. The wheel there, you see, is attached to the millwheel up above, and these rods and levers are what's left of the tentering gear. It's what the miller used to adjust to get the gap between the two millstones just right.'

'Two millstones? I thought there was just one.'

'Hardly,' Michael smiled. 'It wouldn't work like that. Come on upstairs, I'll show you.'

He led the way up a wooden staircase to the first floor. This room was a similar size to the first, but much more comfortably furnished. There was a soft carpet on the floor, a widescreen TV against the wall, a leather sofa and armchair, and some chairs round what looked a like a circular dining table. But unlike other dining tables, this one had a sturdy iron pole rising up from the centre of it, and disappearing through the ceiling above. And when Sarah bent down, she saw that the table had no legs, but was resting instead on two massive circular stones, one mounted above the other.

'There you are - those are the millwheels,' Michael said, 'that's how the grain was ground, between these two.'

Sarah stared at them, intrigued. 'How, exactly?'

'Well, the grain would come down a chute, from the trapdoor above, into a sort of wooden tray, a hopper, just above the millwheel where this table is now. Then it would trickle down from the hopper through a hole in the upper stone - the runner stone, it's called, that's the one that moves - into the gap between the two stones.'

'The runner stone turns? How?'

'That's what this metal shaft is for, you see,' Michael said, slapping it with his hand. 'The shaft was connected to the sails, so the runner stone turned, while the bottom stone stayed still. And the grain was ground between the two stones into flour. Then it would be collected in sacks in the floor below.'

Sarah had never thought about this. 'Is that why they call it stone ground flour, then, like you buy in the supermarket?'

'Exactly. There are a lot of phrases connected to this. For instance, if the miller wanted to know if the grain was the right temperature, not getting too hot and burning, do you know what he'd do? Put his nose to the grindstone.'

'Really?' Sarah laughed. 'I always thought that sounded rather painful.'

'It probably was, if he got too close. But he only did it to sniff the grain, that's all. Another way of testing the quality of the flour was to rub a little bit against his fingers with his thumb, like this. Testing by rule of thumb.'

Michael looked enthusiastic, like a child with a new toy.

'But you're not actually planning to grind flour here yourself, then?' Sarah asked.

'Oh no, that would be far too much hard work. Anyway, there's no money in it. If I tried to restore it as the conservationists wanted, I'd be bankrupt in a few years. No, as you see, my plan is to convert it into a house, keep the millwheels and few original parts as a feature, and link the sails to a generator to provide electricity. Very eco-friendly. And much more appropriate to the twenty-first century, don't you think?'

On the far side of the room was a new, freshly varnished door, with glass in its upper half. Michael walked across and threw it open. 'Take a look outside.'

Sarah stepped out onto a wide wooden balcony. It was nearly three feet wide, and ran right round the outside of the tower. Standing on it, she felt she was floating in midair. She was only one floor above the ground, but that ground swooped down almost immediately in front of her several hundred more feet to the valley below. She looked up and saw, a couple of feet above her head, the end of one of the four great sails. Close to, it looked even more massive than before. It was like a giant finger three stories long, reaching down to her from the hub in the roof of the tower. Above the hub another sail stretched a similar distance into the sky, far above the roof of the mill. Two more sails reached out like enormous arms on either side. A pair of rooks, startled by the sudden appearance of two people on the balcony, launched themselves from the right-hand sail and floated effortlessly down into the valley, cawing indignantly as they went.

Sarah reached up to touch the end of the sail. 'Why doesn't it move?' she asked.

'There's a brake on the top floor. Anyway, as you see, they're made of lattice work too, to let the wind blow through when we don't want to use it. In the old days, if they wanted more power, they covered the lattice work with a cloth, to give more power, like the sails of a ship. But we don't need that now.' He pointed to a long loop of chain hanging down the side of the tower, fastened to a cleat. 'That operates the brake.'

'So if you let that off, the sails would move?'

'Probably.' Michael hesitated. 'I've only done it a couple of times before.' He sucked his finger and held it up in the air to feel the wind. 'But it's a fairly calm day. I guess we could risk it.' He unfastened the chain. 'Stand back against the wall then. Each of those sails weighs a ton, and they can move at thirty miles an hour at times. Quite a few millers have had their heads knocked off, over the years.'

With both hands on the chain, he pulled down hard on one side of the loop. Something creaked high above their heads, and for a moment nothing happened. Then, with a weary arthritic groan, like an old man being awakened from sleep, the sail above their heads began to move. Slowly at first, shuddering slightly, it moved away to the left, rising steadily into the air. Awestruck, Sarah watched it rise from horizontal to vertical; and as it did so, the second sail descended inexorably to take the place of the first. Moving slightly faster, this sail crossed just in front of her and above her head, before it rose away to the left, to be replaced by the third.

It was a stirring sight. Sarah watched in awe as the sails swished round, faster and faster until they settled into a steady, regular rhythm. She had thought it was a calm day but the power the sails were generating, even on this relatively windless afternoon, was impressive. The draft from each passing sail blew her hair across her face. Machinery in the tower above her groaned and creaked dramatically. On the ground below the balcony, the workmen came round the outside of the building to watch.

'Running the lights, then, are you, Mr Parker?' one called.

'Just a short demonstration,' Michael answered. 'To let this lady see it working.'

The man's eyes assessed Sarah thoughtfully. 'You'll be all right on your own, will you? We'll be leaving soon.'

'I'll manage. I'll shut it down at dusk.'

'Right then.' The men walked back round the side of the tower.

Michael put his hand on Sarah's elbow. 'Let me show you the rest.'

They climbed another wooden staircase to the third floor. 'This is where they used to store the grain, before feeding it down to the millwheel below,' Michael said. 'But as you see, I've decided to store myself.'

It was his bedroom. There was a soft blue carpet, with a double bed, an armchair, a reading lamp, a chest of drawers, and a wooden wardrobe. The metal drive shaft from the floor below, Sarah noticed, was missing here. She asked about it.

'We cut it off,' he answered. 'The remains of the shaft below are just for decoration, but here it would have gone right through the bed. I'd have had to wrap my feet around it.'

Sarah listened thoughtfully to the rumble of the huge sails turning outside. Every few seconds one darkened the window as it swished between her and the setting sun. 'But those sails,' she said nervously. 'Aren't they driving anything?'

'The new electricity generator, I hope,' Michael said. 'It's on the fifth floor, just under the cap. Come on, I'll show you.'

The fourth floor, just above, was clearly intended as Michael's study. 'I haven't moved everything in here yet,' he said. 'But when I do, I'm going to really enjoy it.' There was a brown carpet, a desk with a computer and printer on it, a filing cabinet, and a comfortable leather armchair beside the window. Sarah went to the window and looked out. The view from up here was even better. She opened the window to get a better look. The sails swished by a few feet from her face.

'Those cooling towers in the distance,' she asked. 'With the cloud above them. Is that Drax?'

'That's right. Must be all of what? Twenty five miles away. And if you look to the right - there - you can just see the tower of York Minster.'

Sarah stared for a while, entranced, as the sun sank slowly towards the distant horizon. She was soothed by the hypnotic rhythm of the sails, and the steady rumble of the gears above her head. All around the mill, she realised, everything was peaceful and silent. There was no traffic, no streetlights, no TV chatter or children playing in the road. The only lights were those in the distant valley far below. She could hear rooks cawing around the treetops below as the dusk closed in. On the ground below an engine started, and a cone of light burrowed through the woods as the workmen drove away in their van.

She turned back from the window. Michael was watching her with a quiet smile on his face. 'And there's another floor above this?'

'Yes. The last one.'

They climbed a final flight of steps into the space beneath the roof. Here she found the source of the rumbling. There were two large wooden cogwheels moved steadily round - a vertical one mounted round an axle connected to the hub of the sails, and a massive horizontal wheel called the spur wheel which, Michael explained, had originally turned the shaft to drive the millwheels below. Now, although the drive shaft was disconnected, the spur wheel still rotated, and some smaller gears linked it to another heavy millwheel whose weight slowed it down, and a modern generator which took up most the remaining floor area. The rumble of the gears, and the hum of the generator, meant that they had to raise their voices to be heard.

'That vertical wheel is the brake wheel,' Michael shouted. 'You see this mechanism here? When I pull that chain below that tightens around it to stop the sails from moving. Like a huge brake shoe on a car wheel.'

'And right now this is powering the house? The electric lights in all these rooms?'

'Yes, that's right. Free electricity from the wind. I can store a certain amount in those batteries there. But if I kept the sails running all day it wouldn't just power the house, you know. I could sell it back to the national grid. Enough to cover council tax, at least.' He caught her eye thoughtfully. 'Do you want to go out on the roof?'

'All right.'

When he asked, she had not appreciated what she was letting herself in for. The room they were standing in, under the cap, was only a little higher than the height of a man. Michael had to bend his head slightly as he opened a small door at the back. Sarah followed him through, and gasped in shock. She was standing on a tiny balcony, eighteen inches wide, with a handrail no higher than her hips. Behind her, the smooth metal roof rose to a conical point about twice the height of her head. Below her - an aching long way below - she could see Michael's car, a little matchbox toy, and rooks circling over treetops in the gathering dusk. She clutched the rail convulsively and took her bearings. The door they'd come through was on the side of the cap, she realised. To her left the huge dark sails revolved remorselessly between her and the setting sun. To her right, above the woods and Michael's car, was a second smaller set of sails, mounted at right angles to the cap.

'What's that?' she asked. She detached one hand to point briefly, before re-attaching it firmly to the handrail.

'The fantail. It keeps the sails pointing exactly into the wind. So if the wind shifts, the cap moves round slightly and ...' There was a sudden lurch beneath Sarah's feet. '... like that.'

'What the hell happened then?'

'The wind shifted slightly, like I told you, and the cap moved round.'

'The cap ... you mean this whole roof we're standing on *moved*? It isn't fixed?'

'No. Sorry, I should have warned you. The cap - the roof - is circular, right, and it's resting on a set of wooden skids. The fantail's attached to the cap but connected to the tower by a cogwheel that runs round outside the skids. So when the wind shifts, like it did just then, the fantail moves a couple of notches along the cogwheel and drags the cap around so the sails keep facing the wind. Clever, isn't it?' He laughed.

'Very.' Sarah drew a deep breath. She was determined not to show herself afraid. 'And what's the point of this balcony?'

'Suicide.'

'What?' She stared at him, uncertain if she'd heard right. His face was shadowed, between her and the setting sun. 'What did you say?'

'Suicide.' He raised his arms by his sides, in the position of a swallow dive. 'Don't you think it would be a good way to go?'

'Michael, stop it. You're crazy.'

He flexed his knees, as though about to jump. 'Perfect. Two seconds sheer terror, then certain death. Can you imagine a better end?'

Sarah shuddered. I'm alone on the roof of this tower, she thought, with a man I scarcely know. What if he turns out to be a maniac?

'Michael, don't be silly! Stop it.'

Releasing her grip on the handrail, she clutched his arm, staring with horror at the sheer drop below. When he didn't move, she tugged his arm again.

'Michael!'

Instead of moving, he linked her arm with his, forcing her to stand beside him. The sails whisked behind them, turning a little faster than before. A rook flew beneath their feet, cawing loudly. I'm linked to him, Sarah thought; if the cap lurches again we'll lose our balance and fall. He's much stronger than me - *what the hell is he doing?*

Michael looked down at her. In the dusk, his face was hard to decipher. The wind blew her hair across her eyes. We're all alone here, she thought again, there's no one else around for miles. *Is this how it ends?*

He relaxed, reached his arm round her, and guided her back through the door. 'I'm sorry,' he said, as they came down from the cap to his study. 'You were scared. I shouldn't have done that.'

'Of course I was scared.' Sarah's fear turned to anger. 'What the hell were you doing up there? It was dangerous.'

'I'm sorry, it was stupid. It's just that ... I like heights, I always have. But I shouldn't have inflicted it on you. I apologise.'

'But *why*, Michael? What's the attraction?'

'Oh, I don't know. The air, I suppose, the wind in your face. The height. The sense that you've got to keep control of yourself or else ... If I did ever want to die, that would be the best way to go, wouldn't it? Very quick.' He studied her apologetically. 'But don't worry, I've no intention of dying. Not for years and years. Especially now I've met you.'

'I'm glad to hear it,' Sarah said coolly. If that's his idea of a compliment he can keep it. 'Michael, it's late, and I've got some papers to read before court tomorrow. Do you mind if we go back?'

On the drive home his good spirits revived. He apologised again and set himself to lighten the atmosphere with a long involved story about how as a boy he'd once got marooned on an island to which he'd rowed to climb a cliff. 'There were gannets all over this island, and when I got down I found they'd pecked holes in my rubber dinghy. I was half a mile from the shore and no one knew where I was. I had visions of myself living on gannets' eggs and rainwater, and growing a long beard and grey hair like Robinson Crusoe.'

'A ten year old with a long beard?'

'Yes, well I wasn't sure how beards grew in those days. I thought it was something to do with the sea. It was mostly sailors who had them, after all. Like the one who picked me up in his fishing boat.'

Sarah smiled. The thought of him as a ten year boy, scrambling barefoot over rocks at the seaside, was an appealing one. Perhaps that was what attracted him to heights, she thought. A sense of reliving his youth. And young boys did do silly, dangerous things - she remembered her own son, Simon, coming home covered with blood after speeding downhill on a bicycle. The game had been to hit the hump-backed bridge at the bottom of the hill at full speed, apparently, to see how far you could fly through the air without hitting the ground. Simon had broken the record and his arm simultaneously. Sarah had been furious and shocked, both at once.

But her son had been nine or ten at the time, not in his forties, like Michael. She wondered, later that evening, what it all meant. He was a nice man, clearly, and liked her - he'd said so, just once. But why play the fool on top of the windmill like that? And what sort of man jokes about suicide?

29. Dividing the Equity

APPROACHING KING'S Square in Leeds, Sarah walked past Leeds Town Hall, where she and Bob had been married. It had been her second wedding. She had been 17 years old, a young mother with a baby. Her own mother had offered to look after Simon during the wedding, but Sarah had refused. 'He's marrying me *and* the baby, Mum!' she'd said fiercely. 'That's the whole point. He doesn't want me to give him up - unlike you!' So the three of them - Sarah, Bob, and little Simon - had walked up the steps of the registry office together, a family before they were even married. She'd held Simon in her arms throughout the ceremony, only passing him to Bob when she signed the register. Her mother, who'd wanted to put him up for adoption, hadn't held him at all. Sarah didn't regard her mother as family after that. Bob and Simon were her family, she'd felt; when she needed support she could rely on them, no one else. No one else but herself.

Now she had only herself.

She crossed the square, a slender figure in a black coat, quite alone. Her back was straight, her face pale and determined. Her heels clicked briskly up the stone steps into the offices of Ian Carr, the divorce lawyer Lucy had recommended. He came to reception to meet her, holding out his hand in greeting. 'Mrs Newby, isn't it? Come upstairs, please. I have fresh coffee in my office, or herbal tea if you prefer. Your husband and his lawyer are due here in an hour. We should be ready for them by then, I hope.'

He was a pleasant young man, with the right touch of sympathy in his smile. He'll go far, Sarah thought, admiring the effortless, efficient way he put her at ease in his office - an office considerably more luxurious than her own. I should have gone into civil law, she thought. No, I haven't the style.

'Your main interest, I believe, is to keep your house,' he began, handing her coffee. 'Sadly, as I told you on the phone, our options here are limited. If your daughter - Emily, isn't it? - had been a year younger, that would have helped, but now she is over 18 and legally an adult she is no longer dependent on you to house her. If your husband were to agree to let you stay on we could come to an arrangement, but I regret to say ...'

'He won't.' Sarah thought sadly of Emily's desire for a room of her own, of her love for the house by the river. Term would be over soon - she would be home, Sarah supposed, for Christmas. 'So what are my options?'

'Either to sell the house, or buy your husband out. Under Section 15 of the Trust of Land and Application of Properties Act, you should get the house valued. Fifty per cent of it is yours, fifty percent is your husband's. So either you pay him 50% of the valuation or you sell the house and divide the equity. How are you paying your mortgage?'

'We each pay half,' said Sarah, thinking of the huge tax bill she'd have to meet next April. 'What if I increase my payments to cover the full amount now - can't I stay in the house then?'

'Not unless your husband agrees, I'm afraid. You'd be denying him his share of the equity. But house prices have been rising, so he might be persuaded to wait, in the hope of more later. He has somewhere to live, I take it?'

'Oh yes, he has somewhere to live,' she said grimly, thinking of the photograph she had found last week, in his files on their computer. A young woman with long brown hair - rather thin, Sarah thought, for her taste, and with slightly buck teeth - but smiling ecstatically, and clutching her three young children to a long, full-length skirt. She looked happy, but when Sarah had enlarged the photo and focussed closer on the young woman's eyes, she saw something - what was it? - insecurity, anxiety, greed? Something desperate anyway, yearning behind the smile. Or was that just her own jealousy, defacing what she saw to justify her own furious rage? Her hands had shaken so that she could hardly grip the mouse.

There had been other photos, and several had shown a small semi-detached house - perfectly adequate, but a step down from what Bob had grown accustomed to. She doubted he would stick it for long.

So it proved in the meeting an hour later. They sat in a conference room, either side of a gleaming mahogany table. Bob, to her surprise, looked different. He'd had a recent haircut and instead of his usual rumpled suit was wearing a new powder blue jumper and leather jacket - clearly intended to make him look younger. She detected a faint scent of aftershave, too. Only the bags under his eyes made him look old. He responded badly to the suggestions about delaying the sale.

'No, of course I need it now - Sonya's house is rented, it's up for renewal in March, and it's much too small anyway. The real point we need to settle is the size of each share.'

He glanced at his lawyer, a small, round man, who began apologetically. 'Mr Newby claims 65% of the equity, on the grounds of the history of the investment. When the couple originally bought the house he paid the entire deposit himself, and all the interest on the mortgage for the first three years when his wife's earnings were low.'

Sarah's lawyer laughed. 'That won't wash, Mr Snerl, you know it won't. Even if Mrs Newby had been staying at home looking after the children ...'

'Looking after the children!' Bob broke in bitterly. 'As if!'

'... and paid no money at all, she would still be entitled to 50% of the equity. She was contributing an equal share by looking after the family.'

'But she wasn't!' Bob said. 'She was pursuing her education - at my expense!'

'That's irrelevant in the eyes of the law ...'

'I cared for my children, Bob. Don't you dare say I didn't.' Sarah's eye met her husband's for the first time. There was something in her gaze, and the cool incisive tone of her voice, that dried the indignation on his tongue. They measured each other, and for a moment the lawyers were not there. Sarah wondered afterwards if they had continued talking, and she'd heard nothing. *How did you come to this, Bob,* her eyes asked, *after twenty years of marriage?* All based on trust, and the promise that it would continue for ever. Did you change all that with your clothes and hairstyle?

But he was a different man - at least one she had not seen before. There was a bitter wariness in his eyes, and a trembling determination not to back down, however strong his sense of guilt. He looked fragile, she thought; younger not just because of the clothes, but because of his desperate need to deny the truth, and believe he was in the right. Would she want this man back? Not really, no. Not without love. And there was no love left, in the eyes that met hers. None left at all.

She turned back to the lawyers. 'What do we need to do?'

'Well, Mrs Newby,' her own lawyer said. 'The sensible thing is to come to an agreement. Get the house valued, put it on the market, and agree an equitable division of assets. That way there's least pain and expense to you both. Otherwise, if we go to court - well, you're a lawyer, you know where the money will go.'

'Yes, very well.' The discussion continued for a while, the lawyers explaining the procedure and setting up a timetable. Then, it seemed, they were done. Her memory of the Town Hall returned. There should be a crowd of people, friends and family outside - doing what? Her mother maybe, saying *I told you so, you should have listened to me in the first place.* Her father looking sad and pathetic. Her children ...

Outside on the steps Bob said: 'Shall we go for a coffee?'

She stared at him, incredulous. 'What? After that?'

'It won't hurt. There's a Starbucks round the corner.'

And somehow, the loneliness awaiting her seemed so final that any delay seemed a straw worth clutching at. 'OK. Why not?'

In Starbucks there was a brief embarrassment as the cashier asked if they were together. 'No,' Sarah said. 'I'll pay for myself.' They sat opposite each other in the window.

'So, how are you?' she asked.

'Oh, fine.' The leather jacket was new; it still creaked. She preferred the powder blue jumper. It was the sort of thing she might have bought him for Christmas; but his Christmas had come early this year.

'Really?' She sipped her cappuccino. 'You're looking a bit tired.' It was true. The lines on his face had deepened and there was a greyish tinge to his skin. To her surprise he took out a cigarette and lit it.

'You haven't started that?'

'Just a few,' he said defensively. 'It's up to me.'

'Oh, sure. You're a grown man. Do what you like.' She shook her head in disbelief. *Has it really come to this?* 'How are the children?'

'At the school, you mean?'

'No. In your new home.'

'Oh, John, Linda and Samantha? They're great. Really nice kids. Easy to talk to. Of course, it's a little hard for them, having a new man in the house ...'

'Their own father left?'

'Yes. And there was another guy for a while, but ...'

'So you're third in line, are you?' Sarah raised a pitying eyebrow. 'They're probably wondering how long you'll last.'

The shaft went home. 'Look, Sarah, I didn't come here to quarrel ...'

'Who's quarrelling? I just asked ...'

'Yes, well it's my business, not yours. They need a new house, really. This one's only rented, as I told you, and it's ... in a poor state.'

'Oh. So I should sell quickly, you mean? Before March - that would suit you, would it? And Sonya.'

'If you did, there's be less pain for everyone. We could both make a new start.'

'Really.' Rage seethed inside her, but she held it down. 'I hear you phoned Emily.'

He nodded. 'She took it hard, I'm afraid. Understandable, of course. But I think, by the end, she saw my point of view.'

'Which is what, exactly?'

'You know, Sarah. What I told you before. We had twenty good years, but we've grown apart. We're different people now than we were before.'

He's right about that, Sarah thought bitterly. It's not just the clothes and the cigarette - something's changed in his mind. It must have been there before, growing like a cancer in the darkness behind his skull - but now it's burst into bloom and sent its spores through his whole brain. This isn't the man I married. It isn't even someone I want to be married to any more.

I loved him once. We shared half of our lives together. And this is how it ends. Not with a whimper, with scorn. Without finishing her coffee, she got to her feet.

'Goodbye, Bob.' She held out her hand, then changed her mind and took it back. 'I'll let you know about the house as soon as I can.'

She walked out of the café alone.

She took the train back to York and strode into the first estate agent's she saw. Yes, he could value the house next day, he said. On reflection she arranged for a second to come the day after. That's what Michael would have done, she realised. Some of Saturday's conversation came back to her - tales of wildly different estimates from estate agents, builders, and plumbers. It was the sort of decision she'd once left to Bob; now she'd have to manage these things on her own.

Entering the house she looked round, and thought how untidy it was. The washing up wasn't done, the bin in the kitchen was full, there was a pile of clothes waiting to be ironed. There were lines of fluff on the treads of the stair carpet, a litter of make-up and moisturisers by the bathroom basin, a smear of lipstick on the mirror, and limescale on the shower screen. Well, she'd never been much good at housework. She normally had cleaners in to take care of it, but there'd been a problem at the agency - her regular cleaners had left, two others had been ill. So she'd told them not to worry, she could manage on her own for a while. After all there was only her.

But clearly she couldn't manage as well as she thought. Not at present, anyway. Drearily, she put on an apron and set to work. She didn't want to be embarrassed in front of the valuers. After all, a good impression might make the difference of a few thousand pounds. Yes, she thought, but not for me - half of that goes to Bob, the bastard. She jabbed viciously at the stair carpet with the vacuum cleaner. Why isn't he here to clean his own house, if he wants to profit from it? That's men all over. File for divorce, swan around in new clothes, turn your ex-wife into a cleaning lady.

They're all the same, she thought, scrubbing energetically at lipstick on the bathroom mirror. She remembered how it had got there. She'd slipped on the bathroom floor while hurrying with her make-up because Michael was due in ten minutes. So excited she'd been, and why? Because a man was calling for her! I should know better.

That had been a good day, though, for much of the time. She'd enjoyed the drive, the visit to the farm development, the lunch, the new found friendship. But then there'd been that scary incident on the roof of the windmill, and awkward silences on the drive home. So he isn't perfect either. Maybe he thinks the same about me. When they got home she'd asked Michael in for a coffee - meaning just that, coffee, no more - but he'd declined. Looking round critically at her house now, she was glad he hadn't come in.

She'd gone to bed gloomy, her mood not enhanced by a phone call from Emily who'd just spoken to her father. Predictably, he'd put the blame on Sarah, and poor Emily, listening, had felt her loyalties torn.

'Couldn't you have tried harder, Mum?' she'd asked, and Sarah, for once in her life, had been stumped for an answer. It had been the pain in her daughter's voice, more than the injustice of the question, that had hurt the most. So Sarah had agreed to go down to Cambridge to see her next weekend, before the end of the university term. Her chance, it felt like, to make amends - for a break-up she hadn't wanted in the first place.

She'd wept when that phone call had ended, and felt like praying and cursing both at once. Losing a husband is bad enough, she thought, but if he turns Emily away from me as well, then ... that will be just too cruel.

She finished cleaning the house and looked around. It was a family home, she realised - that's what she'd told the estate agents. Four bedrooms, spacious living room and kitchen, nice views across fields to the river, secluded rear garden where children could safely play. Only there were no children, not any more. No family either - Simon rarely visited, didn't like the country, Emily was starting her new life, and now Bob was gone as well. It's not the right house for me, she thought, not any more. Maybe I really will be better off starting again.

She'd talked over some of this with Michael, when he'd phoned, earlier this week. To her relief the odd, unpredictable silences of Saturday had gone. He'd been cheerful, chatty even, and interested in all her problems. He'd invited her out on a date that Thursday - another meal, at a different restaurant he knew. She'd been unreasonably pleased - relieved to have something to look forward to. But then, on the very evening of the date, when she'd come home early to change, he'd rung to cancel.

'I'm really sorry, but there's been a crisis at the farm development. I'm still there now - I'll be here all evening, I expect. I do apologise, but it's got to be sorted. Maybe at the weekend?'

'I'm going down to Cambridge to see Emily,' she'd said stiffly. 'It doesn't matter. You do what you have to. I understand.'

'Yes, well, all right then. I'll be in touch.'

But something in his tone made her wonder if she'd have a long wait.

30. Body in the Hall

THE CALL came at ten in the morning. Jane Carter picked it up. Her face changed as she listened. She put the phone down and turned to Terry. 'Possible suicide in Crockey Hill, sir. Shall we go?'

The house, when they came to it, was isolated. About fifty yards down a rough track on the edge of a small hamlet. It was a two storey double fronted detached house, with a small lawned garden and fields beyond that. Behind the house and to the right were woods, the trees standing bare over their dank fallen leaves. There was a circular gravel area in front of the house, on which were parked a Tesco delivery van, two marked police cars, an ambulance, and a muddy green Rover. The paramedics and the uniformed officers were clustered round the front door. When Terry and Jane went inside, they saw why.

They entered a hall with doors leading into two front rooms on either side. There was a narrow window beside the door, in front of the staircase, which was on the left. The hall continued past the staircase to the back of the house and the kitchen. The floor was paved with old red Yorkshire stone tiles, cracked in places and worn in the centre by many years of passing feet. Halfway along the corridor was a wooden dining chair lying on its side. On the tiles beside the chair, with her feet towards the kitchen, lay the naked body of a woman.

Terry stared at it, the shock, as always, draining the blood from his face and making him fight down the urge to vomit. There was no dignity in a death like this. She was a plump woman, he noticed, with brown pubic hair and a varicose vein in her left leg. Her face was dark purple and there was something tied around her neck. There was a puddle of what looked like urine around her legs, and the stink of faeces. As he stared, a cat scurried down the stairs and ran past the body into the kitchen.

'What happened here?' he asked.

'Suicide, looks like, sir,' one of the young constables said. 'Delivery man rang the bell and when he got no answer he peered through the window and saw a leg hanging in the air, a foot above the floor.' He indicated the driver of the Tesco van, who was sitting on a garden bench with his head in his hands, talking to a paramedic. 'The door was locked, so he called us and we got in through a loo window at the back. The paramedics cut her down, but there was nothing they could do.'

'Dead for several hours, I'd reckon,' the second paramedic said. 'The doctor will confirm that, but her limbs were already stiff.'

'You've sent for the doctor, have you?' Terry asked the young constable. However obvious it was, only a doctor could officially confirm death.

'Yes, sir, he's on his way.'

'Good. Well, we'd better have a look.' He glanced at Jane, noticing the pallor of her face and a grim determination around her jaw. 'Come on. Let's see the worst.'

The woman's face was, indeed, very bad. The tongue and eyes protruded, the face was suffused with dark purple blood. Round her neck, so tight that it bit into the skin, was what looked like a patterned silk scarf. The end was frayed, as though it had been cut, and when Terry looked up he saw the other end dangling above their heads. It was fastened by a knot to the banisters halfway up the stairs. The chair lay on its side beneath the dangling scarf.

'She must have stood on the chair, then kicked it away,' he said hoarsely. 'She'd be hanging with her feet off the ground.'

'Or someone else kicked it away for her.' Jane's eyes, dark with horror against the pallor of her face, met his across the body. The same thought occurred to them both. *Is this it? Could Peter Barton have been here as well?*

Terry nodded. 'That's the first thing we have to establish. Whether it's suicide at all.'

A car drew up on the gravel outside, and the doctor, a stout man in tweed suit and brogues, lumbered in, breathing heavily after the short walk from his car. For form's sake he felt for a pulse, but the cold wrist told a tale beyond doubt. He peered at the face and the scarf round the neck and shook his head sadly.

'Can you give us any idea of the time of death, doctor?' Terry asked.

The doctor felt the legs and arms, lifting them slightly to estimate rigidity. Then, wiping a smear of faeces out of the way, he lifted the pelvis to insert a thermometer into the rectum. When it came out he pursed his lips thoughtfully and looked around. 'Well, given that it's pretty cold in here anyway and the poor dear's quite bare, I would suggest somewhere between ten and twelve hours. Might be longer.'

'So she was hanging here all night until the delivery man found her,' Jane said thoughtfully. 'Poor woman. What a dreadful way to go.'

'It was that Tesco driver who found her, was it?' the doctor asked, getting to his feet and stepping carefully round the puddle of urine. 'I thought he looked a bit wobbly when I came in. I'll check him over before I go.'

'We'd better get a statement from him too, Jane, when he's fit,' Terry said. 'You'll arrange a PM, will you, doc?'

As Jane and the doctor went out, Terry called up a SOCO team on his mobile. Then he stood for a moment, alone in the hall, thinking. Just himself and the soiled, pathetic body at his feet. *Who are you, lady*, he asked her silently. *What happened here last night? What would you tell me if you could speak?*

He turned his head slightly and was startled by the sight of his own reflection in a mirror on a wall facing the staircase. He looked at himself - a tall, thin man in a crumpled double breasted suit, with a puzzled frown on his face. Behind his head to the left, he saw the frayed end of the scarf, swaying slightly where he must have brushed it as he stood up. A second shock came to him, a refinement of the horror of finding the body. She didn't just hang there, he realised, *she could see herself hanging in the mirror!*

Jane came back into the hall, stepping carefully around the body. As she did so the cat came out of the kitchen and rubbed itself against Terry's legs, miaowing hopefully.

'I've spoken to the driver. He arrived here shortly after nine with a delivery of groceries, he said. The uniforms will take him in for a statement after the quack's given him the okay.'

'Good.' Terry showed her the mirror. 'What d'you make of this?'

Jane studied it, awestruck as the implications sank in. 'She watched herself die?'

'Yes. She must have done. Couldn't avoid it unless she closed her eyes, and ...'

'How long do you think it would take?'

'What, hanging like that?' Terry glanced at the body and shuddered. 'Not an easy death, no way. No fall to break her neck. She was strangled, suffocated. Could have been three, four minutes even, before she lost consciousness.'

'And all that time fighting for breath?' Jane said slowly. 'It doesn't bear thinking about, does it? Even if you did it to yourself you might have second thoughts.' The cat got under her feet and she shooed it into the kitchen.

Terry bent down, to examine the woman's throat. 'No claw marks, that I can see.'

'What?' Jane looked uncomprehending, appalled. Terry realised she'd misunderstood.

'Not the cat. I'm talking about her own claws - fingernails. If she'd had second thoughts or just panicked as anyone would if they couldn't breathe, then what would you do? You'd try to tear this thing away from your throat, and probably draw blood in the process. But there's no sign of that here.'

'Maybe she did want to die, then,' Jane said.

'Her body didn't,' Terry said. 'She was scared shitless. Quite literally.'

'But that's just a physical reaction.'

'Exactly. That's my point, sergeant, don't you see? Even if she wanted to kill herself she couldn't control these basic bodily reactions brought on by the terror of dying. So how come her hands didn't react in the same way and try to tear herself free?'

'Perhaps she was drunk - or doped. I'd knock myself out, if I was going to do something like this.'

'Maybe,' said Terry doubtfully. 'The post mortem will tell us that. And I suppose it's also possible she lost consciousness straight away, and the shit and the piss came afterwards.' He shook his head thoughtfully. 'Unless someone helped her, of course.'

'A single woman living alone,' Jane said.

Their eyes met for a long, thoughtful moment. *Is this really suicide, or another one in the series? Out here in the country, a single woman dead in her house. Hanged with a scarf.* Terry bent to examine the woman's wrists, then shook his head slowly. 'No sign of anything here.'

'No sign of what, sir?'

'Restraint. Rope, tape, anything to tie her wrists so that she couldn't reach her throat. That's what you do, isn't it, when you hang people - tie their wrists first. Otherwise they fight, try to escape. Maybe she really did want to die, after all.'

Jane, like Terry before, was staring at the mirror. 'I don't get it, sir. I can't imagine it, somehow.'

'What?'

'Well, if I was going to kill myself ... I don't think I'd do it like this, not after I've seen this body ...' she shuddered. The smell in the hall was still strong. They were both struggling to keep down their nausea. '... but then maybe she didn't know, not what it would be like, I mean. But even so, one question we haven't asked, is why is she naked? Especially in front of a mirror. I mean, it doesn't look as if she was a particularly beautiful woman and even if she was, well if you're going to do *that* to yourself, why look? I mean why would anyone take all their clothes off first and do it in front of a mirror? It doesn't make sense - especially if you think of people like us.'

'People like us?'

'Yes, all of us.' She waved her arm towards the back door, where the uniformed constables and paramedics still hovered. Beyond them, a white SOCO van was parking on the gravel. 'All of us, the doctor, the uniforms, the SOCOs - you must know someone is going to find you and all this investigation is going to take place. And most of the people will be men, they always are. So why take all your clothes off? Most women would be embarrassed. I would.'

Terry smiled. It sounded like typical female logic to him. 'If you're going to die, it hardly matters, does it? We come naked into this world, and go naked out of it.'

'No sir, you don't get it. It's humiliating. Just because you want to kill yourself doesn't mean you want to humiliate yourself too. Whereas a man ...'

'A man wouldn't mind humiliating himself, you mean?' A vision came to him of himself, hanging naked in front of this mirror and how it would look. Light began to dawn. 'No, a man wouldn't do this either. Not a normal man.'

'Not to himself, sir, no. But to a woman he would.' Jane stared at him triumphantly. 'Don't you see? If he hated her enough to want to kill her, he might want to humiliate her as well. Especially like this. Probably get a kick out of it too.'

Terry nodded. 'I see your point, sure. It's hardly proof to put before a jury, though, is it?' Two men in white overalls climbed out of the SOCO van outside the front door. 'But there's something not right about this. Maybe these lads can find what it is.'

He went to the front door, where the leader of the SOCO team stood observing the scene. 'Suspicious death, Bill. Looks like suicide, but until we know better, I want you to treat it as a potential murder case.' He stumbled as the cat rubbed between his legs, purring. 'And someone ring the RSPCA, about this poor cat.'

31. Sarah and Emily

TRAVELLING SOUTH to Cambridge again, Sarah reflected on the past few weeks. As the train pressed her back into her seat she thought, my life is like this, I'm being carried to a new destination by forces stronger than me, that I can't control. A memory entered her mind of a poem, by Shakespeare she thought, of the seven ages of man. *Man*, of course - nobody thought women mattered back then - but anyway the point was clear. There was an illustration, she remembered, of man starting out as a baby - a 'mewling puking infant' - at the foot of a bridge which arched across the page to the right. A few steps higher up the bridge was a schoolboy, and then a young adult, both looking stronger and more confident than the one before, and then the adult man stood on the arch of the bridge - Man at the height of his powers, master of the universe, monarch of all he surveyed. After that - she wasn't quite sure what came next, it hadn't seemed relevant at the time - but it was all downhill, she knew that. Presumably the man getting older and weaker and more frail, until he stumbled off the foot of the bridge on the far side, a geriatric old hunchback in slippers, dribbling like a baby, crippled with arthritis, waiting for death.

Great. Nice one, Sarah. Very cheering thought. She pulled a face at her reflection in the window, and thought that's not going to happen to me, not ever, not for a hundred years. Not yet anyway. But she did feel her life going downhill at the moment, accelerating out of control, as if she'd slipped on a ski run and was sliding to the bottom on her bum. No, that's another image of disaster, she told herself firmly; I've got to get control of this somehow. How about a roller coaster? Yes, that's a better image of life. We rise to a peak of achievement, then relax, glide down for a while, but there are other peaks ahead, some small, some even higher than before. That's it - I must use the momentum of change to climb the next peak.

She sipped her coffee and looked around. There were people reading, texting, typing on their laptops. All different lives, all separate dramas. Not many people actually talking to each other or travelling together. Well, I'm like that too, just now. Alone if I have to be. Strong all the same.

Still, I do have family. Simon's been round twice in the last fortnight, bless him. More than in a whole month before that. He's clearly concerned, though he doesn't say too much. But then he never was a great one for talking. And Emily. Well, I'm going to see Emily now.

She'd been upset when Emily told her she was going on a skiing holiday in the New Year. It meant less time at home. But that's what you hope your children will do at university, she told herself firmly - meet new friends, have new experiences. She'd see Emily at Christmas, after all; that was good news. Only for a few days, though - she was going to London at the end of term, and then Birmingham with Larry, coming home only on Christmas Eve. That was why Sarah was going to Cambridge now. She'd booked a long weekend so they'd have ample time together.

Arriving late Thursday evening, she booked in at the Garden Court Hotel. She ordered a salad from room service, phoned Emily to arrange a time to meet tomorrow, had a bath and went to bed. Next morning, at breakfast, her mobile rang. Glancing at it, she saw a number she didn't recognise. 'Hello?'

'Hi.' A man's voice - Michael! She hadn't programmed his number into her phone, she realised. 'How're you doing?' he asked.

'Oh, all right. Eating breakfast.'

He sounded cautious, and she wasn't surprised. She'd been brusque and offhand when he'd cancelled their date on Wednesday, and had deliberately expunged him from her thoughts since then. Her voice now was cool, neutral. She picked a dried apricot and chewed it while waiting to hear what he'd say next.

'I was just ringing to apologise again for standing you up like that. It was unavoidable, but unforgivable too.'

'Yes, well, I was a bit surprised.' If it's unforgivable, don't expect to be forgiven, Sarah thought. 'Did you get your house problem sorted out?'

'More or less. It took ages.' He hesitated, and she picked another apricot, not caring if he heard her chewing. 'Anyway, I wondered if we could meet some time next week. Make amends, if you'll let me.'

'Maybe. I'll check my diary. I haven't got it here at the moment.'

'Oh.' He sounded discouraged. 'Where are you now?'

'In Cambridge. At the Garden Court Hotel.'

'Really? What are you doing there?'

'Visiting my daughter. I'm going to see a play she's in.'

'But that's fantastic! I'll be in Cambridge tomorrow. I'm driving down to meet Sandra. On the same errand as you, really.'

'Oh, I see.' Her heart fluttered. She saw where this was leading, and wasn't sure how she felt. On the one hand it would be nice to see him, on the other - not in front of Emily, surely! She had come to spend time with her daughter, not this man. She could feel him thinking it over as well.

'Yes. I'll be taking Sandra Christmas shopping, I expect. Maybe we could meet?'

'I'm not sure. I don't know what Emily's plans are and ... how she'd feel.'

'About me, you mean? I see the point. Still, maybe we could meet tomorrow evening, or Sunday. I could give you a lift back.'

'I don't know. Let's see how things go.'

'All right. I could come to your hotel, if you like. The Garden Court, you say?'

'Yes. Look, give me a ring tomorrow, will you? I'll decide then.'

She clicked off her phone and stared out of the window, thinking. She wasn't sure whether to frown or smile - her face in the window looked weird, distorted like a reflection in a fairground mirror. Two days ago he'd stood her up; yet here he was keen and friendly once again. I ought to refuse him, she thought, and yet ... where's the harm? It's not as though I have so many friends I can afford to turn new ones away.

And last time I was here, Emily actually encouraged me to attract a new man. So how would she react if I introduced her to Michael? Sarah trembled at the thought. Highly unpredictable - that's the only reliable prediction I can make.

She finished breakfast and crossed town to meet Emily in her college. Her daughter's room was chaotic, but more homely than she remembered it before. Music throbbed from a CD player, there were posters on all the walls, and incense from joss sticks perfumed the air. Emily looked pink-cheeked and healthy, but a little distracted, Sarah thought. They embraced, and Emily stood back to look at her.

'Same old smart mother,' she laughed. 'No one would take you for a don or a student.' Emily was barefoot in jeans and teeshirt, her hair damp and tousled as if she'd just emerged from the shower. Sarah wore her new spiked suede boots, and a dark skirt and jacket under a long woollen coat.

'Well, I'm not a student, obviously,' she said. 'I'm your mother, a visitor from the real world.'

'Yes.' Emily turned the music down and put a kettle on. 'How's that going, Mum?' A careful, sympathetic look appeared on her face.

'Am I surviving on my own, you mean? Yes, very well, I think, in the circumstances. I met your father this week.'

'And? How was he?'

'Different. He has a new leather jacket and haircut.'

'Dad? In a leather jacket?' Emily looked astonished. 'Why?'

'Trying to look younger, I suppose. Starting a new life.' She felt sudden tears prick in her eyes, and peered out of the window to hide them. 'Maybe he even *feels* younger.'

'Oh Mum, I'm sorry.' Emily put an arm round her mother in an awkward embrace. 'That must have been awful.'

'It wasn't the best day in my life.' She hugged Emily tightly for a second, then stood back and smiled. 'How about that coffee?'

They sat either side of the gas fire, Sarah in a battered armchair, Emily on a purple beanbag, and sipped their coffee. Sarah described her meeting with Bob, and how she had agreed to put the house on the market. 'I don't want to, darling,' she said. 'But it's like you said before, I have no choice, really. And when you're faced with something really nasty, it's best to get it over as soon as possible.'

'But you're a lawyer, Mum - can't you fight it?'

Sarah shook her head. 'Not that sort of lawyer, unfortunately. Anyway, I don't want to get into a legal fight with your father. We did love each other once, after all.'

'Yes, but he left you, Mum.'

'I know, and he's not coming back. I'm beginning to accept that now, but it's hard, of course. It's just ... if I keep moving ahead, start a new life, that seems the way forward. So I want to sell the house now and get shot of it, since I have to do it anyway. If I look back I'll be lost. Just collapse into a sentimental puddle on the floor.'

'*You,* Mum? I don't think so.'

Sarah smiled ruefully. 'You think I'm tough, don't you? Not tough - hard. You've always thought that.'

It was a little too close to the truth. Emily struggled for words. 'You're strong, Mum, that's what I meant. Stronger than most other girls' mums.'

'Am I? Well, thank you for that. But I tell you, I don't feel strong a lot of the time. If I thought I'd lose you, too, or Simon ...' She stared into the fire. 'There's a limit to how strong anyone can be on their own.' She looked up. 'You *are* coming home for Christmas, aren't you? I won't have sold the house by then.'

'Of course I am, Mum, I told you. But - there's London first, and then Birmingham. You don't mind, do you?'

'Not as long as you're with me at Christmas.' Sarah sipped her coffee. 'What are you doing in London?'

Emily smiled. 'You'll see tomorrow night. It's this band I'm in. Adrian's got us some gigs in London. It's scarey, but lots of fun too. I sing, you know, as well as play the flute.'

To Sarah's relief, the talk turned to Emily and her new student life. Not only was she in a play - *A Midsummer Night's Dream*, which Sarah was booked in to see this evening - but she had joined some of the actors in a rock band, which performed cover versions of well-known songs as well as a few original compositions by the group's leader, Adrian. 'We're meeting him for lunch, Mum,' Emily said. 'With Brian, Rachel and Helena. You'll be amazed, he's terrific. Ten ideas a minute - most of them mad, but his mind never stops.'

Emily's work, Sarah noticed, wasn't mentioned; but the girl looked more full of life, energy and happiness than she could remember. The sulky fifteen-year-old who had hated her parents and run away from home seemed a distant memory; but so, too, did the intense, committed campaigner against environmental pollution and global poverty. Sarah wondered about Larry, her boyfriend in distant Birmingham.

'You're going skiing with this Adrian and the others after Christmas, are you?'

'Yes.'

'Is Larry coming too?'

'I hope so. We're going to practise on the indoor ski slope in Birmingham. We've booked some lessons.'

'What does he think about this Adrian? Isn't that a bit difficult?'

Emily gawped at her mother in astonishment, then laughed. *'Adrian?*

No, Mum, you've got the wrong end of the stick entirely there. Adrian's gay - about as gay as you can get - so's Brian. That's why they're such fun to be with, probably. All the girls love them because they're no threat, and they keep the other guys from pestering us. So you don't have to worry about me and Larry - not because of that.' She smiled. 'What about you?'

'Me?'

'Yes. Last time you were here I gave you a few tips, Mum, remember. Have you met anyone yet? Tried them out?'

There was an anxious silence. Emily's smile faded, as she thought no, I shouldn't have said that, it was tactless, Mum's only just left Dad after all, she's still grieving.

Sarah looked down at her hands, thinking what will she think if I tell her about Michael? Well, is there anything to tell? Not really, but he *is* here in Cambridge. How would Emily react if I introduced them? Bad idea, or brave new world?

She looked up, a shy smile on her face.

'Well, as a matter of fact, darling, yes. There *is* someone.'

32. Alison Grey

CROCKEY HILL was a small hamlet which had grown up around a busy road junction. There were no pubs or shops, just half a dozen houses, a garage, a pine furniture warehouse, and a small roadside café. The dead woman's house was near none of these, but set back a hundred yards from the road, near some woods. Nonetheless, by lunch time Terry had found a neighbour to perform the grim duty of identifying the body. The dead woman's name was Alison Grey, the neighbour confirmed faintly, trembling with shock at the swollen, purple face. She had lived alone in this house with her cat for eight or nine months.

'What did she do?' Terry asked. 'For a living, I mean?'

'She wrote school books, she said. She didn't have a regular job, anyway. She spent most of her time at home with that cat. Poor Kitty - who's going to look after her now?'

'Perhaps you would,' said Terry hopefully. 'Otherwise it's going to a cattery.'

'Yes, perhaps I can. I'll feed it anyway, see how it goes.'

'Tell me about this Alison Grey,' Terry continued. 'What was she like?'

'Very quiet, really; kept herself to herself. Friendly enough when you met her, but not seeking company, if you know what I mean. Bit posh for round here.'

'Did she have any friends, regular visitors, people like that?'

'Men friends, you mean?'

'Any kind of friends. People we might ask.'

'Well, I suppose she must have - I mean everyone has *some* friends, don't they? But no one I know of. We're not in each other's pockets round here, you know, twitching net curtains and such, if that's what you're asking. I can't even see her house from my kitchen - not that I'd want to. Live and let live's my motto - always has been, always will.'

'No one's accusing you of spying,' Terry persisted, wondering what secrets the woman herself had to conceal. 'It's just that now she's dead ...'

'Killed herself, didn't she?'

'It's possible, but we have to investigate. So anything unusual you noticed, anything at all ...'

'Well, I didn't see her that much, to be honest with you. I doubt if anyone did. There's no shop here, you see, so if you don't use the bus ... we all use the car. Last time I spoke to her was in the surgery in Escrick.'

'Really? When was that?'

'Oh, about a fortnight ago. She looked quite white, as it happens, quite faint. I didn't ask her what was wrong; well you don't, do you? But I did wonder. I wish I had now. Perhaps if I'd said something then ...'

'Thank you, Mrs Phillips. You've been most helpful.'

The house was a crime scene, surrounded with blue and white tape. Jane and Terry donned protective gloves and overalls and walked carefully in covered boots to protect the floor. The house looked like the home of a single woman. There was a glass, a plate and a few mugs drying beside the sink. One comfortable armchair in the living room had newspapers, books, and a TV Times spread around it. There were three bedrooms upstairs - one full of suitcases and boxes piled on a single bed with a bare mattress; a study, with a desk, computer, and bookshelves; and the third, comfortably furnished with wardrobes and a large double bed.

They looked in the study first. The desk was littered with files and papers, some of which spread onto the floor. The computer was on, humming quietly to itself as it waited for its owner to return. Jane sat at the desk and clicked the mouse. A text appeared on the screen: half a dozen short paragraphs about two young tourists visiting York. They went to the Minster, walked on the walls, visited the Jorvik Viking centre and took a boat down river to the Archbishop's Palace. The text was followed by a number of questions and vocabulary exercises about the events in the story. While Jane was reading them Terry picked up a book. It was glossy, colourful, expensively produced.

'This is her, isn't it?' he said, pointing at the cover. *'First Class,* by Alison Grey. *An English language course for beginners, with listening cassettes and video clips on DVD.* Look, here's a photo of her on the back.'

They studied the photo of a smiling young woman. The text under the photo read: *Alison Grey is an experienced teacher who has taught English in many countries around the world. She is now a professional writer who lives in the north of England.*

'That's her,' Jane said. 'Who's it published by?'

'Oxford University Press.'

'She'll have an editor there, then. Probably communicates with her by e-mail. Yes, here we go.' She clicked on the computer's inbox and found five unread e-mails. One from Marks and Spencer, two from clothing companies, one from a bookclub, and one from a woman called Jennifer Barlow. It was a long, cheerful, encouraging e-mail full of detailed comments about a previous chapter of the book.

'That's someone to get in touch with, then,' Terry said, reading the e-mail over Jane's shoulder. 'But it sounds as though her work was going well. No reason to kill herself for that, then. We'll take this computer in as soon as the SOCOs have dusted it.'

'I'll e-mail this stuff to the station, shall I?' Jane said, smiling at Terry's look of surprise. 'Saves time, and it won't hamper the SOCOs.'

While Jane was doing that Terry browsed through some of the letters on the desk. 'Look at this, sergeant,' he said, holding up one. 'Here's a motive.'

The letter was on headed hospital notepaper. It was dated two days ago, and came from the radiology and oncology department. *Dear Ms Grey,* it read. *Following your consultation with Dr Chandra last week, we write to confirm that your first appointment for chemotherapy will be at 10.30 a.m. on Thursday 4th December.* There followed instructions about not eating anything for six hours beforehand, and directions as to how to find the department. Terry's eyes met Jane's.

'So she had cancer, poor woman. And if this is her first appointment she can only have found out about it when? A week ago - maybe two? Probably when that neighbour, Mrs Phillips, saw her in the doctor's surgery. She said her face was white as a sheet. She'd probably just got the bad news. Maybe that's why she did it.'

'Surely not, sir,' Jane said. 'The whole point of chemotherapy is to make you better.'

'You say that, young woman, but think what it means. Your hair falls out, you get bloated, you feel sick, and even then it doesn't always work. To some people, chemotherapy can be as scarey as the disease.

Particularly if you're a single woman on your own, with no one to care whether you live or die. Maybe she just sat here, scared, lonely, and depressed, and took the quick way out.'

'You don't know she was lonely,' Jane said. 'You're just guessing.'

'True,' Terry said. 'But look around this place. What do you see?'

'I live alone too, sir,' Jane insisted stubbornly. 'But I'm not lonely. Maybe she liked it like this. A peaceful country cottage, a quiet place to write.'

'Until someone tells you you've got cancer, yes. That would change everything, wouldn't it? Then you'd need friends, emotional support. Maybe she didn't have any.'

'Maybe. We don't know. Her e-mails may tell us.'

'That and her phone bills,' Terry agreed. 'We'll check those, of course. See who she phoned and how often.'

As they were talking, the cat strolled into the room, its tail erect like a flag. It rubbed itself against Jane's leg. She picked it up and stroked it.

'That's another thing,' she said. 'What about this cat?'

Terry looked at her, surprised. 'The cat?'

'Yes. Maybe she *was* lonely, as you say, but she had this cat for company, at least. And she was probably fond of it, most women are. Especially single women who spend a lot of time at home. So what did she think would happen to the animal if she topped herself? I mean, I know it's a trivial thing, but if I was going to kill myself, I'd make arrangements for kitty first. You know, have a word with a neighbour, mention the cat in her will, leave a note with a supply of Whiskas. Why didn't she do that?'

'Perhaps she thought it could fend for itself,' Terry suggested. 'Cats do.'

Jane looked sceptical, slightly offended. '*You* may think that, sir, but a woman wouldn't. Not most women, anyway.' She put the cat on the floor and let it run downstairs.

Terry shrugged. 'It's a point. Let's check out the rest of the house.'

They moved on to the main bedroom. It was a large, comfortable room with a double bed facing the window. The bed was neatly made, covered by a dark red flowery duvet with matching pillowcases and sheets. Thick pink curtains were drawn across the window, and a bedside lamp was still on. There were small pine bedside cabinets either side of the bed, and a pine wardrobe and chest of drawers, one either side of the window.

The top drawer of the chest of drawers was open, showing a selection of female underwear. There was a full length mirror on one wall, and a smaller one on top of the chest of drawers, where there was a jewellery box, hairbrush, and a number of items of make-up. There was a dark grey carpet on the floor, and a wicker clothes basket heaped with dirty washing in the corner. There was a wooden chair next to it, piled with jeans, cardigan, teeshirts, and bras, and on the carpet between it and the bed lay a flowery cotton nightie, as if it had been dropped.

'No sign of a struggle, is there?' Terry said. 'I mean, if someone did break in and surprise her, you'd think there'd be a fight. Things would get knocked over.'

They stood, studying the room. It looked peaceful, quiet, lived-in, as if the owner might return at any time. Jane picked up a book from the bedside table.

'What's that?' Terry asked.

'Alex Comfort,' she said. '*The Joy of Sex.*' She turned the pages, frowning at the drawings of a bearded man and a woman in a variety of complicated positions.

Terry smiled. 'The classic bible of free love. Before your time, probably, sergeant.' He opened one of the drawers of the bedside cabinet, and there, amongst a litter of tampons, tissues and panty liners, was a packet of ribbed condoms. Two of the three were missing. 'Well, well. Maybe she wasn't so lonely, after all.'

He crossed the room and pulled back the curtains 'I wish I had a view like this.'

'Yes sir, but think what you're looking at,' Jane said, pointing to the woods. They were on the far side of the field, about seventy yards away. 'Someone could be watching us right now from amongst those trees, and we wouldn't know he was there. And there's a bridleway in those woods. People run or cycle through it from Fulford. You can cross the A19 and go down to Naburn and the cycle track.'

'You're thinking of Peter Barton, aren't you?' Terry said. 'Coming here, breaking in. Doing what you've always worried he might do.'

'It's has to be a possibility, doesn't it, sir?' Jane said grimly. 'This might be the next in our series - the disaster we've been trying to avoid.'

'Bit of a step up for the lad, wouldn't you say? From stealing knickers to murder? Anyway, it may be suicide, just as it seems. But even if not ...'

'A woman on her own, living near a bridleway. Biggish coincidence, sir, isn't it? Who else could have done it? If it *is* murder, that is.'

'Well, it looks like she had a lover, for a start,' Terry said. 'The fellow who read that book with her, and wore those condoms.'

'You think he killed her?'

Terry shrugged. 'We don't know anyone did, yet. What if she had a row with this lover - he dumped her perhaps? She already knew she had cancer, remember? Maybe that was the last straw. She felt scared and abandoned, so she hanged herself.'

'If this guy existed at all.'

'Quite. We'll have to find out. Maybe he didn't dump her - he just wasn't here when she needed him. That could have done it.'

'You'd leave a note, wouldn't you?' Jane said. 'If you wanted to blame someone?'

'Yes, probably. Perhaps we'll find something on the computer when we check it.'

Terry walked into the bathroom, and stood silently for a moment, looking round. 'Do you notice anything about this room?' he asked.

'Make-up remover,' Jane said slowly, looking at the splash top beside the sink. 'She hasn't put it away.'

'Would you normally do that?' Terry asked.

'Depends how tidy you are. The rest of the room looks fairly neat, though. Maybe she was interrupted before she finished.'

'Which means she was wearing make-up in the first place. No doubt the pathologist will be able to confirm that.' Terry shuddered, shocked by the grotesque image of mascara, rouge and lipstick on that purple swollen face and bulging eyes. 'Which adds to the possibility that she might have been entertaining a male visitor.'

'Maybe she just liked to keep up appearances,' Jane suggested.

'Alone out here with her cat? Seems unlikely. Anyway, there's something else you've missed, sergeant.' He nodded towards the bath. There was a selection of soaps and conditioners, and an open packet of luxury foam bubble bath salts.

'You think she had a bath before she died? That would explain why she was naked.'

'Maybe. But look at the shower head.'

The shower head was mounted on a sliding chrome rail on the wall above the bath taps. Jane stared at it without understanding. 'What about it, sir?'

'How tall would you say that woman was?'

Light dawned. 'Five foot two, five three? Not very tall.'

'Not as tall as you. If you got in that bath - don't do it, the SOCOs haven't been here yet - would you have the shower head that high?'

'I doubt it, sir.' The shower head was at the top of the chromium rail. 'I might be able to reach it but I'd probably pull it down, if it slides freely. And she's shorter than me.'

'Exactly. So what does that suggest?'

'Maybe she just liked to have the shower that high. Not everyone likes it close above their head.' Jane shrugged, meeting Terry's eye. 'Unless someone taller used the shower. A man perhaps.'

'So was he the last one to use the shower, this man? Last night, when she died?'

They walked downstairs, to the hall where the body had been found. There were chalk marks on the floor, and a SOCO officer in overalls showed them carefully where to step. 'A single woman living alone out here with a cat,' Jane said, frowning at the front door. 'She should have had a burglar alarm fitted. A simple thing like that could have saved her life.'

'Not if it was suicide,' Terry said. 'Anyway, it wouldn't work. That damned cat would set it off all the time.'

'Then a dog instead. That would have given her protection.'

'True.' Terry shrugged. 'But the real point is, did she die alone?'

'Or was there an intruder? And if so, how did he get in?'

Terry nodded, stepping outside. 'The front door was locked, wasn't it? No sign of a break in anywhere else. So if there was an intruder, he climbed in through that loo window like the uniforms did. The SOCOs are checking for prints there, first of all. And outside. For footprints and bike tracks.'

Terry walked to the SOCO van and peeled off his overalls. When he was dressed normally he stood on the lawn, deep in thought. In the field next to the house a team of tractors were harvesting carrots, one stripping the straw that protected them from the frost, while a second pulled a machine that dug them out of the ground and sent them up a conveyor belt into a large trailer pulled by a third. 'So we have at least two possibilities, it seems to me. Or possibly three.'

'What's that, sir?'

'Well, firstly, this is suicide, just as it appears to be. Second, more scarey, she was murdered by this young pervert who we still can't find. And thirdly, well ...' He hesitated a moment. '... it's too early to say, but if she *was* murdered, it could be the normal thing. Like nine murder victims out of ten.' He looked up and met Jane's eyes. 'Not killed by a stranger, but by someone who knew her well. A husband, if she had one. Or failing that, a boyfriend or lover.'

33. Seduction

SITTING IN the theatre, watching *A Midsummer Night's Dream,* Sarah felt strangely moved. Emily was playing Titania, the fairy queen. Sarah had seen Emily on stage - as the Virgin Mary in infant school, clutching the hand of a six year old Joseph with a cotton wool beard, and then later playing the flute in secondary school concerts - but had never felt like this. Indeed, she'd had often been faintly bored, affecting polite attention while silently running over some book or legal problem in her mind. Bob had accused her, more than once, of being present in body but not in mind.

'This *is* your daughter, Sarah,' he'd snapped. 'She's doing her best. You could at least pay attention.'

Now for the first time she understood what he'd meant. On Friday she'd met Emily's new friends - the witty Adrian, his boyfriend Brian, and two sweet girls called Rachel and Helena - and seen Emily in a way she'd never experienced before. She was happy, vibrant, full of laughter - she made several good jokes of her own - and was clearly valued and appreciated by the others. They'd all been very nice to Sarah, taking her out to their favourite restaurant for lunch, asking about her work, including her in the conversation, explaining the hilarious incidents that had happened that term. It was a light-hearted lunch; she felt privileged to be welcomed to their company. And yet at the same time she was oddly aware of being old, a little lumbering, out of date. A parent to be cared for. A visitor from a real world that moved more slowly, seriously, with none of the effervescence that fizzed in these students' minds - a jacuzzi of new ideas and opportunities.

It was a life she had never known for herself. She was delighted to see her daughter take to it so easily. And yet she envied her, for what she had missed. At their age, she thought, watching the young people wonderingly, I had two babies, I'd been divorced and remarried, I was doing A levels with toddlers underfoot. I always worked, I never laughed. Not like this.

She watched the play, and realised for the first time that it was *funny*. She'd studied it for exams, of course, but somehow it had never seemed funny on the printed page - merely bizarre. Now she laughed, with the rest of the audience, both at the predictable slapstick and the up-to-date topical references that the students sneaked in. She loved Emily's costumes, and was genuinely, absurdly proud of the way she not only remembered her lines but delivered them with real sensitivity and timing. That's *my daughter* up there, she wanted to tell everyone round her. Clap louder, she deserves a bouquet.

After the play she went out with the cast for a meal and a raucous party that was still going on when she called a taxi at one in the morning. On Saturday, she met Emily at eleven and took her out for a snack lunch. They were eating baked potatoes on a bench when her mobile rang. She balanced the food in her lap and fumbled the phone from her bag.

'Hi. It's Michael. How're you doing?'

'Oh, fine. I'm having lunch with my daughter.'

'Snap. I'm about to do the same. Spent all morning buying presents.'

'Good.' Sarah forked a mouthful of potato into her mouth, wondering what was coming next.

'What're you doing this afternoon?'

'Going to the theatre. My daughter's in a play.' To Emily's surprise and amusement, Sarah had insisted on seeing the play again. It was the last day, and the evening performance was sold out, but she'd managed to get a seat for the matinee.

'Oh.' Michael sounded disappointed. 'What about this evening? I was hoping we could meet.'

Sarah thought for a moment. Emily would be on stage again, and after that there would be another party, probably even wilder than the night before. She wasn't sure she had the stamina for that. 'What did you have in mind?'

'I thought we might meet for a meal somewhere. Maybe at your hotel?'

'That sounds nice. What time?'

'Seven? Say seven thirty. I'll meet you in the foyer.'

'Okay.' She clicked the phone off and glanced, somewhat shyly, at Emily.

'Who was that?'

'A friend. This ... man I told you about.'

'Oh really?' Emily grinned. 'He called you then, did he?'

'Yes. I said I'd meet him tonight at the hotel. While you're on stage for your final performance. If you don't mind, that is.'

'Mum, why should I mind? Go for it, why not? It's your life, after all!'

The matinee was just as good as Friday night - better, in some ways, because the cast seemed more relaxed. Perhaps it was because they were near the end of a successful run, or perhaps it was just Sarah's perception of it. She remembered the play from the night before, and noticed subtle differences - places where the young actors forgot their lines and covered up, or deliberately ad-libbed for the hell of it. All the way through she could see they were having fun, and rejoiced that Emily was part of it.

Afterwards she went backstage to give Emily a hug. 'That was terrific, darling. I enjoyed every minute.'

'Really?' Emily laughed. 'But you saw it last night.'

'Yes, but you see little things that are different.'

'Like when Adrian nearly tipped me out of that hammock, the sod? I've told him if he does, I'll put chili in his codpiece. I've a good mind to do it anyway, just to see what happens.'

'Tell me if you do. I've a good mind to cancel this meal tonight, and sneak in at the back.'

'Nonsense, Mum,' Emily said firmly. 'You go, give this guy a chance. Then you can tell me all about it tomorrow.'

'You'll be bored,' Sarah warned. 'There'll be nothing to tell. I can promise you that.'

Back at the hotel she showered, changed and spent some time sitting quietly in front of the mirror thinking as she did her make-up. Or rather, not thinking exactly, but feeling. This past twenty four hours with Emily, she realised, had been one of the best days she'd had for months. Her anxiety about Bob - her long drawn out dread that something was wrong, followed by the terrible discovery that she was right - had faded. She was going to be divorced, and was coming to accept it. Her greatest fear had been the effect the divorce might have on Emily. It could so easily destroy the girl's confidence, wreck her university career. But none of this seemed to be happening. Far from it. At university, Emily had shed the awkward, sullen chrysalis of her teenage years, and was spreading her wings for the first time.

It's worth a celebration, Sarah thought. The relief and pleasure in this discovery had brought her as close to happiness as she could remember. It would have been nice, of course, to share it with Bob, but that was not to be. At least I'll have someone to talk to tonight, she thought. Michael's been divorced, so he should understand.

She spent little of her time actually thinking about Michael until she came downstairs and saw him in the foyer. But he looked as gratifyingly tall and handsome as she had remembered. He wore a dark blue woollen blazer, open-necked shirt and jeans. Sarah wore slim pointed heels, a black trouser suit with a short jacket which flattered her hips, a cream silk blouse, and a gold necklace and earrings which her son Simon had given her last birthday. She'd wondered if the look was too formal, but when his face creased with a welcoming, appreciative smile, she felt glad she'd made the effort. He'd booked a table in the restaurant, and while they ordered, she told him about Emily and her play. He listened appreciatively.

'I'd love to see Sandra in something like that one day,' he said. 'She's just entering the teenage tunnel of horrors, though. She sees Dad as a bit of an embarrassment. Nice to have his money, pity about his company. And you tell me it gets worse?'

'It can do, yes. Did you have a hard day?'

'Let's just say ... I wasn't completely sorry to get back here. I needed a swim and a sauna to put me in a better frame of mind.'

'Back here?' Sarah said, surprised. 'I thought you stayed in your old college in Cambridge - St John's, wasn't it?'

'I did, last time, but to be honest, it's a bit primitive. And when I heard you were here wallowing in the lap of luxury I got jealous and thought well, if they're even taking lawyers these days, maybe they'll have a broom cupboard somewhere for a poor property developer. So I rang, and yes, they did. Not the largest room in the world, but still.'

Sarah raised an eyebrow. 'You share it with a cleaning lady, do you?'

'No, I threw her out. She flew off on a broomstick, screaming and waving a dustpan.'

Sarah laughed, conscious of a faint tingle of excitement at the base of her spine. So he had a room in this hotel too. What would Emily say to that? Thoughtfully, she sipped her wine, feeling the warmth of the alcohol spread through her veins. 'So what happened exactly with Sandra?'

'How long have you got?'

For the next hour or so she listened to the complications of his daughter's emotional roller-coaster, and tried to offer advice from her own experiences with Emily. All the time she was measuring, wondering how good a father he was, trying to work out what his stories revealed about his character. She asked how Michael and his former wife had managed things since their divorce.

'Oh, fairly amicably,' he said. 'We both more or less agree about things like schooling and access and so on - now, at any rate. It was bit sticky at first, but then Kate met the man of her dreams and to be honest, I think I provided a welcome childcare service while she got on with her romance. And now that she's pregnant - well the same thing applies.'

'Pregnant? Isn't she a bit old for that?'

'Well, she's a couple of years younger than me, but yes - last chance I suppose. She looked blooming when I saw her today. Better than I've ever seen her.'

'You still meet and talk then?'

'Oh yes. We don't hate each other. Not any more.' He twirled his wineglass thoughtfully. 'We did once, though. Or at least she hated me. So she said.'

'Why was that?'

He grimaced, trying to deflect the question with humour. 'Because I'm a monster. I used to tie her to the bedpost and whip her every night. And then refuse to take the rubbish out in the morning.'

Sarah said nothing. She wondered if Bob might divert questions in with a similarly flippant response. Maybe this Kate had every right to be angry, she thought. And yet this man seemed ... so charming, so ironically aware of his own failings. She wondered how much further she could probe. Michael met her eyes, seeming to realise what she was thinking. He sighed.

'She fell in love with someone else. She's married him now.'

'And you didn't?'

'Not then, Sarah, no.' He smiled at her across the table.

'I mean - you don't have to answer this if you don't want to - but did you leave her, or did she leave you?'

'Well, that's not so easy to say.' He put his wineglass down and ran a finger thoughtfully around the rim. 'I think we both left each other, really. Just drifted apart. I mean, you start out madly in love, all wedding and lace, and then somehow you wind up with this great yawning gap between you in bed, and no words spoken that aren't cruel. The truth is, I suppose, we were both spending a lot of time at work, and none with each other. She thought I was having an affair when I wasn't, and then bang! One day I come home and find a stranger in my bed. And it's all *my* fault, she says. By that time I was past caring. I didn't even want to punch the guy. I just turned on my heel and left.'

'Why did she say it was your fault?'

Michael watched her keenly, as if realising the significance of the question for her. 'Because,' he said carefully, 'I'd been spending some time with an old friend, a woman, from university days. It wasn't an affair, we were just good friends, really. But Kate didn't see it like that.'

'So what happened to the old friend?'

'She went to live in Indonesia. That's what she does, she travels the world.' Michael paused, as the waiter brought the bill. 'Shall we take our coffee over there?' He indicated a bar adjacent to the restaurant, where a small band was playing dance music. 'We can watch other people take exercise.'

'Or do it ourselves,' Sarah said, as they entered the bar, where two couples were attempting to jive.

He looked at her quizzically. 'I can't do that.'

'Can't you? I can,' she said cheerfully, taking his coffee and putting it on a table beside hers. 'One of my few skills. Come on. I'll teach you.'

'Oh no.' He pulled back. 'I really can't, you know. I've got two left feet.'

'Nonsense. All the man has to do is stand still and let the woman spin round him. You're not scared, are you?'

'Only of looking stupid.' He let her pull him reluctantly to the floor. It was true, she discovered, he had little idea of the jive, but Sarah pushed and pulled him into place and spun round energetically, enjoying herself in a way she had once done with Kevin. He'd been a real live wire, though, not wooden and clumsy like Michael, who accompanied her as best as he could with amused embarrassment.

The dance ended, and they sat down to get their breath and finish their coffee. After another jive, the music changed to a waltz. 'Now this, perhaps I *can* manage,' Michael said. He stood up, holding out his hand. To the relief of both of them, he was right. They danced cautiously but competently around the small floor. He held her more firmly than Bob used to do. She found it exciting and reassuring.

Sarah's mind, as they danced, was alive with excitement. The happiness she had felt earlier in the evening was still with her, enhanced by the wine. This man may have been a bastard to his wife, she thought, but nonetheless he's good company, intelligent, amusing, and physically attractive. So how far could she - *should she* - let this go? She thought back over the men she had known: Kevin, her violent, impetuous first husband; Bob, so kind and supportive but well, a little dull in situations like this; Terry Bateson, the tall, lean detective, the last man she had danced alone with in a hotel. That wasn't such a great memory, though. Sarah recalled ruefully how it had turned out. She'd drunk too much, and made a fool of herself in front of him in a hotel bedroom. Not really something to be proud of. Terry had been a perfect gentleman about it, but Sarah had felt utterly humiliated. Sadly, she doubted if he would ever be able to think of her in that way again - certainly she'd never dared give him the chance.

That mustn't happen this time. If anything does happen, that is.

After the waltz they sat in the bar. Sarah ordered a cocktail and drank it slowly, with the intention of making it last. She'd already drunk enough to loosen her inhibitions - any more and disaster might follow. After a while they danced again, closer this time. And Sarah knew that the choice was hers. If she wanted something to happen, it would. When they sat down again he asked her what sort of a room she had.

Her eyes met his, answering the question he hadn't asked. 'Oh, just an ordinary hotel bedroom. All very neat and compact. Ensuite bathroom, minibar, immaculate desk with hotel notepaper on it. Double bed.'

'Ah. Does it have a view?'

'What, the bed?'

'No, the room. Mine looks out onto a brick wall and a row of dustbins, you see. And the shower doesn't work.'

'Poor you. Mine has a view over the river and a sort of park. And a nice powerful shower.' The tingle in her spine was more electric now; a pulse was throbbing in her throat. She drew a deep breath, and smiled. 'Perhaps you'd like to try it?'

34. Doctor and Priest

'YES, I spoke to her about eight days ago, something like that.' Doctor Clarey clicked the mouse on his computer. 'Here we are, 26th November. I called her in personally to explain the results of the tests to her. We always do that, you know, with something serious like this.'

'So how serious was it, doctor?' Terry asked.

The doctor peered at him over his half moon spectacles. He had a rather pleasant, caring face, Terry thought - lined and crumpled somehow in a way that matched his old linen jacket and baggy cord trousers. He seemed out of place in this modern, purpose built surgery, with its fitted carpets, airport chimes, and computerised waiting list. But all the more reassuring for that. If there's a nice way to tell someone they have cancer, this man probably knows what it is.

'Fairly serious, I'm afraid. She had ovarian cancer, and it rather looked as though it had spread to the lymph glands.'

'Could that have been cured?'

'I told her it could, of course. There'd be no point in the chemotherapy otherwise. But she was an intelligent woman - very nice lady, in fact. She asked questions. And so ... well, I told her the truth. Most of the truth, anyway. As much as I thought she could bear.'

'And that truth was?'

'Well, it's a matter of statistics, really. Probabilities - what she could reasonably anticipate, in terms of life expectancy, recurrence of the disease, and so on. It's much harder, you see, when the disease has spread beyond the original site. You can't just cut it out by surgery, you have to subject the whole body to a pretty unpleasant, poisonous regime, in order to kill the cancer wherever it is. And for a woman of her age, in her condition ...' Dr Carey spread his hands apologetically. 'The chances of a complete cure are about 50-50. I told her 60-40, I think - we always err on the side of optimism, where we can. It's psychologically more motivating, as well as just kinder, I think.'

Kinder, Terry thought. To be told you have a 40% chance of dying rather than 50%. Well, maybe. He imagined the shock, the sheer terror Alison Grey must have felt, sitting in front of this man, hearing this news. No wonder her neighbour said she looked white.

What a job it must be, Terry thought, to tell people such news. How often? Once a week? Once a fortnight?

'How did she take it?'

The doctor grimaced, and rubbed his ear before replying. 'She was scared, of course. Everyone is, it's a natural reaction. I tried to answer her questions, and told her about the treatment - how long it would last, what it would be like, the need for people to care for her and so on. She didn't seem to have many friends up here, unfortunately. But we have a practice nurse who can visit - I offered her that.'

'Doctor, I have to ask you this. Was there anything in her reaction that suggested to you that she might take her own life?'

The doctor shook his head slowly. 'No. She never mentioned it. But then you wouldn't, would you, to a doctor? Not unless the disease is terminal, which hers wasn't - not yet. She did seem quite shocked, but that's normal, in such a situation. It's not normal to kill yourself. Are you quite certain it's suicide, then?'

'Not yet, no. We're still waiting for the post mortem.'

'Well, they'll find the cancer, for sure - be able to tell you how bad it was. Not that it makes much difference now. She was in here for quite some time - twenty minutes or so. I wanted to be sure she was calm enough to drive home on her own. And she did say one thing, now I think of it, that might help.'

'What was that?'

'Well, she was a Christian, I think, but she wasn't quite satisfied with our local church. Nothing to do with the vicar, I gather - it was more to do with doctrine. She'd been planning to be received into the Catholic church, she said, and had been taking instruction from a priest in York.' He smiled sadly. 'She even tried to make a joke of it - that's when I knew she was getting over the initial shock. She said this would give her something really big to talk about next time she met the man of God.'

'Do you know who this priest was?' Terry asked.

'I do as a matter of fact. I recognised the name when she told me; I've met him before. Nice man. Father Roberts, at the Catholic church in York.'

Father Roberts was in his early thirties; brisk, friendly, serious, with a pleasant Irish accent and a twinkle in his eyes which suggested that despite all the problems in the world he, somehow, had found the secret of inner peace, and was happy to share it with anyone who was interested. The perfect recruiting agent for the church, Terry thought; no doubt that was why he had been given the job.

'Alison Grey? Yes indeed,' he said, sitting quietly in a corner of the Catholic church near York Minster. 'I met her several times. A tragedy - how did she die?'

'That's what we're investigating,' Terry said. 'It looks like suicide, but there are several unanswered questions. That's why I've come to see you. Did she say anything ...'

' ... to indicate she might take her own life? Not to me, Inspector, surely. I would recall something like that, you can be quite certain.' Father Roberts frowned. 'She had a number of troubles, it's true, but ... well, for one thing, suicide, you know, it's a mortal sin. I imagine she would have known that.'

'What does that mean, exactly, a mortal sin?'

The sparkle faded from the young priest's eyes. He met Terry's gaze gravely. 'A sin from which there is no redemption. After death, most of us go to Purgatory until our sins are redeemed by time, suffering, and the prayers of those left behind on earth. But there are some sins so serious that they cannot be redeemed. Suicide is one of those.'

'So what? She would stay in this - what do you call it? - purgatory for ever?'

The priest drew a deep breath. 'She wouldn't go there. If you believe in the full doctrine of the church as I do, her soul would go straight to hell. Unless - it is possible there were circumstances known to God which would make forgiveness of such a sin possible.'

'Let's hope we find some then,' said Terry grimly, shocked by the stark horror of the pronouncement. 'Do you really believe in that?'

'It's not fashionable to talk about heaven and hell these days but yes, Inspector Bateson, I'm afraid I do. And I would have told her so had she asked me. Unfortunately she didn't.'

'Why exactly did she come to meet you?'

'For instruction in the Catholic faith. She had been toying with a number of eastern religions, I believe, and attending the Church of England, but found them all unsatisfactory in some way. So she told me, anyway. We were halfway through a course of instruction. She was due to meet me again next week.'

'Did she seem depressed in any way? Worried about anything?'

The priest hesitated. 'There is an issue of confidentiality ...'

'For Christ's sake, man! The woman's dead! What I'm looking for are some of those mitigating circumstances which may help us to understand the reasons for her death, and from what you say, keep her soul out of hell!' Terry's voice echoed in the vast cavern of the church, and several heads turned curiously. He realised his outburst was blasphemous, but didn't care; he found the whole discussion somehow obscene.

'Forgiveness comes from God, not man,' the priest reproved him gently. 'But yes, I understand your motives, inspector. And since she was not yet received into the church I learned nothing from her under the seal of the confessional. She was a troubled lady, certainly. Much of our discussion was around the theme of sin and forgiveness. This seemed very important to her. She never told me why, exactly, but it seemed to be both an attraction and a barrier to her hopes of conversion.'

'How do you mean?'

'As if there was some great sin she wanted to confess, but dared not. I tried to describe the relief that confession and absolution can bring. She seemed attracted by this notion, but afraid of it too. She cried once or twice, in our discussions.'

'Did she tell you what this sin might have been?'

'No. I was not her confessor, and ... I doubt if she was ready.'

'What about her health?' Terry asked. 'Did you know she had cancer?'

'Yes, she told me. She had visited her doctor the day before, and received the diagnosis. She was anxious about it, naturally.'

'What did she say?'

The priest stroked his chin thoughtfully for a moment. 'Well, naturally she was afraid - anyone would be. Not just of the disease, but of the treatment - it's no picnic, this chemotherapy. I've seen the effects. But you know, in a strange way I think she was looking forward to it.'

'Looking forward to it? How?'

'I know, it sounds odd. But it's something she said. What was it now? *We all get what we deserve in the end. That's how God works.* Something like that, anyhow.'

'What do you think she meant?'

'Who knows? Only God can be certain in the end. But as I told you, she mentioned this sin that she dared not confess. And so, when God inflicted this dreadful disease and its treatment on her, maybe she saw it as a punishment that she deserved. Maybe even a punishment that would absolve her, in the end.' The priest shrugged. 'It's probably all in my imagination.'

'Not necessarily. You knew her, after all, and I didn't.' Terry thought for a moment. 'If you are right though, Father, and part of her *was* looking forward to this treatment, then it's less likely that she would avoid it by killing herself, isn't it? Particularly if she believed, like you, that suicide is a mortal sin?'

The priest nodded. 'That would make sense, surely. Let us hope, for her soul's sake, that she didn't do that.'

'Yes, quite. Maybe you should pray for her as well.'

'Oh, I will, of course. I have done so already.'

Terry got to his feet and held out his hand. 'You've been very helpful, father. Thanks for your time. But if she avoided the sin of suicide, as you hope, then someone else committed a worse one. Of murder.'

35. Location, location

ON MONDAY morning Sarah put her house on the market. It was a straightforward process - absurdly simple, she thought, for such a momentous decision. She chose the estate agent who had given her the highest valuation, and that was it. The family home that had once been the pinnacle of her and Bob's shared ambitions, the symbol of their joint success, was to become a commodity, an advert in a window, a photo on a website, a signboard in the garden. She shouldn't expect an immediate sale, the estate agent warned - this was the dead season, after all, between autumn and spring - but even so he had a few clients on his books who had expressed interest in that sort of property. He would ring them today, if she had no objection.

And so it began. Another change - where would it lead? She picked up a few brochures, of smaller houses and flats which she might afford if the sale went through. But none seemed quite real to her yet. She walked back towards her chambers feeling strange, light-headed, slightly scared. How easy it was to change your life! You just walked into a room, took a decision, and bang, everything was different.

She stopped on Ouse Bridge, and leaned on the parapet, gazing down river. It was a crisp sunny day, a few degrees above freezing. An icy breeze froze her face, blowing dark strands of hair across her eyes. She looked at the old warehouses beside the river, converted into modern luxury apartments, and imagined herself living in one. It seemed an attractive idea. It would be simple, modern, convenient, close to the court and her chambers.

I could walk everywhere, she thought - to the court, the station, the shops. I'd have no need for the bike. I could drink and walk home. I could lie in bed late in the morning. I'd be young again without responsibilities. I'd be a totally different person.

But then I'm a different person already. Aren't I?

A boat came upstream, and passed under the bridge. Two tourists, wrapped up against the cold, waved to her from the upper deck. Sarah waved back. She felt the smile on her face broaden, and let it. Why not? She felt happy - she'd felt happy all morning. Or at least *I think that's what it is*, she thought, still smiling as she walked on, hands thrust deep into her coat, collar turned up against the cold.

If I'm not happy, what am I? Scared? Losing control, behaving like a piece of flotsam on the water? A prey to unstable emotions, acting like a crazy teenager? In *love?*

No, Sarah told herself firmly, not that. Saturday night was an experiment, that's all. A liberating one, certainly - it puts another barrier between me and Bob. I don't need him any more, not for company, not for sex. I've found another man already - look, it's easy! This must be how other people behave, all those young girls in magazines who hop from one bed to another, trying on a new man for size! She giggled to herself. Well, exactly, to see if they fit. It's an important point, after all. Michael had fit nicely, as far as that went. And his body - the rest of it - had been satisfactory too, in fact she'd enjoyed looking at it and touching it as much as the actual sex. He was quite strong, fitter and more muscular than Bob, with less of a belly. Unlike Bob his chest and back were hairless, and most exciting of all his buttocks were smooth too - she had loved the bunched powerful feel of them in her hands and his sudden cry and jerk as she'd drawn her nails across them at his climax.

He'd enjoyed that all right - she hunched her head inside her collar, letting her hair blow forward across her face to hide her smile from two businessmen walking towards her. She half-recognized one of them, and thought *no please, not now*, deliberately avoiding his eyes and hurrying past. She didn't want to meet anyone with this silly smile on her face. She was convinced they'd see right through into her mind - a mind which was entirely, shamelessly occupied with replaying this bedroom movie.

It hadn't been all perfect. There'd been some clumsy, embarrassing moments as well. She'd been surprised when he'd insisted on showering first - it would prolong the excitement, he said, and make them smell beautiful for each other. Sarah had just wanted to get on with it. They'd almost done it in the shower itself, but somehow made it to the bed, where he'd delayed again, spreading a towel to avoid getting the sheets wet. Then he'd come too quickly and she'd begun to feel cold and damp before he'd worked himself up to doing it again.

But she guessed that sort of surprise was to be expected with a stranger - she and Bob had been together so long they knew each movement by heart. This man hadn't kissed her as much as she'd expected, or let her take charge as Bob often had. At times he'd been quite rough and forceful. But that, she found, she'd enjoyed - she'd felt nothing quite like it since Kevin. She remembered the moment when he'd lifted her onto the counter in the hotel bathroom, doing it with her back pressed against the mirror and her legs wrapped round his waist. Bob had never done anything like that. Afterwards they'd showered together, their skins smooth and slippery with the soap. The memories made her feel quite warm and damp between the legs, so that she had to take another turn around the park before she felt cool enough to enter her chambers.

So is this love? She asked herself, settling at her desk and kicking off her shoes as she unwrapped the red ribbons round the papers of the case she was to present tomorrow. No, surely not, she told herself sternly - just a one-night stand, a brief liberating affair. The trouble was, unlike the young people and celebrities in magazines, Sarah had very little experience of such affairs. Her heart, she felt, with delightful, guilty panic, was for once in danger of ruling her head. And that wasn't the way she ran her life, never had been. Not since she was a teenager, anyway, and the wonderful sexy catastrophe of Kevin had swept into her life and almost ruined it for ever. That couldn't, surely, be happening again.

Could it?

When she'd met Emily for lunch on Sunday she'd given her a brief, carefully edited version of her date. It was a curious role reversal; she felt like a teenager hiding the most important part under a mass of spurious detail. So she told Emily about Michael's job, his divorce, his character - even a little about his appearance, but only when he was fully clothed. Nothing about how small and brown his nipples were and how she had bitten one and sucked it to make him cry out. None of that - but she felt herself blushing all the same so that Emily laughed and said: 'Mum! You've fallen for this guy, haven't you?'

'No, he's just a friend, darling,' she'd protested earnestly. 'It probably won't come to anything but at least it's a change.'

'From Dad, you mean?'

'Yes. No, just from being lonely and abandoned, out of date, on the shelf. It's nice to feel ... someone thinks you're attractive.'

'Yes, well, that's good, Mum.' Emily had studied her thoughtfully. 'But you will be careful, won't you? I mean ...'

'Careful how, Emily?' Sarah laughed. 'I do know about contraception, if that's what you mean, darling, I ...'

'Mother!' Emily's eyes widened. 'You haven't, have you?' Their eyes met. When Sarah didn't answer, her daughter's eyes widened still further. 'My God, you have!'

'Is it that obvious?'

'You haven't stopped smiling and blushing since you came in here. Oh my God, Mum - what's going on?'

'Do you mind, Emily? I don't want to hurt you. That's the last thing I want.'

The warm pleasurable memories in Sarah's mind shrank beneath an icy douche of fear. *If I lose Emily because of this I'll never forgive myself - never!*

'No, Mum, why should I be hurt? It's your life, not mine.'

'Yes, but I want you in it, darling. More than anything - much more than any man.'

'Yes, well - I'm not going away. After all you're a free woman - it's not as if you're betraying Dad or anything.' A slow smile spread across Emily's face. 'My God, Mum, you did it! You really went to bed with this guy!'

'Yes.' Sarah smiled shyly, like a child forgiven. 'I didn't mean to, it just happened.'

'Was it good? What was it like?'

'Oh Emily, I'm not going to tell you that. I can't.'

'No.' Emily nodded sagely, as though on reflection she didn't want to know either. 'But it was good, anyway, was it?'

'On the whole it was a good experience, yes.'

'Well, good for you, Mum. This deserves a toast.' Emily pulled a bottle of port out of a cupboard, with two glasses.

'I didn't know you drank port, Emily.'

'Adrian gave it to me.' They clinked their glasses together. 'There is one thing, though, Mum, and I know it's a cheek of me to say it. I mean, you're a lot older than me and all that but ... you *are* in the middle of a divorce, and this guy ... it would be easy to fall for him on the rebound and

... I mean he may seem fine *today* ...'

'But not tomorrow, you mean, when I've had time to think? Yes, darling, I do realise that, of course. Just because I went to bed with him once, it doesn't make him the love of my life or anything like that. Who knows, it may all fizzle out. It's just that, right now - it may seem callous to say it, but he's just what I need.'

'After what Dad did, you mean?'

'Yes. To make me feel like a woman again, and not some shrivelled old husk. A kind of therapy, I suppose.'

Emily laughed. 'You didn't tell him that, did you? That you were using him as a sort of health cure?'

'No.' But Sarah wondered, later, whether Michael had realised all along. She'd turned down his offer of a lift, and travelled home on the train - ostensibly so that she could spend more time with Emily, but the real reason was to give herself time to think. Had she been wise, or incredibly foolish? She didn't know. She might be a mother and a successful barrister, but she had little experience of love affairs. The clear mental focus that brought her such success in the law normally kept her clear of such messy entanglements. She worked with logic, not emotion.

The nearest she had come to anything like this was with that detective, Terry Bateson, and that had ended awkwardly. Nonetheless she caught herself wondering, in the train, what Terry might have been like in bed. Would he have been brusque and masterful, like Michael? Was that what she wanted in a man? At the moment, she decided, she did. She must do - she couldn't get him out of her mind.

Entering her chambers, she spoke briefly to her clerk before closing her office door behind her. But at her desk she found herself, for the first time in years, reading whole pages of her brief without understanding a single word. *Come on woman*, she told herself, *get a grip*. Or you'll look a complete idiot in court tomorrow.

She returned to the first page and started again. In the matter of the Crown vs Hartson the muscles of his thighs were ... *stop it! Concentrate.* Her witness, a shopkeeper, confronted an intruder in his shop when - Sarah's phone rang. *Is it him?* She picked it up nervously.

'Good morning, my love.'

'Oh.' Sarah let her breath out slowly. It wasn't a man's voice, as she had expected. It was a woman's. 'Lucy, it's you!'

'Of course. Who'd you think it was - King Kong?' Lucy Parsons laughed. 'Are you okay? Did you have a good weekend?'

'Yes, quite eventful, thanks. I saw Emily in Cambridge. She was in a play - *A Midsummer Night's Dream*. It was excellent - I saw it twice. Emily was Titania.'

'Well, good for her. Isn't she the hussy who marries a mule?'

'More or less. Puck sprinkles dust on her eyelids, and when she wakes up she falls for the first man she sees.'

'Never happens to me. Each morning I wake up and see Derek, snoring and farting like a pig, and I think - whatever happened to love's young dream?'

Sarah laughed. 'I'll get Emily to send you some fairy dust, shall I?'

'Do that. Ask her to post it first class.' Lucy paused awkwardly, remembering Sarah's divorce. 'How are you, anyway?'

'Not so bad. I put the house on the market this morning.'

'Really? I wish you luck. Listen, Sarah, I've been talking to the police again. DCI Churchill - remember him? Every girl's dream escort.'

'I bet he was pleased to hear from you.'

'Oh, he was, he was. I really made his day. But even so, I managed to squeeze a few more facts out of him about Brenda Stokes - you know, the poor girl they found under the motorway. They've finished the post mortem and the good news is that they've no plans to bring any further charges against Jason Barnes. Not at this stage, anyway.'

'That's tremendous,' Sarah said. 'You mean they're actually beginning to think that someone else killed her after all?'

'They didn't quite go that far, no. But they admit that the evidence isn't conclusive, which is something. Obviously the fact that she was throttled with a scarf came as a surprise to them - they've released that to the press, and they've got a slot on Crimewatch next month about it. So our man Churchill gets his fifteen minutes of fame - he'll love that. But there's no evidence that Jason had anything to do with it, no more than before. None of his DNA on the scarf, for instance. And the injuries to her arm, they're a puzzle too. They look like crush injuries, apparently. One theory is that her arm was run over by a car. But here's the big thing. It seems a couple of her fingernails had still survived, and they examined the dirt still attached to them, in the hope that they'd find microscopic traces of Jason's DNA there from when she scratched him. A long shot, but you know that stuff takes centuries to decay, so it was worth a try, they thought.'

'It wouldn't prove much, would it? He admits they had a fight.'

'Well, that's what I thought, but they did it anyway. And hey presto, guess what they found?'

'What? DNA from a fox?'

'Close, but no. They found human DNA all right, but not from Jason! So the last person whose face she scratched was *someone else*. Not him at all!'

'Goodness! Whose was it?'

'There's the mystery. They checked the national DNA database but didn't come up with anyone. So of course it doesn't prove Jason was innocent but it certainly helps his case. Especially if you put it together with the evidence of that girl Amanda whatshername - Carr - who says she saw Brenda an hour or more after she ran away from Jason by the river. It begins to look more and more as if someone else killed her, not him. Even your pin-up Will Churchill is beginning to accept that, it seems. Grudgingly of course, with the worst possible grace.'

'Great news, Luce. So our first appeal court victory isn't about to be overturned as soon we've won it, after all. Have you traced our charming client to tell him?'

'No can do, I'm afraid. I left a message with his cousin, but he hasn't come back, apparently. Vanished into the wide blue yonder.'

'He didn't leave a forwarding address?'

'Nope. Not a dicky bird.'

'And no mobile number either, I suppose?'

Lucy laughed. 'This lad's been in prison for 18 years, remember. They didn't have mobiles when he went down. He's probably still wondering why he sees so many people in the street talking to themselves and holding their ears.'

'So we have no idea whether he knows Brenda's body's been found, or not?'

Lucy sighed. 'No, 'fraid not. No idea what he feels about it, either. But he hasn't been arrested for any new crime, so far as I know. So the good news is, he's still free. And not guilty too, it seems.'

'Always a bonus. Thanks, Lucy love.' Sarah smiled, and put down the phone.

36. Necessary Ghoul

THE BODY, as usual, looked horrific. More like meat in a butcher's shop than human. Terry had been here many times in the course of his career, and always loathed it. As a young officer, he had shielded himself against the horror by somehow denying the humanity of the bodies on the pathologist's table. They were not human but corpses, meat, a corpus of evidence, something to be examined and studied but not loved. Love was for the relatives, who were shown a body tidied and covered and prettified as much as possible, with only the face showing and of course - crucially for identification purposes - still in its normal place on the front of the skull.

Linda Miles, today's pathologist, seemed untroubled by such thoughts. She was a cheerful, extrovert mother of two whom Terry met at parents' evenings. His daughters had even spent the night at her house when Trude was away. As parents they were friends, but here, in her white overalls, her hair covered by a protective cap, her hands by latex gloves, she looked like a maggot in a meat store. Terry forced down his nausea, and smiled.

'What have you got for us, Linda?'

'Your suspected suicide, you mean?'

'Yes. If that's what she is.' Terry looked at the body on the table. Most of it was mercifully covered by a sheet, but the feet and hands stuck out, lifeless, waxen, still. Like the feet of medieval statues in the Minster - but the souls of those people, if father Roberts was right, must have served their time in purgatory by now and be in heaven, whereas this poor woman's soul might be in everlasting hell.

And where is that, Terry wondered. Under our feet, in some furnace at the earth's molten core? Or here, in this room? He looked around, at the eviscerated body of a man on another table. The skull was sawn open and the brain, heart and liver lay in a set of bloody dishes on the workbench.

Hell is all around us, and we're in it.

'She had cancer, you know,' the pathologist began, brightly. 'Quite an advanced ovarian cancer which had spread - look here.'

Terry glanced, nodded, looked away. 'Could it have been cured?'

'Hm. It was fairly advanced. I wouldn't have put the chances very high, myself.'

'Still, that wasn't what killed her.'

'Oh no. Clearly she was strangled - hanged, I believe, by this scarf.' She pointed to the silk scarf, which had been loosened from the neck and lay in a bag on the workbench, ready to be taken to forensics. 'Pretty fancy scarf. Rich lady, was she?'

'Hardly. Just a writer, living in a rented cottage.' Terry had already given the other half of the scarf, the part still attached to the banisters, to a detective constable to trace where it came from.

'Well, it was the scarf that killed her. No doubt about that.' The pathologist pointed to a dark purple bruise round the neck, where the skin had been crushed and not sprung back.

'Would it have taken long?'

'A few minutes possibly. Her neck wasn't broken, so she suffocated. She'd have lost consciousness within a minute or two, and her heart stopped a short while later.'

'She'd have known what was happening to her, though?'

'Oh yes, she couldn't avoid it. She wasn't drugged or anything, if that's what you're asking. Just a faint trace of alcohol in her blood - a glass of wine, no more than that. She probably had it with her supper.' She indicated a bowl on the side. 'Chicken stew.'

'But she made no attempt to save herself?' Terry asked, averting his eyes.

'No, well, not obviously. There are no scratches on her neck, where she might have tried to claw the scarf away, nothing like that. Just a single small cut, just here, under the chin. Only a couple of millimetres deep, but it could be significant, all the same.'

'Significant of what, exactly?'

'Well, if this was a man, you might wonder if he'd cut himself shaving, in a place like that. But not this lady. Anyway, it's not really a razor cut, more a sharp prick, really, with the pointed end of a knife. Caused before death, not after, not after - there are traces of bleeding. The sort of injury that might be caused by someone holding a knife to her throat. Sticking it in a little so she'd know he meant business.'

Terry peered where she was pointing. The cut, in the pale waxy skin, was scarcely visible. 'Are you sure about that, Linda?'

She raised an ironic eyebrow, as if he were questioning her expertise. 'Am I sure it's a cut, caused with a sharp implement before death? Yes, definitely. Am I sure how it was caused? No, that's less certain. I give you an educated guess, no more.'

'Any other way it could have happened?'

'None that comes to mind, no.' Linda Miles shrugged. 'And then there's this. Look at her wrists. What do you see?'

Again, nothing obvious. Terry shook his head. 'I checked for signs of rope or tape at the time. Is there something I missed?'

She smiled, took a large magnifying glass from the workbench, and held it over the left wrist. 'Try this, detective inspector. Sherlock Holmes carried one all the time.' She focussed a bright lamp on the wrist, and moved a fine pointed needle beneath the lens. 'We've got photos on computer, of course, but I like to use the old methods first. See? Here, here, and here. It's a straight line. She only had fine hairs on her wrist but they've been torn out, do you see. And the same on the other hand too.'

A pulse began to throb in Terry's throat - excitement this time, not revulsion. 'You mean, her wrists were taped?'

'That's what it looks like to me. If you fold her wrists together, behind her back - we did it earlier, and took photographs - then you see exactly where the tape would have run, and where it didn't. There are still hairs where her wrists were pressed together. That's why she didn't try to tear the scarf from her throat. She couldn't - she was bound.' The pathologist's eyes met Terry's, triumphant, excited.

'So this isn't a suicide after all?'

'Not unless you can tell me some way this woman could tape her hands behind her back, jab a knife in her throat, hang herself, and then untape her hands when she'd finished, no.' She studied Terry quizzically. 'You didn't find any tape, did you?'

'No, not a trace. Unless the SOCOs are hiding it.'

'Well, then.' Linda Miles's eyes gleamed with amusement. 'Not only did our suicide have to remove the tape after death, she must have tidied it away neatly somewhere before going back to lie on the floor where she was found. Good ghost story but not very likely, is it? However houseproud she was.'

Terry smiled, relieved. He felt grateful for the efforts of this necessary ghoul. 'You're a genius, Linda. Her soul's probably blessing you now from heaven. Or purgatory, perhaps.'

'What?'

'Suicides go straight to hell - didn't you know? A priest told me. But victims end up in heaven, thank God. After a spell in purgatory, that is.'

'Really.' Her eyes met his. 'Don't mock it, Terry. We only deal with the body here. What happens afterwards, that's not my province. Did she have family?'

Terry sighed, recalling his efforts to answer this question in the past few days. 'No one local - just an elderly mother in Peterborough, who's reluctant to travel. A neighbour identified the body. Before you ...' he glanced at the table '... started your work.'

'No husband then? Partner, whatever?'

'Not so far as we know. Why?'

'Well, there's one other thing you should see. I'll need a hand to turn her over. If you take her legs, there ...' Briskly, Linda Miles slipped her hands under the shoulders of the corpse while Terry, fighting down the urge to vomit, took hold of the cold, waxy legs. 'Ready? One, two three ...' Together, they lifted the body and turned it. For a dreadful second Terry felt his hand slipping, and had a vision of the dead woman falling to the floor; then she was safely over, face down like meat on a slab.

'See there? Those marks, what do they suggest to you?'

Terry looked where the pathologist was pointing, and saw a set of lines, like thin bruises, criss-crossing each other across the pale flabby buttocks. 'Whip marks?' he suggested.

'Exactly. A whip or a cane, something like that, thin and hard. Someone's been punishing this woman.'

Terry thought back, to the dead woman's bedroom. Sex books, condoms, and now this. There'd been no sign of a whip or a cane, though. 'You think the killer caned her first?'

'Someone did. That would fit in with the ritual nature of this hanging, the way you describe it. It could be some sort of sado-masochistic thing, gone wrong.'

'Or perhaps not wrong,' Terry said thoughtfully. 'Perhaps he meant to kill her all along. But punish her first.'

'On the other hand, sadistic rituals like this are often associated with sex,' Linda said. 'And there's no sign of intercourse. I checked.'

'She wasn't raped, then?' Terry said grimly, staring at the bruises. How anyone could do this to a woman for pleasure escaped him entirely.

'No. No vaginal tearing or trauma, nothing to indicate forcible penetration.'

'Can you tell if she had sex at all, the day she died? Did you find semen, DNA?'

'Unfortunately not. If she did have sex that day it was perfectly consensual, and she seems to have bathed afterwards. Her vagina was quite clean - in fact her whole body was clean, apart from the dirt where she fell on the floor and soiled herself. I checked carefully. Traces of soap and bubble bath salts. But no male pubic hairs, semen, saliva, nothing like that.'

'So her killer was a sadist, but not a rapist, is that what you're saying?'

'So it seems.' A sad smile flickered over the pathologist's face. 'Not that that was much consolation to her, poor lady.'

37. Lovers' Gateway

JANE CARTER spent the day in Crockey Hill, interviewing Alison Grey's neighbours. They were hardly neighbours in the sense that people in the town would understand it, but they did live within half a mile of her house. No one, however, knew much about Alison Grey. Most people had seen her once or twice, driving her Rover down the track to her house, but few had spoken to her for more than a moment or two. It was something to do with the isolation of the house, Jane concluded, and the lack of a focal point in the village. No shop, no pub, no school - the only place people were likely to bump into each other was the garage, and then only rarely.

The garage staff recalled her as a pleasant woman whose elderly Rover had needed a new cambelt at its last service. They'd tried to sell her a Toyota Auris, but after a test drive she'd refused. She was comfortable with the Rover, she'd said, it suited her style of driving. They shook their heads at such folly, but were shocked to learn of her death. They had no idea if she had enemies, or any friends either.

Terry had asked Jane to trace any male visitors Alison might have had, but it didn't prove easy. Mrs Phillips, the neighbour who had offered to feed the cat, had seen trade or delivery vans drive up to Alison's house from time to time; there'd been several of those. A small red hatchback had been there for a couple of days, and she'd seen a large black car too, from time to time. But what make the cars were, who they belonged to, or what their owners' business with Alison was, she had no idea - why should she? If she was asked to give a list of visitors to her own house over the last month she would find it difficult.

For Jane, it was the connection with Peter Barton, rather than a possible lover, that set alarm bells ringing in her mind. Here was a woman, dead, with a noose around her neck, living alone in an isolated house near woods with a bridleway running through them. After Peter's earlier assaults on women, all living alone near footpaths or cycletracks - the coincidence seemed too great to ignore. But so far she had no conclusive evidence that the house had been broken into, let alone that Peter Barton had been there. For all she knew, he might be in Australia by now.

She walked down a track behind a transport café, where the bridleway joined the main York-Selby road, by woods north of Alison Grey's house. There was a quiet leafy track running through the woods, and a farmhouse nearby. Behind the house was a paddock with a pony in it, and beyond that a further strip of woodland. Peering through the leafless trees, she could just make out the outline of Alison Grey's house a quarter of a mile away.

She looked around, wondering. The bridleway ran through the woods to her left, before taking a sharp right turn along the track down which she'd come. But what if someone coming from York turned left instead, skirting the paddock and going through the woods behind the house? Could someone approach Alison's house that way? It would be easy enough, surely. No one would see a person doing that, except the occupants of this farmhouse.

She knocked on the farmhouse door. A dog inside barked fiercely. After a few moments a woman opened the door, holding a straining alsatian on a lead. 'Yes?'

'Police.' Jane showed her ID. 'We're making enquiries about the death of your neighbour. A woman called Alison Grey?'

'Oh right. You'd best come in. Don't mind the dog, he's just a pup. Give him a pat, he'll be fine. Max, that's *enough*!'

Jane followed the woman into a spacious, fitted kitchen. A warm scent of stew came from the Aga. The young dog sniffed her legs enthusiastically, chased a cat into the hall, then slumped down on a bed in the corner. The woman grinned. 'Never a moment's peace, with that animal.'

'He's good security though, isn't he, living out here on your own?'

'That's the idea, any road. Scare any burglar shitless, he would. Not that I thought I needed protection out here, until now. What happened to Alison, poor lass?'

'That's what we're trying to find out,' Jane said. 'Did you know her well?'

'Hardly. Met her once when she moved in, that's all. She was renting it to write a book, I believe.'

'It's not her house then?'

'No. Belonged to Cartwrights once, but they retired and moved to Elvington. Sold it to an agency in York. I thought they'd do it up, but maybe they get more for the rent, I don't know. There's not that many wants to live out here these days.'

'Do you know the name of the agency?'

'I don't, I'm afraid. My husband might. He'll be in for his lunch in a bit. Will you have a cup of tea?'

'Yes, thanks.' While the kettle was boiling Jane learned that the woman's name was Carol Richards, and her husband owned most of the woods and fields east of the A19. She asked about the bridleway. At its nearest point it was only about twenty yards from the house. 'Do you get many people along here?'

'Not many, this time of year. A few joggers, kids on mountain bikes, things like that.'

'You haven't noticed anyone suspicious? Over the last few days, especially?'

Mrs Richards frowned thoughtfully as she poured the tea. 'Can't say I have, no. Daft buggers, you'd think they had summat better to do.' She laughed. 'I did catch one lad staring at the house, but Max barked and that were it - gone! Sugar?'

'No thanks. When was this?'

'Oh, three four days since.'

'Would you recognise the man if you saw him again?'

'No, love. Just a lad in a black woolly hat and anorak. He could run though, I'll give him that.' As she handed out the tea a thought struck her. 'Why? You don't think he could have owt to do with Alison, do you? Like yon feller pestering women in Bishopthorpe and Naburn? I read about him in the *Press*.'

'We're checking out all possibilities, Mrs Richards. Did you see this man again?'

'No, can't say I did. But then anyone could go along that bridleway. I wouldn't hear them, so long as they're quiet.'

'What if they went straight on, through the woods towards Alison Grey's house?'

'Same difference. The dog would bark if he heard summat, but he's asleep half time, and pestering cats the rest. Dumb mutt!'

'What about Friday night?' she asked. 'Did you notice anything unusual then?'

Carol Richards thought for a moment. 'Can't help you there, I'm afraid. I was at whist drive in Selby - I go each Friday with my mum. And Ian was out drinking with his mates.'

'So even if the dog saw him and barked himself sick, no one would have noticed?'

'Not while I got back, no.' A tractor pulled up outside. 'Here's Ian. See what he says.'

Her husband, a big bluff man, knocked off his boots in the porch as his wife put his lunch on the table. She offered Jane a bowl of stew too, which she accepted gratefully. Mopping up the last of his stew with a thick slice of bread, Ian Richards told her the name of the property company which owned Alison Grey's house. He confirmed he'd been out drinking on Friday night. He'd seen nothing unusual at Alison's house. But on the way home he'd noticed a car parked in a gateway along the road to Wheldrake, a couple of fields along.

'I thought of stopping because it's one of my fields, see, I don't like folk parking there. They've got no right.'

'But you didn't stop?' Jane asked hopefully.

'Nah, what's the point? I'd only get a load of abuse. Kids, no respect, have they?'

'What time was this?'

'About half eleven. On my way home from the pub.'

Probably over the limit, Jane thought, noting the veins round his nose. But that wasn't the crime she was investigating. 'Did you see anyone in the car?'

'Nay, lass. I only had a glance, but it was all misted up. Probably having a shag on the back seat, randy young sods. Like we did once.' He glanced at his wife and grinned, showing several teeth missing.

'What sort of car was it?'

'Now there I *can* help you. Nissan Primera. Red, five door. My daughter's got one, see. Good reliable runner. Spacious, too, with the back seats down.'

Surprised by the accuracy of the information, Jane noted it down. 'You didn't get the number, did you?'

'No, sorry. It wasn't new though. A few years old.'

'Don't worry. Can you show me this gateway?'

''Course. If you come along with me.' He got up, wiped his mouth with the back of his hand, and gave his wife a smile and a slap on the bottom, before leading the way outside. 'You won't find no car tracks though, love, if that's what you're after. We've been lifting carrots all morning. Follow the tractor in your car, I'll show you.'

He was right. The gateway - really just an entrance to a field with a rope strung across it - had been churned up by tractor tyres. Three huge vehicles were still at work. Part of the field was covered with straw, to keep the frost off the carrots. The rest was a sea of mud. It was pointless to ask the SOCOs to have a look, Jane realised. But the information was interesting nonetheless. She stood beside the gateway, thinking. In addition to Terry Bateson's theory about a lover, she had two more possibilities now - a jogger, and the driver of this car. If Alison's death wasn't suicide, that is.

If it was Peter Barton, he could have come along the bridleway. Either cycling, as before, or on foot. He'd shown no interest in cars, though. So what did this red car mean?

Coincidence, or significance? Courting couple, or killer?

The carrot field extended back to a wood, behind which was the Richards' farmhouse. She couldn't see that from here, but what she could see, on her left towards the village, was the track from the road to Alison Grey's house. She could see the house clearly from here, with the white SOCO van and muddy green Rover parked outside. To her left, the carrot field extended to the barbed wire fence round Alison's garden.

The place where she stood was quiet apart from the tractors, and occasional cars swishing past. A couple of nights ago, she thought, before they started lifting the carrots, this field would have been covered in straw. It would be quite easy to walk from the gateway to the garden, leaving no tracks. In the middle of the night no one would see you coming, or know that your car - a red Nissan Primera - was parked here by the gate. No one driving on the road would think to look for someone walking across the straw field, in the dark. But anyone approaching the house through the field would see by the lights which rooms were occupied. If the curtains weren't drawn he might even be able to see inside.

It might be something, it might be nothing, Jane thought, turning back to her car. I'll ask the SOCOs to check for wisps of straw in the house.

38. On the Carpet

TERRY BATESON tried to shield his daughters from his work as much as possible. Their world, he hoped, was safer and more innocent than the one he worked in. They had their jealousies and squabbles, of course, and Jessica was still not happy with her geography teacher, Mrs Murton, but the violence and cruelty of the criminal world was something he wanted to protect them from if he could. They'd suffered enough with the death of their mother; there was no need to burden them with other deaths and assaults.

For this reason, *Crimewatch* was a programme he usually switched off. But it was different when it featured a case he had been involved in. He briefed Trude to help him get the girls to bed early, read them both stories, and then settled on the sofa for the dubious pleasure of watching his boss make his debut as a media star.

It was typical of Will Churchill to have taken over this case. He had let Terry, quite literally, do the initial spadework - carefully excavating the body of Brenda Stokes from beneath the ring road, fending off complaints from the Highway Authority about traffic disruption, calling in forensic archaeologists to examine the body, checking the files of the original prosecution to see if there was any way the discovery could be used to put Jason Barnes back in prison. But when the interest of the national media was aroused, everything changed. It became a high profile case which it was clearly his duty to lead.

'It's a responsibility shared, Terence old son,' he'd said, with his hand on Terry's shoulder. 'This is too much of a burden, I recognise that. So I'll deal with the media, keep them off your back, while you focus on Alison Grey and these other assaults. After all, it's ancient history, this business of Brenda Stokes. You want to be at the cutting edge, young DI like you, dealing with what really matters to the community.'

So there he was, Terry thought bitterly, having his face powdered by make-up artists in some TV studio in London, while I struggle to get my kids to bed. It was, of course, typical of Churchill to rub in the fact that Terry was older than him and of junior rank. Churchill loved that. An appearance on *Crimewatch* could only help him rise further.

It was a short item, three or four minutes, no more. There was a ghoulish introduction about the discovery of the hand, followed by a clip of the excavations which Terry had supervised, a photo of a young pretty looking Brenda Stokes, a summary of the original trial and appeal, and a short interview with a serious, competent looking DCI Will Churchill. He outlined the forensic evidence they had found - the injuries to her skull and arm, the way she had been dressed, and the mystery about how she had got from Landing Lane, where she had last been seen with Jason Barnes, to the ring road where her body had been found. There was a close-up of the fragments of scarf found round her neck, enhanced to make the pattern much clearer. Will Churchill appealed for witnesses, and then it was over.

Three days later, Will Churchill called Terry and Jane into his office. There had been a gratifying response to the television appeal, but it would take weeks to respond to all the leads they had been given. 'The usual array of nutters and fantasists,' he told them. 'But one or two a bit more promising. So this is going to take a fair bit of my time. Meanwhile,' he said, leaning back in his black leather chair, 'we need some progress on this business of Alison Grey. The *Evening Press* article hinted at suicide, but you're treating it as murder, is that right?'

Terry nodded. 'On the basis of the pathologist's report, yes, sir. That's what we'll be saying to the coroner.'

'In that case I want it sorted - fast. The last thing we need is another horror like this on our patch. It's this same pervert who's been pestering women on the cyclepath, isn't it?'

'That's certainly a possibility, sir, yes' said Terry cautiously.

'More than a possibility, surely,' Churchill said scornfully. 'Single woman living alone, hanged with a scarf from her staircase. Didn't he try a similar trick with that other woman, Lizzie something?'

'Bolan. Yes. Tried to throttle her with her dressing gown cord. But she drove him off.'

'Well, obviously this woman didn't,' said Churchill with heavy sarcasm. 'Hence the result. If you'd caught this young bastard earlier, she'd still be alive.'

Terry bit his lip, controlling his temper with difficulty. This wasn't the first time. Interviews with Will Churchill always made his blood boil. Ever since the man had come to York, parachuted into the job Terry had expected to be his, they had prowled around each other stiff-legged, like two dogs with one bone. Neither liked or understood the other. In his charitable moments, Terry told himself that Churchill must have been a good detective once. But if so, that had been in Essex, not here. Since he'd arrived in York there had been two major cases already in which Churchill had been grossly, spectacularly wrong, and Terry had been right.

'If it was him, sir, yes.'

'So what are you doing to find him?' Churchill demanded brusquely. Jane Carter watched uncomfortably, surprised by the hostility between her superiors.

'Peter Barton, do you mean?'

'No, the Queen of Sheba. Who d'you think?'

'Well, we've got a major search on. All the obvious places.' For the next ten minutes Terry detailed the results of their search. Every known associate - not that there were many - of Peter Barton had been interviewed, without result. His photo, description and fingerprints had been circulated to every police force in England. His mother's house had been watched. All known squats and hostels in York had been visited. Farmers had been contacted, and the woods and farmland around Crockey Hill searched. Uniformed officers had visited cycletracks and bridleways, showing people Peter's photo and asking if they'd seen anyone like him.

'All of which has led to what, exactly?' Churchill asked impatiently.

'A number of leads, but none that proved positive.'

'What about the SOCOs' report on the house? What evidence have you got to nail him when he finally does turn up? If we're not all in our graves by then.'

'Which house?' Terry asked.

'Alison Grey's, of course. I've seen the report on Lizzie Bolan's.'

'Well, that's just it, sir, there's nothing conclusive,' Terry said. 'There were plenty of fingerprints, but none of them were his.'

'So? He probably wore gloves, like last time.'

'Maybe, yes. We can't tell. But if there was an intruder we know where he got in. The downstairs toilet window was open, probably for the cat to go in and out - she didn't have a cat door. There were traces of mud on the floor, but the uniform lads went in that way too, so it could easily have come off their boots.'

'Any other traces? Footprints, fibres, that sort of thing?'

'Same story really. The ground outside the window is gravel, so it wouldn't show much even if the uniforms hadn't trampled all over it clambering to get in.'

Churchill sighed and rolled his eyes. 'Didn't they know it was a crime scene?'

'They're only young, sir. I expect they hoped they were going to save a life.'

Churchill leaned back in his chair, glaring at Terry with blatant hostility. 'What do you mean, Terence *if* there was an intruder? You think she was hanged by a Martian?'

We can do without this, Terry thought. We'll never solve this if it's a pissing competition. He drew a deep breath.

'Well, sir, it's likely that this woman had a boyfriend. Maybe one, maybe several - we don't know. We found a sex manual and a packet of condoms in her bedside drawer. So either this lady liked blowing balloons, or she had an active sex life. And another thing - this scarf she was strangled with. It was pure silk, quite expensive. Much fancier than the rest of her clothes.'

'Any DNA on the scarf?'

'Only hers, sir, unfortunately.'

'Pity. So? What are you saying?'

'Well, maybe this scarf was a gift, sir. From a rich boyfriend perhaps. What I'd like to know is who her partner - or partners - were. Maybe he knows something about this. At the very least he could say what she was like.'

'If young Peter the pervert killed her, this is irrelevant,' Churchill said. 'What are you trying to do? Ruin the poor lady's reputation? Embarrass her lovers for the sake of it?'

That's rich, Terry thought, from a man who has a new girlfriend every month. 'No, of course, not, sir,' he said calmly. 'What I mean is, one of them may have been there on the night. He may even have been the killer. Another thing - her mobile phone's missing. It's not in the house. And the neighbour, Mrs Phillips, mentioned a couple of cars she'd seen there occasionally - a small blue hatchback and a large black saloon. We need to check those out too.'

'Drop it, Terence, for Christ's sake.' Churchill shook his head incredulously. 'What are we, the morals police? What does it matter, who this lady did or didn't screw, whether they were married and so on? The most likely thing is, she was topped by this nasty little pervert who assaulted the other women. The one you should have caught earlier.'

He smiled in grim satisfaction, leaning back in his leather chair while Terry and Jane stood on the carpet like two guilty schoolkids, waiting to be dismissed. 'What do you say, Sergeant Carter?'

'Well, sir, I agree that Peter Barton's top of our list,' Jane began cautiously. 'But as far as we know he gets about by bike - this mountain bike of his - and we haven't been able to turn up any sign of that so far. No tyre tracks on the cyclepath, even - and the farmer's wife, Mrs Richards, hadn't seen any cyclists round there ....'

'He has got feet, this lad, I suppose?' Churchill sneered. 'He can walk?'

'Yes, sir, of course, but that's the trouble. We haven't been able to turn up any footprints as yet, despite all the mud in the fields round about. Because of it, in a way.'

'Really? Tell me about that.'

Jane spread a map on the table in front of their boss. She showed him Alison's house, and the Richards' farmhouse separated from it by a strip of woodland. The bridlepath came towards the farmhouse from Fulford and turned right towards the A19, so anyone approaching Alison's house from it would have had to go through the woods first. The woods had been searched for footprints but none found. And the field between the woods and the house was being harvested for carrots, it was hopeless. Parts of it were covered by straw, the rest was like the battle of the Somme. 'So,' she shrugged. 'No joy there. It's the same for our third possibility.'

'What third possibility?'

'The car the farmer saw in the gateway. A red Nissan Primera.' Jane pointed out the spot where the car had been parked. 'Anyone approaching the house from the gateway would either have to walk down the road, where people could see him, or cross the carrot field in the same way as someone coming from the woods. The only faint clue that he might have come that way are a few wisps of straw on the kitchen floor. But as the

SOCOs pointed out, they might just have blown in when she opened the back door.'

'But it could have been your intruder?'

'It could have been, sir, yes. Whichever way he approached the house, from the woods or the gateway, he'd have had to cross that carrot field with the straw. And got scraps of it on his shoes.'

'Hm.' Churchill drummed his fingers on the desk. 'Any TWOCs on this Peter Barton's record? Does he have a licence, a car of his own?'

'No sir. He doesn't seem to be interested in that.'

'You can probably forget about the car then. Got a licence number?'

'Just two letters, sir. Probably XB.'

'Well, check it out of course, but it's probably just coincidence. Couple of teenage lovers, something like that.'

That was typical of Churchill, Terry thought. Jumping to conclusions instead of carefully sifting through the evidence; dismissing details before evaluating them. To judge by her expression, a similar thought was passing through Jane Carter's mind. The longer he had worked with this young sergeant, the more he was coming to appreciate her. She might not be the most charming or decorative of female detectives, but her work rate was second to none. And she was unlikely to forget about that car, until its presence was fully explained.

'Anything else I should know about?' Churchill asked.

'Well, there is one other thing,' Jane said hesitantly.

'Yes, what's that?'

'There's a barbed wire fence between the garden and the field. So anyone entering the garden from the field would have to climb over it, and back out again too. So I got the SOCOs to check the barbed wire and they found a small scrap of cloth, snagged on the wire. Whoever climbed that fence has a hole in his pants. The lab are checking it for DNA.'

Churchill nodded approvingly at Jane. 'Which would nail young Peter if it's his, wouldn't it?'

'If it matches the sample I took when I arrested him, sir, yes. But they weren't too hopeful. It was only a small scrap of cloth, but if he'd been sweating ...'

'Let's hope he was,' Churchill glanced at Terry with contempt. 'Your sergeant's moving ahead of you, DI Bateson. She'll have your job next.'

For a moment no one spoke. Terry and Jane were both embarrassed, for different reasons. Jane was pleased by the praise, but felt it was devalued by the man it had come from. Perhaps she'd joined a duff department, she thought; both her superiors were incompetent. Well, if that was so, it could be an opportunity - if she solved this murder on her own, it might help her a step up the ladder. Unless one of these two snatched the triumph from her, to use in their own private feud. Well, she'd cross that bridge when she came to it.

Terry was annoyed that the old rivalry between himself and Will Churchill had surfaced so obviously in front of a promising, young detective like Jane. Churchill had relished humiliating him in front of her, and some of the barbs hurt.

But there was one great relief. Terry had fully expected Will Churchill to end the interview by taking over the case himself. But he hadn't done so. Leaving the room, Terry wondered why.

Perhaps his boss was simply too busy. His real talent, after all, was not detective work but networking, arselicking, climbing the greasy pole to become Chief Constable before the age of fifty. He'd been on far more courses than Terry, had a CV many pages longer. Maybe he was waiting until the case was eventually solved, and planning to take the credit then. Without even getting out of his expensive leather office chair.

Or could there be another reason? Churchill was devious, but not entirely stupid. All his comments had focussed on Peter Barton. Catch Peter, Churchill seemed to think, and you'd catch the murderer. It had been virtually an instruction. But what if Churchill knew, or suspected, that the case was more complicated than that? What if he was deliberately sending them on a false trail, so that he could take over the case later, when they had definitely got it wrong?

It's another possibility, Terry told himself wryly. That's the thing with a murder enquiry. You shouldn't rule anything in, or anything out.

39. Landlord

IN THE days before Christmas the streets near York Minster were jammed with shoppers seeking last-minute gifts. It was a good area to look, particularly if you had a difficult relative or demanding spouse to please; the narrow medieval streets were full of shops selling unlikely and quite useless decorative items such as suits of armour, mediaeval swords, and sets of wooden Russian dolls. But it must pay, Terry Bateson thought; the rents in this area were far too high for any failed enterprise to last long.

He found the door to Alison Grey's landlord - *Town and Country Holdings* - squeezed between a trendy internet café and a shop selling elaborate string puppets from Thailand. There was a narrow window beside the door, with photographs of properties to rent, and housing developments in various stages of completion. Terry climbed a narrow staircase, discreetly lit by recessed spotlights and decorated by framed Victorian cartoons. At the top of the stairs a glass door opened into a brightly lit modern suite of offices. A young woman was talking on the phone. She waved him to a seat. After a couple of minutes she put the phone down and treated him to a bright, professional smile.

'Sorry about that, sir. How can I help?'

Terry showed her his card. The smile faded slightly, to be replaced by a puzzled frown. 'We're investigating the death of one of your tenants, I'm afraid. A lady called Alison Grey? She rented a house in Crockey Hill.'

'Oh. I read about that. Terrible. She hanged herself, didn't she?'

'She was hanged, certainly,' Terry said. 'But we haven't had the inquest yet.' He took an envelope from his pocket. 'We found this contract in her desk drawer. That is your company, isn't it?'

The young woman studied the contract briefly. 'Yes, yes it is. I'm so glad you're here. When I read the story I thought we should do something but couldn't think what. It's so hard to take in and - she's really dead?'

'I'm afraid so.' Terry watched her carefully, wondering how much of the distress and confusion were real. Most of it, he thought.

'Oh dear. Poor woman. I spoke to her a few times on the phone, and she sounded quite normal. Why would she do such a thing?'

'That's what we're trying to find out. Do you have a file on the house?'

'Yes, of course. What do you want to know?'

'When she came, what sort of tenant she was - anything and everything, really.'

'Here you are, then. That's her - Alison Grey.' She turned the computer screen so that Terry could see it from the front of the desk. 'Came - what? - eighteen months ago. Before my time. Regular payment by standing order; we let the house furnished, put in a new damp course, repaired some windows, some trouble with the Aga last year, installed dishwasher and new washing machine - is this sort of thing any use to you?'

'You say you spoke to her on the phone,' Terry said. 'What sort of woman was she?' .

'Ummm - quite a normal, friendly sort of lady I would say. "Teacher/writer" it says here under "Occupation". That's probably why she chose a quiet house in the country.'

'Was she a sociable person? Did she have any friends, partner, that sort of thing?'

The young woman shook her head. 'I'm sorry, I wouldn't know that. It was just, you know, maintenance calls - if a tile blew off the roof, or there was a problem with the plumbing. She'd ring and we'd send someone to fix it.'

'So she never came here, into the office?'

'Hm, not that I remember, no ....' The young woman touched her cheek with a manicured fingernail, thinking. 'She may have come in at the beginning, of course, to see what we had, be shown a few properties. But I only started a year ago, so she'd have met my predecessor, Muriel Hartson. See - there's her signature on the contract. Michael might know more, of course. He usually vets the tenants, you know, to see if they're ok.'

'Michael?'

'My boss. It's his agency really. Do you want to talk to him?'

'If I could.'

The young woman smiled. 'You're lucky. He's usually out on site, while I hold the fort.' She spoke briefly into an intercom, then pointed to a door. 'Through there.'

As Terry walked through the door, the man in the office got up, walked round his desk, and held out his hand. 'How do you do? Michael Parker. You're from the police, I hear.'

'Yes. DI Bateson.' The name meant nothing to Terry. The man in front of him was tall, about his own height, with a square lined face and dark hair greying at the temples. He was in his mid forties but looked fit, as though he worked out regularly and spent a lot of time in the fresh air. He wore jeans, a work shirt and a leather jacket. All of this Terry saw in the first second.

But what his mind couldn't quite process, was where he had seen the man before.

'Have a seat.' The man waved him to a chair in front of his desk, and resumed his own place behind it. 'Maggie tells me you've come about this unfortunate tenant of ours. Alison Grey?'

'Yes, that's right.' Terry sat down slowly, thinking *why do I hate this guy so much?* He must have done something - what is it? He's not on the child abuse register, is he? He felt his heart pumping with sudden, unaccountable fury. He took a deep breath to calm himself, before asking: 'How well did you know her?'

'Know her? Hardly at all.' The man, it seemed, did not recognize him. His face was calm, quiet, controlled.

'But she was your tenant, wasn't she? Your secretary said you would have vetted her when she first arrived.'

'Oh yes, well that would be normal. I like to meet new tenants before handing over the key.'

'Presumably you take up references, that sort of thing?'

'Normally we do, yes, unless ...' He paused, as if thinking. 'I seem to remember she was a teacher, she'd worked overseas for the British Council - would that be right? And she needed somewhere quiet to write books of some kind - schoolbooks, I think. That seemed quite satisfactory.'

'Yes, she did that,' Terry agreed. One part of his mind kept up the conversation, while another was searching frantically through a database of faces, thinking *where have I met this man before, and why do I have such a strong reaction to him?* He must be a conman, a fraudster of some kind; he's clearly not a common thug, not with a business like this. 'Did you speak to her often?'

'Often? No - very rarely.' Something - either the questions or more likely Terry's cold relentless stare - seemed to be getting under the man's skin. He flushed, his initial bonhomie fading. 'She was just a tenant, that's all. She paid her rent on time, contacted Maggie occasionally about repairs, and ... got on with her life. Look, I'm sorry if that sounds callous. Her death is a tragedy, of course, a terrible thing, but we have about thirty tenants here, and three major building projects ongoing. It's the tenants who cause me trouble who take up my time, not ladies who sit at home writing books. Not until they kill themselves, anyway.'

So he thinks it's suicide as well, Terry thought. That *Evening Press* article has a lot to answer for.

'Did she have any friends, do you know? Boyfriends, perhaps?'

The flush faded, to be replaced by a look of cold irritation. 'Look, inspector whatever your name is, I don't wish to be rude but I hardly see it as part of my role to pry into the private lives of my tenants. If they pay the rent, and keep the house clean and tidy, then that's all I ask. This lady Alison Grey, she was a mature person and I'm sure she had friends and romantic attachments like everyone else. But how many and who they were, it's none of my business to know.'

'I understand,' Terry said. 'But she was murdered, you see. So we need to find out.'

'Murdered?' Michael Parker sat back, shocked, in his chair. 'But ... that can't be right. The *Evening Press* article said she was found hanged. I've got it somewhere ...' He fumbled among the papers on his desk, found a newspaper cutting, stared at it numbly 'I thought that meant ... suicide. Doesn't it?'

'No sir,' Terry said briskly, 'I'm afraid not. We did suspect suicide at first, when we spoke to the press. But after the post mortem, we're treating this case as murder.'

'But - how?' The man had gone quite pale, Terry noted. Clearly this meant more to him than at first appeared. 'I mean, what makes you think that?'

'I'm not at liberty to go into details, sir, I'm afraid. But since this is a murder enquiry, I really do need to know what you can tell us about this lady's friends and acquaintances.'

'Yes. Yes, of course.' Michael Parker leaned forwards, his fingers nervously massaging his forehead. 'Poor Alison. What an awful way to go.' He rubbed his brow for a moment in silence, then looked up, meeting Terry's eyes in surprise, as if he had forgotten he was there. 'That was her name, wasn't it?' He forced a wry smile. 'It's surprising how news like this affects you, isn't it? I'd quite convinced myself it was suicide, but this - it makes it all so much worse somehow. Though I don't see why it should. I mean, a death is a death.'

'Murder is a shocking thing,' Terry said quietly.

'Yes, yes it is. I mean, I didn't know her well, as I said, but the fact is I was in this woman's house only what? A day or so before she died. Talking to her quite normally. So of course I wondered why she'd hanged herself but somehow this - it's a second shock.'

Terry studied him coolly, his senses on alert. 'You were in the house, sir? When was this exactly?'

'I'd have to check my diary.' He pulled a small, handheld computer from his jacket pocket. 'Yes, it was a Wednesday. Wednesday afternoon.'

'And why was that?'

'She'd rung Maggie to complain about a problem with the central heating. It wasn't working properly, she said. So I went to check it out. I went all over the house bleeding the radiators and it worked much better. A simple thing but she'd been living in hot countries for years and had forgotten how they worked. She was very grateful. I thought I'd solved her problem.'

'How long did you stay there, exactly?'

Michael hesitated, thinking deeply. 'Oh, about an hour or so, maybe more. However long it takes to check the central heating and drink a cup of tea.'

'So you talked to Alison, did you?'

'Yes. She seemed quite happy. Especially when the house warmed up.'

'What did you talk about, apart from the central heating?'

'Oh, how her work was going - quite well, she said. How strange she found it living in England again after all the places she'd been.'

'Did she say anything about her health?'

'Her health? No, I don't think so.' He frowned, as if puzzled by the question. 'Why, was there anything wrong with it?'

'She'd been recently diagnosed with cancer.'

'Really? How terrible. Poor woman, her luck was really out, wasn't it?'

'She said nothing about that to you?'

'No, she didn't. But that's hardly surprising, is it? It's not something you would discuss with ... just anyone.'

'No,' Terry agreed. 'I suppose not. And you were just her landlord, were you? You didn't have any other sort of relationship with her? A sexual relationship, perhaps?'

Terry watched the man closely as the implications of his question sank in. He faced Terry coolly, not moving a muscle. 'No,' he said simply. 'Nothing like that.'

No strong reaction, no exaggerated protestations of innocence. Was he lying? Terry wondered. It was impossible to tell. Just a simple, blank denial. And those eyes staring at him coolly - the eyes of a man who understood the question, acknowledged it was reasonable, but had answered it and wanted to move on. Terry, however, was not quite ready to drop it just yet.

'So you wouldn't, for instance, have given her an expensive silk scarf?'

'Scarf?'

'Yes, sir. That's what she was hanged with, didn't you know? A Jacques Rocher silk scarf. I'm told they cost around £50.'

'No, of course not. I never gave her anything.' The face didn't move a muscle, but was there the slightest flicker of shock, panic - something anyway - in the eyes? Terry let the silence build, waiting for a further response. To his surprise, none came.

'Very well, sir, since you knew the lady, I have to ask you this. Where were you on that Friday night, 2nd December, from seven in the evening until three the following morning?'

'That's easy.' Michael relaxed slightly, turning back to his handheld diary. 'I was at a farmhouse development we have near Scarborough. There was a crisis there - I'd set up a meeting with the builders to sort things out. I was going to Cambridge next day so it was urgent. I set out from here at about two in the afternoon and was there all evening until about ten. Then I had a meal in Scarborough, walked on the beach for a while, and drove home.'

'Getting home when?' Terry asked, noting this down.

'Oh, I don't know, about one maybe - pretty late anyway, I know that. For heaven's sake, you're not treating me as a suspect, are you?'

'Not at the moment, sir, no,' said Terry blandly. 'These builders, they can confirm you were with them, can they?'

'Yes, of course.'

Terry noted down the names and phone numbers of the builders and the restaurant. 'Thank you, sir. Now, since you were in the house, I'm afraid I'll have to ask you to come down to the station to give your fingerprints, if you wouldn't mind. They're bound to be all over the radiators, at least.' He got to his feet.

For the first time Michael Parker let his irritation surface. 'Does it have to be today? I really am busy, inspector!'

Terry studied him thoughtfully. Still the memory wouldn't quite come. The man was less calm than he'd been a few moments ago, he noticed, sweating slightly under the veneer of assurance. *Was it the question about the scarf, was that it? Or it is me? Perhaps he remembers where we met before, and is hoping I don't? Where was it?*

'As soon as possible, sir, if you don't mind. If you're busy now, this afternoon or this evening will do, or tomorrow morning at the latest. Just explain at the desk when you come. They'll know what it's about.'

'What if I can't make it by tomorrow morning?'

'Then I'll send a car to pick you up. That would be an awkward start to Christmas, sir, wouldn't it?'

'No need for threats, inspector. I'll come. After all, the sooner you get this cleared up, the sooner I get the house back. Look at it that way.'

'How do you mean, sir?'

'Well, I *am* in the property business, you know. It's a terrible tragedy about this woman's death, but since she *is* dead, I'll have to decide what to do with the house. Get a new tenant, or put it on the market, whatever. How much longer will you guys need it?'

'It's a crime scene, sir. I really couldn't say.'

'Well, give me a rough idea. A few days, maybe? A week? I can spare it over Christmas, but in the New Year ...'

'I'll let you know when we're finished, sir. That's all I can say.' Terry turned back at the door. The mystery of their former meeting was still bothering him. 'Do you have a family, sir, or children?'

'No, I'm lucky. I'm divorced. Which spares me all the tantrums round the Christmas tree. Been there, done that, got the teeshirt. I'm visiting my mother, then off to France skiing for a few days. You should try it, inspector. No kids, no packdrill. Breath of fresh air.'

He smiled conspiratorially, and as he did so, the memory flooded back into Terry's brain at last, as if a dam had burst. Of course! This was the man he had seen with Sarah Newby on the quay by the King's Arms. He'd been jogging, and seen Sarah walking towards him with this man's arm round her shoulder, her face looking up at him, flushed with laughter and excitement. Then she'd seen Terry and like a fool he'd stopped to talk, standing there puffing in his woolly hat and tracksuit, while she smiled at him happily.

With the memory came the emotions - rage, jealousy, embarrassment - which had flooded through his mind at the time. He'd deliberately suppressed the incident, locking it in a drawer in his mind, which was why he'd taken so long to recognize this man now, he supposed. No wonder I loathed him from the start, Terry thought, even before I remembered why.

That's probably why he looked guilty just now. Nothing to do with this murder. He's jealous of me just as I am of him.

And now the wretched man is boasting about being divorced, and going away skiing after Christmas. Leaving his kids with his ex-wife to care for, no doubt. If he had any. Terry thought grimly about his own efforts to organize Christmas for his two daughters. He'd had to arrange the whole thing around the demands of the duty roster. Trude was going home to Norway, Mary's mother was coming over for the two nights of Christmas itself, and after that the girls were going to stay with Terry's sister in Leeds - a visit virtually certain to end in tears.

But for all that, Terry thought, Christmas *matters*, particularly for family and kids. Particularly if those kids have lost their mother. You can't just swan off skiing on your own. At least *I* can't.

And then the second thought came. Maybe this man isn't going on his own. Maybe he's going with Sarah Newby. What if she's left her family too? For a man like this!

The thought hurt, much more than it should.

After all, she was nothing to him.

'Make sure you come in for those fingerprints today, sir,' he said coldly, as he turned to go out. 'Unless you want us to fetch you from the ski slopes in handcuffs, that is.'

Now there's a thought.

He smiled grimly as he went down the stairs.

40. Grandmother

AS CHRISTMAS approached Sarah's workload, perversely, seemed to increase. She dealt with a residue of cases committed in summer, months ago. Court staff, huddled beside ancient, clanking radiators, tried crimes committed at seaside resorts and open-air swimming pools. Sarah led snuffling witnesses in scarves through evidence about events which occurred when they'd been wearing nothing but factor 30 and the briefest of beachwear.

She met Michael for a meal the week after Cambridge, and again for a trip to the theatre; but neither date ended in bed. She wasn't sure whose decision this was - he seemed busy, polite, a little nervous. She wondered if it was her - if she had been unsatisfactory, somehow - but he seemed anxious for the relationship to continue.

'It's just ... I have moods,' he said, when she challenged him about it. 'It's not you - I get these depressions sometimes. They soon go; I just ignore them. And I've been having a tough time at work. Being interviewed by the police didn't help.'

'The police? What do you mean?'

'Oh, it was nothing really.' He shook his head, as though pestered by some annoying thought that wouldn't leave him. 'Just that one of my tenants died - you may have read about it in the paper. A teacher called Alison Grey. I thought it was suicide at first - that's what it said in the *Press* - but it seems they're treating it as murder.'

'And they came to see you?'

'Yes, well of course they did. I was her landlord, wasn't I? Nice lady; I even talked to her two days before. It's horrible to think of something like that. But I suppose in your work you meet it all the time.' His eyes met Sarah's briefly, then looked away. There was a hint of tears in them, almost. 'Anyway, the police have a job to do, but it doesn't help, does it? People dying on your property. That's part of the reason I'm so grumpy, just now. All the same ...' He reached across the table for her hand. 'That weekend in Cambridge was so good, I don't want to spoil it. I need a little space for a while, that's all.'

Not the best response, Sarah thought, but what had she been expecting? She wasn't sure; she had too little experience of such situations. Part of her - the physical, emotional part - longed for a repeat performance. Physical memories, the feel of him inside her, his hands on her breasts, her bottom, invaded her mind at the most inappropriate moments - when she was speaking in court, or talking to a solicitor on the phone. But the other part of Sarah - the rational, logical part - told her to back off. You'll destroy yourself, her mind warned. You could throw away everything, career, respect, self-control, for a man you still know little about. If you can't control what's happening, don't do it at all.

Nonetheless, she was disappointed, and wondered how long his depression would last. He was spending Christmas with his mother, she knew, and then skiing with friends in France. He'd asked Sarah to go; she'd considered it, but decided against. It was a step too soon, too far. She liked him, but not that much. She doubted if she could spend a fortnight with any man, just at present. And the risk of embarrassment was high. She had never learned to ski, so she imagined herself stumbling clumsily around the nursery slopes while he went off laughing with his friends, people she'd never met and might not like if she did.

So she stayed at home, preparing for a two-week fraud trial scheduled to start in the New Year. And she went shopping for a Christmas tree and presents for Emily and Simon.

Three days before Christmas, the estate agent phoned Sarah to ask if he could bring some prospective buyers round to view the house. 'They're very keen,' he said. 'It's usually dead this time of year, but the husband's starting a new job in York in January and they're not part of a chain, so ...'

'Yes, of course, bring them round,' Sarah said. But it came like a splash of cold water. She stayed up until midnight the evening before, hoovering, dusting, polishing, and resenting every minute. What right did these people have to turn her into a skivvy, cleaning her home for their inspection? And yet she couldn't leave it grubby, it had to be perfect.

They came on Saturday morning, a few hours before she was due to meet Emily at the station. They were a young couple, in their late twenties.

The wife was pregnant, the husband carried a toddler in his arms. Their faces were smooth - to Sarah they looked scarcely older than her children. 'Are you sure they can afford this?' she whispered to the agent as they stood in the hall while the couple explored upstairs. 'They *have* seen the asking price?'

'Must have,' the man shrugged. 'He's an insurance manager, I believe, quite a high-flier. She has her own business, too. Baby clothes.'

'But they look like they're just out of school.' Sarah met the man's eyes and realised that he, too, was in his twenties, and found the young couple's affluence perfectly natural. The world doesn't belong to me any more, she thought grimly. I struggled for years to afford a home like this, and now it's going to be sold off to children. When the couple came downstairs she smiled at them brightly.

'Would you like to see the garden?'

The young woman had already inspected the kitchen and spoken openly, in front of Sarah, about the need to replace the oven, hob, and units with something more 'contemporary', as she put it. Now Sarah led them across the patio to the garden at the back of the house. There was a large lawn surrounded by silver birch and weeping willow trees in what the brochure described as a 'mature, well-tended shrubbery.' It was a place, Sarah recalled, where she and Bob had been proud to entertain their friends. Now the toddler ran in circles while the young couple peered anxiously over the small rustic gate at the end.

'There are cows out there,' the young man said, almost accusingly.

'Yes,' Sarah agreed. 'They're quite sweet really, they're no bother. You can walk through the field to that stile on the far side, do you see? That takes you onto the footpath beside the river. It goes all the way into York, I believe.'

Sarah was no country girl herself and had never walked that far, but it had seemed an attractive idea when they had bought the house, and she'd always felt proud simply to own the possibility. Perhaps it was a selling point now?

'We see herons sometimes,' she added temptingly. 'I watch them from my bedroom window.'

The young woman turned away, her face frowning. 'There've been stories,' she said. 'In the local paper.'

'What sort of stories?' Sarah asked, surprised.

'Women getting mugged, assaulted, something like that. By some perv on a footpath like that. Wasn't there a murder, too?'

'Oh, that was to the south of the city,' Sarah said lightly. 'Nowhere near here.'

But the couple drove away soon afterwards. Sarah stood with the estate agent, gazing miserably after them. 'Not much hope there, then.'

'Oh, I don't know,' the man said. 'I thought they seemed quite keen.'

'What, with my kitchen dating from the stone age, and rapists on the riverbank? I don't think so.'

'Don't take it to heart. Some people are like that,' the agent insisted. 'It could mean they like the house, funnily enough. They're just talking it down so when they put in a lower offer you'll feel pressured to accept.'

'I hope they don't,' she said grimly. 'The thought of those two living here gives me the creeps.'

'You won't see it.' The young man smiled reassuringly, as if he'd met this resentment many times before. 'You'll be starting a new life, miles away.'

The new life, however - or at least a striking aspect of it - turned up on her doorstep on Christmas Day. Emily was home, happy and exhausted after her trips to London and Birmingham, and to Sarah's delight her son Simon and his girlfriend Lorraine had also accepted her invitation. So the house had a family celebration after all. Sarah, never a great cook, enlisted Emily's help in the kitchen, and the pair of them were working hard when the doorbell rang.

'I'll get it,' Emily said, and a moment later Simon appeared in the kitchen with Lorraine clinging tightly to his arm. Sarah poured some sherry, and the girl sipped it nervously, Simon preferring beer. This was the first time Lorraine had been to this house, Sarah realised; she hoped it wouldn't go wrong. A slim, dark-haired girl, she had seemed cheerful and friendly enough when Sarah met her before. But today she blushed and stammered when spoken to. Perhaps it's the house, Sarah thought; too imposing and wealthy. If so, that's ironic; it won't be mine much longer.

The meal, however, was a success. The despised oven turned out a joint of roast pork with all the trimmings and crackling as crisp as any they could remember, and the young people attacked it hungrily. Emily was determined to be a good hostess, and for once Simon seemed ready to reciprocate. So many times we have quarrelled round this table, Sarah thought, looking at the flushed faces under the paper hats - please don't let it happen today. But there was no sign of that. Emily and Simon talked happily, about her play and her band in Cambridge, nightclubs in Leeds they had visited, music and stars and old schoolfriends they knew. Soon Lorraine joined in, and by the time they sat back, red-faced and replete, with even the Christmas pud nearly gone, Sarah knew it had worked. She opened a small bottle of brandy she had bought for the occasion, and poured four glasses.

'To us all,' she said smiling. 'And may next year be happier than this.'

'To the future,' Simon added. As he raised his glass he met Lorraine's eye, and when they had drunk the toast he turned to face Sarah. 'And now, Mum, Lorraine and I have an announcement to make.'

'What?' Sarah smiled, surprised. 'You're not getting married, are you?'

'No, not that exactly.' Simon flushed, and Sarah instantly wished her words unsaid. So often she'd done this - spoken quickly, let her tongue run away with her while her son struggled to find the right words. His brain was connected to his fists, not his mouth, she'd said once - that's why he was always in trouble at school. Now here he was trying to say something important and what was she doing? Teasing him before he could start.

'What is it then, Simon?' she said as gently as she could.

'It's that - well, Mum, I'm 21 now and I've got a good job, so - me and Lorraine, we're not kids, we can look after ourselves, you know.'

He reached for Lorraine's hand, and she smiled at him encouragingly. The girl looked flushed, Sarah thought, and there was an attractive bloom of health to her skin. Youth, or - perhaps something else. A new suspicion entered Sarah's mind.

'... and so, we decided a few weeks ago, I mean we've got the spare bedroom, we never use it, and ... well, Lorraine's pregnant. I mean, we're starting a family.'

Simon's eyes met his mother's. He looked nervous, awkward, scared of her reaction. Sarah glanced from him to Lorraine, who stared back at her, proud, defiant, but anxious too.

So I was right, she thought. 'How many weeks?'

'Nearly eight, now,' Lorraine said softly.

My God, Sarah thought, they're just kids! This girl's hardly left school - she's younger than Emily, for Christ's sake! But then her mind flashed back to the memory of herself, much younger than this, in a similar situation, only worse. She'd been 15 when she'd stood, proud and defiant in front of her own parents, with Kevin, Simon's 17-year-old father, holding her hand beside her, just as Simon held Lorraine's here now. She could still see every line of the shock and disapproval on her own mother's face, after all these years - so deeply engraved had the memory become. And suddenly she realised what a formidable, frightening figure she must seem to this young girl. No wonder she had felt nervous about coming here.

Don't make the same mistake, she told herself. But there was no need. Unbidden, a smile spread across her face like sunshine. She saw its reflection in the eyes of Simon and Lorraine. Relief, and pride too.

'Simon, that's tremendous!' She got up, and went round the table to embrace them both. 'Are you feeling well?' she asked Lorraine.

'A bit sick in the mornings, and I get tired.'

'Of course. But the sickness will go.' She looked at Emily, relieved to see her smiling too. 'Well, this is a Christmas present and no mistake! Simon, you'll really have to grow up now! Do you think you can manage to look after a child?'

'Of course, Mum. You did, after all. We're going to this evening course in, well, baby stuff. But if we get tired, we thought we'd just bring the baby to court and dump it on you.'

'That will give the judges a heart attack.'

They were all standing now, at the end of the table. She looked up at her son, smiling. This was the baby she had borne so long ago, when she was just a child herself. Now here he was a tall young man, starting the same risky journey. She felt quite frail in front of him.

'Almost forty years old, about to be divorced and become a grandmother,' she thought. 'What else has life got in store?'

41. Terry's Christmas

CHRISTMAS FOR Terry Bateson was bitter-sweet. He looked forward to spending time with his daughters - Jessica and Esther - how could he not? But somehow, since Mary's death, the importance of such family events - birthdays, Christmas, Easter - made them as much a burden as a delight, for all three of them. The day needed to go well, Terry felt - the meal, the tree, the presents, the Queen's broadcast - they had to go through these rituals, to prove they were a family. To show he was a good - or at least adequate - parent. There must be no quarrels, no tears - no sign, when his sister or his parents came to visit, that they weren't coping.

And yet tears, inevitably, lay behind it all. There was the empty chair at table, the memory of the days when there were two adults in bed for the girls to bounce on in the morning with their stockings. A mother who could cook without a recipe book. Who bought her presents early instead of rushing round the shops at the last minute as Terry did. Who'd once been a girl herself.

His daughters tried hard but responsibility burdened them too. The only quarrel came when Jessica insisted that Esther eat up the burnt stuffing on her plate - Terry didn't know whether to applaud her for taking her mother's role, or check her for being too strict. They endured the visit to Terry's sister in Leeds, but were glad to come home for New Year.

Jane Carter had no such concerns. She spent most of her Christmas thinking of murder. Alison Grey's murder, to be precise. She volunteered for duty when older officers were at home with their families; and she used her time well. By the time Terry Bateson returned to work, she had rearranged much of the display in the incident room, and made progress on a number of vital details.

'Firstly, the silk scarf,' she told him, sitting calmly in front of her computer, which, like her, had been working overtime while others relaxed. 'As we established, it's a designer item, by Jacques Rocher. I've been into their catalogue and only 5,000 of that particular pattern were produced worldwide last year. So it's a pretty exclusive item. Retails for anything between £35 and £55 - as much as you can make the punter cough up, it seems.'

'For a scarf?' Terry said incredulously. 'A metre or so of posh fabric?'

Jane grinned. 'It's the cachet, sir, the label. Shows other ladies you've made it. Or so I'm led to believe.'

'So what's that got to do with Alison Grey?' Terry mused. 'Was she into fashion?'

'Hardly, sir, to judge by the rest of her wardrobe. Sensible clothes, mostly - jeans, corduroys, fleeces, a couple of suits from Marks and Spencer, but that's it. Sort of stuff my mum might wear, if she was a bit younger. Nothing fancy.'

'Apart from the scarf, which killed her?'

'Yes, exactly. And here's the other thing. So far as Jacques Rocher knows - that's the company, not the man himself - they're only sold by a dozen or so stores throughout the country. Two in London, one in Leeds - none in York, though - Edinburgh, Oxford, Cambridge, Cheltenham, Bristol, Manchester. That's it.'

'So you've been checking, have you? Who bought one recently?'

'Trying, sir. They're not exactly co-operative, with the sales going on. But ...' She shrugged. 'It may lead to something. In time.'

'Perhaps,' Terry said doubtfully. 'What else?'

'Well, the other thing I've been working on is this car. The red Nissan Primera. It's a long shot, because we can't be sure if it was stolen or not. And all we've got so far is the sighting by the farmer and part of the number plate - XB. Which may be accurate or not. But anyway I've been chasing up the dealers and again ...' She leaned back in her chair, stretching her hands behind her head and cracking her shoulder blades. '... it seems there were 1,206 Nissan Primeras issued with a number plate featuring the letters XB, of which precisely 375 were red. Not an impossible number, I suppose. Given time. I've got two DCs working on that at the moment.'

'Good work,' Terry said. 'What about TWOCs?'

'Well, exactly. So far I've come up with four stolen red Primeras.

One in Leeds, one in London, one in Manchester, and one in ...' she glanced at her notes '... the isle of Skye. Believe it or not.'

'I think we can put that at the bottom of the list,' Terry said. 'Is that the lot?'

'Not yet, sir, no. Most of them haven't replied.'

'Well, keep at it, sergeant. It's a possibility we have to eliminate. But ...' he grimaced. 'You know what our DCI's going to ask?'

'Where's Peter Barton, sir?'

'Exactly. Where is the bastard? Any news on that?'

'None, sir, I'm afraid. We've circulated his description nationwide, but no joy so far. There's more to that lad than meets the eye, it seems. If he can disappear so completely.'

'Do you think it was him?'

'It could be, sir, obviously. We'll know for certain when we get the lab report on that scrap of cloth the SOCOs found on the barbed wire fence. They're still working on that apparently. Staff shortages over the Christmas period.' Jane grimaced contemptuously. 'But he has to be top of the list. These other assaults almost look like he was practising. Working himself up for the big one. In which case, what if he's got a taste for it, and does it again?'

'Then we're in trouble,' Terry agreed. 'But what's his motive?'

Jane frowned. It seemed obvious to her. 'He's a pervert - he was spurned by women in his childhood, so he's out for revenge. He gets his kicks from stalking single women.'

They were sitting in the incident room, its walls covered with photographs and maps of the crime scene and surrounding area. A dotted green line led from the bridleway to Alison Grey's house. A similar dotted line in red led from the house to the gateway where the Nissan Primera had been seen. Terry drummed his fingers on the map thoughtfully.

'I know, there are a lot of similarities with those earlier assaults, but there are differences too. Quite significant differences at that.'

'Like what, sir?'

'Well, for a start, look at this place, Crockey Hill.' He tapped the board with his hand. 'It's not even a village - just a road junction with a few houses and a filling station. Much more remote than the other places he's been. And that bridleway's hardly used. Would you run there now, through all those damp woods? I wouldn't.'

'You're not a serial killer, sir.'

Terry raised an eyebrow. 'Well, thank you, sergeant, for those kind words. But if I *was* a serial killer, or sexual pervert, whatever, I guess my ardour would be pretty much diminished by all the cold damp mud I had to plough through to get to my victim. And there's another point, too. How did he know she was living there alone in the first place?'

Jane shrugged. 'He scouted through the woods, sir, I suppose.'

'You suppose.' Terry turned back to the map. 'Look where this house is, sergeant. It's down a track a hundred yards from the road, with a field and strip of woodland behind it. Young Peter coming along this bridleway is *behind* those woods, isn't he? Where he can't even see this house and has no reason to know that it exists, let alone that it's occupied by a single woman.'

'Maybe he deliberately set out to search for victims, sir. If Mrs Richards hadn't come out with a dog, he might have attacked her.'

'Well, maybe you're right. But you know as well as I do that 90% of murders aren't committed by strangers at all, but by someone well known to the victim. She had condoms in her bedroom, she must have had a boyfriend. What if it was some jealous lover who killed her, not Peter Barton at all? The guy who gave her that scarf, perhaps?'

Jane's eyes met his thoughtfully. 'You may be right, sir, but if she *did* have another lover, he was unusually careful to cover his tracks. I've been through all the e-mails on her computer, and there's nothing even mildly flirtatious. Just gossip to friends and colleagues - most of them in other countries - and a lot of detailed stuff about this book she was writing.'

'So they got in touch by phone, then. Must have done.'

'Right. Only her phone's missing. So if they sent each other texts we can't read those either, not yet anyway. I've got T-mobile working on that, but it's going to take some time. They're going through the numbers on her phone bill one by one. But if they don't come up with anything we've still got Peter Barton to find.' She sighed. 'It's still very possible that she was killed by an intruder. Either someone who came up the bridleway through the woods, or the driver of the red Primera.'

'The first thing to establish, is exactly what happened that night,' Terry agreed. 'And in what order. How, exactly, did the killer - whoever he was - persuade her to stand on that chair, naked, with a scarf round her neck?'

'She'd just had a bath, we know that much. There was a residue of foam around the sides of the tub,' Jane insisted. 'He came upstairs, surprised her in the bath or the bathroom ...'

'Wearing what, exactly, on his feet?' Terry asked pointedly. 'Shoes that left no trace?' The lack of footprints was a weak point in the intruder theory, they both knew. If the killer had come from the bridleway, he would have passed through woods where the ground was damp with mud and leafmould, before crossing a carrot field covered with straw. Yet there was no mud, straw or leafmould in the rooms upstairs.

'There were a couple of wisps of straw downstairs,' Jane said. 'And mud - in the loo and the hall. Quite a lot of it.'

'Dropped by our fine young constables,' Terry said dismissively. 'Rushing through the flower bed to the window. Why none upstairs, that's the question?'

'Maybe he took his shoes off.' Jane suggested. 'In order to make less noise.'

'Then why no fibres from his socks?' Terry asked. 'One of those would be soaked in DNA, if they're anything like mine. We'd have him. Only there aren't any.'

Jane shrugged. 'Who knows? Maybe he never went upstairs at all. Maybe she got out of the bath and came downstairs in her dressing gown, or with a towel wrapped round her, and he surprised her in the hall.'

'Why would she do that?'

'What, come downstairs? To feed the cat, maybe. Make herself a warm drink. Or perhaps she heard a noise and came down to see what it was.'

'Would you do that? Get out of the bath and come downstairs? A single woman, alone?'

'Not if I thought the noise was a burglar, no. But if I thought it was the cat, knocking over a cup or something, then maybe.'

Terry shuddered, imagining the mind-numbing shock poor Alison Grey had faced, if this scenario was true. Alone in that house, half naked, attacked by a strange man in the hall. 'That could explain why there was no sign of a struggle,' he said. 'She'd have been frozen by panic.'

'Quite. Then he taped her hands, made a noose with the scarf, and it was too late.'

'Where did he get the scarf?'

'There's a coat cupboard just inside the front door. Either that, or he brought it with him.'

'And yet there's no trace of his DNA on it anywhere,' Terry mused. 'That's what gets me. He'd be sweating, bound to be. Hyped up with excitement. But nothing. He must have worn gloves.'

'So he came prepared. Like Peter Barton did, in Lizzie Bolan's house.'

'Maybe,' Terry said. 'But I'm still not wholly convinced about this intruder theory. As you know.'

'You think it could have been her lover?'

'Yes. Look at it this way, sergeant. There were those scars on her buttocks, don't forget. That's not the sort of thing Peter Barton's ever done - not so far, anyway. It looks more like some perverted sex game. And there's no proof - no definite proof - that anyone broke into this house at all. He could have come through the loo window, I grant you, but our young constables blundered through there too, so that mud in the hall could have come from them. All this about the woman coming downstairs *could* have happened, I suppose, but it's not particularly likely, is it? If she heard a burglar, she'd have shut herself in her bedroom and phoned 999 ...'

'If she could find her mobile,' Jane said. 'We can't.'

'Well, exactly,' Terry said. 'Maybe she tried, and he snatched it out of her hands. But let's stick with Alison for a moment. If the cat needed feeding, you'd think she'd do it before she had a bath, wouldn't you? Or if she forgot, get herself properly dried and ready for bed before she came down. Whereas your theory has her walking downstairs half naked immediately after her bath, just exactly at the moment the intruder appears, simply to account for the lack of mud upstairs. Whereas if there *was* no intruder ...'

'There wouldn't have been any mud,' Jane said smoothly.

'Which may have come from our constables, sadly.' Terry sighed. 'Look, what if the killer was someone she knew? A man she'd let into the house quite willingly? Someone she was relaxed about having a bath in front of? Someone she might stand in front of naked? Remember, somebody caned her. And the shower head was raised too high for a woman, so it's likely the man took a shower afterwards. Or before.'

'All right, but how come he left no trace? No male hairs in the bathtub? Or on her body?'

'She washed them away in the bath.'

'No DNA on the scarf?'

'He wore gloves. He was careful.' It was Terry's turn to shrug, Jane's to look sceptical.

'He's her lover. A man she trusts enough to stand naked in front of, you say. She lets him whip her. And he's wearing gloves? Sounds kinky to me. Anyway, where's the whip?'

'Maybe he took it with him. He'd guess we could get DNA from it. After she was dead, he'd try to clean up.'

'He couldn't clean everything. There must be traces of him somewhere in the house.'

'There are. There are fingerprints everywhere. Most of them unidentified. None belonging to Peter Barton, remember. The only male ones we've identified belong to her landlord, Michael Parker. He visited her two days before, he says, to check her central heating.'

'So could he be your man, her secret lover?'

Terry shrugged. 'No evidence of that so far. He was near Scarborough when she died, he says, with some builders he employs. She phoned his office a couple of times in the last month, but not often. Still, he's on my list. I'll check on him further ...'

'Well, if it was someone she knew, how did he get to the house, without anyone seeing?'

'By car. He drove there, sometime after dark. No one would notice, why should they? The neighbour's a quarter of a mile off anyway, it's cold and dark, and he parks round the side out of sight.'

'So this man murders his mistress, walks out the front door, drops the latch, and drives away. Is that your theory?'

'Yes. Not switching his headlights on until he reaches the road, perhaps,' Terry said. 'That's what I'd do, in his position.'

'Why?'

'So no one would see me.'

'No sir. I mean why kill your mistress, if that's what she was? Deliberately, wearing gloves to avoid detection? And hanging her up in the hall like that, to make it look like suicide?'

'Or to humiliate her.'

'Or to humiliate her, yes, in front of the mirror. Scare her shitless, in fact, poor lady.'

'Yes. Well, maybe that's the point. He hated her so much, he planned it carefully. He almost got away with the suicide idea, too. He would have, if it hadn't been for the tape marks on her wrists.'

'And the scars on her buttocks, the knife mark on her throat. You think her lover carries a knife?'

Terry hesitated. 'That, I grant you, is less likely.'

'Or gloves?'

'I'm not saying this is a crime of passion - something spontaneous that got out of control. It looks deliberate to me. He came there planning to do this.'

'Which fits the intruder. Peter Barton. Or some other pervert. Someone who just thinks of her as a woman, not a person at all. An object to revenge himself on.'

'Not necessarily. You're forgetting how it was made to look like suicide. And the fact that she was suffering from cancer. A lover could have known that, planned to kill her, and disguise it as suicide, thinking he'd get away with it. He might have, too, if the pathologist hadn't noticed those tape marks on the wrists.'

'But why? What's the motive?'

Terry frowned. 'Could be anything. People do strange things when they're in love. Maybe it was simple jealousy - she'd deceived him with another man, perhaps the guy who'd given her that scarf. Or maybe she threatened to tell his wife - tried to blackmail him somehow. Anything like that. Perhaps love just turned to hate. It happens sometimes, so they say.'

'There's no evidence of any of this.'

'There's no evidence of your intruder.'

'Yes, sir, there is. There's the jogger Mrs Richards saw ...'

'Two days before. Could have been anyone.'

'And the scrap of cloth snagged on the barbed wire, the open window, the mud in the loo and the hall ...'

'Could have been our constables.'

'Or the killer. Then there's the red Primera parked in the gateway.'

'Young lovers, probably.' Terry shrugged. 'You're right, we shouldn't exclude it, I suppose.'

'And most of all, there's Peter Barton,' Jane persisted. 'With a nutcase like him on the loose, all this is a bit academic.'

'I know, I know,' Terry conceded. 'The sooner we catch the young bastard the better. It could easily be him. But it doesn't feel right, somehow. There's something we're missing. Something about the woman herself.' He paced across the room, thinking. 'We need to know more about her. Why she came to live in York, who her friends and enemies were, that sort of thing.' He smiled. 'And who she was sleeping with. That's the lad who did it, in my book.'

42. Quick Sale

THE PHONE call came as a surprise. Sarah was at her desk, deep in preparation for her fraud trial. It was Friday afternoon. The trial began on Monday, and she'd set aside this afternoon for preparation. But her client's bank statements were more complicated than expected, and she had only an hour before she had to leave. She had promised to meet Michael Parker that evening, and was beginning to wish she hadn't. The last thing she needed now was an interruption.

'Mrs Newby? This is Simon Marlow, of Strutt and Pollock.'

'Who?' She didn't recognize the voice.

'Strutt and Pollock, the estate agents, Mrs Newby.'

'Oh yes, of course. Mr Marlow.' She remembered the young man who'd shown people round her house before Christmas.

'We've had an offer on your house.'

'Really? Good heavens.' She'd been so busy over the past few weeks, her thoughts full of Lorraine's pregnancy, this coming fraud trial, and Emily's skiing holiday, that she'd almost forgotten that the house was for sale at all. The sale board in the garden had become an established fixture; on Boxing Day morning, Emily had hung nuts from it for the birds. 'How much?'

'Well, it's ten grand below the asking price, I'm afraid, but we might get them up a little. It's that couple I showed round, you remember ...'

'The ones who were so critical about the oven?'

'That's it - and the footpath. Like I told you, people often make comments like that when they're interested. The good news is, they're not part of a chain. They're in rented accommodation at the moment, with money in the bank.'

Sarah caught the hesitation in his voice, and prompted him to continue. 'And?'

'The bad news is, there's a three day deadline on the offer.'

'What? How does that work?'

'It means the offer's only on the table until Monday evening. After that they withdraw it. They claim they've seen another property almost as good. How true that is, I can't tell ...'

'You say you think they might go up a little?'

She could almost feel the man shrugging his shoulders. 'A couple of grand, maybe. No more. It all depends how quickly you want to sell. If you hang on until April, May, you could probably do better. But then you could easily be in a chain, and not complete till next year. Whereas these people are in a hurry. There aren't many buyers around in January.'

'No, I imagine not. Let me think about this, will you, Mr Marlow? I'll get back to you tomorrow.'

It was hard to concentrate after that. She put down the phone and returned to the file of bank statements, but had to give up with only half of it finished. She got on her motorbike and rode home through the freezing winter wind. As the house came in sight she saw it with new eyes. Not a home, but an asset; something that could be sold and broken up. Half for her, half for Bob. Was that what she wanted?

What I want, she thought, is someone to talk to. Someone who can share this problem and give me helpful advice. As it happens, that's all arranged.

Michael had flown home from his skiing holiday on Monday, and they had arranged to meet today. She'd suggested several restaurants, but for some reason he'd acted picky - he'd eaten too often at one with clients, he didn't like the waiters at another, he thought they used too much pepper at a third - until she cried out in exasperation.

'What's the matter with you, Michael? You're as fussy as an old woman!'

'I'm sorry. I've been eating out all week, I guess I'm tired of it. But I've got an idea.'

Something in his voice told her he was playing a game.

'All right. What is it?'

'Listen, you like home cooking, don't you? Why don't I prepare us a meal?'

'You?'

'Sure, why not? I did a cooking course once, didn't I tell you? One of my minor accomplishments.'

If I go to his house, she thought, that means I'll go to bed with him. At least that's what he thinks, that's what this is all about. Is that what I want? She prevaricated.

'Sounds risky, Michael. You know how critical I am.'

'I'll treat it as a challenge.'

She thought rapidly, trying to decide. Part of her longed to go to bed with him again. The sight of his naked body, the feel of him inside her - she thought of it regularly, daydreaming sometimes in court. But that was also a reason for *not* doing it. Especially not now, with this important case starting next week. She was still not fully prepared. Another night like that one in Cambridge could lead to her acting in court like some dizzy blonde - stumbling over facts, missing vital arguments, struggling to focus on today's trial rather than the excitements of the weekend.

In short, *losing control.*

Ever since her first early mistake with Kevin, Sarah's life had been about keeping control. It was a flaw in her character as well as a strength, but it was what defined her. It didn't mean she was afraid to take risks; she had taken plenty of those. But she wasn't foolhardy. She balanced the benefits against the dangers before deciding. And if the balance came down in favour of caution, she chose caution. Usually.

It was the wise thing to do, after all.

Over Christmas and New Year, she had thought about Michael Parker quite often. There was a lot to like about him, she decided. He was tall, handsome, he made her laugh. He was good in bed, or at least he had been that night. Not as passionate as Kevin, but more exciting than Bob. So that was good. And he was wealthy, a successful businessman. That was good too.

But there were other things about his character that worried her. For a start, he could be moody - quite frighteningly so. She remembered that time on the roof of the windmill, when she'd thought he might jump. That had been weird. Afterwards, he had been quite silent; she had never had a proper explanation. There was some secret there, perhaps, buried deep.

She wondered how much she could trust him.

'What's the matter?' His voice broke in on her thoughts. 'Don't you believe me? I haven't poisoned anyone yet, you know.'

It was a light comment, but he was offended, she could tell. And it's a nice offer, in its way. It's not as though I have many male friends.

There's a risk in playing safe as well. I could lose him and regret that too.

After all, you only live once. And we're adults. I can always say no.

'All right then,' she said. 'You're on. I'll expect cordon bleu standard, mind you.'

It was cold on the Kawasaki, riding out to the windmill, and twice she nearly lost her way in the dark. But it was exhilarating too, with the hint of adventure. Riding down the bumpy track through the woods, she came round a corner and saw the tower with its four great sails, starkly silhouetted against the starlight. Michael's black BMW was parked near it on the grass. Lights of distant houses twinkled from the valley far below. As she parked the bike and took off her helmet, a chilly breeze blustered around her face. She shivered, thinking how lonely it was.

Then the door of the mill opened, throwing a warm glow across the grass, and Michael stepped out. He greeted her with a smile and a kiss on the cheek. She followed him into the sudden warmth of the kitchen. It had progressed, she saw, since her last visit. The cardboard packing and dust had gone from the floor, which shone as though it had been recently mopped. There were framed photos of old windmills on the wall, and an open bottle of wine on the worktop beside the hob where something was steaming. The room smelt of warm bread. There was a small table set for two under the window, with flowers in the middle, which hadn't been there before.

'I thought we'd eat in here, since there's only the two of us,' he said. 'Easier to talk while I'm cooking, and I won't have to carry everything upstairs.'

'Fine.' She smiled, feeling her cheeks flush with the sudden warmth of the room after the chill of the night air outside. 'Is there somewhere I can change?'

'Of course. Through there.'

Sarah went through to the bathroom to peel off her leather motorbike jacket, trousers and boots. She'd brought shoes and a dress with her in a bag. The bathroom was finished now too: the walls were fully tiled, there was a loo, basin, and elaborate shiny shower cabinet. She spent a few moments checking her make-up in the mirror, which had spotlights set artfully around it like those in a theatre dressing room. She smiled cautiously at her reflection. Not a bad face, she told herself firmly - a few more wrinkles than I'd thought, perhaps, and a little flushed from the wind on the ride, but still, with a touch of lipstick and something around the eyes, like that ... I shouldn't scare him too much.

Anyway, it's only a dinner invitation, that's all. No big deal.

She went out into the kitchen and sat on a chair, sipping a glass of wine which Michael poured for her. He was wearing an apron over his jeans and shirt, but even so he'd got flour in his hair. She smiled as she watched him. It was a long time since a man had cooked for her. He took some hot rolls out of the oven and passed one over to her.

He seemed more nervous than she had expected. Perhaps it was the stress of cooking. The rolls were perfect, crunchy and brown on the outside, soft and melting inside, and he'd made little fancy patterned dabs of butter to go with them. But then there was a panic over a cheese soufflé, which collapsed as he put it on the table. He shoved it back in the oven again, and turned the heat up high, which failed totally. In a matter of minutes it turned brown, hard and flat. Michael's brow darkened. He was speechless with frustration.

Sarah laughed. 'No one's perfect,' she said. 'I think you're brave for even trying. I've never made a soufflé in my life.'

'I have. That was my pièce de resistance.'

'Well, it's suffered an internal revolution. Maybe we can cut it up and eat it as crisps.' She picked up a knife and approached the dish.

'No!' Michael snatched it out of her way, nearly burning his hands in the process. 'It's a failure, that's all - I'll trash it.' He scooped it angrily into the bin.

'Sorry,' Sarah said softly, stepping back. 'It doesn't matter, Michael, really.'

'It does to me.' For a moment he stood with his back to her, staring out of the window. She could see his reflection in the darkness of the window. But the double glazing blurred it oddly, as if she were looking at one face superimposed on another. The expression on the combined face was unclear, misshapen, like a painting by Picasso. It looked like a grimace, a snarl - then he turned and she saw it was a smile.

'I'm sorry,' he said. 'Forgive me. I just wanted everything to be perfect.'

'This is real life,' she said. 'It never is.'

'Well.' He drew a deep breath, and made a conscious effort to ease the tension in his shoulders. 'Let's hope I can grill a steak, at least. I thought I'd add some Stilton for flavour. And peppers and onions.'

'It sounds fine,' Sarah said. 'Just what I need.'

'Good. That's what I hoped.' His eyes met hers and she thought yes, that's not the only need of mine he hopes to meet. But his tantrum just now had scared her slightly; the image of that scowl in the window upset her. How much did she truly know about this man, how much was hidden? She remembered that moment on the little balcony above. Did she really want to stay in this lonely tower all night? She shifted in her seat uneasily.

I can always say no, she told herself firmly. Get on the bike and leave. Whether he likes it or not.

He busied himself with steak, onions, peppers, mushrooms, spinach and potatoes, and his mood began to lighten. He told her tales of his skiing holiday. He had successfully completed a black run - the hardest - for the first time ever, he said, at severe danger to life and limb. After which, flushed with euphoria, he had promptly fallen, and slid all the way down on his bottom on a red run, headfirst. Sarah laughed, appreciating the joke at his own expense. She began to relax, and told him about Emily, and the skiing lessons she'd had in Birmingham.

'That should help,' he agreed. 'Gentle slopes and lots of practice. You should try it. There's a place like that in Castleford. I could take you.'

'I'm not sure,' she said. 'I might break my leg.'

'You'd be fine. You managed the skating okay, remember?'

She remembered. That had been a good evening. Fun, exciting, just what she needed. Apart from that unfortunate meeting with Terry Bateson.

'Where's your daughter going?'

'Umm - it's on the tip of my tongue. Morvine, that's it. Somewhere near Geneva.'

'I know it. Good place for beginners. Easy slopes and lots of night life. She'll love it.'

He served the steak. It was perfect - medium rare, just as she liked it, and garnished with a sprinkling of Stilton cheese melted on top. The mushrooms were good too - unusual ones, hot and garnished in butter, with interesting flavours which she wasn't used to. The spinach, onions and potatoes were all exactly right.

'Michael, this is wonderful.' She lifted her glass. 'You are a chef after all.'

He beamed with pleasure. 'Told you I could do it. I get some things right at least.'

'Congratulations. I may even come again.'

'I hope you do.' Once again their eyes met, and she thought, careful, Sarah, let's not go overboard just yet. But it was fun, nonetheless, to be sitting at a candlelit table eating a meal cooked for her by a handsome man. Not a common situation in her life. Bob had seldom attempted any cooking beyond spaghetti or baked beans, and her own efforts were never as good as this. Perhaps, if this relationship did develop, she would eat like this more often.

'What about your daughter, Sandra?' she asked. 'Have you seen her since Christmas?'

'No,' he shook his head shortly. 'Just one phone call, that's all. She has her own life.'

'Oh. Well, I have some family news.'

'What's that?'

'My son's girlfriend, Lorraine, is three months pregnant.'

'Good lord! Is she going to keep it?'

'Of course.' Sarah frowned, shocked by the question. 'She's eighteen, he's twenty one. They're very proud. I'm going to be a grandmother!'

'Well, congratulations!' He laughed, raised his wineglass; then shook his head wonderingly. 'You? A grandmother? You're only a schoolgirl yourself.'

'Old enough to have been divorced twice,' she pointed out, pleased nonetheless with the compliment. 'Or at least I soon will be.'

'True.' He leaned forward, cradling his wineglass in both hands. 'How's that going?'

'In the hands of the lawyers. You know how slow we are.' She shrugged. 'But the house sale, that's making progress. Or it will, if I accept the offer by Monday.' She told him about this evening's phone call, and asked his advice.

'Well, if your agent's any good he ought to get their offer up a little,' he said cautiously. 'But then it depends what you want to do. As he said, you could hang on for a higher price.'

'But that would take months, wouldn't it? And half of the money goes to Bob anyway.'

'So what are you going to do?' he asked, clearing away their plates.

'I'm tempted to accept,' she said slowly. 'It looks like the answer to my prayers, really. A chance to sell quickly, cut the knot and move on.'

'Wise move. Burn your bridges, start a new life.'

'That's the idea.' *I've already started,* Sarah thought. *That's why I'm here. Isn't it?*

He rinsed their plates in the sink and put them in the dishwasher. Then he took two glass bowls out of the fridge and carried them proudly to the table. 'How about this?'

Blueberry meringues with whipped cream, rising to a pyramid and sprinkled with flakes of chocolate. There were long silver spoons to eat it.

'Michael, it looks delicious!'

'I hope it is. Not too fattening either. Melts on the tongue. The blueberries are the latest health craze - mop up your free radicals. I read it in the *Daily Telegraph.*'

Sarah tasted it. 'You're right, it's lovely.' She put out her tongue to lick some cream from her lips. Then an idea came to her and she laughed. 'Typical *Daily Telegraph* health story though.'

'Why?' Michael had been watching her tongue.

'A food that mops up the free radicals. Sounds like cooking for the Special Branch or the CIA.'

'Oh, yes.' His laughter, to Sarah's disappointment, was slightly forced. That was my best joke for ages, she thought, hugging herself secretly. I must remember that and tell Lucy. It'll crease her up.

'I was thinking about your work today,' he said cautiously. 'You remember that case in the Appeal Court? The man convicted of murdering that girl years ago. The one you got off?'

'Yes.'

'What's happening about that?'

'Well, nothing' said Sarah, surprised. 'The man's free, that's all. Why?'

Michael looked down, spooning some meringue carefully into his mouth. 'Well, didn't they find a body, of the girl he was supposed to have killed? I thought perhaps there might be new evidence.'

'None they could link to my client. As far as I know, the police aren't pursuing the case against him. Which is more or less an admission that they were wrong all along.'

'He must be pleased, then.'

'Who? Jason Barnes?'

'Yes. Was that his name - the killer?'

'Michael, *he didn't kill her*. That's the whole point.'

'No, of course. Sorry, stupid of me.' He smiled awkwardly. 'So he'll be seeking compensation, I suppose. Will you handle that?'

'I would if he asked. But he's disappeared.'

'What?' Michael looked shocked.

'Vanished into thin air, with no forwarding address.' She shrugged. 'That's the criminal classes for you.'

'But isn't he on parole? Doesn't he have to report to the police or something?'

'No, the case against him was quashed. He's free to come and go as he likes.'

'But ... don't you have any record of where he is? I mean, the police might want to know. If there was new evidence, or something ...'

'Michael, I'm his lawyer. I don't go shopping him to the police. Why are you so interested in this anyway?'

'Oh, no reason. Just that, you know, I was in York when that girl disappeared. It was a big case then, I remember. Still is, I suppose, if he didn't do it.'

'Yes.' She shivered, realising she had just acted unprofessionally. 'Michael, don't go talking to anyone about this, will you? I shouldn't have told you that, about Jason. He's my client.'

'My lips are sealed.' He smiled, then drew his fingers across his mouth, as though closing his lips with a zip fastener. A grim, determined face stared at her. Then he laughed, and stood up. 'How about coffee?'

'Yes, please.' She finished her meringue while he busied himself grinding beans. 'What about your work, anyway?'

'It's going well, I think.' He set the cafetiere on the hob, and took some white bone china cups and saucers from a cupboard. 'Cream, sugar?'

'No thanks. Just black.'

'Okay. I went out to the farm development yesterday. It's coming on well. They've got most of the wiring finished. That's what holds things up. That and the plumbing. You can't do the floorboards or tiles or plastering until that's done. It's going to look good.' He got up to pour the coffee. 'But what about this house of yours? If you sell it, what sort of place do you have in mind?'

'I was thinking about somewhere in town,' she said, taking a cup of coffee gratefully. 'One of these modern flats, maybe. It's what they're built for, isn't it? Now that I'm a single person, all of a sudden. And then I could walk everywhere. I wouldn't need the bike or a car. I wouldn't have to wear leathers and boots all the time. It's a nuisance, always having to change.'

'Pity, from my point of view. I thought you looked great. Turning up like a Bond girl and then slipping into something feminine and soft.'

'You liked that, did you?' She sipped her coffee, looking at him through the steam from the cup.

'Of course.' He considered her, returning her look. 'You're a beautiful woman.'

'Thank you, kind sir.' She crossed her legs, sitting back in her chair. 'Anyway, that's my idea. Start a new life, get rid of all the baggage - house, garden, all the history and hassle that goes with it. If I'm going to be single, I may as well learn to accept it. Live in a flat.'

'Hm.' He rested his chin on his hand, studying her thoughtfully. 'Sounds attractive. You wouldn't want anywhere too small though, would you?'

'Why not? There's only me.'

'Yes but, with all due respect, Sarah, you've got kids, you're almost a grandmother now. You'll need space for your furniture. And your zimmer frame.'

'Stop it!' she laughed. 'Not quite yet.'

'And somewhere for visitors to sleep.'

'Simon lives in town. I'll need a room for Emily, though. I promised her that.'

'Yes, and?'

'And what?'

'People like - well, me. I might want to visit you. If I was invited, that is.'

'Yes, well, that remains to be seen. Anyway, I haven't found a place yet.'

'Better start looking. We could go round the agents together in the morning if you like. What sort of price range are you thinking?'

'Half of what I get for my own house, I suppose. Give or take. But

Michael, I can't go house hunting tomorrow; I've got this trial hanging over my head. And stacks of files to go through before Monday. I shouldn't even be here now.'

'Well, I'm glad you are.' He looked hurt. 'Aren't you?'

'Yes, of course. I didn't mean to be rude. It was a lovely meal.'

'Apart from the soufflé.'

'Forget about the soufflé, Michael. It was funny.'

'Okay, I'll try.' He closed his eyes, then reopened them. 'There. I'm over it now. Almost.' He smiled, and their eyes met. *This is the Michael I like,* Sarah thought, *Funny, charming, ironic. Not that other one I saw in the window.* She smiled back.

He took a small digital camera from the kitchen worktop. 'I took some photos of the barn development yesterday. And there are all my skiing exploits on here too, for what they're worth. Would you like to see them?'

She hesitated. If I want to leave, this is the moment to go, she thought. Before it's too late. But then, where's the harm? It's a long ride home, in the dark. And he's gone to all this trouble, he'd be hurt. Anyway it was fine last time, in the hotel. And what is there at home, after all? Just two days' solid work. Loneliness. And regrets.

'Yes, all right,' she said. 'I'd love to see them. Why not?'

'Great.' He got up. 'Let's go up to my study, shall we? I can show you them there on the computer.'

43. Garden of Remembrance

THE CITY crematorium was a modern, single storey building set in pleasant landscaped gardens near the archbishop's place in Bishopthorpe. Terry and Jane arrived early, and sat in their car watching people arrive for the funeral of Alison Grey. Attending this funeral was a lot more, in Terry's book, than just good public relations. It could give him vital leads to the investigation; if, that is, Jane was wrong and it wasn't Peter Barton. To everyone's irritation, there was still no sign of the twisted young pervert. What if he had murdered Alison - would he strike again? Terry had woken several times this week from nightmares in which Peter Barton was prodding the dead body of a naked woman hanging from a staircase, causing it to swing to and fro. Mostly the corpse had been faceless, but once - most recently - he had woken in a muck sweat, shuddering at the vision of his dead wife Mary's face throttled by the scarf.

Will Churchill's right about one thing, Terry told himself grimly. I have to solve this soon, if only to regain peace of mind.

A small crowd began to gather outside the solid oak doors at the entrance to the building. They wore dark coats, gloves and scarves, their collars turned up against the cold January wind. A taxi pulled up and a white-haired old lady got out, together with two elderly men, their faces wrinkled and seamed like old parchment.

'That's her mother, is it?' Jane asked, watching sympathetically as they hobbled towards the door. 'Doesn't look too well, poor old dear. Which one's her Dad?'

'He's not here,' Terry answered. 'Died two years ago. Those must be uncles or cousins of some sort.'

They stayed in the car watching as more cars arrived and the group gradually increased. There were several older people of the mother's generation, but there was a fair sprinkling of young people too, from late twenties to early forties. Several of these were black or Asian, and the white people were tanned, as if they had been living abroad. They tended to shiver more than the rest, and paced about restlessly, waiting for the doors to open.

A shiny black limousine rolled smoothly into the drive, coming to a silent stop just in front of the entrance. Four burly pallbearers in black coats got out and smoothly lifted the coffin onto a trolley. Terry and Jane got out of their car, and followed the mourners into a room with wooden panels and deep soft carpets. The chairs were arranged in a semi-circle facing the front, where the coffin waited on a trolley before some curtains. Terry and Jane took their seats unobtrusively in at the back. Organ music played softly. As a priest walked to the front, Jane held her order of service in front of her mouth and whispered: 'See anyone likely?'

'Not so far,' Terry murmured. There was always a possibility that the killer would turn up to the funeral to see his victim safely cremated, silently gloating over his achievement. Or if he'd been her lover, he might even be grieving. But no one stood out from the crowd.

Still, all of them must have known her. There was a rich source of human information here, if they could manage to mine it discreetly.

'You take the younger ones,' Terry muttered. 'When the service is over, see if you can find out how well they knew her, what she was like, and so on. They're probably teachers, a lot of them, like her.'

'I'll do what I can. What about you?'

'I'm going to talk to that woman over there. That's her editor - I recognise her face from a book catalogue in Alison's house.' He indicated a woman two rows ahead to their right - a good-looking middle-aged lady, with red hair greying slightly around the temples. She wore a thick brown coat and sensible fur-lined high boots against the cold. Jane had watched her arrival earlier from their car. Most of the younger mourners spoke to her, and several - especially those who appeared to come from abroad - had quite long, animated conversations, much more than a simple exchange of condolences. She seemed a warm, friendly sort of person; even now, as the service was beginning, one or two of the younger mourners threw glances her way, as if seeking reassurance or sympathy.

Terry wondered if the Catholic priest, Father Roberts, would lead the service, but it was a Church of England vicar who stood before them. He led the assembled congregation quietly and confidently through the service, but when the time came to address them about Alison Grey, it was clear that he had not known her well. He referred constantly to a sheaf of notes in his hand, and despite his best efforts the encomium was somewhat perfunctory. He told the congregation things most of them, no doubt, already knew: how Alison had been born in Leicester, the only daughter of Helen and Andrew Grey; gone to school there where she displayed a particular talent for foreign languages which she'd studied at York university; trained as a teacher in Oxford before going abroad to teach English as a foreign language; how she had travelled the world and made friends in many countries, before returning to England to write teaching books for Oxford University Press. She had been a talented person, he said, but someone who used her talent for the benefit of others. Many people had benefited from knowing her; both her pupils, to whom she had taught English; and her colleagues, with whom she had shared her skill in teaching. She had been a decent, honest, hard-working woman who, if her life had not been so cruelly cut short, would have had many happy years of life still ahead of her.

It was all true, no doubt, and particularly comforting to her elderly mother, who sat listening with bowed head and tears trickling unregarded down her face. But it was only part of the truth. All this man knew was the surface, the public persona, not the core. What was she really like, Terry wondered. That's what we need to know. What about the cancer that was devouring her body? And the secret that she dared not tell Father Roberts? Why did she want to leave the Church of England?

What was it that had made someone kill her?

When he had exhausted his knowledge, the vicar turned to the coffin, and launched into the final prayers of committal. Then he invited the congregation to stand and sing the final hymn. As they ploughed their way grimly through the verses, the final, banal horror took place in front of their eyes. The vicar pressed a button, an electric motor hummed, and the coffin moved slowly forward on hidden rollers. As it did so, the curtains on either side began to move towards it. It was all timed perfectly. The curtains appeared certain to brush against the coffin before it had gone behind them, perhaps knocking off a wreath; but they missed it by millimetres. A triumph of funeral engineering.

As the congregation sang on, Terry wondered what happened next behind the curtain. Did the coffin continue to roll smoothly on by itself, into the sudden, fiery furnace? Or was that part done by hand? By men in boiler suits, pushing the coffin bodily through a fireproof door? There would be a system for sure; one practised a dozen times a day. While the congregation walked slowly out into the garden of remembrance, the coffin and its contents were being reduced to ashes. Ashes which would have to be cleared out, poured into an urn, and labelled, before the next one came through.

They had buried Mary's ashes in the garden here, behind this building, in a small plot Terry had paid for. He had come three times, with Jessica and Esther, to leave flowers above it. But then they had stopped coming; it caused too much distress, he decided, served no purpose. It was a grave smaller than one they had dug for a hamster.

After the final prayers, Terry and Jane followed the other mourners out into the garden of remembrance. They stood around, talking in subdued voices, uncertain what to do next. One of the elderly uncles reminded them that a buffet had been ordered at a hotel on the Tadcaster road, to which all were invited. Alison's mother stared bleakly at the gardens, where the ashes of her daughter would rest, somewhere among the hundreds of miniature headstones among the neatly tended rose gardens. One of the soberly dressed crematorium staff appeared to offer her condolences, and discreetly usher them all back towards the car park.

At the hotel, people helped themselves to sausage rolls and sandwiches and stood around making conversation. Someone had had the foresight to put up a pin board with photographs of Alison on it - as a baby, a schoolchild, a student, and in various countries of the world. Jane joined a group of teachers who were studying it curiously, while Terry approached the woman he had identified as her editor.

'Jennifer Barlow?'

'Yes?'

'Detective Inspector Terry Bateson. We spoke on the phone.'

'Oh yes, I remember. You're looking for Alison's murderer.'

'That's right. So the more we know about her the better. Has anything more come to mind, since we spoke?'

'I'm not sure. Perhaps.' She manoeuvred her way across the room to a corner by a window. 'I'm sorry, it's all been such a rush and a shock; it might be best if you remind me of what I told you before. Then I can fill in the gaps, if there are any.'

She was an attractive woman, Terry thought; a strong character with presence. No wonder these young teachers cluster round her; several were watching now as they talked. She had several large rings on her fingers and bracelets on her wrists, which jangled as she moved her arm. She had a lively active face out of which her large grey eyes scrutinized him intently.

'All right,' he agreed. 'Well, when we spoke on the phone, you told me you met Alison in Oxford on a postgraduate teacher training course. You became friends and taught together for a couple of years in Japan, is that right? But then you went into publishing while Alison carried on teaching English as a foreign language in various countries around the world, so you lost touch for a bit.'

'That's right, yes. We tried to meet when she came home, and we'd write, you know. But those were the days before e-mail, and she worked in some pretty remote places - even Mongolia for a couple of years - so yes, we lost touch.'

'And then you met her at a conference, I believe?'

'Yes, an IATEFL conference - that's the International Association for Teachers of English as a Foreign Language - in Bournemouth, about four years ago. It was great. She gave a presentation about some teaching materials she had written, and as it happened they were just the sort of thing we were looking for at the time. So I asked her to write some more, which she did. She came to Oxford, people were impressed, and it all led to *First Class*.'

'That's the book she was working on?'

'Yes. Or series of books, actually. Quite apart from the tragedy of her death, it's going to be a major headache finding someone to take over. She had a real talent, poor girl.'

'So the books were doing well?'

'Very well. The launch was a terrific success, and the second book's doing even better. It was a great breakthrough for her - a life-changing experience, really. I would imagine she'd already made enough in royalties to set her up for life.'

'That's interesting,' Terry said. 'Enough to buy a house, would you say?'

'Oh, heavens, yes. Quite a good one, too.'

'But she was living as a tenant in a small cottage. Not particularly luxurious. Just her and a cat.'

'Yes, well, that's Alison for you. She didn't really care about money. After all those years of living abroad in rented flats and houses, she probably saw that as normal. I talked to her about buying a house once, and she said she'd get around to it when she'd finished the next book. That was what she was focussed on.'

'What about her private life? Friends and so on?'

Jennifer Barlow shrugged. 'She was a friendly person. Look around you - half of these people are teachers she's worked with or helped in some way. Some of them have travelled long distances to get here.'

'Any of them boyfriends?'

'I doubt it. They all look a bit young to me,' Jennifer surveyed the room thoughtfully. 'But the truth is, I wouldn't know. She had a couple of boyfriends in Oxford, I remember, but neither of them lasted.'

'Why not? Do you remember?'

Jennifer shrugged. 'Usual reasons, not compatible, I suppose. I think she was getting over some undergraduate affair at the time. No one she met in Oxford quite matched up.'

'Undergraduate affair?'

'Yes. She was a student here in York, I think, before she came to Oxford. But that was before I met her.'

'I see. You don't happen to remember his name, do you, this boyfriend of hers?'

'No, sorry, she never told me.'

'What about later, when she went abroad? There must have been other men, from time to time?'

'I think there was a man in Indonesia - a doctor I think - but he was married and it all ended badly. There were probably one or two others, but she didn't tell me about them all.'

'She wasn't bisexual, by any chance?'

'Oh no. When she did talk about that sort of thing, it was always men. She could be quite forthright, on occasion - one or two things she came out with quite shocked me.'

'But not in connection with any man in particular?'

'As I say, there was this doctor - the Indonesian.' She smiled faintly. 'He was quite adventurous, it seems. The whole Kama Sutra. Taught Alison a lot.'

'Do you have a name for him?'

'Again, I never met him.' Jennifer sighed, shaking her head. 'I might have it in an old letter of hers somewhere. If I find it I'll tell you.'

'Thank you, that would help.' Terry studied her thoughtfully, wondering how to phrase his next question. 'I'm sorry to ask you this, but ... these sex games with this doctor; did they include bondage, sado-masochism, anything like that?'

Jennifer Barlow flushed. 'They may have done, yes. He sounded quite adventurous, and Alison ... well, I think she enjoyed it. We had a few laughs at the time.' Her face darkened suddenly. 'Why? What's this got to do with her murder? I thought she was hanged.'

'She was. But how that happened exactly, we don't know. So we have to explore every avenue until we find out, I'm afraid. So if you do remember the name of this doctor ...'

'I'll tell you, of course. But it was a long time ago, and on the other side of the world. I think it ended when his wife found out.'

'A long shot, then.' Terry shook his head. 'Do you know what happened to this old boyfriend of hers? The one from York?'

'Sorry, no, she didn't say. She was always very secretive about him. But it's always possible that was the reason she chose this part of the country to settle, I suppose, when she came back to England. Or it could just have been happy memories.'

44. Homeless Person

THE SALE of Sarah's house went through quicker than she had expected. The young buyers had expensive, efficient lawyers, probably provided free by the man's employers. They made it clear that any unreasonable delay on Sarah's part could cancel the deal. And she felt pressure from the other side by Bob, who was eager for his share of the equity.

Sarah herself was gripped by an uncharacteristic mood of fatalism. She felt swept downstream in a torrent, by events that she couldn't control. Normally she would have fought back, straining against the current, but for once she didn't care. She felt a perverse pleasure in letting go, in feeling all the ties of her former life washed away, so much flotsam on the surface of the stream.

Two furniture vans came on the day of the move. One hired by Bob, to take his share of the furniture, or what they had agreed he could have. An antique writing desk and sideboard he had inherited from his mother, the books, bookcases, filing cabinet and computer equipment from the room he used as a study, and the king-sized double bed which he insisted he had bought in their former house, before she started earning.

They had nearly come to blows about that. It wasn't that Sarah wanted the bed, particularly - it had memories, after all, of their married life together, of the hundreds, probably thousands, of times they had made love, or simply lain together, reading, talking, sleeping, cuddling, caring for each other in sickness and in health. Trusting each other, taking each other for granted, the way married couples do. Knowing and accepting all the intimate embarrassing details about each other - the way Bob snored, grew his toenails longer than she liked, and had hair on his back as well as his chest. All those things, together with the deep-chested, helpless way he'd laughed when she'd tickled him, and the soft scratchy feel of his beard on the top of her head as she'd snuggled up to him at night - all that would come with the bed if she took it. All those memories would surround her at night, like small colourful dreams of the past. Dreams poisoned by his betrayal, turning green, bitter and choking in her sleeping brain.

So for that reason she was glad to be rid of it. Better to buy a new bed of her own, she told herself. Start life afresh, on clean virgin sheets. But ...

Try as she might, she could not rid herself of rage at Bob's reasoning. He'd been quite open about it. 'Sonya's bed is old,' he'd said. 'It sags, she's never had a decent one. And since this is mine, after all, and still has a few years of use left in it ...'

It was that callous phrase that set Sarah's teeth on edge. Her mouth felt sticky when she thought of it, as though she'd sucked rhubarb. It was that *few years of use* that enraged her. Not use by Bob alone, of course, but by him and Sonya. As well as her wretched children, too, no doubt, from time to time. Even a baby, God forbid, if Bob gave her one.

There was the rub. He wanted to sleep with Sonya, make love to her, cuddle her, talk to her, laugh with her probably, share his new bloody life with her in this same bed they'd shared for most of their married life. And he didn't seem to care, damn him! All those memories and associations that came back to her almost every time she lay in the bed - did they mean nothing to him? Had he just deleted them from his memory? Was the bed just a thing - wood and fabric and springs cunningly constructed into a machine for sleeping - and nothing more? Apparently so, in his mind.

There must be something wrong with the man, she told herself.

Well, there is. That's why he left me. So good riddance, that's the best attitude. I'm better off without him, if that's the way he thinks.

Only it hurts. It hurts all the time.

It hurt especially to see the bed being dismantled, lugged downstairs by two beefy men, and stowed in a van beside the rest of Bob's furniture, bound for his new life in Harrogate. New *wife* in Harrogate, too, it seemed. Last time they'd met, quarrelling tetchily about the bed and other items as they toured the house and ticked them one by one off a joint list, he'd let slip that he intended to marry Sonya as soon as the divorce came through. He'd meant it as some sort of justification - a consolation for Sarah, perhaps - to convince her that this wasn't just an affair, but a definite new direction in his life, a permanent commitment. But it felt like a slap in the face. When he persisted, saying he hoped one day she and Sonya might meet, even become friends, she turned her back on him and walked smartly away.

Since then they'd spoken only through lawyers.

When Bob's van was packed and driven away, the van she had hired for her own furniture took all the rest. Annoyingly, there was more than she'd anticipated. All the stuff that neither of them wanted - books, clothes and papers from the loft, old curtains she'd stored in the hope of using them some time, Emily and Simon's old school reports, toys and clothes they'd grown out of - all these had to be cleared out of the house before the buyers moved in, and since Bob didn't want them she was lumbered with them. I've paid too little attention to this, she realised, watching the furniture van fill up with alarming quantities of junk, I've been too busy working to deal with it. She had nowhere to put it either. All her furniture was going into store, at a cost which had already seemed to her exorbitant, even before the amount of stuff had started to multiply before her eyes.

I'll have to find somewhere to live, she thought. More spacious than I'd thought. And sooner, too.

The move had come upon her so suddenly, in the middle of her complicated fraud trial, that she'd had almost no time to look for suitable lodgings. It was only because the move took place on a Saturday that she was able to be here at all, supervising her life's possessions being lugged out of the front door. A few days ago she'd contacted a letting agency, who'd taken her to see a couple of flats one evening, but they'd looked so battered and dreary to her, so lacking in hope, cleanliness, or even basic modern amenities, that the thought of taking either for a six month let, which was the minimum offered, made her feel suicidal. Is this what I've come to, she thought - after all my work, all my study, all my commitment to career and family? A one bedroom flat in a narrow side street, with grimy carpets, grubby shower, and a view over a vehicle spraying business? I can't bear it.

The alternative was to live with Michael Parker. He'd made that offer as soon as she told him the sale was going through, and she'd smiled and said she'd consider it. That was the other reason she'd delayed so long, and been so dilatory about renting a flat. She was tempted. It tickled her fancy, the idea of living with this man in his house - and such an unusual house, too, a windmill. That would show Bob she wasn't on the shelf, abandoned at forty! She was a still a desirable woman, she had a lover already!

But as the time grew nearer, doubts crept in. It wasn't that she disliked Michael, not at all; their lovemaking, that second time, had been as exciting and satisfactory as the first - even more so, in some ways, with less anxiety and guilt. But somehow, the more she thought about it, the more she feared that these events, dramatic as they were, might deteriorate into routine and domesticity. Michael was a good lover, she thought, but it had been the excitement and rarity of their love-making, in a strange bed with a strange man, that had made the sex truly thrilling. The thought of it kept her warm for days.

But, perhaps because of her age, she felt she didn't need it too often. The secret inward pleasure of the memory, the anticipation that in due course it could be repeated - *if* she chose, *when* she chose - were as delightful as the event itself. And the effect on Michael too was important. Coquettish it might be, but she'd enjoyed it when he'd rung her, asking for a date, and she'd had to turn him down, pleading pressure of work. The keener he was, she thought, the better balanced their relationship would be. If she moved in now, all that might change. She might start to seem stale to him, he could take her for granted.

Take her for granted, just as Bob had. *No, forget Bob.* But how could she? She'd had a warning, one of the harshest of her whole life. The man she'd relied on, shared her life with, had got bored with her and left. It was as heartless and terrible as that.

If it happened once, it could happen again.

She'd mentioned her fears to Michael, and he'd been the perfect gentleman, in understanding. Not only that, but he'd come up with a practical solution. Rather than move in with him, he suggested, why didn't she move into the house he'd just left - the miller's house, next to the windmill? That way they'd each have their own space. It was standing empty - it needed someone keep it warm. It was a decent house, with three bedrooms, much more spacious than the windmill, where they'd be bumping into each other all the time, especially on those stairs.

This way she could have her own privacy, but they could meet when she wanted. Of course they wouldn't have to sleep together every night, he'd promised - not at all if she didn't want to. Anyway, he travelled a lot, just as she did, was often tired in the evenings, was too old to be a constant stud.

'We'll eat out, if you like, once a week - put it in our diaries, make it special. Then if we both agree, ok,' he grinned. 'Otherwise not. For the rest of the time we'll walk around each other like strangers. Neighbours, that's all. No touching. Keep up the tension. How's that?'

She laughed. It was tempting. A game she could play with this man. She wasn't sure how well it would work, but after all, she told herself, I can always move out if it doesn't. And it sounds worth a try. Better than these grubby flats I've seen, anyway.

He showed her round the house. It was clean, in need of some modernisation, but decent enough. There was a practical farmhouse style kitchen with an Aga, a spacious living room with a view over the windmill and a small dining room which Michael had been using as an office. It was still cluttered with a desk, books, papers and a filing cabinet.

'I'm sorry, I'll move these out as soon as I can,' he said. 'It's just time and ...'

'Leave it, it doesn't matter. I can work in one of the bedrooms upstairs. There's only me, after all.'

The main bedroom, in fact, was lovely. It only had a single bed at the moment but there was a thick blue carpet, fitted wardrobes, and magnificent view across the short hilltop grass beside the windmill to the valley beyond. She could see the clouds drifting towards her from the distant horizon. She could just pick out York Minster, a tiny white building twenty miles away. Sarah gazed out, enraptured.

'I could sit here all day,' she said. 'I probably will. It could make me late for work.'

'I doubt that, somehow, knowing you.' Michael smiled. 'Let me show you the bathroom.'

This, it seemed, was the one room he had modernized. 'It really needed it,' he said defensively. 'It was one of those terrible English disasters with a carpet round the bath and the loo, soaked with urine, no doubt, paper peeling from the walls because of the steam. But now ...'

Now it was immaculately tiled from floor to ceiling, with a large luxurious bath with taps along the side, cabinet with power shower, low level loo, and a six foot mirror stretching all along one wall over the basin and splashtop. It reminded Sarah of a hotel - her hotel bathroom in Cambridge, in fact, where he had insisted on showering that first time, before they made love.

'It's wonderful,' she said. 'But I'm not sure I could afford it.'

'Don't be silly. You're my friend. There's no question of paying rent.'

'Of course I'll pay rent,' Sarah said. 'I'm not your kept woman.'

For a moment she stared at him, there in the bathroom, and the deal nearly fell through. What do I really know of this man, after all, she wondered? What am I letting myself in for? But Michael seemed genuinely hurt.

'No, no, I didn't mean it like that, please, don't misunderstand me. I'm just trying to help. And since we're, well ...'

'Michael, I'll pay rent,' she insisted. 'I wouldn't consider it otherwise. Even so, it'll seem strange.'

'It won't be strange at all,' he smiled. 'It'll be nice.'

And with that, for the moment, she decided to settle.

45. Burnout

THE CAR was a blackened shell. The windows were smashed, and the tyres and upholstery had vaporized, leaving only the springs, metal frame, and tracery of steel wires behind. Most of the paintwork had burnt off too, so that it was hard to tell what colour it had been. The number plates had been removed. All that could be said for certain was that it was a three year old Nissan Primera.

'You said that's what you were looking for, so here it is.' The mechanic in charge of the Leeds police vehicle recovery workshop stood calmly beside the car, waiting for Jane Carter's response. 'We'll keep it till Wednesday, then it's going for scrap. Unless it's needed for evidence, which I doubt.'

Jane walked around the car, examining it from different angles. 'You're sure it was red? How can you tell?'

'Here, look.' He crouched down to show her a place under the wheel arch which hadn't been burnt. 'A few spots under the bonnet too. Typical Nissan red.'

'They made a thorough job of burning it.'

'You're right there. Whoever torched this had a guilty conscience, for sure. Either that or he just liked the flames.'

Jane poked her head through the window, examining the blackened mess inside. 'Not much you can gather from this, is there?'

'I wouldn't think so. Not unless we put a thorough forensic team on it and even then you'd be lucky. Never justify the cost.' He shook his head dourly. 'Not unless your guvnor's going to pay. Serious crime is it, you're after?'

'Murder,' Jane said shortly. 'Where did you say it was found?'

'Off the edge of a by-pass, at the bottom of the slope. Needed a crane to lift it up, that's why we waited until the New Year. Didn't seem any particular rush. We get dozens of these every month. Joyriders, mostly, young lads. Or robbers using them as getaway vehicles.'

'So far as you know,' Jane said. 'How many do you catch?'

'Not many. Not when they're burned out like this,' the man admitted. 'It's a professional job, I'll give the lad that.'

'He took the number plates too, to make it harder to trace,' she said. 'What about the engine markings?'

'Still there, I think.' The mechanic wrenched up the buckled bonnet. 'I can do a search, if you like. But we know whose it is, without that.'

'How?'

The mechanic shrugged. 'It's a Primera, isn't it? Not the most popular car. There's only one been reported stolen in this manor all year. Red, just like this - stolen three weeks before Christmas. Belonged to a little old lady - her pride and joy, she said. I had her on the phone in tears.'

An idea sparked in Jane's mind. 'Do you have the dates exactly?'

'It'll be on the computer. Through here.' The man set off across the workshop, a vast booming barn of a place, and Jane followed. They wove their way through a maze of similar car wrecks, some burnt out like the Primera, others mangled and twisted by accidents. In a separate barn at the far end, carefully shielded behind plastic screens, were a group of vehicles being meticulously examined for forensic clues. She followed him into a small office, where he tapped away on a computer.

'Here we are. Car reported stolen Monday 5th December. Burnt-out vehicle found by patrol car Saturday 3rd December. There - what does that tell you?'

Jane's spirits sank. 'It was burned out two days before it was reported stolen.'

'Looks like that, doesn't it? But wait a mo, I think I remember ... yes, there we are.' He scrolled down to a report. The old dear, Mrs Hamilton, she'd been up in Edinburgh visiting her grandson. Didn't like to drive, she said, the motorways scared her, so she took the train instead. Left the car parked in her drive and when she came back on Monday, oh dear me, it wasn't there.'

'So how long was she away?'

'Let me see, does it say? Yes, here we are. *'I took the train from Leeds on Wednesday 30th November at 9.45 a.m, arriving Edinburgh at ..'* bla bla - Christ, too much bloody information, these rooky cops can't see the wood for the trees. It's all here, though, sergeant, every last detail. Is that any use?'

It might be, Jane thought hopefully. And then again it might be nothing at all, like so many leads she had checked out already. 'Can I have a print out of that?'

'Sure. Free of charge.'

While he was fetching the paper from the printer she went through the dates in her head. Alison Grey had been murdered near York on the night of Friday 2nd December. The Nissan Primera had been left standing in the old lady's drive since the morning of Wednesday 30th - ample time, presumably, for whoever stole it to realise the house was empty, take the car, and - possibly - drive it to York, park it near Alison Grey's house, murder her, drive back to Leeds, and set fire to the car the next day. She sighed. It did fit, in a way. But it seemed a long shot, even to her.

'What time was the car found, exactly?'

The mechanic checked the printout before handing it to her. 'Ten in the morning. A couple of horse riders saw it on a hack. Said it spooked their horses.'

'So it had only recently been burnt?'

'I guess so.' The man shrugged, obviously losing interest. He nodded at a colleague who was trying to attract his attention through the window of the office. 'So if that's all?'

'Not quite.' Jane was tired, but she'd turned up a faint possibility, at least. Now she had to follow each detail, see where it led. She squared her shoulders, standing between the mechanic and the window. 'Look, I need to be sure about this car. So first, even though the old lady says it's hers, can you run a check on the engine number, please? So we're quite certain?'

'If we have to.' The man looked reluctant. 'Might take a while. We've got a lot on.'

'Please,' Jane insisted. 'Hold the car till that's done. And then ...' she looked at car wistfully. 'I'll see if I can get a forensic check authorized on it, even though it looks a pretty forlorn hope. If it is our car, it was parked in a muddy gateway near a carrot field covered with straw. But any straw would have burned up in seconds, wouldn't it?'

'Sure.' The mechanic thought for a moment. 'Was it very muddy, this gateway?'

'Like the battle of the Somme. Deep mud, as soon as you got off the road.'

'Well, you might have a chance then. Soils are different, you know, these boffins can tell an awful lot under a microscope. They might find a few traces under a wheel arch or on the chassis somewhere that wasn't blackened to a crisp. Worth a try, any road. If it's murder, as you say.'

'I'll do it, then. Now, if you could just show me on the map where it was found? And the address of this lady, Mrs - what is it? - Hamilton? I'll call in on the way back to York.'

Driving out to the by-pass where the car had been found, Jane yawned, wondering if this would turn out to be yet another wild goose chase. Her eyelids drooped; the small adrenalin rush she'd felt in the workshop when the dates had matched had not lasted for long. She needed a break, in both senses of the word. She still had no idea where Peter Barton was, the main suspect in the case; and no idea how he might be connected to this car, if at all.

Still, she wasn't about to give up. The murder of Alison Grey was the biggest crime she'd been involved with since she started her new job in York, and she was determined to solve it if she could. That was how she had always operated: working long hours, tracking down every last detail until she was satisfied. Jane had always known she wasn't brilliant, but she made up for it by being dogged, diligent, indefatigable. In her former job at Beverley she'd been nicknamed the Tortoise. Some people - her enemies - claimed this was because she was shy and tended to retreat into her shell at parties. But Jane liked the nickname. It suggested she was careful, slow, and thorough, unlike her young male colleagues, who dashed around a crime scene like hares, ignoring vital clues on the ground. She'd won her race to be Detective Sergeant, and she meant to stick to her method in York. If she, Jane Carter, could catch this murderer, then she'd gain the respect she craved, and be given more serious cases when they came along. One day, she might be a Detective Inspector. All it took was hard work, attention to detail - and a little luck.

46. Moving In

THE MOVE to Michael's house had gone more smoothly than Sarah had expected. The house was partly furnished, so most of her furniture went into store. The main thing it lacked was a double bed, and that was the one luxury she couldn't do without. Her squabble with Bob had been humiliating enough; after a couple of nights sleeping on a single bed in one of the smaller bedrooms, she went to a furniture showroom and ordered the largest, most comfortable queen-size double bed she could find. Michael laughed when he saw it.

'That looks to me like an invitation,' he said, when the delivery men van had gone. He put an arm round her shoulder.

'You've got your own, in the windmill,' Sarah protested. 'That's why I bought this. So I can really stretch out, by myself. Pure luxury.' She slipped from his grasp, and lay on the bed, fully clothed, looking up at him. 'That's the one great advantage of getting divorced. Having a whole huge bed to yourself, all night. Don't you think?'

Michael's face clouded, like a child denied sweets. She watched him for a moment, to see how he would respond. It felt dangerous, to tease him, but thrilling as well. Her husband, Bob, had been a soft man, thoughtful, intellectual, kind for the most part, and cruel only with words. With Michael, it was different. There was a faint sense of menace. He was normally charming but there was always that sense that he might turn, like that time on top of the tower. And then, anything might happen.

This time, when he said nothing, she took pity on him. She laughed softly, and stretched out her arms. 'Of course, I might invite you to share it with me occasionally. Like now, for instance. If you're not too busy, that is?'

It was a curious experience, for Sarah, this lovemaking. She had been faithful to Bob for so long, and before that, in her teenage years, to Kevin. She had no experience of other men in bed. That first night with Michael in the Cambridge hotel had been wild, guilty, full of nerves and tremendous, overwhelming excitement - a sensation that stayed with her for days, followed her into court, made her blush like a girl and feel foolish and forgetful with clients. Not so much because of the sexual satisfaction as the emotional release. Afterwards, she felt she was no longer Bob's wife; he was history.

And so it was again, here now, on this new queen-sized bed she had bought with her own money and installed in this new different house, nothing to do with Bob at all. Standing in the shower afterwards, she remembered the words of a song, and laughing, sang it out loud. *'I'm gonna wash that man right out of my hair.'* She was free, her own woman, making a new start.

And yet there was a problem, too, about drawing the boundaries between herself and Michael. They lived in different houses, which was important, though both belonged to him. It was crucial that she paid him rent, she felt, and had the status of a proper tenant. For however long she stayed here, she wanted this to be her house, which he could visit when she invited him, not otherwise. To her relief, Michael seemed to respect this. There was that clutter of his books and papers in the small dining room, but it was old stuff which he rarely needed. The windmill, he made clear, was his home, and the house was hers.

The arrangement began to work quite well. Michael was away quite often, travelling round his various projects, and Sarah, as usual, was absorbed in her work. There were days when they didn't see each other at all, or only briefly, going in or out. And then there were evenings when, as he had suggested, they made a night of it, cooking for each other or going out for a meal and sometimes a film or a play and then, like lovers, to bed. Sometimes in his bed, sometimes in hers.

It was a stunning place to live. Sarah had grown up the city, among the back streets of Seacroft, with no view but houses and tower blocks, mostly squalid and run down, where everyone knew each other's business. She had fought to escape that, and succeeded. The one thing she'd loved about the house she'd shared with Bob had been the sense of space. From her old bedroom window she'd looked out across fields to the river, where the heron floated in daily in his solemn quest for food. It had become, without her knowing it, a landscape in her mind. She had drawn sustenance from the changing beauty of the seasons, the big sky, the wide horizons.

But if that had been beautiful, this was spectacular. She could see for twenty miles to the west. She had never realised before how vast the sky was, how varied and beautiful cloud formations could be. On mornings when she didn't have to be in early at work, she sat at her bedroom window, lingering as she brushed her hair and put on her make-up, and watched the weather come towards her from the west. Once she saw a huge rainbow arching like a giant bridge from Selby in the south to the gleaming whiteness of York Minster in the north, where the pot of gold must be. And then a black storm like the end of the world, blotting everything out as it tumbled eastwards towards her.

Travelling to work was a pleasure too. The bike really came into its own, swooping down the long switchback roads of the Wolds. She found several routes, and varied them according to her mood each day. Her confidence in the bike increased, as she got used to the hills and bends. Michael suggested she buy a car, but she refused. The comfort of his BMW was one thing, the exhilaration of the Kawasaki quite another. On the bike she felt free, quite alone, out of time, a black bullet of concentration focussed on nothing but the winding ribbon of road straight ahead.

Her son Simon and his girlfriend came out to see her. Lorraine was blooming. Her skin was smooth, her breasts had swollen, she glowed with an inner beauty that radiated around her. Sarah gazed at the girl in wonder, thinking *I must have been like that once*, before I brought her young man into the world. Now she felt quite sinewy and withered beside her.

Simon brought her some chairs from storage in his van, and fitted a new carpet in the bedroom she had chosen as a study. Michael, seeing how handy he was, offered him a job laying a patio round the outside of the windmill. It was a small job, but Simon needed the money, so he agreed to make a start next weekend.

Sarah guessed that her son did not entirely approve of her new lover. But then, he'd had so many fights with Bob over the years, she hardly expected things to run smoothly. Michael went out of his way to be friendly and welcoming, showing Simon and Lorraine around the windmill, talking about building, enquiring about the baby, and - best of all perhaps - leaving them alone after an hour before things got too awkward. Sarah had noticed Simon beginning to strut like a young cockerel, protecting his mother from another male, and she was grateful to Michael for his tact.

She was not surprised by Simon's question.

'Are you going to settle with him, Mum? Is he ...'

'My new man? In place of Bob, you mean?'

'Yeah. That's what I'm asking, I suppose.'

'Why? Don't you like him?'

'I'm not sure. He seems ... a bit sure of himself, like. A bit cocky.'

'He's a self-made man, Simon. A property developer.' Sarah sighed. This was the wrong tack to take with Simon, who had a chip on his shoulder about all successful people. But it had been getting less in the last year, since he'd had regular work and the responsibility of the baby and Lorraine. The last thing she wanted to do was to drive him back into the envious rage of his adolescent years.

'Honestly, Simon, I'm not sure myself. It's too early to say. But it's good for me to have a relationship with someone else after what your stepfather did to me. That was painful, you know, it really hurt. I lost a lot of confidence when he walked out like that ...'

'You? Lost confidence? Mother, you're the most over-confident woman I know!'

'Yes, well. It may look like that to you, Simon, but it's not always how I feel. Anyway, as far as this relationship with Michael goes ... I don't know.' She smiled, remembering what had happened last night. Michael had filled the giant luxury bathtub with bath salts until the bubbles spilled over the rim, and they had both climbed in and splashed and laughed together like two big children until it began to get cold. Then he got out, dried himself quickly, wrapped her up in a heated white bath towel and carried her into the bedroom, where he gave her slow, luxurious massage with scented oils before they made love. Sarah had never been treated like this in her life before. She'd felt at once deliciously relaxed and on the edge of laughter at the absurdity of it. Remembering it now in front of her son, she felt amused and faintly embarrassed.

'He's a nice man, Simon, and he's made a big difference to me in the past few months. But whether it lasts - only time will tell.'

It was true, she thought, how Michael had helped her. She felt she was reaffirming her freedom, taking the necessary steps into a new and different life. It was vital, she felt, in her healing process not to feel that he, Bob, had taken all the main things from their marriage - the house, their bed, the decision about how and when to part - leaving her stranded like a waif on the shore. Sarah had been a waif once, when Simon was a baby; she never wanted to feel like that again.

As the weeks passed, her relationship with Michael changed. The sex, as they came to know each other's bodies, was better; but the thrill of the first few times faded, into something more like friendship than passion. Or perhaps not friendship either, she thought, as she lay with her head on his chest afterwards, but therapy.

Yes, that was it - therapy, a sort of healing process. Once, years ago, she had fallen off her bike and ripped some muscles in her thigh, and for two months she'd had regular treatment from a handsome young physiotherapist. He'd been a friendly, talkative young man, and over the weeks they'd got to know each other quite well. She'd lain on his table, his long, sensitive fingers massaging the bruised muscles of her thigh, while they talked happily about their different lives. They'd come quite close, or so she'd thought; yet when the treatment was over, he passed her in a supermarket with just a brief smile. I'm one of many, she'd realised; I'm healed, it's done.

Something similar, perhaps, was happening here. There were many moments when she felt close to Michael; and others when he seemed as much like a stranger as ever. There were those dark moods, for instance - not just the moment at the top of the windmill and the time his cooking had gone wrong, but other times too. She'd seen him a couple of times now during difficult negotiations on the phone, and it hadn't been pleasant. There'd been a real scowl, not just normal anger but a hint of violence, of instability within him that had scared her. It was something she remembered from her first lover, Kevin. It impressed her, but she feared it too.

She liked him, certainly, but it wasn't love. He was sexually attractive, entertaining and mostly considerate to be with, but ... he didn't obsess her. She could quite easily imagine life without him, but not yet. After all, he'd done a lot for her - not just given her a roof over her head, but given her back the sense that she was an attractive, interesting woman whom a man was proud and happy to spend time with. Those were things she needed so much that she was prepared to stay, at least until she was healed.

Which I will be in the end, she thought ruefully, putting on her make-up one morning. No bruises last for ever. One day all this will be over. I'll have a new life and a home of my own. And then what?

I may even walk past him in the supermarket as if he wasn't there.

How would that feel?

To her surprise, she found the thought not scarey at all, but comforting. She frowned as she realised this, pulling a face in the mirror. I'll make love to him now, and dump him when I'm healed, she thought coolly.

What does that say about me?

47. Clear as Mud

'LOST IT?' Terry said incredulously. 'What do you mean, you've lost it?'

'I'm not saying we've *lost* it, necessarily,' the voice on the phone replied miserably. '*Mislaid*, more like. It may just be filed in the wrong place. You see we're in the middle of installing a new computer system, and our main office administrator resigned last week, in a dispute about re-grading, so ...'

'This is a crucial piece of evidence in a murder enquiry! My sergeant sent it to you before Christmas. She's had two sets of excuses from you already.'

'I know, I know, and I do most sincerely apologise. It has the highest priority. We're turning the place upside down as we speak. But the fact remains that at the moment, most unfortunately ... we have no idea where it is. It may even have been sent to a different lab by mistake.'

'Jesus Christ!' Terry slammed the phone down. 'Pay peanuts and you get monkeys.' He turned to Jane Carter, spreading his hands in a gesture of despair. 'They've lost it. Our top scientists are very sorry, but they have accidentally posted your key piece of evidence to Outer Mongolia. Or Antarctica perhaps. So we're no further forward.'

Jane groaned. She had pinned a lot of hopes on the small scrap of cloth which the SOCOs had found on the barbed wire fence round the carrot field next to Alison Grey's garden. Will Churchill had praised her for it, and she'd been convinced it was just the sort of small, insignificant clue that would crack the case. All she needed was for the forensic scientists to find a trace of DNA on it. If it matched the sample she had taken from Peter Barton, then that was that - he was almost certainly guilty. If not, it had probably come from the driver of the red Nissan, and she could trawl the national DNA database to seek a match.

The one thing she had not expected, was that the lab would lose the sample.

Terry drummed his fingers on the table. 'It's absurd,' he said. 'The government wastes millions on some over-priced new computer system, and then tries to claw some of the money back by cutting staff pay. So what happens? All the good ones leave and get replaced by halfwits.' He sighed. 'And our murderer gets off scot free.'

He sat with Jane Carter in the incident room. The walls were covered with maps and pictures, the computers were running, the files of statements lay on the table between them. But even before this disaster, there had been a sense of something stale in the room. Nothing personal; his young sergeant's skin glowed with health, if not with beauty, as it had always done, and Terry felt warm and relaxed from an hour in the gym before he had come on duty. No, it was the room itself - not the floors, which had been cleaned, as they were every day, by young women from Poland - but the case itself, and its exhibits. Terry had brushed a wisp of cobweb away from a photo this morning when he came in. Only a small wisp, but it was the photo of Alison Grey's body, hanging from her staircase. And the cobweb had snagged on a corner of the photo, where it had started to curl up.

Time was passing. And the murder was not solved.

'It is of course possible that your scrap of cloth didn't come from the killer at all,' Terry said, after a while. 'It could have come from the Crockey Hill farmer, or one of his workers.'

'We could have checked, and eliminated them,' Jane said. 'This way, we just don't know.'

'No. Well, the only thing to do is plug on with what we do know, that's all.'

They had checked everything obvious. The house had been extensively fingerprinted and searched for suspicious fibres and DNA, without significant result, so far. The pathologist's report on the body was complete and it had been released for burial. Alison Grey's neighbours had all been interviewed. Her computer had been analysed and her emails read. All her email correspondents had been contacted, as had her family and friends who attended her funeral. And her phone bills had been checked. This, to Terry, was the other promising line of enquiry.

'Whoever killed her, took her mobile,' he said, leaning back in his chair. 'Why, we don't know. But she had it earlier that day. We know that, because she rang this number.'

'The one T-mobile say they can't trace?'

'Yes, because it's a pay-as-you go phone. No name, no account, no way of tracing who it belongs to. I've tried ringing it, but it's always switched off.'

'Perhaps he took it, and then dumped it in a ditch somewhere,' Jane suggested.

'Quite possibly. But the question is, who was she ringing?' He pulled a sheaf of papers from a file. They were Alison Grey's mobile phone accounts. Down each page, one number was highlighted in yellow. 'It's the only number that's unaccounted for,' Terry said. 'She rang or texted it, or it rang her, thirty-six times in the last three months. Sometimes two or three times a day, other times not for a week.' He got up and walked to the display board, where a map was festooned with coloured pins. 'And whoever he is, this phantom caller, he gets about. Assuming it's a he, which I do.'

'What about the texts? Haven't they retrieved them yet? That should tell us something.'

'No. They're working on it, they say. Some sort of glitch on the server, apparently. So in the meantime all they can tell us is where the calls were made from.' He tapped his hand against the map. 'Quite a few - including the last one - from York, several from Pocklington, three from Scarborough, and a scattering all over the country. A couple from London, and one from Cambridge as well. What does that tell us?'

'A travelling salesman, maybe?' Jane suggested.

'Yes, but selling what? Schoolbooks, computer paper? That's about all this woman needed.'

'She probably wasn't buying anything from him, if he was her lover,' Jane said. 'You think that's who it was, don't you, sir?'

'Yes. The lad in the big black car - the one that might have been an Audi, a BMW, a Mercedes, or any combination of the three. How I wish we had a nosy neighbour in this case. These people in Crockey Hill didn't see anything.'

'The curious thing,' Jane said slowly. 'Is that he had a big posh car like that, and then used a cheap pay-as-you-go-phone.' She smiled. 'You're a man, sir, why do you think he did that?'

'Probably so that calls from her wouldn't show up on his normal phone bill. So his wife wouldn't find them and ask questions, most likely.' Terry grunted. 'Not my problem, sergeant, as you well know. The only man who definitely did visit her is her landlord, Michael Parker. But he's got an alibi for the night she died. He was in Scarborough, working with builders on a barn conversion project. I've been out to check. They confirm it.'

'What, he was with them all night, was he, sir?'

'Until nearly ten, yes, I checked. There was some sort of crisis on with the barn. They had a big pow-wow - electricians, plumbers, builders, the whole team. Then he went into town with his foreman for fish and chips. They ate it on the beach and he drove home about eleven, the man says.'

'That pretty much lets him off, then doesn't it? He couldn't have been back in York before what - quarter to twelve at the earliest. What did the pathologist say about the time of death?'

'Anywhere between eight in the evening and one in the morning, he thought. She couldn't be more precise than that. So it's not impossible. He could have driven to her house on the way home.'

'And killed her there, after a long day at work? It's not likely, sir, is it? Most men would drive home to bed.'

'Most men don't murder their mistresses.'

Jane met Terry's eyes dispassionately. He looked stubborn, she thought, excited, with a slight flush on his face as though he knew what he was saying was unlikely but was determined to pursue it nonetheless. But then perhaps that was what she saw in his face because that was her opinion about him already. He was convinced Alison had been murdered by her lover, even though, in Jane's view, most of the evidence pointed the other way.

'We don't know she was his mistress,' she said neutrally. 'That phone number, it might belong to someone else. It's not his mobile, is it, so far as we know?'

'No. I checked with his secretary and the builders. He has a mobile with a different number. It doesn't crop up on Alison's phone bill.'

'There you are then. If the prepaid phone did belong to her mystery lover, it wasn't him. It belonged to another guy.'

'Someone who didn't leave any fingerprints or DNA in her house,' Terry said stubbornly. 'Michael Parker's are all over it.'

'It's his house - he's the landlord. Anyhow, there are six other fingerprints we haven't identified. Any one of them could be the lad who owns this phone.' Jane shook her head. 'You may be right sir, it *could* be him. All I'm saying is we'd be straining the evidence to breaking point to say it was. And we have two other suspects we have to eliminate first. Peter Barton, and the driver of the red Nissan. Unless they're the same person. Either way, that scrap of cloth would have helped us find out.'

Jane leafed through a pile of papers on her desk and pulled out a two page report. 'Anyway, sir, look at this. I've had the forensic report on the burnt out Nissan they found in Leeds. It was a red Primera, like I told you, and the dates all fit. It was found smouldering on Saturday 3rd December, the same day we found Alison's body, remember, and it was probably stolen a couple of days before. Most of it was just a heap of ash, but I asked FSS to examine any traces of mud they could find, especially under the wheel arches, and compare it with a sample from the gateway in Crockey Hill. The mud was pretty deep there, so I thought it was worth a try.'

'Did they find anything?'

'They found some, yes. Pretty well-cooked mud, but mud all the same. They don't say it's a perfect match - I guess that would be too much to ask - but they did find strong similarities. There's a list here, look, on page two. Their conclusion is that the mud found on the vehicle is entirely consistent with the sample from the gateway. So ...' She passed him the report triumphantly. 'Put that together with the dates, and the fact that the first two letters of the number plate are XB, which is all the farmer could remember, and I think we've found our vehicle.'

Terry skimmed the report, then looked up. 'We've found a vehicle that *could* be the one the farmer saw, ok. But how far does that take us? Who's to say it wasn't nicked by a couple of joyriders who fancied a trip to York that evening? And who never went nearer the house than a couple of hundred yards across a field?'

'There were wisps of straw in the hall. Which could have come from the carrot field.'

'Or from our constables, blundering in through the window. If you'd found wisps of straw in the car, now ...'

'They were burnt. Obviously.'

'If they were there in the first place.' Terry handed the report back to

Jane. 'Good try, sergeant. It may mean something, it may not. What we do know is that Peter Barton doesn't drive and apparently shows no interest in cars ...'

'That could always change, sir.'

'Unlikely, if he's shown no interest so far. And it seems equally unlikely that Alison Grey's lover was in the habit of nicking clapped out Primeras in order to pay her a visit. Though if the Primera driver did kill her, that would be a good reason for torching it, I agree.'

'So we're not much further forward, that's what you're saying?'

'Looks like it.' Terry strolled across the room, drumming his fingers on the pinboard with the fading photos of the crime scene. 'What we do know is she was murdered, in a particularly bizarre fashion, by someone who seems to have wanted it to look like suicide ...'

'Or wanted to humiliate her ...'

'Or possibly both, yes. Which would suggest that her killer knew her.'

'Unless he was a misogynistic pervert like Peter Barton. A twisted maniac who hated all women, and who'd tried to attack several already.'

Terry sighed. 'We also know that she had a boyfriend. Someone she phoned and texted regularly on a prepaid phone, who probably used her shower, and those condoms we found in her bedroom.'

'So if he was her boyfriend, why would he suddenly kill her? In such a weird sadistic way - beating her with a cane while she hangs in front of the mirror?'

'That can't be how it happened,' Terry said. 'Think of the scene in the hall. If she was hanged facing the mirror as you say, she'd have had her back to the staircase. And her hands taped behind her as well. He couldn't have whipped her there.'

'So what? You're saying he whipped her earlier? Or when she was dead?'

'Not when she was dead. The blood would have stopped flowing, the bruises wouldn't have come out.'

Jane thought about this for a moment. 'But remember, the pathologist said she'd just had a bath; that's why she was so clean. And naked too. So, if he didn't undress her, because she'd just got out of the bath, and those marks on her buttocks weren't inflicted when she was hanging there in the hall, then ...'

'Maybe she was caned earlier in the evening,' Terry said. 'Then she got in the bath, to comfort herself perhaps, and he hanged her afterwards.'

'The same guy? He lets her have a bath, then hangs her? Why?'

'I don't know why. Maybe he had a rush of temper, maybe he planned to kill her all along. I'm just saying this is how it could have happened.'

Jane shook her head, decisively. 'No. I mean, surely if that happened, you'd think the woman would be anxious, wouldn't you? If her lover was planning to kill her - and this doesn't look like a spontaneous killing, does it, it's too weird for that - then surely she'd pick up some vibes. She'd be worried, nervous, especially if he'd whipped her already. I can't see her feeling relaxed enough to lie in a bubble bath while he was prowling around outside. He'd have to be a really smooth, two-faced bastard to persuade her to do that, wouldn't he?'

'Which is why we should find him, soon,' Terry said. 'Before he finds some other woman, and treats her the same way.'

48. Student Memories

SARAH'S WORK as a barrister alternated between periods of extreme pressure and relative idleness. When her fraud trial was over, she found herself dealing with a succession of bail applications and petty thefts, which took little effort and less time. Leaving court at lunchtime one Friday, she rang Michael to suggest they eat in her house that night.

'I'll cook,' she said. 'It's about time I returned the favour. All you have to do is come over on time, before it's burnt to a frazzle.'

He laughed. 'That's an order then, is it, Mrs Newby? Seven sharp, on pain of death?'

'Yes, it is. This is a one time offer, you understand. My meals are a rarity, not to be missed.'

'I'll be there. I wouldn't dare disobey.'

'If you do, you'll regret it.'

She clicked off the phone, smiling at their banter. She wondered if he - and she - would regret it anyway, whenever he arrived. She was no great shakes as a cook, and had a theory that the ingredients of most meals burnt themselves or remained raw on purpose, just to show up her incompetence. Well, things would have to go better today. She'd ride to Sainsbury's on her way home, take what she needed in the pannier bags. She had time, and for once in her life she actually felt like cooking. Perhaps this relationship with Michael would last after all.

The meal - coq au vin - was not difficult but Sarah was determined to get it right. Michael was a gourmet, she knew. She'd seen enough of his behaviour in restaurants to know how critical he was, and she remembered how upset he'd been about his own failed soufflé. She doubted he'd be rude to her if she got it wrong, but she was hoping for praise, not politeness. In the kitchen, however, she had a crisis of confidence. She'd cooked this before, but never without a recipe book propped reassuringly in front of her.

All her own cookbooks were in storage. Anxiously, she hunted around on the shelves and in the cupboards. Surely Michael must have cookbooks too? She'd seen him with one in his hand, hadn't she? But there were none in the kitchen - just clean cupboards, pristine surfaces, tidy shelves. No books.

So where did he keep them? In the windmill, perhaps. But that was locked and he wasn't at home. She crossed the hallway to the room he'd used as a study. It was a moderately large room, still cluttered with much of his stuff. There was an old desk too big to fit in the windmill, a battered filing cabinet, an old leather armchair, and bookshelves all along two walls, from floor to ceiling. She'd only been in here a couple of times. It was the only part of her house he'd kept for himself; his inner sanctum, as he'd once referred to it, and it certainly looked like that - a traditional man's study, with drab colours, subdued lighting, and a decanter of whisky with cut-class tumblers on the end of one shelf. But he did use it; a set of architect's drawings were spread over the litter of papers on the desk, and the waste basket was full. Some of the books, with leather bindings, looked as if they'd been bought by the yard for effect, but there were paperbacks too, magazines about building, and two shelves of books about property law and surveying which looked well used.

Sarah started hunting for cookbooks. At first she couldn't see any, then she saw one on a shelf behind a chair stacked with files and papers. She pulled it out, but it was vegetarian cooking, not what she needed. There were several others nearby, untidily jumbled together. As she pulled out a book on French country cooking, a looseleaf file slid to the floor by her feet. She checked the book's index, found coq au vin, and tucked it under her arm. Then she bent down for the file, which had fallen open by her feet. She glanced at it briefly as she picked it up. It seemed to be full of newspaper cuttings, some loose, some in plastic pockets. She was about to close it when she saw a name she recognized.

Jason Barnes.

She looked more closely. The cutting she was looking at was quite recent - a report of Jason's appeal last autumn. She saw her own name mentioned several times, once highlighted in yellow. She pulled it out of its plastic pocket and stared at it in wonder. There was a photo of Jason coming out of court, with Lucy at his shoulder and herself in the background. What was this doing here? Michael hadn't collected cuttings of her trials, had he? Surely not - they hadn't even met when she won this appeal.

She leafed through the rest of the cuttings. The latest - those at the front of the file - were reports of the discovery of a female body found buried beside the ring road near Copmanthorpe. The first reports described it as curious, a mystery. One report focussed on the sensation of a child's discovery of a skeleton hand, which had led the police to the body. More recent cuttings described how the police were now convinced that the body was that of Brenda Stokes, the girl Jason Barnes had been convicted of murdering, before his successful appeal last autumn. Next to the report was a full page feature about that original trial, complete with pictures of Brenda - an attractive, lively looking teenager - and a scowling Jason Barnes, 18 years younger. Another column reported a police statement. They had no plans to re-arrest Jason Barnes, a senior detective said. But the case file remained open.

Sarah turned to the back of the folder. The cuttings here were brittle and yellow with age. Several, to her astonishment, dated back to the original trial. Michael wouldn't have needed to read the recent retelling of the case - it was all here, in much greater detail. There were cuttings from the *Yorkshire Post,* the national press, and magazines. Here and there, phrases were underlined or were marked with stars in the margin, suggesting they had been read carefully before they were filed away.

Sarah put the file down on the desk, wondering. It was very thorough, everything arranged in chronological order. Why was it here? Michael had done a postgraduate degree in York, of course - there was a framed certificate on the wall. She remembered discussing the case with him a couple of times; almost arguing about it once. She tried to remember what the potential argument had been about. Michael had thought Jason was guilty, that was it. She remembered changing the subject, to avoid a row. But it had all seemed quite casual, nothing to suggest the level of interest displayed in this file. What did it mean?

Whatever it meant, she decided, it was best discussed on a full stomach. She put the file back on the shelf and returned to the kitchen, the cookbook open at the recipe for coq au vin.

Sarah's cooking was a success. She followed the recipe slavishly and, for once, everything worked out as it should. Perhaps it was the Aga, which magically seemed to cook everything well without burning; perhaps it was because she had more time than usual; or perhaps the ingredients felt sorry for her and decided to co-operate - she didn't know. But when Michael came in the kitchen was full of a rich, enticing smell, with the chicken bubbling in its pot, a bottle of wine open on the table, and some hot rolls coming fresh and crisp from the oven. She smiled triumphantly.

'Voila, monsieur! French country cooking at its best.'

'Tremendous. You're an angel. Just what I need after a day like this.'

'Why? What happened?'

'Let me just wash my hands and I'll tell you.'

For a while, as they enjoyed the food, he told her: how the joiners in his farm development had put up a ceiling with the wrong insulation, and the drains to the septic tank didn't have enough fall and would have to be relaid. 'And then, to top it all, the planner is saying we may not get a certificate because the window frames aren't traditional enough. I ask you! It was a *barn* before, for heaven's sake! With a tradition of no glass and fresh air!'

'So what will you do?'

'I'll get around it somehow. Sweet talk him if I can, go and see his boss if I can't. There's always a way, if you're patient. That's one thing I learned long ago. Don't lose your rag or you're lost. They hold it against you for years. Especially in Yorkshire.'

'Why? Were planners different in Cambridge?'

'A bit, yes. Less pig-headed and stubborn.'

'More civilized in the south, then?'

'You could say that.' Michael smiled. 'Present company excepted, of course.'

She studied him quizzically over her wineglass. 'One thing you never told me, Michael. Why did you move up here?'

'To York, you mean?'

'Yes. I mean, you weren't born here, were you?'

'No. I was born in a place called Six Mile Bottom, if you must know. A village just outside Cambridge. You can imagine the ribbing we used to get. Kids finding the name in the phone book and ringing up from all over, just for a laugh. "Hi, there. We're a company in Kansas, and we sell giant toilet seats. We thought you guys might be interested."'

Sarah laughed. 'Sounds grim.'

'It was. We became quite thick skinned. There's another joke there, if you're looking for it.'

'So why York?'

'To get away from Kate, I suppose. I'd done a postgraduate course here, as you know, and I liked the place then. So when our marriage went pear shaped, I thought, why not?' He shrugged. 'I needed a fresh start. You can understand that, can't you?'

'Of course.' Sarah ran her finger round the rim of her wine glass. 'But most of your youth was in Cambridge, then?'

'In and around, yes.'

'Tell me,' she said. 'I've always wondered. What's it like, being a student in a place like that? I mean, I've seen Emily there, but what was it like for you?'

He grimaced. 'A bit different, I should think. For a start, there weren't many girls, not like today. Your Emily would have had to have been very brilliant, or very lucky, to get in then. The girls' colleges were Newnham, New Hall, or Girton. All the rest were male. And so of course for us lads ... well, the hunt was on.'

'What, for girls, you mean?'

'Yes. There weren't many around. So ...' he smiled wryly. 'If you'd been there, you'd have had the time of your life.'

'I had that in another way,' Sarah said ruefully, thinking of her late teens spent wheeling baby Simon round the slums of Seacroft in Leeds, from social worker to supermarket, doctor to dentist, playgroup to infant school, and all the time desperately taking evening classes to catch up with her GCSEs. 'So how about you? Did you have a lot of girlfriends, before you met Kate? If you were anything like my son, that was the main focus of your life. Far more important than studies.'

'There were a few girls, yes. But as I told you, they were thin on the ground. And I was quite shy, you know. Pretty naive. The girls used to run rings round me.'

'So when did you meet Kate?'

'Oh, that was later. After I'd left York, and I had my first job in Lincoln. I used to go back to Cambridge sometimes. I met her there.'

'So, when you were a postgrad here in York, did you have a girlfriend, then?'

'I had one or two. But they didn't last.' Michael looked at her warily.

'Why all these questions suddenly?'

'I'm just curious, that's all.' Sarah paused, then brought out her bombshell. 'This Brenda Stokes - the girl Jason Barnes was supposed to have murdered - she wasn't one of your girlfriends, was she?'

This question, as she had expected, hit him hard. Michael's face paled slightly, his body tensed. His voice changed from the relaxed, bantering tone of a few moments ago.

'Why on earth do you ask that?'

She smiled, affecting not to notice his change of mood. 'Oh, nothing. It was only that you seemed so concerned about the appeal when we talked about it before. And the day her body was dug up, when we saw it on the TV news in the restaurant. You told me you'd met her, remember? I thought perhaps she meant something to you, that's all.'

Sarah's senses were fully awake, as they were during cross-examination in court. Michael looked away from her for a moment, before answering.

'I ... I met her a few times, like I said. And yes, I did fancy her, as it happens. But she wasn't interested in me. So that's as far as it went.'

Sarah affected gentle feminine concern. 'It must have been dreadful for you when she was killed. What was she like?'

'Oh, very pretty, very vivacious.' Michael relaxed slightly, responding to the gentle, feminine concern in Sarah's tone. 'Promiscuous, too, as a matter of fact. Into sex, drugs and rock and roll. Not my type at all, really.'

'You were fairly straight, were you?'

'Yes. Even wore a tie to tutorials, at first.'

'So how come the attraction to Brenda?'

'Oh, well, opposites attract, they say. She was that sort of girl, wasn't she? She had all sorts of men flocking round her, she was used to it. Including that lowlife Jason.'

'Jason Barnes? You knew him, too, did you?'

'I met him once or twice, yes. Unfortunately.'

'Why unfortunately?'

'Well, he was a slob, wasn't he? A thug. And he killed her, too, for heaven's sake. Or at least that's what everyone thought. The police, the court, everyone. Until you won his appeal for him and let him out. It's all very well for you, Sarah. You didn't know what he was like.'

'I *have* met him, Michael. He was my client, after all.'

'Yes, well, he won't have changed, I'll bet, not even after 18 years.'

'He's not the most charming character, certainly,' Sarah conceded. 'Full of bitterness and anger. But then, if he was wrongly convicted, who can blame him?'

'*If* he was.' Michael had regained his composure now. He looked at her coolly. 'Did you really prove his innocence, Sarah, or just get him off on a technicality?'

You *know* the answer to this, Michael, Sarah thought. You've got all the details of his appeal in your file. 'The judges decided his conviction was unsafe,' she said. 'Technically, that's the same as not guilty. It means the evidence was too flawed to sustain a guilty verdict.'

'But it doesn't prove he didn't do it?'

'No. As with all not guilty verdicts, it means the prosecution are unable to prove that he did.'

'So it's like the Scottish verdict of not proven, is it?'

'You could look at it like that if you want to. But that's not how Jason looks at it, of course. He thinks he's not guilty - he's always maintained that, apparently. And as far as I know, even though Brenda's body has been recovered, there's still no move from the police to prosecute him again. Which they could, if they'd found significant new evidence.'

'I hope they do,' Michael said bitterly. 'I'm sorry, Sarah, but I still think he did it. And if he could do that sort of thing once, he could do it again. Now he's out, no woman he meets is safe.'

'Well, let's hope you're wrong.' Sarah looked at him carefully, wondering whether to mention the file she'd found in his study. She decided against it, for the present anyway. She seemed to have strayed onto sensitive ground. 'Let's talk about something different, shall we? I dropped in at an estate agent's this morning before court. There's a flat for sale in one of those warehouse developments by the river. Quite pricey, but I might be able to afford it. I've got the brochure, for you to give me an expert opinion.'

49. Intruder

THE HOUSE in Crockey Hill remained empty. The SOCO teams had finished their work and returned the keys to the office in Stonegate, but the landlord seemed in no hurry to find a new tenant. Scraps of black and white chequered police tape fluttered from bushes it had snagged when the SOCOS ripped it down. The wind tore its ends into ragged shreds, so that only fragments of the words 'Police Crime Scene. Keep out. Authorized Personnel only' could be read. But anyway there was no one to read it. Every day or so a police car stopped by to check the locks and see no windows were broken. Apart from that it was deserted.

The grass, uncut since last autumn, sprouted molehills and snowdrops in odd corners. Rabbits crept cautiously through the hedge at dusk, noses twitching, eyes and ears alert for the danger of dogs, cats or humans. Finding none, they ventured further, nibbling down the grass, stripping the flowerbeds of anything edible. It seemed a new paradise, fortunately discovered at the end of winter. More rabbits appeared. Then the stoat came. He ripped out the throat of a young doe. Her fur, blood and bones defaced the lawn.

It was the house's second murder. The killer slunk satisfied away.

The rabbits were more cautious after that. They stayed alert, close to their escape routes. Thumped the ground and fled at the least hint of danger. So the fox, sniffing round the doors, marking his territory like a dog, seldom saw them. He heard the rustle of a vole in the grass, the squeak of rats in the dustbins which they'd long stripped bare. The rats climbed through the toilet window which the cat had once used, but the fox didn't follow, as a man might have done. The rats began to explore and colonize.

The cars at the end of the track swished by, fifty yards from the house. One or two each minute, in the mornings as people drove to work, or returned in the evening. Fewer at night. Even before midnight the road could be silent for five minutes at a time. Even longer, after twelve. Hedgehogs crossed, stopping halfway to scratch. Owls cruised soundlessly between trees, watching for the sudden scurry of a vole on the tarmac. A car droned in the distance, humming gradually nearer. The wildlife tensed, waiting. The car approached, rushed into view and was gone. A pulse of music in a cone of light, hurrying away through a hole in the dark. The silence slowly returned.

The rabbits heard the man long before he was near. There was the bark, first of all, of the dog in the farmhouse. It barked twice, short and sharp, then the farmer swore and it stopped. But even at that distance, a third of a mile, the rabbits heard. Ears pricked, they rose on hind legs, and waited. Sure enough, there was more. The crack of a twig, the rustle of leaves. Distant at first, but approaching. When the man was a hundred yards away they began to move. When he was fifty yards from the house they were all gone. Passing the man on either side, unseen. Scampering away to their warrens at the edge of the wood. While he, emerging from that same wood, filled the night air with his human stench, the rasp of his breath, the squelch of his shoes, the rustle of his clothes. Even before he briefly flashed his torch, he shone bright as a lighthouse to their senses.

The rats heard him too, as he clambered clumsily across the fence. They heard him curse as he snagged his jacket on the wire. And they scurried quickly to their nests in the kitchen cupboards and under the beds, to wait in safety until he was gone.

Never thinking for a second that he would climb through the toilet window just like them. Never expecting him to flash a torch on their hiding places, open doors, expose their precious babies to the horror of his boots, his stick, his foul swearing. Never expecting to end up fleeing for their lives, out of the window, across the lawn, back into the woods from whence they came.

Leaving the man in the house alone.

50. Warning

'FLATTERER. I'LL see you tonight then. Bye.'

Sarah clicked off her phone and crossed the foyer of the court, still smiling from a conversation with Michael. The meal the other night had gone well; he had taken it as a challenge to cook even better for her next time. This new relationship, it seemed to her, was improving by the day. She felt lucky: somehow, at her age, she had managed to find a lover who was good in bed, interesting to talk to, and kind and generous in the way he treated her. He had spent the weekend looking at flats with her, but they found none she liked - perhaps, she realised, because she was enjoying her stay in Michael's house too much. It was the perfect arrangement - alone on the hilltop, with beautiful views over the valley, and her lover in the windmill next door. She could invite him in when she needed company, be alone when she didn't. And each evening together, it seemed to her, was a little better.

He still had strange moods which worried her. He'd been so cool and dismissive towards her questions about Brenda Stokes that she hadn't dared bring up the subject of the file in his study. Perhaps he'd loved the girl, Sarah thought; if so, that would make his attitude and the morbid file of yellowing newspaper cuttings more easily understandable. What mattered at the moment was the warmth of the attention he was lavishing on her. There was a spring in her step, a sparkle in her mind. This affair is like a bubble in time, she thought. If I'm lucky, it will expand to encompass my whole future - *our* future together. But I must enjoy it while it lasts.

It could burst at any moment.

At the door, she bumped into a man. A tall, loose-limbed man, in a faded double-breasted suit. He put out a hand to restrain her.

'Hello, Sarah.'

'What? Oh, hi - *Terry!* I didn't see you.'

'No. You look busy.'

'So - so. An easy case today for once.'

She stepped past him through the door into the sunshine, on the wide stone veranda overlooking the grassy circle called the Eye of York. To her right and straight ahead was the eighteenth century women's prison, now the Castle Museum; to her left the Norman castle, Clifford's Tower, on its circular grassy mound. Terry followed her out.

'Lucky for some.'

'Yes.' She brushed a wisp of dark hair from her eye, looking up at him. He looked well, she thought. Fit, but quite tense. A little tired. 'You busy?'

'No peace for the wicked. Or at least, I hope there isn't. Still running a murder hunt. Among six other things.'

'Not that murder at Crockey Hill? Haven't you got anyone for that?'

'Not yet, no.' Terry smiled ruefully. 'So ... we're still looking.'

'Oh. Well, good luck.'

'Thanks.' His eyes studied her carefully, seeing the trace of a smile linger on her lips. It wasn't a smile for him, he felt sure. 'You look well.'

'Thanks. So do you.'

'I heard you split up with ...' At the vital moment he couldn't recall the name of the wretched man. '... your husband?'

'He left me, yes. I'm getting a divorce.'

'I'm sorry.'

'Don't be. What's done is done. My life's started a new chapter, that's all.' She lifted her chin in that brave, unconscious movement of assertion that he remembered so well. It set off a symphony of memories inside him - the defiant mother who'd defended her son against all the world; who'd insisted, when he doubted himself, that he had to do better. She was the only woman, since Mary, who he'd ever seriously tried to seduce, and he'd almost succeeded. The only one he could never fully get out of his head, however seldom he saw her.

And now she was getting divorced.

'So ... you're all alone in that house, then?'

'I've sold it, Terry. I've moved out.'

'Oh, I see. So where ...?'

'I'm staying with a friend. Michael Parker. You met him, I think. He's renting me a house. Out in the country, on the Wolds.' Her hazel eyes met his coolly. *Don't ask, Terry, please,* was the message. *If you do I'll bite your head off.*

'I see. Was that who you were phoning?' *And smiling for,* Terry thought bitterly. The news hurt, like a knife in the ribs. A light punch at first, spreading pain thereafter.

'As it happens, yes.' She raised an eyebrow at his impertinence. 'What about you?'

'Me?'

'Yes. Your girls. They must be growing up.'

'Yes, they are.' Terry drew a deep breath, answering randomly, scarcely hearing what he said. 'Jessica's in her second term at Fulford now, loving it so far. Esther's jealous of course, but she's growing all the time. She's got a guinea pig, and a rabbit as well ...'

'That's nice.'

'It's a lot of trouble. You've no idea ...' He stopped, gazing at her sadly. He didn't want to stand here talking about rabbits and guinea pigs. She probably didn't want to hear about them either. She'd never been a very domesticated woman, as far as he could make out. She hadn't even been a particularly good mother, from what he'd witnessed of the tempestuous arguments with her son and teenage daughter a couple of years ago.

Not a good mother, at least, until the chips were down. Then she'd been superb.

But then, a woman who could defend her son in court wouldn't necessarily be any good as a stepmother helping a nine-year-old care for a rabbit and guinea pig, Terry told himself sternly. Even if there was the remotest opportunity for that. Which, clearly, there wasn't.

But there was something, all the same, that she ought to know.

'How about a coffee?' he said, recovering himself. 'If you've got time, that is. In your busy professional life.'

Sarah smiled at him fondly, comparing him to Michael in her mind. He came out of the comparison quite well, she thought - robust, manly, straightforward, with a few rough edges that appealed to her. She couldn't imagine him fussing about having a shower before they made love. But then, there was no need to fantasise about making love to Terry, or anyone else. She had a lover already. One she was going home to tonight.

'All right. I suppose I could spare a few minutes.'

Sitting at a table in Starbucks, Terry reverted to the point that was worrying him.

'He's ... a landlord, isn't he, this Michael Parker? Property developer, that sort of thing.'

'Yes, that's right.'

'I met him. It's his house this woman was killed in.'

'I know that, Terry. He told me.'

'Yes, well. We're still looking for her killer.'

'Well, I hope you nail the bastard,' Sarah said. 'He's one of the reasons I moved. Not the main one, of course, but he contributed.'

'What?'

'Well, I was living alone in a house backing onto a public footpath, wasn't I? Just like all these women who got attacked. It's not a great feeling.'

'That doesn't sound like you,' Terry said. 'I thought you were tougher than that.'

'Tough? Well, maybe, but we all have our limits. Who knows, perhaps this woman who was murdered was tough as well. Or thought she was. Anyway, how's your case going?'

'Well, that's what I wanted to talk to you about.' Cautiously, he began to fill her in on the details of the case - the way Alison had been found hanged, apparently after taking a bath; the early suspicions of suicide, disproved by the tape marks on her wrists discovered by the forensic pathologist; the frustrating search for Peter Barton; the bruises on her buttocks; and the two remaining leads: the red Nissan, and the possibility that Alison might have been murdered by a lover.

'It sounds intriguing,' Sarah said. 'Which do you think it is?'

'Well, I keep an open mind, of course ...'

Sarah laughed. 'Oh come on, Terry, this isn't a public statement for the press. What do you *think?*'

Terry frowned. 'I think it was her lover.'

'And? What are you looking at me like that for? *Terry?*' Sarah smiled, perplexed. So far the conversation had seemed to her to be going well. 'Come on, we're still friends aren't we? Spill the beans.'

Terry drew a deep breath. 'You're not going to like this, Sarah, but ... there's something you should know.'

'Which is?'

'It's not completely impossible that her lover was Michael Parker.'

'What?' The friendly atmosphere froze. Sarah felt as if an icy waterfall had fallen on her head out of a clear blue sky. She stared at Terry in shocked disbelief. *'Michael?* You can't be serious!'

'It's only a possibility, you understand. One we can't exclude.'

'But you must have proof. Evidence. What is it?'

'Well ...' Her face was sharp, as intent as he had ever seen it. Those clear hazel eyes bored into his like lasers. Carefully, he began to count off the points. '... firstly, of course, he's her landlord. So he knew her. In fact he was there two days before she died. He admits that himself.'

'Why was he there?' Sarah's voice was cold, hard, intimidating - the tone she kept for a hostile witness in court.

'To fix the central heating, he says. And his prints are all over the house.'

'Well, they would be. It's his house.'

'Yes. On the radiators certainly. But they're in the bathroom too. And on her bedside table.'

'He might have used the bathroom. Touched the table when he furnished the house.'

'He might. But it would have been smudged over time, or dusted off when she cleaned. This looked fairly recent.'

'What else have you got?'

'Well, he drives a black car, I believe ...'

'A BMW, yes ...'

'... and one was seen there quite often. And then, there's the absence of any other plausible lovers. And the question of why she came to York in the first place. She spent most of her life abroad, you see, teaching, until she started writing school textbooks. She needed a house to rent but she could have found one in Spain or Morocco or anywhere if she'd wanted, somewhere sunny and warm. So why come to York? Her editor thinks it had something to do with an old boyfriend from her student days.'

'Where was she a student?'

'In York. She studied foreign languages.'

'Well, there you are then. That's why she came.'

'Michael Parker did a post-graduate course here too, in 1991. That was Alison Grey's final year. He didn't mention her to you, did he, by any chance?'

'Only as his tenant, the woman who was murdered.' Sarah stared at Terry coldly. For some strange reason the memory of the file she had found in Michael's study the other night flashed briefly into her mind, confusing her. But that was about the murder of Brenda Stokes, 18 years ago. Nothing to do with this, surely.

'Have you got any evidence whatsoever to suggest that this old boyfriend, if he actually existed, was Michael Parker? That she even met him here in York?'

'Not so far, no. But ...'

'You've tested the body for DNA, have you? Pubic hairs, semen, that sort of thing?'

'Of course. But she'd had a bath. Quite a luxurious one, in fact, with bath salts and candles and so on, before she died. So if he did have sex with her he didn't leave a trace. Just these whip marks on her buttocks.'

'You found the whip, then?'

'No. We looked, of course.' Terry shrugged.

'And that's it?'

'All we have so far, yes.' Terry lowered his gaze for a moment, glancing down at the table to avoid the furious accusation in those blazing hazel eyes; then looked up again doggedly. 'I have spoken to your friend Michael.'

'And?'

'He denies anything other than a purely business relationship. He last saw her two days before she died, he says. On the actual day of her death he spent the afternoon and most of the evening with building workers at a housing development near Scarborough. I checked. He was there. Till about ten in the evening.'

Sarah thought back. That was the night he cancelled their date, she remembered. The day before she met him in Cambridge. And took him to bed.

'So that puts him out of the frame, does it?'

'Not completely, no. The pathologist puts the time of death anywhere between about eight at night and one in the morning. So if he'd hurried back from Scarborough, he might just have had time. You don't happen to know when he got back, do you?'

'No. I was still in my old house then.'

'Pity.'

'But you've no proof. No one saw his car, for instance? Just this red Nissan?'

'That's right.'

'Michael doesn't drive a red Nissan, Terry, not his style. Anyway, how would he have got into the house?'

Terry described the downstairs loo window. 'Could have been that way, who knows? But since he was her landlord, he probably had a key. Especially if he was her lover. He could have opened the front door, done the deed, locked it again on the way out.'

'No burglar alarm?'

'No.'

Sarah shuddered. Terry's use of the word *lover* hurt her deep inside, as though she'd been punched just below the heart. 'But *why*, Terry? What possible reason could Michael have for doing a thing like this?'

Terry shook his head. 'Lover's quarrel, perhaps. You know this man better than me, Sarah. Would he be capable of it?'

'Oh come on, now!' Sarah stared at him for a second, trembling. Then her fury flared up, like a vixen defending her cub. 'Terry, you don't like Michael, do you? Have you considered you might have got this totally, horribly wrong? That you might be accusing an innocent man of murder? You're stretching this much, much too far. For a start he's not a sadist - I think I'd know about that. Let's look at it, shall we? What evidence have you got? A few easily explained fingerprints, and the occasional sighting of a black car - is that it? No DNA, no other forensic evidence of any kind. No proof that he ever had any relationship other than a business one with this woman apart from the fact that they once studied in York together, along with 5,000 other students. A pretty good alibi, and nothing to put him anywhere near the scene of the crime. Are you even sure it wasn't suicide?'

'Her wrists were taped together, Sarah ...'

'Were they? Where's the tape? You haven't got that either, have you? Or any proof that her wrists were taped at the same time - the same *day* even - that she died? What if she was wrapping up a parcel, and she stuck the sellotape to her wrist while she was folding the paper - have you never done that?'

'Don't think so. Not to both wrists, certainly. Anyway, where's the parcel?'

'With her publisher, maybe, I don't know. Maybe she posted a manuscript or something ...'

'She'd use a Jiffy bag ...'

'Perhaps, who knows.' Sarah shook her head furiously, feeling rage overpower her judgement. 'Look, I haven't studied the case, you may be right about the tape. The point is, Terry, I'm living in this man's house, I like him, I've trusted him up to now, and just because you're jealous, you come to me and throw these accusations around, on evidence that wouldn't stand up for a second in court, not if I had anything to do with it anyway...'

'Who says I'm jealous?'

They paused, staring at each other. Sarah's face was flushed, her eyes blazing with anger. She breathed deeply, forcing her emotions to die down.

'Well, I don't know, I thought maybe ...'

'You're right, I am.'

'Really?' She shook her head, still flushed and angry. She didn't care how he felt.

'Yes, of course. To see you with a man like him ...'

'He's got a lot of good points, Terry. He's been very kind to me. Helpful, understanding.'

'Has he.' Terry spoke flatly. It wasn't really a question.

'Yes, actually, he has.' Sarah flicked her hair from her eyes, facing him coolly, realising the focus of the argument had shifted. She had no reason to want to hurt him. But this - this was intolerable. She watched him struggle for a response.

'Well, I suppose I should be glad to hear it, but if we're speaking the honest truth here, Sarah, I'm not. Because ... well, okay, I admit I haven't got a lot of proof, but I'm still trying to eliminate possibilities. Detectives do that, it's what we're paid for. And for another thing ...' Terry hesitated, searching for words.

'Well?'

'I *do* care about you, as it happens. You should know that. I thought you *did* know that, as a matter of fact. Clearly I was wrong.'

'No, you weren't wrong, Terry. You just ... presume too much.'

'About Michael or you?'

'Both, I suppose.' She shook her head. *My bubble is bursting,* she thought. *How can it ever survive this?* 'Look, Terry, this is a difficult time for me. I'm going through a divorce, I'm selling my house, I'm trying to keep my head together, and now you come and tell me the man I'm having a relationship with may be a sadist and a murderer. It's not easy, you know.'

'Since when was life easy?'

'I don't know, but it should be. Easier than this, at least. Look, if you are right, then I suppose I should be glad you told me. Well, maybe not glad, no, not that. Grateful at any rate.' She looked at him regretfully. 'Even if you are jealous.'

'Better to know before than after.'

'Yes. What do you suggest I should do?'

He hesitated. 'Well, there are two answers to that, I'm afraid. The cautious one, and the bold one.'

'Really? You've thought this out then?'

'To an extent. The cautious answer, the sensible thing for you to do, is to get out now. Leave him, move into a hotel if you haven't got anywhere to go, come and sleep on my sofa if you like ...'

A bitter, ironic smile flickered briefly on Sarah's lips. 'This is objective advice you're giving me, is it?'

'A friendly offer, that's all. Or I sleep on the sofa and you have the bed. Whatever ...'

'And the bold option?'

' ... is that you weigh up the risks, and if you feel safe enough, you check things out. Ask a few questions, look around his house, do a few things that I couldn't do without a warrant. If he's innocent, there'll be nothing to find, he'll have good explanations. If it doesn't look so innocent, let me know. I'll give you the number of my mobile, in case you need help. It's always with me, day and night.'

Sarah shook her head, astonished. 'You're suggesting I spy on my ...' she suppressed the word *lover* ' ... landlord?'

'Yes. I'm sorry, I know it's difficult. But ...' Terry watched her face closely. 'I'm afraid I am. I'll understand if you refuse.'

'Too right you will.' Sarah thought about it furiously, thoughts chasing each other around her brain like demented rats. *I can't spy on Michael, that's awful. But then, if he has nothing to hide, there'll be nothing to find, he won't know. And what if he **was** having an affair with this murdered woman, this Alison - what the hell am I doing renting a house off him? Alone, out there in the country. I should run, leave now. Or* *is this a ploy of Terry's, to turn me against him? He's **jealous**, remember? Christ, men! If I leave, and Michael's innocent, I'll ruin my relationship for nothing. But I have to check to prove he's innocent. Otherwise there'll always be this suspicion, now Terry's raised it. Damn, I wish I hadn't met him. I don't want this choice. I can't escape it now.*

The memory of the file she had found the other night came unwanted into her mind. *Why was it there? Why did he collect all those old cuttings? Why was he so cool to my questions? What year did Brenda Stokes die?*

1991. When Michael and Alison Grey were both here in York.

Just a coincidence, surely. I can't tell Terry that yet.

But her bubble of love was bursting. In the warm sunlight, she shivered.

Watching, Terry saw her frown, and then that unconscious lift of her chin. She was angry, all right. But she wasn't going to run away. Not now. Not Sarah Newby.

That didn't happen.

'Okay. What exactly do you think I should look for?'

51. Local Bobby

MURDER IN a country village is a rare event. The local community constable had little experience of it. Most of his time was taken up with community relations - maintaining the neighbourhood watch scheme, getting to know local people. The farms, hamlets and villages between York and Selby were a low crime area, and the residents wanted to keep it like that. They were pleased to see their constable, in his blue and white Range Rover, but they didn't expect to see him every day, or indeed every week. The area was too large, the villages scattered. Much of the crime he dealt with was minor - quarrels between teenage youths, thefts of garden equipment or farm machinery. The most dangerous offenders he faced were lampers - poachers shooting deer and rabbits at night in the glare of high-powered headlights. These men were armed and well organised - the constable needed back-up to deal with them, and tried to catch them as they were leaving, with the carcases in the back of a van, rather than risk pursuing them through the midnight woods.

But murder, of a woman alone in her cottage, was a different category of crime altogether. It sent a ripple of horror through the countryside. Community Constable George Graham, driving around the farms and villages, found people talked of little else. Who could it be, they wondered - a local or a stranger? Where would he strike next? How could anyone feel safe in their beds until he was caught? What were the police doing? Did the dead woman know her killer, or not? What was she doing, all alone in the country? Was she a wholly innocent victim, as it appeared? Or had she somehow brought her death on herself?

Constable Graham could answer none of these questions, however often he was asked. To his immense chagrin, he'd been off duty on the day Alison Grey's body had been found, visiting his mother in Scarborough. When he returned, two days later, he felt he'd been sidelined. His local knowledge was ignored by CID, who seemed to feel they already had the answer. All they asked was where the killer might be hiding - a question which seemed to him preposterous, in the dark days of midwinter. It was damp in the country, and cold - surely no one in their right mind would hide in the fields and woods at this time of year.

But then no one in their right mind would break into a middle-aged woman's house to kill her.

So Constable Graham spent days searching fields, barns and copses where there was a slight chance the killer might be hiding. It was futile, frustrating work, especially since he scarcely believed in it. But he did it diligently nonetheless, partly to cover his back, but also in the faint hope of success - the sort of dogged defiance of the odds which leads people to buy a lottery ticket each week. And also, it meant he could talk to his wife and kids about the murder enquiry he was involved in, however slightly.

His other link with the investigation was the visit he made most days to the crime scene - the house in Crockey Hill.

The house was empty, so the landlord had asked him to keep an eye on it. All he usually did was drive his Range Rover down the pot-holed track to the house, get out, and look around. Most days he strolled around the building, checking that the doors were still locked, peering in at the windows to see nothing had been disturbed. He sometimes imagined going inside to see if he could find some evidence that had been overlooked; though what that could be, after the SOCOs had spent two whole days lifting every fingerprint, vacuuming up each fibre and speck of dust, he had no idea. Anyway he had no key.

Most days he stood there for a while, thinking, seeking answers to the same questions the locals asked him. Who could have done this, and why? What was the dead woman like, to choose to live here? Constable Graham could see the attraction. For someone who loved peace and quiet, it was ideal. Set back a hundred yards from the road, surrounded by fields and woods, with views in each direction. Perfect for a woman alone with her cat and computer. It would be lovely in the spring, he thought, though she would never see it. Even now, the first tips of daffodil shoots were making a tiny, tentative showing around the edge of the lawn. Later they would be beautiful.

Alison Grey must have liked birds, the constable concluded. All around the house there were bird-feeders, hung high in the branches away from her cat. But they were empty now, the nuts all eaten. He watched a bluetit land on a bird feeder outside the study window and cling there, swinging for a second, before flying off. A pity, he thought, to abandon the birds now, with the cold on its way. He took a sack of peanuts from the boot of his car, bought earlier at the request of his wife. Would it do any harm to feed the birds? Surely not, he decided. After all, since he'd been asked to make these pointless visits, he could at least get some pleasure from them.

It was when he was filling the second bird feeder that he saw the movement. It was somewhere behind him; he only just caught it in the corner of his eye. With his left hand he was holding down the long, whippy branch of a birch tree, while his right twisted the lid of the bird feeder to get it free. Something moved inside the house. Just a shadow inside a window; there for a second, then gone. As if a bird had flown across the sun, but it wasn't that. A cat, maybe, inside the house - but it had been larger than that. Moving quickly, as though to escape detection.

Inside the house!

Constable Graham might be only a village bobby, but he wasn't stupid. His early training had been on the streets of Chapelfields in Leeds, where a quick furtive movement like that meant only one thing. Particularly when a uniformed officer was outside the house.

Guilt! Someone trying to escape.

He let go of the branch, which sprang back into the air, the bird feeder swaying wildly above his head. He ran to the window and peered in, staring right and left to see who was there. No one - but it was the kitchen window, and on the table was something which had not been there before.

A plate. A plate with crumbs on.

If he hadn't peered through the windows almost every day for the past week, he might not have been so sure; but now he was certain.

Someone was inside the house!

The problem was, the doors were locked and he had no keys. So how had the intruder got in? Constable Graham had already walked round the house and checked the doors - *did this person have a key?* Surely not; that would mean they had legal access and in that case he would have been informed. Or at least he should have been; procedures didn't always work perfectly, especially when it came to informing lowly rural constables about the details of a murder investigation on their patch. But then if this person had legal access why would he hide? And anyway - the realisation flashed electric blue in his brain - *there was no car outside, so how had he got here?*

Or she. It could always be a woman. Less likely though, unless he'd seen the ghost of the deceased. Constable Graham wasn't superstitious; he dismissed that idea in a second. And even as these thoughts crowded in his mind he was running round the house, peering in a second window and then a third, trying to find a person he'd only glimpsed for a second. Out of the corner of his eye.

No face, no silhouette even. Just a movement.

Another man might have doubted himself, but George Graham seldom did that. He wasn't superstitious or imaginative. As a young policeman he'd been taught to keep his eyes and ears open and trust his own senses, and that's exactly what he did. Above all, when chasing a suspect, his trainers had said, don't just chase blindly, *think ahead*. The suspect knows you're after him, what's he likely to do next? In this case, Constable Graham thought, *escape*. He can't hide in that house, he's trapped in there. He knows I could call up reinforcements at any time. I will in a moment, if he doesn't come out. But if he's looked out the window he knows it's only me on my own. So his best chance of escape is now. He'll want to get out of the house and run. And if I can't catch him he'll get away. So that's what he'll do.

How's he going to get out of the house?

From the downstairs loo window, the one the dead woman left open for her cat. That's how he got in, that's how he'll get out.

Even as this thought came to him Constable Graham was turning the corner to the back of the house where the window was. And he saw what he should have seen earlier.

The window had been pushed up, wider than before.

Wide enough to let a man climb in.

Or out.

He stood there, hesitating. Had the man - or woman - already climbed out, and got away? He didn't think so. There hadn't been time, and anyway, the window looked out across open fields, and there was no one there. No one running, no one trying to hide. The intruder must still be inside.

What's best to do, Constable Graham asked himself? Wait here until he comes out? Call for back up from the car? Or go in after him?

If I go to the car he may run off while I'm doing it. If he sees me waiting here he may smash a window and get out somewhere else. I could stay here all day, just waiting. That might be wise, but ...

Constable Graham's blood was up. If the intruder was connected to the murder, this could be the most important arrest of his career. He decided to climb in through the window.

It was a small window and he was a big man. But it was hinged from the top, and if he pushed it right up there was room. He swung his feet through onto the toilet, then stepped down to the floor. He was straightening himself up, and moving into the house, when he heard a sound. It was only a small sound, just a click. But Constable Graham recognised it. It was a sound he heard every day. It was the sound of a Yale lock, being opened from inside.

The intruder was leaving by the front door.

Sarah went back into court for the afternoon, wondering if she'd made the right decision. The case she was involved in was a minor shoplifting one, but she was so absorbed in her thoughts that at one point the judge had to reprimand her. What is going on here? she thought. First I lose my husband, then my house, and now I'm involved in this crossfire between two men vieing for my favours. Except that I've already granted them to one to the extent that now I'm almost a hostage in his house.

What if Terry's suspicions are right? Could Michael really have killed this woman Alison Grey? Why would he do it? The one thing Terry didn't come up with in our conversation was a motive. After all what could that possibly be? A man doesn't just go round killing women for no reason. Not unless he's a psychopath. And Michael isn't like that.

Is he?

No, of course not. He's a charming, polite man - friendly, helpful, rather too neat, obsessive and controlling perhaps, but nobody's perfect, not even me. I probably seem like some sort of messy disorganised tomboy to him, but he doesn't complain, not all that much.

Why did Terry say that woman was naked? Because she'd been having a bath, he said. A bubble bath, apparently, they found traces of scented oils in the tub. So if she was killed by an intruder he broke in and surprised her while she was in the bath.

Yes, but what if it wasn't an intruder? What if Terry's right and she was killed by her lover who was in the house all the time - a man who knew she was in the bath, watched her, maybe even ran the water and poured the bath oil for her? She would have trusted him, felt safe, even happy to have him fussing around her. And then, what? He asks her to get out of the bath, holds up a towel for her perhaps, with a roll of tape in his pocket to wrap round her wrists when they're dry - is that how it happened? Was the scarf already tied round the banisters, the chair in place in the hall? Did he prepare all this while she was relaxing comfortably in the bath?

Sarah shuddered as she tried to imagine it. She couldn't quite make the details fit, the sequence slipped from moment to moment. Sometimes the man was naked, sometimes he was fully dressed. Sometimes the woman in the bath was nervous, other times she was unsuspecting and relaxed, enjoying the warm water, the cossetting, the comfort. But one thing was constant - the face of the man holding the towel, smiling as she stepped out of the bath. It was Michael. *He'd done the same thing for her.*

This is nonsense, she told herself. Michael has no motive, concentrate on that. Why would he do such a thing? Surely he wouldn't whip her, I can't imagine that. Terry Bateson's wrong, he has to be. It wouldn't be the first time he's got things wrong and it won't be the last. He's jealous, he's just trying to scare me so I'll run off to him instead. I could sleep on his sofa, didn't he say? As if ...

Come on, Sarah, you're a rational woman, a professional lawyer, focus on the facts, not the fantasies.

The snag is there are some important facts. Facts that require an explanation.

Fact 1. Michael knew this woman. He was her landlord and he'd visited her a couple of days before. His fingerprints are in the bedroom and bathroom as well as on the radiators.

Fact 2. On the night she was killed, he cancelled a date with me at short notice. Why? Because of a building crisis at Scarborough, he said. But couldn't he have dealt with that next day? On the other hand he did go there. Terry said he'd checked.

Fact 3. Alison Grey was a student in York, at the same time as Michael. Well, what does that prove? Nothing, if they never met. But then there's this other thing ...

Fact 4. Michael keeps a file in his study about the case of Brenda

Stokes and Jason Barnes. I found it. And several times he's asked me about Jason's appeal. Why is that? Simple curiosity, or something deeper?

Sitting in her office that evening she turned over these facts in her mind. The one possible connection, she realised, was that all these people - Alison, Jason, Brenda and Michael - had been in York at the same time, 18 years ago. Michael admitted that he'd known Brenda slightly, and was convinced Jason was guilty of her murder. And Alison Grey would have known about this murder too, if she was a student at the university then. It would have been a big story.

But did she know Michael, or Jason, or Brenda? Sarah didn't know.

She remembered how touchy Michael had been when she started to question him about these things the other night. Why was that?

What if Michael *had* met Alison in York when they were students, and was lying to Terry about his relationship with her now?

Sarah shook her head, bemused. Why would he do that?

She had no idea. Anyway, that didn't make him a murderer, did it?

52. Gotcha!

THE DOWNSTAIRS loo was at the back of the house, in an extension built onto the kitchen. Community Constable George Graham stepped out of it into a utility room, with a washing machine and tumble dryer. From there he went directly into the kitchen. The click he had heard was very quiet; if there had been any background noise - the hum of traffic, a radio or TV playing - he wouldn't have heard it. But out here in the country there was nothing. No tractors, no traffic, not even birdsong just then. His own footsteps, the breath in his lungs, sounded clear. So the intruder in the house would have heard him, for certain, as he scrambled clumsily through the window, breathing heavily and trying not to tear his trousers on the window catch. The intruder knew he was there anyway. He would have seen him drive up, fuss with the bird feeder, and walk round the house peering in the windows when he saw a movement inside. His thoughts would have mirrored Constable Graham's. What's he going to do now? Stay outside, call for help, or climb in? When George Graham started to haul his heavy body through the window, the listening intruder would have made his own decision. Time to go. So he'd clicked open the Yale lock and opened the front door.

    The constable rushed into the kitchen, his boots slapping on the tiled floor. He dodged round the table, knocked over a chair, and hurried into the hall. It was a short, tiled hall, perhaps four yards long, and the front door hung open at the end of it. Outside the door, in the cold winter light, was a man in black tracksuit and trainers. A youngish man with long dark hair.

    All this George Graham saw in the first second. But what surprised him, as he sprinted along the hall, was the young man's hesitation. Instead of sprinting away down the drive, he turned to his left, out of sight. George thought, *why's he going there?* A microsecond of thought, and the answer was plain.

He's seen my car. With the keys still in it!

As he ran out of the front door a cry came from his chest. The fierce shout he intended came out like a groan - of horror and apprehension. *Don't touch that car!* If he drives off in a state of the art Range Rover worth what - £30,000? - my career will be ruined. I'll never live it down - George Graham the car salesman, stop me and get one free.

He turned the corner of the house and saw the nightmare happening. The man was in the driver's seat, turning the ignition. The engine started. The constable sprinted up to the car just as the man reached out to pull the driver's door shut. But George was there, his arm inside. The door slammed on his shoulder, hurting like hell, but it didn't shut. With his other arm George wrenched it open, reached in, and grabbed the driver round the neck. At the same moment the man let the car into gear, and it lurched forward, dragging George off his feet.

Off his feet, but only for a moment. His legs took huge, lunging strides to keep up, while his arms refused to let go. George was a strong man, fit, he played rugby at weekends, he knew how to grip his man round the upper body and drag him to the ground, though not usually from a car. The young man fought back. He pushed his elbow into George's neck, forcing his head back, so that his spine above his lungeing legs was arched like a bow. But the young man was half out of the car too. He pulled hard on the steering wheel to save himself, and at the same time his foot went down on the accelerator. The Range Rover leapt forward, in a long wild swerve to the right. Gravel sprayed in the air.

George lost his footing altogether; he felt his legs dragged backwards across the ground. Any moment now I'll be under the wheels, he thought. But I'll take this bastard with me. He had the young man by the neck, the hair, they were both leaning right out of the car, which turned faster, wheels on full lock, engine roaring ...

... and crunched straight into the wall of the house.

The impact threw George and the driver hard against the open driver's door, which was wrenched off its hinges. They collapsed on the ground and lay there, stunned, a tangle of legs, arms and trunks. But George, luckily for him, had fallen on top of the young man, and he got his elbow across the wriggling youth's throat and pressed his full body weight down. The face beneath him darkened with blood, eyes opened wide with fear.

'Stay fucking still lad, you're nicked!'

He kept up the pressure, just this side of throttling the boy, adjusting his weight to keep the lad pinned down. His own arms and legs, he was glad to find, still worked. When the resistance beneath him lessened he released the pressure from his elbow. The young man drew in deep, rasping breaths of air. George turned him roughly onto his face and jabbed his knees into the small of his back. He reached for the handcuffs at his belt, pulled the boy's arms behind him and cuffed his wrists together. Then he looked at the car.

It was wrecked. Less than three months old and the bonnet and driver's side wing were half their normal length, concertinaed like cardboard. The driver's door hung off at a crazy angle. Air hissed from one of the tyres. The engine had stalled with the impact but the ignition lights were still on.

George got cautiously to his feet. He kept his right foot firmly in between the young man's shoulders, pressing him flat into the gravel.

'You stay right there, son,' he said. 'Don't move a muscle.'

He reached into the car with his left hand for the radio microphone. To his delight, it still worked. He recognized the voice on the other end.

'Dave,' he said. 'This is 791 George Graham. Backup required, Crockey Hill. I think I may have arrested a murder suspect.'

53. Holding Hands

WHEN SARAH got back that evening Michael's car was already there. She saw his light on in the study on the third floor of the windmill. She parked the bike, went into her house, and cooked herself some pasta and salad which she ate at the kitchen table while watching TV. Just as the ten o'clock news came on, there was a knock on the door. Before she could get up Michael opened it and looked in, a friendly smile on his face.

'Mind if I come in?'

'No ... I mean yes, of course. Just for a few minutes, that's all.'

As he came in she got up nervously and took a glass out of a cupboard. 'I was just going to have a whisky. Would you like one?'

'Why not? Just what the doctor ordered.'

Sarah poured him a drink and they sat down opposite each at the kitchen table. He looks a lot less anxious than he ought to be, Sarah thought, if Terry's theory has anything in it. But there can't be, this is all nonsense, I wish I'd cut the wretched detective dead in the first place. Then I'd never have had coffee with him and he wouldn't have planted this worm of doubt in my brain. I'd be calm and relaxed here with Michael instead of ... what?

Nervous. Angry. Afraid.

'Cheers.' She raised her glass. 'Have a good day?'

'Busy. A few complications. How about you?'

'Oh. I got a shoplifter sent down for six months. Out in three. Total cost to the taxpayer - including legal aid, police time, prison accommodation and transport - of about fifty grand, at a guess. My good deed for the day.'

Michael winced. 'Someone has to do it, I suppose.'

'So they tell me.' She smiled. 'It pays the bills. Mine, at least.'

He sipped his drink, and looked at her thoughtfully. 'You look tired.'

'I am, a bit.' She muted the TV and leaned back. 'Early night.'

'Good idea.' He raised his glass, then looked pointedly at her rumpled work clothes. 'The water's hot. Why don't you slip out of those while I run you a bath. I discovered a new massage oil in Fenwick's today. Relieve your tensions, ease your troubles.'

Sarah cringed. No doubt it was kindly meant but he could hardly have made a worse suggestion. The image of Alison Grey came into her mind. Stepping out of her bath, soap bubbles sliding down her naked body, into a warm towel held by - who?

'I think, if you don't mind, I'll skip the bath this evening.'

'Really?' He frowned. 'You disappoint me. I was thinking perhaps tonight ...'

'I'm tired, Michael. I've had a long day, and I've got a bit of a stomach ache. But the whisky will deal with that, if I just take a few minutes to unwind. Then all I want to do is get into bed, pull the duvet over my head, and dive into the land of dreams. If that's all right with you.'

She looked at him, making sure he'd got the point. No sex, and she was sleeping alone tonight. Separate bedrooms, separate houses. That was the agreement.

'I see.' His bonhomie faded. 'I thought a hot bath and massage would help you relax, that's all. Help us both, matter of fact.' There was hurt and anger in his face, quickly mastered. 'But it's your choice, of course. In that case I'll say goodnight. I've had a hard day too.'

'Oh, really? What happened? Stay and tell me about it, if you like.'

'Not now. It's too long and complicated anyway. Maybe tomorrow night, if you've got more time. And your stomach isn't troubling you.'

'All right.'

He knocked back his whisky, got up and left. Sarah sat quietly, listening to the sound of his footsteps fading across the grass. An owl hooted in the woods; his front door closed. Looking through her window, she could see the lights from the windmill reflected on the grass outside. She sipped her whisky and waited. After about half an hour the downstairs lights went off, and there was a single light in his bedroom, on the third floor. She waited a while longer.

Ever since she'd met Terry she'd been wondering: what else is there here, what else can I find? The only specific thing he'd asked her to look for was a mobile phone, but Michael always kept his in his jacket. Anyway she'd told Terry his number and that wasn't the one he was looking for, apparently. Why on earth should Michael have two phones? The more she thought about it, the less likely it seemed.

The only other thing she could think of was that file on Brenda's death and Jason's trial. It had seemed meticulously kept, but she hadn't had time to study it closely, and it had seemed odd, rather than important at the time. Curious, perhaps, but not worrying.

She still didn't see what relevance, if any, it had to this investigation of Terry's. After all, she knew just about everything about Jason's case and his appeal - she'd seen all the case papers. But those were prepared with a particular end in view - first Jason's conviction, then his acquittal. That's what she and Lucy and the lawyers before them had focussed on - the facts most relevant to their client. But now it occurred to her that Michael may not have seen it like that - certainly he hadn't collected his materials for that purpose. So if he had another purpose, what was it? Some passages in the texts, she remembered, had been highlighted in yellow. What were they?

She waited until the light in Michael's bedroom went out. Then she walked quietly into the dining room, took out the file from behind the cookbooks where she had found it, carried it to her own study upstairs, and began to read.

For about ten minutes she read swiftly, all her attention on the file, as she'd learned to do as a barrister. But the answer to her question eluded her. Several passages were highlighted, but they were the ones you'd expect - the key items of evidence, the lawyers' main arguments, quotations from the police, the judge's decisions. Nothing she didn't know already.

Then, at the beginning of the file, she came across some yellowing cuttings from the *Yorkshire Evening Press*, and the *Yorkshire Post* - ones she hadn't seen before. The content of the articles was nothing new or obviously useful - early stages of the investigation, quotations from the anguished friends and family of Brenda Stokes. Not things she would need for the appeal. But there were also a few photographs - one in particular which caught her eye. It was of a memorial service, held in Brenda's memory - not a funeral, since without her body, there was nothing to bury. Her family were there, clustered outside a church, and behind them older people. Policemen - she recognised Robert Baxter, the detective superintendent who'd cursed her in court. So young he looked here! And behind him, younger people, Brenda's friends presumably, in the strange fashions of the 1990s. And then, there it was.

One face stared out at her from the photo, different from all the others. A young, skinny version of a face she knew well. A face she'd touched, kissed, seen on the pillow beside her own. It was Michael, she was sure of it. A young student Michael with long hair and a foolish, droopy moustache, but Michael for all that. She couldn't be wrong.

So he didn't know Brenda just vaguely, she thought, as he told me. *He lied about that.* He knew her at least well enough to attend her memorial service, with what - a dozen other young people at most, in the photograph anyway. She picked up a magnifying glass from the desk and studied the expression on the face of the young man in the photo. But it was hard to decipher - calm, controlled as usual, the lip hidden by the droopy moustache. He looked serious, but that befitted a memorial service. *Why was he there?*

She was about to put the magnifying glass down when she realised something else - the girl standing next to Michael was holding his hand. Not just with her left hand that was beside his right, but with her right as well - she was reaching across to clutch his arm tightly with both hands as though without his support she'd fall over. And the expression on her face was much easier to read. Not just grief or respect but something stronger, like horror perhaps, or shock.

Why shock, Sarah wondered? It seemed strange at such an occasion, excessive, unnecessary. Grief would be more appropriate, sorrow. After all, Brenda must have been missing, presumed dead, for several months.

Sarah peered at the yellowing photo closely, moving it directly under the table lamp and holding the magnifying glass to get the best possible magnification.

It wasn't just shock, Sarah decided, it was fear. The girl looked terrified. As if something awful was going to happen to her at any moment. As if she expected it, almost. And she was hanging on to Michael for dear life. *Why?*

And who was she?

Sarah got up. She had guessed who it was, but to be sure she needed to compare the photo of this girl with the one of Alison Grey that had been published in the *Yorkshire Evening Press* several times over the past few weeks. There was a pile of newspapers on the floor beside her desk. She had meant to throw them out, but never got round to it. She leafed through them quickly, searching for the photograph she remembered. At last, at the bottom of the pile, she found it. Just as she had remembered.

The woman in the picture was older, of course, and looked much happier, as murder victims always do. The press seem to choose the prettiest picture they can find, perhaps to comfort the relatives slightly. This is how she was in her good days, before she died.

But the hair was the same, the shape of the face, everything. There was no doubt. The girl holding so tightly on to the youthful Michael as though he was her only support in the world, was a younger version of the woman who had been found hanged the hallway of a house belonging to Michael, eighteen years later. Alison Grey.

She was his girlfriend first, and then his tenant, Sarah thought.

Just like me.

54. Interviewing Peter

'I WANT a lawyer,' Peter Barton said. 'I can have one, can't I?'

'Of course you can, Peter. A very wise decision, in my view.' Jane Carter smiled at the boy. Not a kind smile; more like the eager grin of a bitch watching a rabbit. 'These are serious charges you're facing.'

When George Graham had learned the name of the young man he'd arrested, he'd been delighted. It was Peter Barton, the lad they'd all been looking for. The attitude of the CID officers, Terry Bateson and Jane Carter, brought him further relief. He'd arrested a murder suspect, that's what mattered to them. The car could be repaired. He hoped his uniformed superintendent would take the same view.

'He went back then,' Jane Carter said, while they waited for the doctor to attend to Peter's bruises. 'Like a dog returning to his vomit.'

'It looks like it,' Terry agreed. 'I wonder what he was doing there.'

'Gloating, probably,' Jane answered. 'Trust me, this is one sick kiddo.'

The sick kiddo turned up an hour later in an interview room. He sat beside the duty solicitor, Rachel Horsefall, a young woman with spiky copper brown hair and a thin elfin face, which was currently creased in an earnest frown appropriate to the seriousness of the case. She clasped her hands firmly together on the battered interview table and leaned forward, her green eyes focussed sharply on Terry Bateson.

'Before we start this interview, Detective Inspector, my client has a complaint. He believes he was arrested with undue violence. He was nearly throttled and sustained several injuries.'

Terry sighed. 'What injuries? Could I see them?'

Peter Barton rolled up his sleeve. There was a gauze bandage taped to his forearm. His face was grazed on the left temple where some ointment had been applied.

'Several cuts and bruises, as you see,' Rachel Horsefall insisted. 'It was clearly a violent arrest.'

'He was trying to steal a police car, Miss Horsefall. He caused a serious accident. Placing the arresting officer in danger of his life.'

'Does that justify brutality? My client was nearly strangled. His throat is bruised.'

Terry peered across the table. There was the faintest of marks on Peter Barton's neck, under the tracksuit top. Possibly mud, possibly a bruise. Either way ...

'I note your complaint, Miss Horsefall, and if you put it in writing it will be investigated. In the meantime, this is a murder enquiry.'

'My client has no knowledge of any murder.'

'Really? Perhaps *he* could answer a few questions.' Terry inserted two cassette tapes in the recorder, checked that it was working, issued Peter with a caution, and recorded the time, date, and names of the people in the room. 'What were you doing in that house, Peter?'

'Which house?'

'The one in Crockey Hill, where you were arrested.'

'Nowt.' Peter stared at him sullenly. 'It were empty, so I dossed down there. Then this copper tried to kill me.'

'How long had you been there?'

'Since last night. What's it to you?'

Terry looked at him coolly. There was more to this lad than first appeared, he decided. But then there would be, if he was as guilty as he seemed.

'So you just decided to break in?'

'There were no lights on. I were cold.'

'That house was someone's home, Peter. What if the owner had been there? What would you have done then?'

'But she weren't, were she?'

'*She?*' Terry let the word hang in the silence for a moment. Rachel Horsefall, he was glad to note, was looking worried. 'How do you know it was a she?'

Peter shrugged. 'Women's things, all over't place. Make-up and such. I just thought.'

'Thought what?'

'That a woman lived there.'

'And that's why you broke in, is it? Because a woman lived there on her own?'

'No. I told you. It were empty.'

'Why did you doss down there? Why didn't you just go home?'

'*You* know why.'

'No, I don't. Tell me. Why don't you?'

Peter's lips moved, but he said nothing. He just stared at Terry, shaking his head. Terry let the silence build for a while, then he said: 'It's because you're on the run, Peter, isn't it? You skipped bail, and you're on the run from a different crime.' He sat back, nodding at Jane. 'DS Carter has some questions for you about that.'

Jane leaned forward, her arms on the table, her face a few inches from Peter's. He gazed back at her anxiously.

'Peter Barton, two weeks ago a man wearing a mask broke into a house off the Tadcaster Road, just by the Knavesmire. A woman lived in this house, a young mother called Elizabeth Bolan. She'd been out for a run and was having a shower before her child came home. When she was drying herself after her shower a man came into her bedroom. A man with a mask over his face, and latex gloves on his hands. Can you imagine how terrified she was?'

Peter shook his head slowly, not speaking. Jane stared, forcing his eyes to meet hers.

'The man knew she was in the house. He came prepared to assault her. He held a cord in his hands, like this.' She reached beneath the desk and pulled up a plastic evidence bag. 'I'm showing Mr Barton a pink dressing gown cord which was found in Ms Bolan's bedroom. Do you recognize this, Peter?'

Silence. Another shake of the head. A bead of perspiration began to form on Peter's left temple.

'Mr Barton is shaking his head. The next thing that happened, Peter, was that this man assaulted the woman. He put the cord round her neck, and tightened it so she couldn't breathe. He held her like that in front of the mirror for a moment, and then pulled her towards her bed. But she was a brave woman, and she fought back. She pulled his mask sideways and he let go of the cord. Then she found a pair of scissors, and threatened him with them. That must have been a shock for the man, don't you think? Not what he expected.'

Peter made no response. But his face seemed paler than before, the perspiration more pronounced. The solicitor grimaced, as if she had eaten something nasty.

'Not as brave as you thought, were you, Peter? Didn't fancy being stabbed with those scissors. Might have got you in the balls, mightn't she? Cut off your prick?'

Peter winced, and Rachel Horsefall intervened. 'Detective sergeant, is that necessary? You have the right to question my client, not harass or insult him.'

Jane ignored her. Her eyes stayed focussed on Peter, who was sweating quite noticeably now. His right thumb was trembling, as if detached somehow from his body.

'You don't like that idea, do you, Peter? Don't like the idea of being hurt in your sexual parts. But that's what you meant to do to that woman, wasn't it? Hurt her sexual parts. Drag her onto her bed and rape her!'

'I didn't want ...' The words burst from his mouth involuntarily. He looked shocked, as if he hadn't known he was speaking.

'Didn't want what, Peter?' Jane's voice was quiet, cool, controlled.

'Didn't want ... nothing. I weren't there.' He glanced at the solicitor on his right, recalling where he was.

'You weren't there?'

'No. No, it weren't me. She couldn't see. It were ... it were a man in a mask. You said that.'

'You're quite right, I did.' Jane smiled, and reached below the table for another evidence bag. 'This mask.' She held the transparent bag above the table, with the mask - the tortured copy of Edvard Munch's painting *Scream!* - facing Peter and his solicitor. Peter looked scared, his solicitor shocked. 'I'm showing the defendant a facemask found near the scene of the crime. Do you recognise this, Peter?'

The boy's face was paler now, the droplets of sweat more pronounced. 'No. It's not mine.'

'Who said it was yours? Did I say that?'

He shook his head, wordless. Terrified now.

'No.'

'So you don't recognise it? Really? That's surprising. You see, this mask was found in a ditch in the little wood just behind Ms Bolan's house. We believe her assailant threw it there in his hurry to make his escape. You see, her neighbour brought her little boy home from nursery school in the middle of this assault. When he heard them, the intruder ran downstairs past them, got on his bike and rode away. Why did you do that, Peter? Were you scared of a little boy?'

'No. I never saw him.'

'Never saw him? He was on the stairs!'

A look of deep cunning spread across Peter Barton's pale, sweating face. 'I never saw him, because I weren't there.'

'So it wasn't that you was scared of being cut with those scissors?'

'No.' A quick shudder. 'I weren't there.'

'I think you were, Peter.'

'I weren't.'

Jane paused, watching him coolly. Terry Bateson could see she was enjoying this. But the silence tempted Rachel Horsefall to try to earn her fee.

'Sergeant Carter, I must ask you again not to browbeat my client. He's answered your questions fairly; he says he wasn't there. So unless you have any evidence to prove that he was, I must ask you to drop this charge.'

'Well, there are a couple of things,' Jane said, with a mocking smile. 'In the first place, we've tested this mask for traces of DNA. You know what that means, Peter, don't you? You've heard of DNA?'

He nodded, slowly, dumbly. His eyes fixed on hers. Like a rabbit watching a stoat.

'What is it, then? Tell me.'

'Stuff from your body. To tell if it's you.'

Jane laughed. 'Good enough, Peter, yes. Stuff from your body. I took a swab from the inside of your cheek last time you were arrested, remember? So if this was your mask there'd be more stuff from your body in it, wouldn't there? And the two would be the same.'

Jane watched him silently for a moment, allowing the tension to build. 'Remember breathing in this mask, do you, Peter? Deep breaths - you were excited when you attacked that woman, weren't you?'

Peter mumbled something inaudible - something like 'nnmi.'

'What? Speak up, I can't hear you.'

'Not me. I said it weren't me.'

'Not you wearing this mask. Is that what you say?'

'Yeah.'

'Really? Well, let me explain something, Peter. You see, Peter, the chances of your DNA matching someone else's are - I don't know - something like sixty million to one. Virtually impossible, in other words. And I have a report here, from the forensic science laboratory, that says that the DNA found in this mask was identical to the sample I took when you were arrested before. You understand identical, Peter? It means it was exactly the same.'

She paused again, giving him time for her words to sink in. 'You wore this mask, didn't you, Peter?'

Another dumb shake of the head. Jane persisted.

'Oh come on, Peter - we've got proof. So if you want to save time, you can admit it right now. That might help you in court with the judge. Get you time off in prison. You assaulted that woman, didn't you?'

He tried to hold her gaze, but she was too intense, her face just inches away, her eyes boring into his own. He looked down at his hands, then at his solicitor, then back at Jane again. A trickle of sweat ran down his forehead.

'Let me tell you what else we know, shall I, while you think about it. We believe that the intruder approached the house on his bike. But he wasn't wearing this mask when he rode through the streets; that would have drawn too much attention to himself. And it was a warm day - quite sunny in fact. Perhaps that was why Ms Bolan decided to go for a run. Anyway, the intruder didn't wear gloves on his bike, when he was cycling. We know that for a fact too, you see, because of these.'

She reached below the desk for another evidence bag, and placed it on the table. This one contained a sheet of paper, with some swirls and smudges on it, arranged side by side. 'See these, Peter? They are photocopies of fingerprints. The ones on the left - these here - are the ones we took from you when you were arrested before, when you assaulted a young girl near Bishopthorpe. Remember that? Now look at the fingerprints on the right. Do you know where we found them? On the garage window sill outside this lady's house. The lady who was assaulted by the man wearing this mask. So how did they get there, do you think?'

'Dunno,' Peter muttered. His voice was faint, hoarse, scarcely audible. Jane smiled coolly.

'Well, we think the man cycled up to the house, you see. That's how he came. And he wasn't wearing gloves, as I said, because it was so warm.

But when he arrived, he propped his bike against the garage and rested his fingers on the window sill for a second. By accident possibly, he wasn't thinking clearly. Or he was excited by what he was going to do next. Either way, he left these prints on the window sill, and *after that* he put on the gloves and the mask before going into the house. That's what happened, isn't it, Peter? Remember?'

Silence. Peter ground his teeth slowly, staring grimly at the paper.

'And the thing is, Peter, the really interesting thing, is this. These fingerprints from the window sill match yours perfectly. Just like the DNA from the mask. They're both yours, Peter, there's no point in trying to deny it. You broke into this young mother's house and assaulted her in her own bedroom, didn't you? Wearing this mask which has DNA from your spit in it.'

She paused, letting the hammer blow sink in.

'Do you want to tell us about it?'

Two hours later they had a full confession. Yes, Peter Barton admitted, the *Scream!* mask was his. He'd bought it at a Party Games shop in town. He'd liked it because it looked so scarey - and perhaps, though he didn't admit this, because its portrayal of desperate loneliness spoke to something in his soul. But mainly it was the horror of the thing, and the thought of the panic it would induce in anyone who saw him wearing it. He had noticed the woman, Elizabeth Bolan, on one of his cycle rides to and from work. She'd been out running, and he'd followed her, without coming close. He often did that, he said, looking up appealingly. Nothing wrong with that, was there?

'You mean you follow women without them noticing?' Jane asked softly.

'Yeah. It's not a crime, is it?'

Well, yes, it is, Jane thought grimly. But no need to emphasize that now. 'Why do you follow them?'

'To see where they live.'

'And you saw where this woman lived, did you? Elizabeth Bolan?'

'I didn't know her name, like.'

'But you guessed that she lived alone. Just her and her little boy?'

'I went back to check, yeah. Looked through the windows.'

'When was this?'

'Late at night. If there'd been a man there like, I'd have seen.'

The sick nastiness of it filled Jane with fury. Here he was, this hulking, half-brained moron, skulking outside women's homes at night. Probably tossing himself off in the bushes afterwards as well. And not just fantasizing about the women either, but planning to do something far worse. She glanced briefly at the young solicitor and saw her feelings were shared. Rachel Horsefall looked appalled, disgusted; she had unconsciously shifted her chair a couple of feet away from her client. No more interventions for a while from that source, then.

Peter admitted assaulting Elizabeth Bolan just as she had described. He hadn't meant to hurt her with the cord, he claimed; just control her so she couldn't fight back. But she *had* fought back. He hadn't expected that, and had been shocked when she threatened him with the scissors. He'd pleaded with her to be reasonable, he claimed; but she'd taken no notice. He'd been wondering how to get the scissors out of her hands when he'd heard the neighbour returning with her child from the nursery. He had panicked, run downstairs, and cycled away through the little wood onto the Knavesmire. He had torn off the mask, meaning to stuff it inside his jacket, but it had fallen in the ditch. He had thought of picking it up, but had seen a man approaching with a dog, and so pedalled away into the distance instead.

'What would you have done, Peter, if you hadn't been disturbed?' Jane asked, as softly as she could. Her tone was gentle, but her aim was quite the opposite - she wanted to gain his trust, not to help him but to get him to admit to as much perversity and evil intent as she could. She wanted his statement read out in court, to get him locked away for as long possible. But Peter was too dim, or repressed, to help her. Or perhaps not so dim, after all.

'I dunno,' he said slowly. 'I wouldn't have hurt her.'

'Wouldn't have hurt her? You had a cord around her neck!'

Silence. Peter stared down at his hands.

'You wanted to have sex with her, didn't you? Against her will?'

He looked around the room - at the ceiling, at the floor, the table, his own hands. Everywhere except at the three people who were listening.

'I wouldn't have hurt her,' he repeated at last, desperately. 'Not really bad.'

'She was in fear of her life, Peter. She thought you were going to kill her.'

'No!' He shook his head fiercely. 'I wouldn't do that. Never do that.' He looked down again at his hands. 'I'd have let her go. After.'

'After what, Peter?'

Silence.

'After you'd raped her. Is that what you mean?'

Slowly, Peter nodded his head. As Jane described this fact for the tape, she noticed tears - *tears!* - in his eyes. What kind of self-pity was this? She pressed on relentlessly.

'You're agreeing with me then, Peter, are you? You intended to rape this woman, and then let her go?'

'I wouldn't have hurt her. Not hurt her.'

'I understand that, Peter, I hear you.' Jane kept her voice calm, as unconfrontational as she could. She noticed the young solicitor shifting in her seat, as if screwing up her courage to intervene. But Jane needed this last admission. 'You wanted to have sex with this woman, didn't you? That's what you intended to do?'

He nodded slowly. 'Yes. But she wanted it.'

Jesus! Jane drew a long, deep breath, counted to ten in her head. One hundred, two hundred, three hundred, four ... 'She was in her own house, Peter, she was scared out of her wits, and you break in, wearing a mask and try to put a noose round her neck, and you say *she wanted it?* She was screaming, Peter, telling you to stop. Didn't you notice that?'

'Yeah, but ... you don't understand.'

'I don't understand? Explain it to me.'

'She ...' There was a long silence. 'She weren't really frightened.'

'Not frightened? Peter, I've interviewed this woman. Trust me, she was terrified.'

'I didn't notice.'

'Didn't notice? Not when she picked up the scissors?'

'Mebbe then, yeah. Not before.'

'Didn't she say anything? When you threw her on the bed?'

'She screamed a bit, like. *Go away. Let me alone.* It don't mean owt, though.'

'It doesn't mean anything? Is that what you're saying?'

'Yeah.' He looked straight into her face for the first time. '*You* know that, don't yer?'

'Right, that's it.' Jane sat back, then got to her feet. Without consulting Terry Bateson beside her, she said, 'Interview suspended at 16.43. I think we need a break. *I* do, anyway.' She walked straight out of the door.

55. Hut of Horrors

AFTER TWO days of interviewing Peter Barton, Terry and Jane's cup was half full. They had a detailed, believable confession to the assault on Elizabeth Bolan, and Peter had admitted, under pressure, that he had also burgled Sally McFee, and stolen her necklace and underwear. 'So where is it?' Jane asked, at the end of a long second day.

'In my hut.'

'Your hut,' Jane asked. 'Where's that?'

'Where you couldn't find it, that's where.' A flicker of weary insolence crossed the boy's face. It was the last thing, it seemed, he had over them. Or the last thing but one. 'You've been searching for me for weeks, you lot. Never found nothing.'

'We've found you, now, though, haven't we?' Jane said. 'Look, Peter, you've admitted to this burglary. So the judge will probably look kindly on you for that, give you a shorter sentence for a guilty plea. But only if you do this last thing.'

'What's that?'

'Give the necklace back, of course. If you've still got it. Have you?'

A short hesitation. Then a nod.

'Well then, tell us where it is.'

After a few more minutes' hesitation he agreed. A couple of hours later he directed their police car down a long country lane south of Heslington, then through a small coppice and across a field with a dyke along which Peter claimed he'd crawled to keep out of sight of the farmer. From there they progressed to another wood at the end of a disused airfield. Just inside this wood was a small brick shed with a tin roof. From the outside it looked disused and abandoned. The door was rotting and half off its hinges. There were bits of wire and broken branches strewn around, and tall weeds had grown through the concrete at the edge of the old runway.

'I never knew this was here,' Terry said.

'No. No one does.' Jane shook her head. 'Except the motorcyclists, and they don't care.' The hut was out of sight of the nearest farm, and the only other buildings in sight were half a mile away, on the far side of the airfield. The disused runway, Terry knew, was used for motorcycle races at weekends, much to the annoyance of villagers two miles away. No doubt the bikes zoomed past this hut on their circuit, but the lad was right - none would stop or give it a glance. And since he hadn't known where it was, he doubted any local constables had either. So it hadn't been searched.

They pushed open the door and stepped inside. The interior was dark, but quite different to the image of ruin conveyed by the outside. The concrete floor was swept clean, and there was a battered wooden table and chair against the wall on the right. On the table was a small camping stove, an old milk carton full of water, an aluminium saucepan, plate and cup, a torch, and several tins of food. Against the opposite wall was a mountain bike. Across the end wall was a camp bed, with a sleeping bag stretched out on it.

There was a small window in the right hand wall of the hut, with a dusty metal grill across it. The glass was too filthy to see in or out, but let in a certain amount of light nonetheless. By the light from the window and the open door they could see the display on the opposite wall. There were two large posters, like the ones in Peter's bedroom. The one on the right was of a big-breasted fantasy female warrior fighting a losing battle with a giant lizard. The one on the left featured another naked, big-breasted woman who was tied to a tree. In front of her gambolled a group of hellish, dwarf-like monsters, armed with jagged knives and blades, clearly intent on doing her harm. But what really caught Terry's attention, far more than the lurid sadistic fantasy, was what was around the woman's neck.

It was an expensive gold necklace.

Not a necklace that was part of the poster. A real gold necklace, that had been pinned on top of the poster. A necklace identical to that described by Sally McFee.

On the rest of the walls, pinned up roughly here and there, were a number of newspaper cuttings. They were all from the local newspaper, the *Evening Press*. They were reports of the assaults on the women living near the cyclepath in Bishopthorpe and Naburn. There was a detailed report on the assault on Lizzie Bolan. And there was a front page story of the house in Crockey Hill, where Alison Grey had been murdered. A house, Terry realised from his study of the map on the way here, that was no more than one or two miles at most from this hut.

Peter Barton looked at them, a sort of shy pride on his face.

'This is it,' he said. 'Never would have found me here, would you?'

'Hi,' Michael said. 'I'm in Scarborough. Can you hear the seagulls?'

'Maybe. Is that what that screeching is?' Sarah answered. 'Oh yes, there's one.'

'Lots of them. Great big buggers, sitting on the harbour wall and scavenging everything in sight. Including my ice cream if I don't watch out. Listen, I've had a bit of luck.'

'Oh? What's that?'

'I was at the farm development and then I came down to the harbour just as a fishing boat was coming in. So I bought two sea bass fresh off the deck. I thought I could cook them for us tonight. What do you think?'

'Yes, well, maybe ... I've got a lot on today, though ...'

'You've got to time to eat, haven't you?'

'At your place, you mean?'

'In the windmill, of course. I'm heading back there now.' He paused, waiting for a response. 'You don't sound too sure.'

'No, that's fine.' There was no point backing away, Sarah decided. Troubles only pursued you if you did. 'I'll look forward to it. What time?'

'About seven? I've got an idea to put to you as well.'

'Oh? What's that?'

'Wait and see. It's one best approached on a full stomach.'

'Okay.' Sarah drew a deep breath. 'See you there then.'

She clicked off the phone and leaned back in her office chair, thinking. Ever since she'd met Terry Bateson outside the court she'd been in a turmoil about her relationship with Michael. A cocktail of emotions swirled inside her - on one side anxiety, irritation, jealousy, and anger, battling with something like love on the other. No, not love, she told herself firmly - her attraction towards Michael wasn't passionate enough for that, not yet, anyway - but she did feel warmth, gratitude, strong affection towards this man who had taken her under his wing. He'd not only offered her a house when she was homeless, but far more than that, he'd given her back a sense of herself as a desirable, attractive woman, just when she'd needed it most, during this traumatic period of her divorce. At a time when she could so easily have sunk in self-pity she'd found a new friend. Not just a sexual partner, but someone she could have fun with too.

So at least she told herself in her better moments. Michael wasn't perfect, she had seen that from the beginning. He'd divorced his wife, for a start, just like Bob, and for a similar reason, that he'd played away, just as her own husband had done. He had unpleasant moods, when he could be abrupt and distant, and others when he could be downright frightening, like that scarey moment on the roof of the windmill when he'd joked about suicide. For a moment she'd feared he might jump, and take her down with him. And try as he might to be pleasant to her son Simon, even employing him to lay a patio outside the windmill, she could tell the young man didn't like him.

But then Simon had seldom got on with Bob either. People are difficult, Sarah told herself, we all have rough sides as well as smooth. Every day in court she saw how hard human relationships were, how seldom one person meets another's every need. She herself was no angel. If she'd ever had any fantasies about her own moral perfection, her husband, Bob, had stripped them away long ago. She had a cold self-centred heart, he complained; she was obsessively focussed on her career to the exclusion of husband, family, or anything else which might get in her way. Once he'd even accused her of having no tongue in her mouth but a knife, so sharp and wounding were her arguments.

'Aren't you just describing yourself, Bob?' she'd responded coolly. 'Seeing me as a mirror for your own failings?'

For in her own eyes, Sarah's obsession with her career was a virtue, the one thing that had raised her from poverty and kept herself and her children safe in a cruel, uncertain world. Once Bob had admired her for that: he'd called her sharp and hard like a diamond, with qualities to be treasured, not despised. No longer, it seemed.

But now she had Michael instead - a man who could be kind, generous, attentive, even amusing on occasion - what more could she want? However long this new relationship lasted, it was doing her good. Was it to end so soon?

Everything had been going well until she met Terry Bateson outside court. Part of her wished she'd said hello briefly and walked on. But it's no good building your life on a fantasy, she told herself sternly. Especially if the truth underlying that fantasy is as dangerous as well, murder.

But what if the real fantasy is in Terry Bateson's mind, and the truth about Michael is entirely innocent? That's what I want to believe, Sarah thought. That's what I hope.

After all, Terry's made plenty of mistakes before. He thought Simon was guilty once; I had to prove that wasn't true. He's a decent man but maybe he's suspicious of Michael because he's sweet on me. He admitted being jealous after all, the other day. I care for you, he said. That's nice.

Sarah smiled ruefully, recalling that one time she and Terry had almost made love. If I hadn't been sick and made an exhibition of myself I would have, too, she thought. I wanted to all right, and so, I'm sure, did he. He's a decent man - good-looking too. Who knows - perhaps if I'd met *him* on a train that week Bob walked out, instead of Michael, things might have turned out quite differently ...

She shrugged. But they didn't, so now I have this situation to deal with. Tonight Michael's going to cook for me and make some kind of proposal - God knows what that can be - and I have to decide what to do about all these suspicions. At the very least I have to ask him about that file I found in his drawer and what his real relationship was with that woman who was murdered - Alison Grey.

They certainly looked like close friends 18 years ago, at that memorial service for Brenda Stokes. Were they lovers then? Possibly, but that doesn't matter much. It's none of my business really. But what if Terry's right, and they were lovers here in York, right up until the time she was murdered? And Michael never mentioned it, not even to me?

That would be a little harder to swallow.

'So what do you think now?' Jane asked, queuing in the station canteen for lunch before interviewing Peter again. 'He's admitted all that - it's got to be him who murdered Alison Grey as well, hasn't it?'

'It certainly looks that way,' Terry agreed. 'But we still need evidence. He would never have admitted assaulting Elizabeth Bolan if you hadn't confronted him with the fingerprint, and the DNA from the mask.'

'If only FSS hadn't lost that scrap of cloth, the halfwits - I could have used that in the same way.'

'I'll ring them again before we go in. That's all I can do, short of mounting a dawn raid on their wretched laboratories.'

Sitting together in a corner to eat, they discussed tactics for the next interrogation. 'So what do we do now?' Jane asked. 'It has to be him, everything points that way. But without evidence he'll just sit there and deny it.'

'There may be another way,' Terry said thoughtfully. 'You saw how proud he was of that awful shed. In his own mind, he's a hero. We may have to flatter his ego a bit.'

Jane shoved her sandwich away, a look of disgust on her stolid face. 'That's all very well, but he's a brutal young pervert, this lad. Every time I see him I want to be sick.'

'Well, keep your mouth shut then,' Terry smiled. 'Let me do the talking.'

'All right. But if had my way I'd cut his balls off and feed 'em to the pigs.'

'Leave it to me, will you? You've seen how he hates women, poor sap, that's his problem. So he's more likely to confide in me, as a man. He thinks I understand his anxieties.'

'Ok, guv, my lips are sealed.' Jane rolled her eyes in ironic acceptance. 'But if you really do understand him, that only goes to show one thing. Which I suspected all along.'

'What's that?'

'You're all sick bastards. The whole hopeless gender, the lot of you. You could all be replaced by a syringe; that would make this world a better place. That's what we need - no more perverts, just pure female perfection.'

56. Windmills in Spain

BY THE time Sarah got home it was already dark. The Kawasaki followed the beam of its headlight up along the quiet, empty road at the top of the Wolds. Wind blustered around her, the occasional stronger gust cuffing the bike sideways. Dark treetops swayed overhead as she turned off the road into the woods, and dead leaves skittered across her path.

Halfway through the woods she saw headlights coming towards her. She slowed the bike and pulled in to the side to let the vehicle pass. Then, as it came closer she recognised the number plate and raised a gloved hand in greeting. A battered white van slowed to a stop beside her and her son Simon wound down the window.

'Hi, Mum, how're you doing?'

Sarah tugged off her helmet, and was immediately assailed by the roaring of the woods all around her, like the surf of the sea. The wind whipped her hair across her face.

She raised her voice to be heard.

'All right, Simon. Glad to be home. Has this storm been blowing all day?'

'No, it just blew up in the last hour or so. I could see it coming across the valley before it got dark.' He grinned. 'Hell of a place to live.'

'Yes, but it has its points. How's the patio going?'

'Good. I've got most of it done now. Another couple of days' work at the most. I was hoping to finish it tomorrow before this blew up.'

'It may blow over.' Sarah smiled. 'How's Lorraine?'

'Great. In fact she looks lovelier than ever. I never knew pregnancy did that to girls. She sort of glows when I look at her.'

'Lucky her - and you. Well, look after her, Simon - that's my first grandchild she's carrying, you know.'

Simon laughed. 'I'll do my best, Mum. Why don't you come round and see us sometime? We'll have a celebration when I'm paid for this patio.'

'I'd love to, Simon. Just send me a text.'

She rode the last hundred yards to the mill with a smile on her face. Whatever else had happened in the last few months, her relationship with Simon was improving. His affair with Lorraine, and her pregnancy, seemed to have matured him. Out of his surly, resentful teenage chrysalis was emerging a friendly, trustworthy young man, with shoulders broad enough to bear his new responsibilities.

Or so, at least, Sarah hoped. She wished her husband Bob could have seen it. But then, it was really only since Bob left her that Simon had begun to take up the role of the man of the family.

Coming out of the woods, she had another surprise. Lights were blazing in every room of the windmill. But that wasn't the surprise - something was moving on the far side of the tower. It was hard to see at first, but whatever it was it was it was huge and powerful. Sarah stopped the bike and stood, peering into the darkness beyond the glare of the lights. What on earth could it be? Above the tower, a quarter moon appeared briefly from behind racing dark clouds, and then, almost immediately, a huge dark shape crossed in front of it, blotting it out for a second. Then another, and another, in a swift steady rhythm, and Sarah understood. Of course - it was the sails! Michael must have released the brake, and in this high wind they were turning, faster than she had ever seen them before. Perhaps that accounted for the unusual glare of lights; they must be generating a phenomenal amount of electricity. But was it safe? Well, he must have studied it. He'd had engineers here most of last week. She hoped he knew what he was doing.

She watched for a moment longer, then wheeled her bike across to the house. She could see Michael moving around in the windmill kitchen. He didn't seem concerned about the storm. She imagined him working hard in the irritable, nervous frenzy which seemed to characterise his cooking, and checked her watch as she went indoors. 6.30 - just time to shower, change, and make it without annoying him unnecessarily by being late.

As she crossed to the mill later the wind whipped her skirt around her legs, but it seemed gentler than before. She glanced across the valley and saw stars appearing in the far west, beyond the clouds. There was a flurry of rain, and she stepped carefully across Simon's patio, to avoid tripping over a pile of bricks or putting her foot in a pool of damp mortar. To her relief, the work looked good, as far as she could tell. She asked Michael about it in the warmth of the kitchen.

'Yes, it's coming along fine. He's a grafter, your son, I'll give him that. When he manages to turn up, that is.'

'Well, he's got other jobs, as well as this. I suppose he fits it in when he can.'

'Don't they all?' Michael was busy chopping herbs on the side. He glanced at her briefly, and changed his dismissive tone. 'I'm sorry, I didn't mean it like that. He's doing fine, really. Doesn't talk to me much, but then that's not what I'm paying him for. Sherry? Wine? Juice? What d'you fancy?'

'Juice, to start with, anyway.' Sarah wanted to keep a cool head, if she could. She was only half convinced that she was wise, to be here at all. But then, what she really needed was to resolve her doubts. If Terry Bateson was right and there really was something suspicious about Michael, then the sooner she found out about it the better. Then, if necessary, she could make the decision to leave - find another place to live and cut him out of her life altogether. But if Terry was wrong, as she hoped, and this man was as decent as he seemed, then well - he was the best thing that happened to her for ages. Ever since things went so badly wrong with Bob. The last thing she wanted to do was to shipwreck a friendship that had so recently been launched.

But how could she decide, without revealing her suspicions? How would Michael react, if she told him she had been speaking to Terry, or that she had been examining the file of newspaper clippings in his study in her house? He'd be angry, she felt sure. Hurt, angry and betrayed. Even if he had a perfectly reasonable answer to her questions, he'd still feel she'd been spying on him behind his back, discussing him with the police as though he were some sort of criminal. No man would react to that kindly, she felt sure - certainly not a man like Michael who, for all his good points, had already shown several frightening flashes of temper in the short time she'd known him.

But if she didn't reveal the reasons for her suspicions, how could she get answers to her questions? Sarah had puzzled over this all afternoon, ever since Michael had rung her from Scarborough. She had never been good at feminine wiles; she was more used to cross-examination in the courtroom, with precise, detailed, questioning based on evidence that was out in the open for all to see.

This time, she thought, she would have to try something different. Get answers, if possible, without asking too many obvious questions. She was far from certain that she would succeed.

She asked him about the sails, and he smiled. 'Yes, stunning, aren't they? I thought I'd test them in a moderately strong wind, and they're holding up well, just as the guys told me they would. We must be generating enough electricity to light up a whole village - and we will do, too, once the grid people pull their fingers out and get us connected properly.'

'It's like a giant propellor. I'm surprised the building doesn't take off.'

'No wings, or it would. Don't worry, the wind's forecast to die down this evening. Anyway, it's been here three hundred years, it's seen worse than this before now. Though it's probably a good idea the grindstones aren't connected any more. I read about a hurricane one year - 1750 or sometime like that - when several mills spun so fast for so long that they caught fire. I guess the friction made the stones red hot.'

'That can't happen to us, can it?'

'Let's hope not. Anyway it would be a spectacular way to go, don't you think?'

He seemed in a good mood, Sarah thought. Slightly tense, perhaps, but then he was often like that, when he was cooking. No hint of the guilt or anxiety she might have expected if Terry's suspicions had been true. But then, how well did she really know him? There'd been several times before when he'd started out like this, then changed suddenly for no apparent reason.

The sea bass, at least, was a success. Light, fresh, steamed on a bed of green beans with a white wine, vanilla, cream and garlic sauce, with new potatoes and sprinkled with celery leaves, set off with a crisp dry Chablis.

'Your best so far,' Sarah said appreciatively. 'You're becoming a chef.'

'Not me - Jamie Oliver. I'm glad you like it.' He sipped his wine, watching her thoughtfully. 'I hope you like my next idea too.'

'Which is?'

'Tell you in a minute. Let me fetch the sweet first.'

They were eating on the second floor tonight, at the circular dining table with the two redundant millwheels underneath. While Michael went downstairs Sarah strolled to the glass door leading onto the balcony, and watched the sails revolving steadily between her and the stars. Were they going a bit slower now? Their power unsettled her. But the night sky looked a little clearer. She could see stars around the Moon. What was this idea he seemed so keen about? She had a miserable feeling she was about to disappoint him, even before she probed for information. And she still had no idea how to do that.

Michael came up from the kitchen with a tray carrying apple pie, whipped cream, and a cafetiere with coffee cups and saucers.

'My idea,' he said slowly, putting the tray on the table, 'is quite simple really. I'm thinking of moving to Spain.'

'What?'

'I've a friend who's into property there, and I've been talking to him. He's been there for years now, already made a fortune, and says there are plenty of opportunities left - not on the coast where the lager louts go, but inland, the more select areas where smaller operators like me might move in. For expats looking for the real Spain, in villages and old farmhouses like I've been converting here. He's even found several old windmills, believe it or not.'

'But why would you want to do that?'

'Oh, I've been thinking about it for some time ...' Sarah listened in wonder, putting a few questions here and there, while he developed his idea. It was nothing like what she'd been expecting. He seemed enthusiastic, she thought, but nervous too. As though he was trying to convince himself as well as her. The crux came over coffee. '... if I really put my mind to it, I reckon I could sell up here in about six months, a year at most, and begin again over there. We'd have plenty to live on, you wouldn't have to work, only ...'

'We?' She put her cup down, with a clatter.

'Yes. I'm sorry, I'm not explaining this well. The reason I'm telling you this is that I ... well, I was hoping you'd want to come with me.'

From where he sat, with his back to a spotlight in the wall, half his face was in shadow, but the eye she could see watched her eagerly. There was a shy smile on his lips.

'Michael, I have a career.'

'Yes, I know, but they have lawyers in Spain, don't they?'

'I'm not qualified to practise in Spain. I don't know the law or the language.'

'You could learn. Anyway, as I say, you wouldn't need to work. I could earn enough for us both.' He reached forward across the table for her hand. 'Sarah, I'm asking you to come with me.'

She let him take her hand for a moment, but then withdrew it. 'I'm very flattered, Michael, but ... I've never thought about leaving this country. Or my career.'

'Well, I'm asking you to think about it now. Of course it comes as a surprise, I understand that. You don't have to decide today. I'm just laying out my plans, and saying, I suppose, that I'd like you to be part of them. I really would. That's all.'

There's no way, snapped a little imp in Sarah's mind, *no way in hell that I would ever give up my career and put my life in the hands of a man, not this man or any other, not while I have breath in my body.* But she didn't say it. She gagged the imp swiftly as other, contradictory thoughts came rushing in. *He is a nice man after all, a good lover, and this is the best offer I'm likely to get, at my time of life; I should consider it at least.* And then, more subtly: *this is my opportunity, this is my way in, if I was to think of going with him, it would be natural to know more about his past, wouldn't it? If I turn him down flat I never will.*

So she said, very cautiously: 'It is a surprise, Michael, let me think about it. I can't decide on a thing like this, to change my life, in a day.'

'So let's go over it again,' Terry said, when they had got Peter in an interview room. 'Why did you go to Crockey Hill?'

'I went out for a walk.'

'What, in the middle of the night?'

'Yeah, why not? It's the best time. Nobody sees you.'

'Why would it matter if people saw you?'

A look of deep cunning crossed Peter Barton's face. 'Well, you know that, don't you? I were on the run.' He made it sound glamorous, like Robin Hood or Bonnie and Clyde.

'I see. So it was exciting, was it?' Terry kept his tone as neutral as he could. As he'd explained to Jane over lunch, he didn't want to antagonise Peter by pointing out the evil of his ways; what Terry wanted was his co-operation. If that meant pandering to the boy's fantasies, even seeming to understand and approve them, then that's what he would do. He needed to build up a bond of trust with him.

So far, Terry thought, so good. The first really difficult hurdle for Peter had been his confession to the sexual assault on Lizzie Bolan. When he'd finally completed his statement he'd been sweating and trembling so much he could hardly hold the pen to sign his name. His solicitor had even called a break for medical attention. Part of Peter's problem seemed to be that he expected punishment to follow immediately - he would be locked up in some cold dark cell, tortured, chastised. When none of that happened - he was given a decent meal, a night's rest, even a congratulatory half-smile from Terry - a tide of relief flooded through him. He relaxed, seeming to regard the three of them - Terry, Jane, and his solicitor - if not as his friends, then at least as his audience, witnesses to what he had done. Perhaps he deluded himself that they approved, even applauded his achievements, who knows? At any rate, this mood had lasted long enough for him to agree to show them his hideout; and that, Terry had to admit, *was* a triumph, of sorts - for Peter to have eluded the search efforts of the whole York and Selby division for so long. Local farmers had been on the lookout for him, too; but not the owners of the airfield, who were legendary for their lack of co-operation with the local community.

Jane sat silent, her chair pushed back a little from the table, while Terry leaned forward encouragingly to Peter. What interested him was the proximity of Peter's hideout to Alison's house in Crockey Hill. No more than a couple of miles cross-country at most - much of it through woods and open scrubland, far from the nearest farmhouse.

'It must be quite interesting, walking in the country at night.'

'It is. You get to see things.'

'What sort of things?'

'Owls. Deer. I saw a fox once. And badgers.'

'What about people?'

'Not many people about that time of night. See them through windows, though.'

'You watch people through windows, do you?'

'Sometimes. It's better than TV. You get surprises.'

'What sort of surprises?'

Peter smiled, and glanced pointedly at Jane. 'She'll say it's wrong.'

'Don't worry about her, Peter. Talk to me. I understand.' Terry leaned forward further, willing Peter to look back at him, meet his eyes. 'Ever see any women through windows at night, Peter?'

'It happens.' A cunning, troubled look crossed the young man's face. 'They want me to, but I don't. I don't watch. Not always.'

'They want you to watch, you say?'

'Yeah, course they do. They think they look good, don't they? They want everyone to see. They don't realise what it's like.'

'What is it like, Peter?' Jane asked quietly, from behind Terry's shoulder.

He stared at her sharply, a surge of anger in his voice. 'Ugly, of course. Fat like you. Not pretty like they think.' He paused for a second, then turned back to Terry almost as an ally. 'That woman who was hanged in that house, now. She was in front of a mirror, wasn't she? She got to see. How ugly she was, at the end.'

A chill came over the room. Terry looked at the tape recorder to make sure it was functioning properly. Peter had had newspaper reports of Alison's death in his hut, but the detail about the mirror, he was quite sure, had never been released to the press.

'How did you know about the mirror, Peter?' he asked quietly.

'Dunno. Can't remember. Why, what's it matter?'

'Do you remember what the woman looked like, hanging in the hall?'

'Yeah, it was in the paper. Naked, wasn't she? Hanged by a scarf from the staircase. Showing her tits and all in the mirror.'

'Were her feet touching the ground?'

'Couldn't have been, could they? She wouldn't have hanged else.'

'So how did she get to be there, hanging in the hall with her feet off the ground?'

'Must have stood on a chair or something, and knocked it over.'

Ideas chased each other like rats in Terry's brain. Peter's eyes were bright, eager - he was clearly excited by this conversation. Was it just because he was a sad sick pervert, turned on by such horrors? Or was it because he had been there, and wanted them to know? Was he trying to admit to the murder, perhaps? The detail about the scarf had been in the *Evening Press,* but not about the mirror. *How did he know about that?* Was it just that he'd seen it in the house and worked out how it had been? *Or had he been there when Alison died?*

'It must have been difficult to kill a woman like that, don't you think?' he said, as conversationally as he could. 'I mean, she might have fought back. When she knew she was going to die.'

He watched Peter's eyes closely. As he expected, there was a flicker, as his delicate shaft went home. Peter had tried something similar with Elizabeth Bolan, and failed. Not just failed - he'd been humiliated. He might have some admiration for a killer who'd succeeded. *Or was he the killer himself?*

Peter looked down at his hands, thinking for a moment. Or remembering, perhaps. 'He used a knife, I reckon,' he said at last. His voice was flat, trance-like - not excited, but calm, dull, monotonous. 'That put the fear into her, that would. Tell her he'd cut her throat or stick it in her tits, that makes her freeze. Then tape her hands behind her back nice and tight. Scarf round her neck, march her downstairs, stand her on a chair in front of that mirror, and you've got her, it's all too late. Reach up, quick, tie the scarf through the banisters. If she moves, you pull it tight; if she don't, leave her standing on the chair till it tips. Or just kick it away when you like.'

He paused, and the room fell silent. Neither Terry, Jane, nor the solicitor Rachel Horsefall sitting beside him said a word. Peter looked up at Terry and smiled.

'That's how it happened. I reckon.'

'That's how you killed her, you mean? Is that what you're saying?'

Another long silence. The nervous, trembling grin on Peter Barton's face widened slightly. There was a tremor in his left cheek. But none of the perspiration or fear that had accompanied his confession yesterday, to the assault on Elizabeth Bolan. There was something almost ecstatic about him - a beatification, almost.

'How I killed her?' he said at last. 'Yes, that's how I did it.'

57. Confessions

'AND NOW I've won a case in the Court of Criminal Appeal,' Sarah said. 'That's another feather in my cap. Of course I'm proud of it. But you don't approve, do you?'

'It's not that I don't approve, of course not. I just don't believe that man Jason Barnes is innocent, that's all.'

Michael spoke softly, but when Sarah looked up she saw a slight frown on his face. He was sitting on the sofa in the first floor room in the windmill. Sarah lay stretched out with her feet on one end of the sofa, and her head in his lap. The lights in the room were low, and Mozart was playing quietly on the CD player. Outside, the night sky was bright with stars, washed clean by the passing storm. The wind had fallen, and the sails turned slowly now, a quiet comfortable rhythm. They had been talking companionably for an hour or more, Sarah telling him about her past, the events and decisions that had brought her from being a teenage single mother in the slums of Seacroft to where she was today.

She was aware, as she spoke, that the conversation was less natural than it seemed. There were two motives behind it. The first was to make it clear to him, in a quiet non-confrontational way, how central a role her career had played in her life, and thus how difficult, almost impossible, it would be for her to abandon it and follow him to Spain. And the second, even more subtly perhaps, was to invite him to respond in kind, with details of his own life story. Especially, she hoped, those connected with the picture in the file she had found in his office. Of Michael holding hands with Alison Grey.

Now, she thought, they had reached the moment when this might happen. If it was ever going to, that is. This was why she had introduced the subject of Jason Barnes' appeal. Whenever this subject had come up before he had dismissed it, as if it didn't matter to him. But the file in his office suggested it did. Sarah wanted to find out more, without revealing what she knew about the file.

'You knew both of them, didn't you?' she said softly. 'Jason Barnes and Brenda Stokes.'

Lying as she was across his lap, she felt his body tense slightly as he breathed in.

'A little, yes.'

'It must have been a big event at the time. Was there a funeral?'

'A funeral? No, there couldn't be. They never found her body.'

'A memorial service, I mean. I bet hundreds of people went.' She kept her voice as relaxed, as disinterested as she could, but her mind was on high alert.

'Yes, there was.' He paused, and she thought he would say no more. To her relief, at least there had been no angry reaction. Then he said: 'I was there, as a matter of fact.'

'You were there? At Brenda's memorial service?'

'Yes. It wasn't as big as all that. Forty or fifty people maybe, no more. She wasn't ... that nice a person, really.'

'So why did you go?'

'Curiosity, I suppose. And shock. You don't expect someone you know to be murdered, do you? Even if she wasn't very nice.'

'No.' Sarah breathed slowly, willing her body to stay relaxed. She listened to the music in the room, letting almost a minute pass before she spoke again. She tested the words twice in her mind before speaking them. 'I read somewhere that this other woman who died, this Alison Grey, was a student in York at the same time too.'

This time the tension in Michael's body was palpable. He breathed in sharply; she could feel the muscles in his legs contract, as if preparing to run. If she hadn't been lying across his lap he would have stood up, she felt sure. But she stayed where she was, totally vulnerable, apparently unconcerned.

'Yes. I ...' He looked down at her for a moment, forced a smile. 'D'you mind getting up for a moment. I'd like another drink.'

'Of course.' She sat up, as calmly as she could. 'Pour one for me too, if you would.'

He stood with his back to her in the shadows, pouring the drinks. It seemed to take a while. He brought hers back and went to stand beside the window. 'As a matter of fact I did know Alison then too. Rather better than Brenda, as a matter of fact.'

'Oh?' Thank God, she thought, he's telling the truth. *I know this, Michael, I've seen you holding her hand in the photo.* So if he's not lying to me, perhaps everything in that file has an innocent explanation. 'Was she your girlfriend?'

'For a short while, yes.' He gulped his whisky, and went to pour himself another. 'It was a long time ago.'

'Did she know Brenda?'

'A little, yes. They weren't friends or anything, though.'

'It must have been hard for you, then, when Alison was killed in your house.'

He came and sat down beside her, on the sofa. It was clear this wasn't something he wanted to talk about. 'Look, she was an old friend from university, that's all. We hadn't been in touch for years. Until she came back to York looking for a house to rent, that is.' He sighed, and where the lamplight caught his face she thought she saw a drop of sweat glistening on his forehead. 'What really upset me about it was when the police came to see me. It was that detective friend of yours, you remember - the one we met jogging on the quay once. I'd thought it was suicide up until then, but he told me she was murdered. That was a nasty shock.'

'I can see that.' Sarah frowned. 'But ... weren't you upset when you thought she'd killed herself?'

'Of course I was, but murder is worse, isn't it? I mean, last time I met her she told me she was ill. She had cancer, you know, and she was scared of the treatment. So when I read that article in the *Press*, suggesting it was suicide, I thought, well, she'd taken the quick way out.' He shrugged. 'We all have to go sometime, after all.'

'She was found hanged in her hallway, wasn't she?'

'So they say, yes. Look ...' Michael bent forward, running his hands through his hair, then looked up and smiled. '... do you mind if we talk about something else? It's not very pleasant, thinking about someone being murdered, is it? Especially someone you knew. So I'd rather ...'

'You've no idea who did it, then?' It was a risky question but Sarah had to ask it. She expected an angry response. Instead, to her surprise, Michael laughed.

'Well yes, they think they've caught him. Didn't you know?'

'What?'

'I heard it on *Radio York* tonight, while I was cooking. They arrested a man yesterday, in the house where Alison lived. They've already charged him with all these assaults on other women, and they're interviewing him about Alison's death too.'

He smiled, and lifted his glass. 'So I think we should drink a toast to the police, don't you?'

The problems with Peter's confession were in the details. Over the next six hours, they went over it again and again. By the end of that time, Jane loathed him even more than before. His solicitor had demanded a psychiatric assessment. And Terry Bateson had still not charged him.

After Peter's first, dramatic statement in the interview room, Terry took him slowly, carefully back through all the details, step by step. Very occasionally, Jane asked a question, but mostly she just sat silent in the shadows, listening, letting Terry lead the way. Peter preferred that, she could see. Man to man, he told Terry how he'd stalked an innocent woman, and murdered her. Because she deserved it.

Peter admitted he'd been upset by the way his assault on Lizzie Bolan had gone wrong. He hadn't expected her to resist, he said; he'd been shocked by the way she'd fought back, and humiliated by his own failure to act quickly and control her. He had cycled swiftly away across the Knavesmire, terrified at the thought of being caught, and furious with himself for his own lack of nerve and planning.

Since then he'd been hiding in his shed on the airfield. He had stored food there, so he wasn't hungry, and he stayed inside until after dark. He was cold, of course, but that was part of his 'survival training'; he had his sleeping bag and thermal underwear. After dark he crept out to roam around. He knew the area well - he'd been coming here since last summer, when he'd first found the shed. It was close to York, but wooded and remote - few people went there, especially at night in midwinter. He saw animals; set snares for rabbits, though he failed to catch any. But his main interest was spying on people in houses.

Cross-country, it was about two miles from his hut to Crockey Hill. Most of it was through woodland - plantations and copses of one sort and another. He only had to cross a couple of open fields, and some uncultivated marshland behind a golf course. People in remote houses, he'd discovered, sometimes left their curtains undrawn at night. He'd watched Mrs Richards one evening, but been scared away by the dog. He'd spied on several other houses too, lying quietly hidden in a hedge at the end of their gardens, imagining himself in hostile territory, a soldier in the SAS. But most houses had men or dogs in them; he steered clear of those.

Then he came across Alison Grey's house. This was perfect for him. She lived alone. She often worked late at night. She was careless about curtains. And her house was remote, with no neighbours nearby.

He'd reconnoitred the house once, and came back again. This second time he'd crept through the hedge into the garden, watching the house carefully. Nothing happened; no dog barked, no alarm rang. No one saw him. And then something moved.

It was a cat, he told Terry with a half smile. A cat sticking its head out of a downstairs window. It looked around for a while, sniffing the air, letting its eyes grow accustomed to the darkness. Then it leapt lightly to the ground and ran away into the undergrowth, on a hunt of its own.

This, Peter claimed, was too tempting. An open window, a woman alone upstairs. He remembered his failure with Elizabeth Bolan; but he remembered, too, the excitement he had felt - the overpowering thrill of entering the house of a woman who didn't know he was there. He wanted to experience it again. And this time, surely, no neighbour or child would burst in and disturb him. She would be alone, helpless, in his power.

From the lights he guessed she was already upstairs, getting ready for bed. He crept up to the window and lifted it with his gloved hand. It moved up easily, leaving plenty of space for a man to climb in. So he did, cautiously, quietly, his movements silent, his heart beating like a drum in his ears. He wore gloves as before, careful this time to leave no prints on the sill. But he wore no mask, just the hood on his anorak. When he was in the kitchen he drew a hunting knife from its sheath. No danger, he told Terry - I won't fall for that scissors trick a second time.

It's not a second time, Terry thought - *this is a different woman.* But he made no challenge. He just quietly asked Peter what happened next, with as little hostility as he could manage. And listened, while Peter warmed to his tale, his words coming quicker now, in short, eager bursts of excitement. The women, Jane Carter, and Rachel Horsefall, remained silent. Their faces stony, distant, disgusted.

I climbed the stairs, Peter said, and the woman was just coming out of her bath. They met right there on the landing, between her bathroom and bedroom. She was naked, steaming from bathwater, wrapped in a towel. But unlike Lizzie Bolan, she'd offered no resistance at all. She'd been terrified, of course. He'd held the knife to her throat, and she'd stood there shivering, in front of him. Frozen with fear. Unable to move. A naked woman at his mercy.

'So then what?' Terry asked softly. 'What did you do?'

'Do?' Peter drew a deep breath; the light in his eyes, shining, ecstatic. 'I shagged her, of course.'

That was the moment when Terry ceased to believe him. Jane leaned forward urgently, but he put out a warning hand to restrain her. He knew, as Jane did and Rachel Horsefall did not, that Alison Grey had *not* been raped. Murdered, yes; raped, no. Not if the pathologist was to be believed. There'd been no sign of vaginal tears or bleeding. No forced penetration. No male hairs or semen to be sent for DNA testing.

Terry's mind raced to remember whether this fact had been made clear in the newspaper reports. He thought not. They had focussed on what *had* happened to her, not what had not. Very quietly, Terry asked: 'How did you do that, Peter?'

Peter described it, as he had described everything else so far. Graphically, and - given his limited range of vocabulary - with striking detail. He spoke slowly, sometimes looking down at the table or his hands, at other times staring directly into Terry's eyes. As though it was important that he, the man, understood. He ignored the two women completely.

'I tied her hands behind her back with this scarf I found. I didn't want no trouble, see, not after last time. Then I shoved her back on the bed, told her to spread her legs, and ... did it. I shagged her senseless. Bitch.' His eyes met Terry's, shining with triumph. 'She couldn't do owt. Not a thing.'

'And how did that feel?'

'Feel? It were great.' For the first time, a shadow of doubt, a fear of mockery perhaps, or disbelief, flickered in his eyes. 'What d'you mean, feel?'

'I just wondered how it felt, to have shagged a woman like that. When she couldn't fight back.'

'It served her right.'

'Served her right?'

'Yeah. It felt good. She didn't take all my strength.'

'Take your strength?' Terry frowned, puzzled.

'No. Not that way. Like they do.'

'All right.' The kid's insane, Terry thought. He had no idea what he was talking about, but he saw, or thought he saw, the boy's fragility crumbling under the facade of his tale. Terry didn't want to break it down, not yet. He affected a faint, reassuring smile. 'You had your knife in your hand?'

'Yeah. At her neck.'

'Did you use any protection?'

Here, Terry thought, the story would crumble. There'd been condoms in Alison's bedroom. A type called a *Tickler*. No rapist would bother with that.

'Aye.' A sick, cunning grin crossed young Peter's face. ''Course I did. What d'yer think? I wanna get Aids or summat?'

Terry groaned inwardly. *Could this be true?* 'You used a condom?'

'Yeah. Keep myself clean.'

'What type was it?'

'I dunno. Normal sort. What you buy in supermarket, like. You've seen 'em.'

'So what did you do with it afterwards, Peter?'

'Flushed it down t'loo. What d'yer think?'

Terry glanced sideways at Jane, shaking his head slowly. The cottage wasn't on mains drainage, as he remembered; it had a cesspit. The thought of asking someone to trawl through years of accumulated sewage to retrieve a used condom made his heart sink. Even if they found it, it would probably be too filthy to provide any useful evidence. He gazed back at Peter. His story *could* be true, a lot of it fitted. Almost fitted. Yet Terry was reluctant to believe it.

'So what happened next?'

'Well, then ...' There was a long, thoughtful pause. Peter looked down at his hands, then up at the wall behind Terry's back, then down at the table again. Somehow the sparkle seemed to leach out of him. He sagged, deflated, then raised his head. There was an appealing look in his eyes. Terry thought he was about to admit he was lying, but instead he said: 'She had to die, you see. After that. I couldn't help it.'

'Why, Peter?'

'She'd seen my face. And she knew ...' He looked down again, struggling for breath. 'She knew what I'd done.'

Or hadn't done, Terry thought grimly. But it wasn't time to pursue that, not yet. 'So how did you kill her?'

'Well, I dragged her up. After I'd done it, like. Dragged her up to her feet.'

'And she didn't resist?'

'Didn't have no choice, did she? I still had me knife, see. Not like last time. Said I'd stick it in her tits if she moved. So she didn't. Not till I said, like. Then when I were good and ready I told her to walk down t'stairs. In front of me, like, me holding end o't scarf. Like a bitch on't lead. With me knife in her back, 'case she tried owt. Then I stopped her in front o't mirror. Shaking she were.' He grinned, relishing the image in his mind.

'What happened then?'

'I fastened t'scarf round her neck, like a noose. It were that long, it were easy. With me knife at her throat, like.'

Peter drew a deep, shuddering breath. He looked up, the sparkle returning to his eyes. He seemed to pump himself up with excitement at the thrill of the tale he was telling.

Or inventing, Terry thought. *Can any of this be true?*

'She didn't like that. She stood there weeping, staring at herself, the fat slag, in't mirror. See what a great fat whore she were ...'

Beside Peter, the young solicitor's face was pale, greeny white.

'... then I got this chair from a room, put it in't hall, and stood her up on it, in front o't mirror. I fastened t'loose end o't scarf through't banisters, and pulled her head back tight, so she had to stand there on tiptoes, on top of this chair.' He grinned. 'It were too late then. She were weeping. She shat herself.'

Oh my God, Terry thought. *He **was** there after all, he must have been. There's no other way he could know. Not about that.*

'What happened then?'

'I kicked the chair away.' All the sparkle had returned to Peter's eyes now. The confidence, the macabre delight. He smiled almost shyly at Terry. In triumph, it seemed. *I did this!*

'And then?'

'She swung. Like a pendulum, you know. It were odd. I shoved her a bit, to make it last. You don't think that'll happen, do you?'

Silence filled the room. For over a minute, no one could find anything to say. For Terry, it was like being trapped in a dream. Not his own nightmare, but that of this young monster before him, with the sparkling eyes and shy, appealing grin. And superimposed on that face - quite an attractive face, in its way, despite the ingrained dirt and spots on his forehead - he saw that last, terrible image. A hanged woman swinging to and fro on her own staircase. A small, dumpy, middle-aged woman, with varicose veins on one thigh. Watching herself die in her own mirror. The woman he and Jane had seen dead in her hallway.

And suddenly Terry, like Jane earlier, could take no more. He got to his feet.

'That's it,' he said. 'I think we all need a break. Interview ended at 1.47 a.m.'

He turned and walked grimly from the room.

58. Picture Phone

SARAH'S RELIEF at the knowledge that someone had been arrested was immense. Ever since she'd met Terry outside court, his suspicions had been preying on her mind. As time passed, she tried to separate her emotions from the facts. By this evening, she had decided there were two distinct questions that worried her.

The first was Terry's suggestion that Michael had been having an affair with the murdered woman. Sarah's initial response to this was jealous rage. Michael was *her* lover, no one else's. If he'd been having an affair with this Alison, then he'd deceived her. But slowly, grimly, she had forced herself to look at this more logically. She and Michael weren't married, they had made no vows to each other. The first time they had become lovers, in Cambridge, Alison Grey was already dead. And in fact their relationship had only really developed over the months since then.

So, in one sense, even if Michael *had* been having an affair with Alison, he had not been unfaithful to Sarah while doing it. She, Sarah, had come to fill the gap in Michael's life that Alison had left. That was hardly a flattering way to see herself, but Sarah thought she could live with it. After all, whether the affair lasted or not, it had already given her a great deal. Michael was clearly fond of her, or he wouldn't be so attentive, wouldn't have cooked meals for her, wouldn't have asked her to go to Spain with him. Wouldn't have found her a house, wouldn't make love to her the way he did. Wouldn't have given her a life after her husband Bob had left her.

The more she thought about it, the more she realised how lucky that chance meeting on the train had been, and how much her life had changed because of it. She liked Michael, she was grateful for his affection, she owed him a great deal.

So this evening, when she had asked him about Alison, she hadn't questioned him as thoroughly as she normally would. Thinking about it later, lying in bed beside him, she wondered at herself. It wasn't like her, to allow someone to evade something like that. But there were at least three reasons, she thought, why she hadn't asked him the direct question: 'Were you having an affair with her?'

Firstly, because of moments like this. *His warm body curled against my back, his strong arm round my waist, his breath whispering against my neck as he drifts off to sleep. I like it, I'm happy and content. I don't care if he had an affair with Alison, she's dead, she's no challenge. I've got him now.*

And then secondly, it would just have made him angry. When she'd asked him about Alison he'd become nervous. *If I'd pressed him any more we'd have argued*, she thought - *we've never have made love, or had this blissful peace after. And I need it - it's his gift to me, and mine to him.*

The third reason was much the same thing. *These suspicions aren't mine*, she told herself, *they came from Terry Bateson. He put them in my mind because he's jealous. He's fond of me too, so he can't bear to see me with Michael. So it would have been* his *questions that I'd have been asking, not my own. About an affair that doesn't matter to me any more, because it's over.*

Not for the first time, she felt anger against Terry Bateson for having put her in this position. What had he asked her to do? Investigate her own lover, for heaven's sake! And she, foolishly, had agreed. *Why?*

Michael rolled over onto his back, and Sarah lay beside him, wide awake, her thigh pressed against his. His sleeping breath made a counterpoint to the steady rhythm of the sails turning outside. *Why* had she agreed? Because Terry had suggested that Alison's lover - whoever he was - might also have been Alison's murderer. And that of course put a quite different light on it. This lover - Michael perhaps - might have run Alison a bath, full of luxury bath salts, as Michael had done for her before now, then waited until she got out, warm and naked and presumably cleaned of all traces of male semen or hair from her previous love-making, and hanged her with a scarf in the hall.

Sarah shuddered. That might have been this man lying next to her - that's what Terry had suggested. Only it wasn't. That seemed certain now, and Terry must know it too. Michael had switched on the radio at ten o'clock so she could hear for herself the item on *Radio York* that he had heard earlier - a 24-year-old man had been arrested in an empty house in

Crockey Hill, charged with a number of assaults on women in the York area, and was being interviewed in connection with the murder of Alison Grey.

So it was nothing to do with Michael after all, Sarah told herself. I can relax. Just as I relaxed my defences when he asked me to come up to bed. And I'm glad I did that. It was better than ever tonight; it seemed to matter more to him. Even if he leaves me and goes to Spain we've both had this. I'm happy here now. Warm and comfortable and safe.

But somehow, she couldn't relax. The tension of the evening wouldn't leave her. She lay awake, listening to Michael's breathing and the steady swishing of the sails. They hadn't drawn the curtains - no need out here, so high up - and the moon crept round the corner of a window and shone first on her pillow, then on her face.

She felt thirsty, and searched for a glass of water beside the bed. But there wasn't one - in the heat of passion neither of them had thought of such things. It's no good lying here, she thought, I can't sleep anyway and I need a pee too. Carefully, so as not to wake Michael, she slipped out of bed, dressed herself in his shirt, and crept downstairs past the living room to the kitchen and the bathroom.

Coming out of the bathroom she put the kettle on and sat at the kitchen table listening to it boil. It was quiet and peaceful; just the low lights under the kitchen units. The kettle boiled, and she got up to make a cup of tea. She found cups, milk and teabag, then hunted around for a teaspoon to stir it with. She wasn't used to this kitchen; she didn't know which was the cutlery drawer. She pulled open one, full of dish cloths, then a second. It was full of batteries, candles, phone chargers, matches, an old mobile phone.

She was about to close it when she stopped, her heart pounding strangely. *An old mobile phone.* That was what Terry Bateson had asked her to look for, wasn't it? The one item he had been specific about. The number of an unidentified mobile had cropped up frequently on Alison Grey's phone bill, and the police wanted to know who it belonged to. Well, maybe it was Michael's, Sarah thought, after all, he's admitted he knew her.

Maybe he *was* her lover, and this is the phone they used. *So what, what does it matter, he didn't kill her and the woman's dead.* Her hand trembled as she reached for it, then drew back. *Leave it alone, why don't you?*

But she couldn't. It's better to know, she thought, then I'll be certain. If there are texts on here I can read them, know a little more. Maybe it's all innocent anyway.

She picked up the phone and pressed the *On* button. The screen lit up. Sarah gave a guilty start as a welcoming jingle played - louder than she had expected. She looked round nervously, but she was alone. She searched for *Inbox*, and found a string of little icons of opened envelopes. Beside each one was the same word - *Alison*.

Sarah's heart began to pound in her throat. This is like reading someone's diary, she thought, it's snooping, no good ever came of that.

*Don't look. Okay, Terry was right, Michael **was** having an affair with her, so what? It's none of my business, put it back.*

But she had to know. She pressed the button for the first message.

As she did so, the kitchen door opened, and Michael walked in.

'Do you believe him?' Jane asked, as they stood outside by the coffee machine. It was the middle of the night and they were both exhausted.

'Not about the rape, no,' Terry said, pressing the button for black coffee. 'And the story about the scarf is odd, too. He doesn't mention the whip marks either. But he knows most of the rest.'

'What rest?'

'The mirror. The chair, the way she lost control of her bowels. He couldn't have made that up if he hadn't seen it.'

'So it has to be him.'

'Looks like it, doesn't it? The young bastard.'

'So why lie about the rape?' Jane asked. 'She wasn't raped, we know that. That proves he's lying, doesn't it? If he'd raped her the pathologist would have found semen, pubic hairs - got his DNA from that, weeks ago.'

'No, he never touched her.' Terry sipped his coffee, grimacing as it scalded his mouth. 'Not that way.'

'Then why tell us he did?'

'Male bravado, I guess. He wanted to, poor sad sap. That's what he said about Lizzie Bolan, isn't it? He went there meaning to rape her, but he was interrupted. Couldn't do it. So this time, he wants us to think he got his revenge.'

'Only he didn't.'

'Not sexually, no. But you could say, he punished her for it in every other way. Poor woman. If he's telling the truth.'

'Punished her for what?' Jane frowned. 'She'd done nothing. Not to him.'

'She was a woman, wasn't she? That's what she'd done. He hates women, that's his problem. Any woman's a target for him. Probably never had a girlfriend in his life.'

'He's sick. I can hardly stand being in there with him. Leering at you like he does.'

'He wants to impress me. Make me think he's a man.'

'You're all sick, the whole lot of you.' Jane shook her head vigorously. 'If that's what being a man is, count me out.' She met Terry's eyes, and shrugged apologetically. 'I'm sorry, I didn't mean you.'

'You think *I* like him? He needs mental help.'

'That's the worry, isn't it?' Jane said. 'He'll get away with an insanity plea. I could see the wheels spinning in that brief's mind as you talked.'

'That's why we've got to nail him down to the details. Go through it all again, piece by piece. Build a case as solid as we can so there's no way he can wriggle out of it by changing his plea. Because you're right. That's exactly what she'll do. If she's got any gumption.'

Jane sighed, looking at the clock. It was nearly two in the morning. 'Now?'

'It's late. Start again tomorrow morning. If we go on any more his brief will claim harassment. Maybe the details will become clearer to all of us after a night's rest. And I'll ring that wretched laboratory again.' Terry tipped up the paper cup, swigging the last dregs of his coffee, or whatever it was. 'Cheer up, lass. We may have solved our murder case, at last.'

Guiltily, Sarah tried to hide the phone behind her back. She'd had no time to read the message. Michael's hair was tousled, he wore a blue dressing gown loosely tied around his waist. 'Sarah? What are you doing?' he asked.

'Making a cup of tea. I'm sorry, I didn't mean to wake you. It was the moon, I couldn't sleep.' Stop babbling, she told herself, you've done nothing wrong. 'Would you like one?'

'Okay.' He sat on a chair at the kitchen table. Sarah turned to make the tea and put down the phone casually beside the kettle. Perhaps he hadn't noticed it, after all he was half asleep.

'Where do you keep the spoons? I couldn't find any.'

'In that drawer there.'

She made the tea and joined him at the table. It was cold in the kitchen; she clasped her mug in both hands and watched the steam rise before her face. Michael sipped his tea, and then, to Sarah's surprise, got up, opened the front door, and stepped outside. His voice carried in from the night. 'Storm's gone, at last. It's a beautiful night. Come and see.'

She followed him to the door, and looked outside. He was right. The wind had dropped and the moon and stars shone down crisp and clear out of a jetblack sky. Far below in the valley, she could see the distant lights of remote farmhouses scattered in the darkness. Above their heads, the sails turned lethargically, almost motionless. An owl hooted from the woods behind.

Sarah felt cold and vulnerable standing there in his shirt. After a moment, she turned back into the kitchen. It's okay, she thought, he was too sleepy, he didn't see the phone. I'll put it back in the drawer before he notices.

She picked it up and wondered whether to switch it off. If I do it'll play that jingle again and attract his attention, she thought. But if I don't he may find it switched on and realise I've touched it. Which to do? Leave it switched on and come back to switch it off later or ...

She hesitated, looked down at the phone, and her world fell apart.

There was no message on the screen. Just a photo of a naked woman, hanging from the banisters in the hall of her house.

59. Two Suspects

IT WAS two a.m, and the station was almost empty. Jane Carter left, escorting the young solicitor out to her car. Terry Bateson took Peter Barton downstairs to the custody sergeant, who looked him away in a cell for the night. He watched as the boy was led away, pondering the details of the confession they had heard. There was a swagger in the boy's walk that disgusted him. After all these years, he was still shocked by the depths to which human beings could sink. This is the world I try to protect my children from, he thought. My God, if I could only lock up all these bastards before Jessica and Esther grow up, that would be something worth doing.

But I never will, of course not. There are plenty more where he came from. Breeding in some swamp somewhere.

He shuddered, and went back upstairs. He longed to go home, but dreaded it too. The girls would be asleep, hours ago. Trude, not he, would have read them a story and tucked them in. He didn't want to go in now and wake them, with the filthy aura of this murder still about him. He needed to chill out first, let his mind settle and recover some equilibrium.

He sat at his desk, thinking over the day. Jane Carter, he thought, had done well. Like him, she'd been appalled and disgusted by the lingering pleasure, almost pride, in Peter's voice as he'd relived the details of his crime. But she seemed satisfied too. After all, she'd always suspected Peter, and now, it seemed, she was right.

Or was she? Terry leaned back in his chair, thinking. Most of the details of the confession were right, but not all - she hadn't been raped, for instance. A defence barrister would make a great deal of that. But it wasn't just that. Even though most of the boy's story was accurate, there was something it that Terry found hard to believe. He closed his eyes, trying to pinpoint what it was. He thought back to the previous crimes the boy had confessed to - knicker theft, molesting a jogger on the cyclepath, the attempted rape of Elizabeth Bolan. They all seemed so muddled, so incompetent, in comparison. In each case Peter had fled, at the first sign of trouble. Whereas here, if he was to be believed, he had dominated Alison Grey from the start. She'd been terrified; well, that was understandable, but surely at some point she'd have realised she was about to die, and tried to escape. At which point Peter, if he was true to form, would have fumbled the knot, dropped the knife, knocked something over, run ....

None of which had happened.

But then, if Peter was lying, how did he know so much? An idea formed in Terry's mind. What if only the first part of Peter's tale was really true - the part where he sneaked out of his hut, late at night, to spy on women through their uncurtained windows? Terry could believe that. Was it possible that Peter had been there, outside Alison's house, and seen *someone else* commit the murder in the way he'd described? And that he was now confessing to it out of the perverted sense of bravado that Terry had detected in the interview room? Because he'd seen another man do something that he, Peter, was not brave enough to do himself?

That would explain why he'd gone back later, to imagine what it might have been like. That would be when he'd seen the mirror, and the bathroom. It was all possible, Terry thought, but far fetched. Jane would be annoyed when he suggested it. But he'd put it to Peter nonetheless, Terry decided, when they interviewed him tomorrow morning before deciding whether to charge him. A confession alone, after all, wasn't enough to secure a conviction. They needed evidence, to back it up. And there was still the issue of the red Nissan, and the scrap of cloth on the fence, to be cleared up.

It was too late to ring the forensic services now. Terry switched on his computer, and sent an angry e-mail for them to find first thing in the morning. Then he went downstairs and got into his car.

Driving home, he thought briefly about Sarah Newby. She'd been cold and distant with him last time they'd met. But that was hardly surprising, given the suspicion he'd tried to plant in her mind. He wondered if she'd found anything. She probably didn't bother to look, he thought, given how besotted she is with that man.

Ah well, I was probably wrong about him. If she had found something, she'd have rung by now. Anyway, I'll probably know more in the morning.

Sarah stared at the phone in horror. This was Alison Grey, it had to be. And here was a photo of her dead body *on Michael's phone!* Terry Bateson had been right all along, she thought - more right than he knew. What had he said, that day in the coffee bar, when she'd asked him who killed this woman? *'I think it was her lover,'* he'd said. *'And it's not completely impossible that her lover was Michael Parker.'*

But I refused to believe him, Sarah thought. I gave Terry such a hard time. I accused him of being jealous and having no evidence, all because I wanted to take this man to bed, as I have done, to let him run his hands all over my body, inside my body, let him run warm baths for me and stand there smiling while he wrapped me in a towel just as he must have helped this poor woman out of a bath and - what did he do then?

Tied a scarf round her neck and hanged her from the banisters till she was dead.

Jesus Christ! And he's out there in the darkness right now. If he sees me with this phone he'll ...

'Where did you get that?'

'What? No, I ...' Sarah leaped involuntarily backwards.

'Give me that phone!'

'No! Get away!'

But he was too quick. Even as Sarah backed away Michael grabbed her wrist, and yanked the phone out of her hand. 'You mustn't see - oh my God. No.'

He released her wrist and stood there, staring at the picture on the phone. As soon as he let her go Sarah backed further away, as far from him as she could. But there was nowhere obvious to go. He was standing between her and the open doorway, and the bathroom door was only a couple of paces to his left. No point going into the bathroom anyway, that's just a trap. I might make it to the stairs, she thought, but how would that help? I'd be going up into the tower. He could just follow me up and up to the roof and what would I do then? Jump?

My only hope is get past him somehow, run out into the night, and either hide in the woods or get onto the bike. But how? The bike keys are in my house, on a hook inside the front door - I'd have to sprint over there, grab them, run back to the bike, climb on, and start it, all before he follows me and knocks me down. I can't do it. I'll have to use cunning.

Out of the corner of her eye she saw a knife block by the fridge, a yard to her right. She began to edge her way towards it, watching Michael all the way.

He looked up from the phone. 'I'm so sorry you saw this.'

'Yes. You must be.'

'You know who it is, don't you?'

'Alison Grey.' She inched another foot to her right. 'Your tenant. The woman you had an affair with. The one before me.'

'What?'

'Don't lie to me, Michael. She was your lover, wasn't she? Your tenant, your mistress, your victim - just like me. What happened - did you get tired of her?'

'What are you talking about, Sarah? She was nothing like you.'

'Because I'm alive and she's dead. That's the only real difference, isn't it?'

'Sarah, please! Let me explain ...'

He took a step towards her and she lunged wildly to her right. Her right hand seized the handle of the largest knife in the block and dragged it free so roughly that the rest of the block flew across the room, scattering knives over the floor. Sarah pointed the carving knife at Michael's chest.

'Stay away from me!'

'All right, all right.' He backed away, raising his hands with the palms towards her. One of them still held the phone, with the dreadful picture on the screen. 'Look, this isn't what you think.'

'I know what it is, it's a picture of a dead woman. A woman you murdered, and then took a photo of with your phone. Stay away from me, Michael. I'm not going to be your next victim. I'll kill you first.'

Sarah hadn't been in a fight since she was ten, and that was only screaming and pulling another girl's hair. Her first husband Kevin had bruised her face and nearly broken her arm, but that wasn't really a fight, just a beating, all over in a few seconds, which convinced Sarah of two things: men were far stronger than women, and speed is as lethal as strength. So if I'm to have any chance I must stab him first, she thought, before he grabs me. Which is the best place - the throat, or the stomach? Maybe the thigh - that's a big target.

The blade trembled in her hand as the adrenalin coursed through her.

'Sarah, I didn't kill her.'

'Don't lie, Michael.' He was backing away from the knife, she realised with relief - three more yards and she could reach the front door and run.

'I'm not lying, for Christ's sake! How do you think that photo got on the phone?'

'Because you took it.' Another step back. Two yards to safety.

'No. It's a picture message. It was sent to me.'

'What?'

'Have a look if you don't believe me. Here.' He bent down, and slid the phone across the floor to her feet. 'Pick it up. I'm not going to hurt you.'

Carefully, keeping her eyes on him all the time, she bent down and picked up the phone. It's a trick, she thought. He thinks I can't look at him and the phone at the same time. When I stop looking at him he'll rush me.

'Look, I'll sit down, okay? I'm not going to hurt you, I promise.'

Michael sat on a chair at the kitchen table. Cautiously, Sarah moved to the open doorway, and stood with her back to it, looking in. I can run any time I want, she thought. Slam the door in his face and sprint for safety. With the knife in her right hand, she held the phone in her left and pressed buttons with her thumb.

'Look. It's not saved on the phone as it would be if I'd taken it, is it? It's in a text message I've received.'

Grudgingly, she realised that he was right. Her racing heartbeat slowed, from a wild gallop to a canter. 'A text from Alison? But she's dead.'

'Yes, obviously. She didn't take it.'

'So who did?'

'The man who killed her. Don't you see? He must have taken it with her phone.'

'And then sent it to you? But why would he do that?'

Michael sighed. 'Because he hates me. Look, it's a long story and I ... I can't tell you, I'm sorry. It's private, between me and Alison.'

'But Alison's *dead*, Michael. She was murdered.'

'Yes, I know, but I still can't tell you.'

Sarah stared at him, as coolly as she could. Her pulse was throbbing in her throat, like a drummer boy going to war, but she could see he was nervous too. His face was pale, his eyes sunken, shadowed, gazing at some distant, dreadful memory. I have to understand this now, Sarah thought; he can't just shut me out and pretend this doesn't matter.

She picked up the knife and phone and got to her feet. 'If you don't tell me what all this is about, Michael, I'll take this to the police. I've no choice, really - it's evidence of murder.'

'But I didn't do it, Sarah - I swear to you!'

'Then who did? Explain it to me, Michael, or I'm going.' She stepped towards the door, pointing the knife boldly at him in case he should rush her.

But Michael looked defeated, diminished, rather than violent. He spread his hands in appeal. 'All right, all right. Don't go, please. I'll tell you if ... if I can find the words. It won't be easy. You deserve an explanation, but you won't like it much. Look, Sarah, you're scaring me with that knife. I didn't kill Alison, I promise - I've never killed anyone in my life. Why don't you just sit down, and I'll try to explain what's happened. Or what I think has happened, anyway.'

60. Midnight Story

IT WAS cold in the kitchen. The door was still open to the night air and all Sarah had on was Michael's shirt, which she had picked up when she got out of bed, a hundred years ago it seemed. She stood with the carving knife in one hand, the mobile phone in the other.

'Sit down, please,' Michael said, indicating the chair opposite him at the kitchen table. 'I can't talk if you stand there like that.'

'You stay there then.' Cautiously she crossed the room and sat down, the knife on the table in front of her. 'All right, I'm listening.'

Michael looked haggard, his eyes sunken, his face pale and lined. He met her eyes briefly, then looked down at his hands. Twice he seemed about to speak, then stopped.

'It's very difficult, Sarah. I don't know how to say this.'

'You could start by telling me why you had this phone, and why Alison sent you messages on it.'

'Yes, well, that's not so easy, you see.'

'She was your girlfriend, your mistress, wasn't she? Just like me.'

'Nothing like you, Sarah! Nothing at all!'

'Really? What was the difference?'

'Well, for a start, I'd known her a long time ...'

'Since you were students in York, right?' The photo from the *Yorkshire Post* came into Sarah's mind, the one she had found in the file in the other house. Young Alison clinging onto a younger Michael at the memorial service for Brenda Stokes.

'Yes, since then. She was my girlfriend once, back then. And ... it never really ended, so when I got married, she used to come back to see me, write letters, make phone calls, and ... of course my wife didn't like it, so ... I bought that phone.' He pointed to the phone on the table in front of her. 'I told her she could only ring me on that. It's pay as you go, you see - no account, no phone records, nothing. So Kate wouldn't know how often she rang. No one would. Or that's what I hoped.' He looked up to see if he was making sense to her.

'You had a separate mobile, just to ring Alison? So your wife wouldn't know?'

'Yes.'

'But Michael, you're divorced! So the only person you're deceiving now is - *me!*'

'Not just you. Not you at all, really.' A faint smile crossed his lips.

'It's not funny, Michael. It's bloody deceitful ...'

He shook his head wearily. 'It's nothing to do with you, Sarah. Really. At least it wasn't until now. This has been going on for years. We just ... got into the habit of it. It seemed wise, in the circumstances.'

'What circumstances?'

'That's ... just it.' There was a long silence, so long that Sarah thought the conversation was over. She shivered in the draught from the door, and hunched her arms across her breasts for warmth. An owl hooted outside in the woods. Michael stared down at the table, so lost in thought that she wondered if he remembered she was there at all. At last he sighed and looked up.

'I've never told anyone this, Sarah. No one. If you hadn't found that photo on that phone I never would. Look, if I tell you, will you keep it secret?'

'I can't do that, Michael. It's evidence in a murder case.'

He stared at her earnestly. 'Please. You do care for me, Sarah, don't you? A little, at least?'

I did, Sarah thought. *Until all this happened.* Now, she wasn't so sure. A few moments ago she'd been terrified of him, now he was pleading with her. The respect and gratitude she'd felt for him was leaking away. But she had to know the truth about that photo. So she said: 'Yes, of course. You know I do.'

'Then I'll trust you. If I tell you, perhaps you'll understand. And if not, well ... all life ends sometime.'

Sarah didn't like the sound of that. *Not my life*, she thought. *Not yet. Not if I can help it anyway.* Her fingers touched the handle of the knife.

'What I need to know, Michael, is why that photo is on your phone. You say the killer sent it to you as a picture message. Who is he? And why?'

'That's exactly what I'm going to tell you.' He drew a deep breath. 'You see, it's all to do with me, and Alison, and Brenda Stokes - you know, the girl whose body they found beside the ring road before Christmas. You see, I know how it got there.'

'What?'

'You asked me before if I knew Brenda. And I told you I'd met her and your client, Jason Barnes, when we were students here in York. Well, Alison was my girlfriend then, as you've guessed. We were a couple, though she was fonder of me than I was of her - it happens like that, sometimes. Anyway, nothing would have come of it, probably - we'd have split up, met other people, and led perfectly normal lives, if it hadn't been for this one terrible day which changed everything.'

He gazed past Sarah at the window, his eyes focussed on the memory he was about to describe.

'You see, our affair was coming to an end, and I'd met this girl Brenda, who was very sexy, in a busty, provocative sort of way. Anyway, I fell for her - she was exciting, after Alison, and I was flattered that a stunner like her could fancy me, even for a moment. I didn't realise what a bitch she was, I was blind to that, at first. So I made my big mistake. One day she told me it was her birthday, which turned out to be a lie, I only found that out later. But I panicked, and thought I have to give her something decent, so she'll like me. And the only thing I could think of was a silk scarf, which I'd already bought for Alison, who really did have a birthday later that month. Brenda probably knew that, about Alison's birthday, that's why she lied about her own. That's the sort of bitch she was. She'd pull guys just for the hell of it, to rub their girlfriends' noses in it. Then dump the boys after.'

Michael sighed. 'Anyway, I was too naive and besotted to understand all this, so I gave her the wretched scarf, which cost me a lot of money in those days, it was a good one. But what I didn't realise was, Alison had already seen it - she'd found it in a drawer in my bedroom, and guessed I was saving it for her birthday. So when we went to that party, the day that changed all our lives, that scarf was at the heart of everything.'

Michael ran his hands through his hair. 'You see, I went to this party with Brenda, proud as a little peacock, with about as much brain as a peacock as well - and she was wearing this scarf I gave her. But when Alison saw it, all hell broke loose. They had a catfight in the ladies' loo -

God knows what happened, but Alison came out with the scarf in her hand, and Brenda came out with a face like thunder and wouldn't speak to me. By the end of the evening she was totally pissed and when I tried to talk to her she spat in my face and drove off with a young thug called Jason Barnes. Who you know.'

Michael spread his hands on the table, looking down. 'So I slouched off home, full of self-pity, and that would have been that, just another teenage tragedy, if only ...'

An owl hooted outside, a gust of wind blew in through the door. Sarah shivered as she sat there in the shirt.

'... if only things had been slightly different. I've thought about this so often. Only one thing had to be different, and none of our lives would have been blighted. Brenda would never have died, Jason wouldn't have gone to prison, and Alison and I wouldn't have tormented each other for the next eighteen years. That photo would never have appeared on that phone.

'You see, I went home - I lived in a village outside York, called Stillingfleet, with a couple of guys who were away at a rugby match somewhere. So I went to bed, feeling sorry for myself, but about five in the morning I was woken by someone hammering on the front door. It was Alison, in a dreadful state. Hysterical, weeping and angry at the same time. She dragged me outside to her car, and there in the front seat was Brenda. Or Brenda's body, rather.'

'She was dead?'

'Quite dead. It was horrible. There was blood all over her face and hair, one of her arms was broken, and her eyes and tongue were popping out.'

'What had happened to her?'

'Alison had killed her. Without meaning to, but she had.'

'How could she kill her without meaning to?'

'Well, it was another appalling coincidence. After the fight at the party Alison had gone somewhere else, to another party I think, and then at about half past four she was driving home to Naburn, where she lived, when she saw a girl walking alone along the road. She didn't realise who it was at first, so she stopped to offer her a lift. And then Brenda got into the car. And somehow or other the fight started again. I don't know who started it, I wasn't there, but according to Alison Brenda picked the wretched scarf up off the front seat and put it on, saying it was hers and Alison had stolen it. Then Alison tried to shove her out of the car. When she thought she'd got her out she drove off, meaning to leave her there by the side of the road. But the scarf had got caught in the door as she pulled it shut. So when she drove on she pulled Brenda off her feet and dragged her along the road beside the car, with her head banging on the road and the scarf throttling her round her neck. The car must have driven over her arm too, which broke her wrist. Alison was accelerating away in a rage, so by the time she realised something was wrong, it was too late. She'd dragged Brenda a hundred yards along the road. She was dead, it was hopeless. So she heaved her into the car, drove to Stillingfleet, and hammered on my door for help.'

Michael shook his head slowly. 'So it all had this dreadful inevitability.'

The story certainly explained a lot, Sarah thought. It explained why the police had been unable to decide between two possible causes of death, strangulation and blows to the head. It explained why the hand had come away from the wrist so easily. It also showed that the trainee nurse, Amanda Carr, had been telling the truth about the young woman she'd seen on Naburn Lane that night. If only *she'd* offered Brenda a lift before Alison came along, none of this would have happened.

It also proved, beyond any doubt, that Jason Barnes had served 18 years in prison for a murder he hadn't committed. Something that Michael had clearly known all along. Sarah shivered, but not from cold this time. *This is the man I've chosen to comfort me. The man I've taken to bed.*

'What happened next?'

'Well, I suppose you can guess that.'

'Not really. You'd better tell me,' Sarah said bleakly. Up to this point, the story could be construed as an accident. But not afterwards.

'Well, it's simple really. She was in hysterics and I was in shock - we both were. I mean, you never know what you'll do in a situation like that until it happens, and then ... well, whatever you do stays with you forever. It can't be undone, not easily anyway. Of course I thought of calling the police, we both did, but it looked so awful - I mean, even if it was just manslaughter Alison would go to prison. She was desperate, and in a way it was all my fault - I mean, if I hadn't given Brenda the wretched scarf none of this would have happened, and we both hated Brenda at that moment, we could see what a bitch she had been, and in a way it was her own fault that she was dead, at least that's what we told ourselves, so ...' Michael drew a deep breath. '... I said I'd help her hide the body. As it happened I'd had a holiday job labouring on the road works, and I knew they dug a lot of trenches there which they filled in with concrete, so I thought if we just buried her in one of those we might be lucky and the body would never be found for a hundred years. So we found a couple of spades in the garden shed, drove there, and did it. And we very nearly got it right. After all, if that fox hadn't dug up her hand, she'd still be down there now and no one would ever know. Next day we washed all the blood off her car, took it to auction, and sold it.'

He looked across the table at Sarah. 'We swore each other to secrecy. We promised each other we would never, ever, tell anyone. And neither of us ever has, until now.'

'So when Jason Barnes was arrested ...' Sarah prompted, neutrally.

'We said nothing. How could we, without incriminating ourselves?'

Sarah's eyes met his. She touched a key on the mobile with her fingertip. The screen, with the shocking photo of Alison's body, lit up. 'What I still don't understand, is how all that relates to this.'

'Yes. Well, that's the second part of the story.'

61. Rough Love

'YOU UNDERSTAND something now, at least, don't you?' Michael asked, gazing bleakly across the table. 'You see how we were bound to each other? Not because I loved her or anything like that, that all ended the day Brenda died - on my side at least. But we shared this one terrible secret, that we could never discuss with anyone else, ever. Until you.'

Michael rested his head in hands, gazing down at the table. He sat like that, silent, for over a minute. A fox barked in the night beyond the open door, and somewhere far away down the valley, the sound of a distant car engine rose through the stillness.

'I never imagined I'd have this conversation,' he said at last. 'Not with anyone. It's good of you to listen, at least.'

Sarah said nothing. She was not a woman given to sympathy - her life, and the career she had chosen, had left little room for that. Until now, she had respected Michael for qualities she recognised in herself - the way he had created his own business out of nothing, ran it efficiently, took responsibility for his own decisions. Now, as his story progressed, she felt the last vestiges of respect leaking away from her mind. In its place was a growing sense of horror for what she had heard, and self-disgust for the intimacy she had shared with such a man.

But she needed to understand, so she stayed silent and listened.

'It would have been better, probably, if we'd split up and never met again,' he continued. 'I could have managed that, but she couldn't. You see, from the beginning she was fonder of me than I was of her, and after Brenda's death, well, she thought I'd saved her from prison, which I suppose I had, so then love, or whatever she felt, was mixed with gratitude in her mind, and she could never stay away.' He sighed, shaking his head. 'Oh, she tried, of course. I got married, and for a while she respected that. She trained as an English language teacher, and went as far away as she could - Saudi Arabia, Indonesia, Japan, even Outer Mongolia for a year -

but she always came back, and it was always the same. She'd met some man, a doctor or foreign student or teacher, but the affair always broke up because he didn't match up to me, that's what she said. So then we'd meet in a hotel or go away for a short holiday and ... you can imagine.' He looked at Sarah ruefully. 'No, actually, you probably can't. It was too nasty, too violent for that. Because she loved me and I didn't love her - that's how it all went wrong in the first place, of course, with the scarf - and also because she, on top of this, felt guilty for killing Brenda, well ... often the only way I could satisfy her was to punish her.'

'How, exactly?' Sarah asked quietly.

'With punishment, bondage, domination - all that S & M stuff. She liked it, she found it exciting, and so did I, in a way. After all, it expressed the way we were together; not lovers, exactly, but well, partners in crime.'

Sarah said nothing. Thank God he never tried that with me, she thought.

'And then at other times I'd try to be really nice, to break out of all that. So I'd make her a bubble bath, give her a massage to heal the bruises, you know, like ...' He met her eyes, appealing for understanding. Sarah looked down, at the photo on the mobile.

'Is that what you did here in York?'

'Yes. Both of those things. But it was before I met you, Sarah. Remember that.'

With an effort, Sarah looked up and met his eyes. 'That first time, we ... had sex ... in Cambridge, that was the day after she died, wasn't it?'

'I suppose it was, yes.'

'Did you know she was dead, then?'

'*No!* Of course I didn't - what sort of a monster do you think I am? Damn it, Sarah, the only way I could have known that would be if I'd killed her, and I've told you I didn't - you have to believe me!'

'So when was the last time you had sex with her?'

'I ...' he let out a long, slow breath. 'I told the police it was two days before - I mean, I didn't tell them I had sex with her then, I said that was the last time I saw her, when I went to fix her central heating. But in fact ... the last time I saw her was on the morning of the day she died, before I drove off to Scarborough.'

'And what happened then?'

'Oh ...' he shook his head miserably. 'It was a terrible conversation, as a matter of fact. I wish I could make you see it, how it was.'

'Try,' Sarah said coolly. Her small stock of sympathy was almost used up. *Whatever happened that morning,* she thought, *the very next day he drove to Cambridge intending to seduce me. Which he did, that Sunday. Thinking this Alison was still alive and waiting for him in York.*

Alison saw the BMW as soon as it turned off the road. She watched it crawl slowly down the drive, a farmtrack about a hundred yards long, and disappear around the back of the house. Michael always parked there, out of sight. Her nearest neighbour, Mrs Phillips, lived a quarter of a mile away across a field, and Alison hardly knew her, anyway, so there was no real reason to hide these visits, but the habit of secrecy had become engrained with them both over the years. Alison always used Michael's special phone, never sent him emails, never told his secretary she was anything but a normal tenant. Indeed, when the last secretary had suspected it, she'd been replaced.

It was all part of the punishment she'd endured for eighteen years. Michael would only visit her, he insisted, if no one else knew about their relationship at all. If even one person guessed what really bound them together, everything would unravel uncontrollably. And they both had too much to live for to allow that.

Or at least, they *had* had too much to live for. But Alison had just visited her oncologist. He had been kind, sympathetic, professional - and had confirmed her worst fears. The cancer was inoperable; it was too far gone for that. Without treatment, she might last three months, maybe four - with chemotherapy, maybe a couple of years. No more. And the chemotherapy, she had heard, was dreadful. The thought of it terrified her, almost as much as the thought of death itself.

Either way, she had little left to live for. The English language teaching books she was so proud of would be published and sell worldwide, bringing in thousands, perhaps hundreds of thousands, of pounds, but she had no idea who to leave the money to. Her father was dead, her mother was 80. She was an only child. She had no husband, no children, no current lover except for Michael.

And she didn't even really love him. That wasn't the nature of their relationship any more. It was deeper and darker than that.

But since it is death that I have to face, she thought, as she went to open the back door, perhaps he is the best person to talk to. He knows more about me than anyone else. And before I die, one thing has to change.

They sat round an open wood fire in the small front living room, while she told him what the cancer specialist had said. Her cat climbed onto her lap and she stroked it to soothe herself, keeping her voice as calm as she could.

'It's terrifying,' she said, 'but it comes to us all, in the end. In a dreadful sort of way, it's good to know the truth. It concentrates the mind. There's one thing I have to do before I die.'

'Which is?'

He guessed the answer, she could tell by his face. But she told him all the same. 'You know I'm planning to become a Catholic, I told you that before. I've been taking instruction. But there's one thing an applicant has to do before he or she's received into the church, and there's no point doing it unless you do it properly, with your whole heart. You have to confess your sins.'

'No,' he said firmly, 'you can't do that. We've kept this secret all our lives, we have to take it to the grave.'

'But that's a cold and lonely place,' she said with a shudder. 'Or perhaps not so cold for me, if I don't confess. This is my eternal soul I'm talking about, Michael. It's all right to tell a priest, they're trained to keep everything secret. You know that.'

'You can't be sure,' Michael said. He frowned, thinking hard. 'Anyway, at the very least they'll ask you to atone for it in some way. And how could you do that, without going to Jason or Jason's lawyer and explaining why he's innocent? And what would come of that? We'd both end our lives in prison.'

'My life's about to end anyway,' she said softly. 'I'm thinking about what comes after.'

'But what about me? I've got thirty or forty years left. Do you want me to spend that time behind bars?'

'No, of course not, Michael, but I don't have to involve you. After all, *I* killed her, you didn't. I can just confess to what *I* did. I won't even mention you.'

Michael got up, and stood with one hand on the mantlepiece, glaring down at her. It was a familiar anger; she had seen every facet of his temper, down the years. She deserved it, she knew that, but she hoped it would not follow her beyond the grave.

'They'll know though, won't they?' he insisted. 'Brenda was a heavy girl, bigger than you. No one will believe you carried her from the road to where we buried her on your own. They'll guess you had help. So then they'll talk to people who knew us at the time, and ask who you would have trusted to help you and keep your secret. The answer will be obvious, won't it? *Me.*'

Disturbed by his anger, the cat sank its claws in her thigh. Alison winced, lifting it up and stroking it gently to soothe it. 'What are you talking about?' she asked. 'Who is this *they?* I'm not going to tell a lot of people, certainly not the police. I just want to confess to a priest, that's all. To take this burden off my soul.'

'You can't,' he insisted flatly. 'You can never tell anyone. Neither of us can. We agreed that 18 years ago.'

'I know. But now I'm dying ...'

'It doesn't make any difference. There's nothing beyond the grave, anyway. Just silence, and peace ...'

'How do you know that, Michael? How can you possibly know?'

'I don't know, it's just obvious, that's all.' He threw a log on the fire, and watched the woodlice scurry to escape the flames. 'We're all animals; this religion of yours is so much claptrap people invent to comfort themselves. Think about it, Alison - how is it comforting to believe in eternity? Especially for you and me - an eternity in which we can never forget what we've done. Is that what you want? With Brenda up there too to make your life ...'

'*Hell.* That's what you were going to say, isn't it? To make our lives hell?'

'Exactly.' He smiled - an odd, mocking grin which he intended to be comforting. 'But you don't have to worry about that, Ally, you see, because it's all nonsense. There's nothing after death, just silence. Ashes to ashes, dust to dust. You remember what Brenda looked like - do you think she had a soul? She didn't; she was just a body. Dead, gone, finished. That's all it is. Silence. Think about it for a moment; isn't that more comforting? You never have to worry about anything ever again. There's no *you* to worry any more. Nothing. No guilt, no recriminations, nothing at all. Peace and silence for all eternity.'

'That's even more frightening. I don't think I could cope with that.'

'You don't have to cope with it. It just happens.'

They sat in silence for a while, looking at each other, appalled by the prospect they'd been discussing. In a sudden smooth leap, the cat sprang from Alison's lap onto the floor. She looked up at him defiantly.

'I've made an appointment with a priest on Tuesday.'

'You can't do that, Alison.' A note of menace, familiar to them both, entered Michael's voice. 'You know that. I would have to punish you.'

'No, Michael, please. Not this time.'

'Yes. You know you deserve it; this time more than ever. It's the only way you'll get any release.' He seized her wrist, dragged her up out of the chair to her feet.

'No, don't. You're scaring me.' She struggled to escape. Not hard; she knew from long experience that it was impossible.

'You deserve to be scared,' he insisted. 'You've been a bad girl. You want it really, that's why you've been telling me all this.'

'I don't want it.'

'You do. At least if it hurts, you'll know you're not dead. Not yet, anyway.'

'And that's how you left her?'

'Yes. I knew she was ill, so I wasn't really rough. I just whipped her a few times with a cane I kept in my car. It was punishment, sexual humiliation, something she enjoyed. Therapy, in a way. I told you, she was used to it.'

'She was dying, Michael.' Sarah struggled to keep the disdain out of her voice.

'Not then. She was fully alive when I left her. Happier, in fact, than when I arrived.' He gazed at her dejectedly across the table. 'I knew you wouldn't understand. I should never have told you.'

'Did you run a bath for her too? Before you left?'

'No. I was in too much of a hurry. I had a shower, but she didn't. Maybe she ran a bath for herself later. She often did that, to comfort herself.'

And to wash all traces of you off her body, Sarah thought bitterly. I could do with a shower myself, right now. All trace of her affection for Michael was gone. She understood, but did not sympathise.

'And that was the last time you saw her?'

'Yes. I swear it. I drove out to Scarborough, spent the evening in conference with the builders, and came straight back here. Next day I drove to Cambridge. I had no idea she was dead until Monday.'

Sarah turned the phone towards him. 'So who did this, then?'

'Your client, Jason Barnes. The man you freed from prison.'

'What?' This idea had never occurred to Sarah. 'What makes you think that?'

'It's pretty obvious, don't you think? Who else would want to kill her, a single woman like that? Nothing was stolen, as I understand it, she wasn't raped. She had no other enemies. Besides, look at that photo. What do you see?'

Sarah shuddered. 'A naked woman hanging from the banisters.'

'Yes, and what's round her neck?'

'A scarf.'

'Yes, exactly - an expensive looking scarf, too. Not the kind of thing Alison would own; in fact she hated scarves, since Brenda's death. But it's exactly the sort of scarf that killed Brenda, isn't it?'

'I wouldn't know. I never saw it.'

'Well, I'm telling you, it is, so far as I can make out on a small screen like that. Similar colour, similar style. Her killer must have brought it with him.'

'But why ...?'

'And the other thing you can't see, but you'd know if you'd been in the house, is the significance of *where* she's hanging. She had a mirror in the hall directly opposite the stairs, she was hanged facing that. So whoever killed her, wanted to humiliate her first. Let her see herself hanging in the mirror.'

'It was a ritual execution, you mean?'

'Her final punishment for what she'd done.'

'But how would Jason know that Alison killed Brenda? It's always been a mystery - he spent 18 years in prison convicted of it himself. If he'd known who really killed her he would have told his lawyers, wouldn't he! I'd have used it in court, myself!'

'He didn't know then, don't you see?' Michael sighed sadly. 'It was only when that fox found her hand that everything started to unravel. The police dug up her body and went on *Crimewatch* with the remains of the scarf, asking for information. As soon as I saw that I knew we were in trouble, Alison did too. I asked you about Jason, remember, and you said he'd disappeared. I hoped he'd gone to Australia or somewhere, but no, he must have seen *Crimewatch* just as we did and started to think. He knew Brenda had fought with Alison about the scarf, she couldn't stop talking about it. And he knew Alison had snatched it back. So if the scarf round her neck had killed her, then the only person who could have put it there was Alison. Once he worked that out all he had to do was find Alison, and make her pay for what she'd done.'

'But what about this photo on the phone?'

Michael groaned. 'That's what really scared me. I only saw it a couple of days ago, because I'd switched the phone off and thrown it in a drawer. I wish I'd never switched it on again, then we wouldn't be having this conversation now!'

'But if he killed her, why send the photo?'

'Don't you see?' He shook his head despairingly. 'After she died, I buried my head in the sand for while, thinking even if it was Jason, he's only after her, not me. Maybe he thinks she killed Brenda all on her own. After all that's what Alison was going to tell the priest, so perhaps that's what she told him, if she got the chance to speak. Nothing about me at all. But obviously he found her phone, took a photo of her body, the sick bastard - and read some of the texts I'd sent her on it. Maybe she told him everything anyway, before she died. So he sent me this photo as a warning. A threat, probably, too. To say that he knew.'

He looked at Sarah with a bleak, hopeless smile. 'That's why I thought of moving to Spain. To get away and hide before he finds out where I live. But it's probably futile. He'll follow me there too, won't he? Unlike you.'

There was a sad, pleading look on his face. Sarah gazed at him steadily, thinking of her client who'd spent 18 years in prison for a crime he didn't commit. 'You can't be sure about all this, Michael. This could just be guilt and paranoia speaking. She may have been killed by that young man the police have arrested.'

'Do you really believe that? After all I've just told you?'

Sarah struggled to be fair. 'It's not a question of what I believe; what matters is the truth. You have to take that phone to the police tomorrow morning. Tell them all you know. Let them sort it out.'

'I can't do that, you know I can't. They'd send me to prison.'

'You let someone else go to prison for 18 years.'

'Yes, but he's a murderer!'

'Not then he wasn't. Alison was, and you were an accessory. But if Jason did kill her, then it's your duty to bring him to justice. You may even get credit for it, from the judge.'

'If I give myself up, will you act as my lawyer?'

'No.'

'Why not? You defended your son, when he was accused of murder!'

'That's different, Michael. He was innocent. And he was my son.'

'Come to Spain with me, Sarah. Please. Forget all this, leave it behind.'

'We could never forget it. Michael, I'm not going to throw my career away for you or anyone else. I'm an officer of the court, and that phone is evidence. I have to take it to the police. Your best bet is to come with me. The worst they could charge you with is being an accessory to manslaughter, not murder. You'd be out in five years.'

'I'll never go to prison. I'll kill myself first. Sarah, please. Come to Spain. You know all this now but no one else does.'

He reached across the table for her hand, but Sarah recoiled instantly.

'I'm not coming, Michael.' She picked up the knife and stood up. If he wants to stop me, she thought, this is when he'll try to do it.

But he stayed slumped at the table, watching her walk to the door.

'It's up to you,' she said. 'I won't tell anyone about this until the morning. Make up your mind by then. But if you leave, you leave without me.'

Outside, in the cold night air, she walked swiftly, her bare feet stumbling across the stones of Simon's half-finished patio and the damp grass beyond. She glanced over her shoulder, feeling an urge to run, but she could still see him through the open doorway, sitting at the table. Inside her own house, she locked and bolted both doors, closed all the windows, and went upstairs to her bedroom. The light was still on in the windmill kitchen, she saw, and the door was still open.

I left my phone over there, she thought, with my bag and the clothes I was wearing. But I have the keys to the bike; I can escape if I want to. And I can ring for help on this phone, if I need to. Terry said I could ring any time.

But it's late, he has kids, I can manage.

For half an hour she sat on the edge of her bed, staring into the dark, watching to see if Michael would get in his car, and drive away. Or come across the grass, bang on her door, smash a window even, drag her outside.

But nothing happened. The door to the windmill stayed open, no one came out.

At last weariness overcame her, and she crawled into bed to sleep.

62. Sailing High

WHEN SARAH woke it was still dark. She fumbled for the clock beside her bed, and pressed the screen to light it up. 5.45. Something woke me, she thought. She lay still for a few moments, listening, trying to work out what it was. Someone in the house? No; the house seemed silent enough. No surreptitious footsteps on the stairs, no doors opening or floorboards creaking. Just a slight rattle of wind on her bedroom window.

Something outside then. A car perhaps? The memory of what had happened earlier came back to her in a rush. Maybe Michael was leaving. She swung her legs out of bed and peered out of the window. To her surprise, the lights were on in the windmill. Not just the kitchen - all of them, on every floor. The light blazing out in the darkness illuminated the grass between the buildings, and Simon's unfinished patio outside the open kitchen door. But it cast the area nearer the woods into deeper shadow, so that she couldn't see if Michael's car was parked there or not.

He must have gone, she thought. I gave him that chance; he's taken it. That's what I heard - Michael driving away in the BMW, to Spain or South America or wherever he thinks he can hide. He switched on all the lights to pack what he needed, and left the door open because he's never coming back.

She felt relieved and depressed, both at once. Relieved, because she wouldn't have to face the trauma of persuading him to come into York and give himself up. She had wondered how to do that last night; should she risk getting in his car, or follow on her bike? Both plans had their problems, but it didn't matter now. She felt depressed, though, because his flight diminished him further in her eyes. He was less of a man than she'd thought, she decided. All his life he'd been running from the truth, and here he was doing it again.

She'd fallen asleep in Michael's shirt. She threw it off, and dressed quickly in jeans and a warm jumper. She was fairly certain he'd gone, but she wanted to make sure. Then I can ride into York and show Terry Bateson that phone, she thought. He'll be pleased. Smug bastard; he never liked Michael in the first place. Oh well.

A sudden rush of pain constricted her lungs as she realised Michael had gone, and she'd never see him again. He's a coward, she thought, but he had good qualities too, I liked him. He was kind to me, generous, a good lover - I wasn't a total fool to fall for him, was I? She remembered how nervous and excited she had felt that first time they had made love in Cambridge, and the dizzy thrill of walking round York the next day, unable to concentrate on anything except the way he'd touched her, the way he'd felt. He gave me that, she thought; something I never expected to feel again. I even considered starting a new life with him.

But he wasn't worth it. At the crucial moment, when he was forced to decide, he made a catastrophically wrong decision. The sort which defines your character for ever. And now, he's done it again.

Or has he? Halfway to the windmill, on the edge of the patio, she saw several things at once. Firstly, Michael's BMW was still there. It was parked at the edge of the woods, a little further away than she'd remembered, in the shadows just beyond the range of the lights from the house. That's why she hadn't seen it. But something else was lighting it up now - a red glow somewhere behind the car in the woods. What was that? A fire? Surely not. The sun rising in the east? But it's too early, isn't it? In the west the sky is still black.

But when she looked to the west, she noticed the second thing. Which drove everything else out of her mind.

Something was hanging from one of the windmill's sails.

She first saw it out of the corner of her eye and within a second she could look at nothing else. The sails were moving slowly in a light wind, with a hesitant, slightly jerky motion as if they were unbalanced; and as the lowest sail came into sight from behind the tower and rose, or tried to rise, to the horizontal, Sarah saw what was holding them back.

It was a body, hanging from the end of the sail.

The sail dragged the body across the lower balcony, around the first floor of the mill, and as it rose into the air a foot got caught on the balcony rail, so that for a moment the body was stretched between the sail, trying to drag it upwards by the neck, and the foot, holding it back. Then a shoe fell off the foot and the body swung free, swaying left and right like a pendulum as it rose higher into the air.

Sarah screamed. It was the body of a man, hanging by his neck from the sail. As the sail rose to the vertical his arms flopped loosely beside him and the light from the windows caught his face. His eyes seemed to be staring straight down at her and his tongue stuck out of his mouth, like a gargoyle. Michael, it had to be him.

Then the sail passed the vertical and the body vanished behind the mill in the night.

Sarah screamed as she ran into the mill, straight up the stairs to the first floor. She was screaming all the time without knowing, but her mind was racing as well. *I must stop it*, she thought, *he may still be alive, I must put on the brake. How do you do that? He showed me, there's a cord, a rope, something you pull.* She dashed through the first floor room to the balcony door, opened it, and saw the dreadful sight of Michael, descending slowly towards her, swaying slightly in the wind. *I've got to stop it*, she thought, *where's the brake, here, here, it's this rope isn't it, what the hell do you do?*

She was fumbling with the rope when something brushed against her back. She turned and saw Michael's face, a few inches from hers. Eyes protruding, tongue lolling, it jerked past her like a ghastly marionette, and began to rise again into the air, the legs flopping over the balcony rail.

Sarah screamed again, tugged futilely on the rope, then abandoned it in despair. Either she was doing the wrong thing or the sails were too strong, turning remorselessly with the power of the wind against everything she could do. Anyhow, what did matter? She'd hoped somehow she could save him but she was clearly too late. He was dead.

And I let him do it, she thought grimly. What did he say last night? *'I'll never go to prison. I'll kill myself first.'* That was the one alternative she hadn't thought about, that he might actually do it. But I should have, she realised, of course it was a real possibility. Remember that moment on the roof, when he joked about suicide - I thought it was a joke at the time, but it wasn't. And the way he talked about death with Alison. Peace and silence for all eternity. It's been on his mind the whole time.

Only I didn't see it. And now this. She felt a sudden, desperate urge to vomit, and stumbled downstairs to the bathroom.

Coming out of the bathroom, Sarah thought, I need help. I can't let his body carry on going round like that in the wind, it's obscene. But I'm not strong enough to stop it; either that or I'm doing something wrong. Anyway I'm not sure I can face this for long on my own.

She remembered she had left her mobile in her bag with her clothes in Michael's bedroom, so she climbed the stairs to get it. Her legs shook with each step, but she forced herself to climb. When she reached the bedroom, she stopped and stared. It was chaos. Clothes were flung everywhere, drawers were opened, bedclothes on the floor. That's not like Michael, she thought, he's usually so neat. But then he was in a terrible state last night, he must have had a breakdown or tantrum before he decided to do this. If I'd stayed here he might have killed me too.

Or not done it. If I'd stayed he might still be alive. Maybe he killed himself because I abandoned him.

Don't think like that, it gets you nowhere. This was his own decision, not mine.

Was it? Are you sure?

Of course I'm sure.

What if you'd stayed, shown a little compassion? You condemned him for the decision he took, ages ago. How are you going to feel about this, in five year's time?

I'll cross that bridge when I come to it. Shut up, please, I've got things to do.

Sarah found her bag, on the floor beside a pillow, and took out her phone. I ought to ring the emergency services, she thought, but how do I explain all this? She felt a wave of weakness pass over her, and a desperate need for strength and sympathy. On impulse, she pressed the number for her son, Simon. He answered on the second ring. His voice sounded sleepy.

'Hello. Mum? Is that you?'

'Simon, I need your help.'

'Why? What is it?'

'Something terrible. It's Michael. He's dead ... and I can't get him down.'

'What? Mum, what the hell are you talking about?'

'Please, Simon, get here quickly. I need your help. Just hurry.'

'All right, but what is it?'

'I can't ... Michael's killed himself. Please.'

A wave of nausea gripped her and she clicked off the phone. She collapsed to her hands and knees, retching, then staggered to her feet and stumbled down the stairs. *I must phone the emergency services*, she thought, *but which - police, ambulance, firemen? Someone's got to stop the sails and get him down.* She tried to press 999 but her thumb was clumsy and when she peered at the phone through a blur of tears she saw she'd pressed 666 instead. She was fumbling with the buttons to press *Clear* when she came into the kitchen, looked up, and saw ...

... a man in the doorway.

'Thank God!' she said. 'Please - I need help. There's a man, hanging out there ...'

'I know. He deserves it.'

'What?' At first her brain was too tired to believe what she'd heard, then the adrenalin kicked into overdrive and she backed away, towards the stairs. *I know this man*, she thought, *I've seen him before, but who the hell is he?*

'It's a pity you screamed,' he said. 'I was just leaving. I thought he was alone.'

A short, stocky, man with muscular arms that hung heavy by his side like a weightlifter's. He wore a dark sleeveless teeshirt, jeans, and trainers. His head was shaved, his face had the bitter resentment and pallor of the long-term prisoner.

'*Jason!* Jason Barnes!' Of course! What had Michael said last night? *'I thought of moving to Spain to get away and hide before he finds out where I live.'* Her mind was racing; in an instant everything fell into place in her mind, like a kaleidoscope changing. That's why the bedroom looked wrecked - there must have been a fight. Jason must have crept into the house in the night - that was the noise that awakened her, his car arriving, perhaps. He sent that photo to Michael as a threat, a warning - to say *I know who killed Brenda, it wasn't Alison alone. You'll be next.* Now here he was. That's how Michael died.

'You killed him, didn't you?'

'He deserved it. After what he did to me.' Jason stood poised on the balls of his feet, ready to spring at her; but a frown crossed his face. 'I know you, don't I?'

'I was your brief,' she said. 'Your barrister, at your appeal. Remember?'

'Fuck me, so you are. What are you doing here, darling?'

'Calling the police.' It was a stupid thing to say, she realised that immediately. He was halfway across the room in a second, reaching for the phone. She flung it in his face, and ducked to her left, under his outstretched arm. He turned, trying to grab her as she backed away against the worktop. Her hands fumbled behind her and seized the first thing she found, a plastic kettle. She threw that at him too, spraying him with water, and screamed. 'Leave me alone! I saved you, didn't I? I set you free!'

He stood in the middle of the room, staring at her, shaking his head to clear his face of the water from the kettle. 'It doesn't matter, you stupid bitch, you shouldn't be here. What were you, his dolly bird?'

'Mind your own business.'

'My business is to stay out of gaol. You know I killed him now, so unless you're prepared to keep your mouth shut ...'

'You know I can't do that.'

'Then I'll shut it for you.' He lunged for her again, and Sarah dived desperately towards the door. She was almost through it when his hand caught her shoulder, spinning her round, so that she crashed backwards against the door frame. But at the same time his hand let go as he fell flat on his face. He had stepped on one of the knives from last night and his foot slid from under him on the wet floor. He groaned; he'd hit his head on the fridge.

I should run, Sarah thought, he'll be up in a minute. But if I run he'll just catch me, he's too quick. She glanced round wildly, snatched up a frying pan from the hob, and smashed it on his head just as he was getting up. He dropped like a log to the floor.

Oh my God, I've killed him, Sarah thought, standing there with the pan in her hand. No I haven't, he's still breathing. Perhaps I should hit him again.

But then he'll really be dead, and what then?

A memory flashed into her mind, of a client who'd been charged with manslaughter for killing a burglar with a baseball bat, and she thought no, I mustn't do that, I just hope he's out cold. So she threw away the frying pan and ran.

The keys to her bike were in her house, just inside the front door. As she came out of the door she saw Jason, stumbling out of the windmill. He looked groggy and was holding his head, but when he saw her he broke into a shambling run. Sarah sprinted for her bike, fumbled the key into the ignition - *what's wrong with my fingers, why won't it go in?* - and turned it.

Nothing happened. *What's the matter, what now?* She glanced over her shoulder and saw Jason ten yards away, moving faster. She looked down and realised she hadn't disconnected the immobiliser. *What the hell was the code?* 157- 3, was it, or 4? She often had trouble with pin numbers, especially in moments of stress. She closed her eyes, and let her fingers remember for her. Her muscles should know, even if her mind didn't. 1573. She opened her eyes, saw the light change from red to green. *Thank God!* She turned the key in the ignition and the engine fired.

'Come here!'

'No!' As she let in the clutch his hand grabbed her leg. She twisted the throttle but the bike skidded sideways around in a circle so she almost fell off. She looked round and saw him sliding, face down on the grass but still clutching her leg. She leaned away from him, twisting the throttle hard, and there was a wild lurch as his hand let go and she almost fell off the bike on the other side. Then she was away, skidding across the grass.

As she turned onto the track through the woods she glanced over her shoulder and saw Jason back on his feet, sprinting towards Michael's BMW. Then she turned to look where she was going and screamed. Right in front of her was the smouldering wreck of a car. She swerved, trying to avoid it, but she was too late. Her front wheel bounced off its side and the bike fell over on the track.

Sarah lay under it, stunned. For a moment she thought her leg was trapped but with an enormous surge of adrenalin rushing through her she wrenched her leg free and heaved the bike up. She flung herself back into the saddle just as the BMW began to move towards her across the grass. She twisted the throttle and roared down the track, bouncing over potholes towards the road.

What the hell was that, she wondered. A burnt out car in the woods? Then she understood. It must be Jason's car, the one he came in. That was the fire I saw earlier, which I thought was the sun coming up. He must have torched it when he saw the BMW and decided to nick that instead, the greedy little bastard.

She turned left at the gate and roared down the road as fast as she could. She had no helmet, no leathers, and the icy dawn wind knifed through her thin clothing as though it wasn't there, freezing her hands and face and streaming her eyes with tears. The sky was lighter in the east, she saw vaguely, she could make out the blurry shapes of fields. But when she twisted round she saw the dark shape of the BMW, closer, much closer than she'd hoped.

She was heading down a steep hill which rose in a switchback on the far side. At the bottom, she remembered, there were two field gates where cows often crossed, leaving mud on the road. She throttled back slightly, not daring to put on the brakes, but as she did so, Jason came alongside. He swerved the car towards her, trying to drive her off the road. Sarah screamed, and twisted the throttle back as far it would go. The bike zoomed ahead, flying down the hill, faster than she'd ever been before. At the bottom she hit the mud, and felt the back wheel slide, left, right, then straight again, and she was still upright. She laughed with relief, and roared up the hill, the BMW a distance behind.

But at the top there was a tight bend and then another steep descent to a series of zigzags before a T junction. As she approached this there was a loud clang from her front wheel, and the bike slowed and swerved abruptly. Sarah wrenched it upright, but she couldn't maintain her speed, and the BMW drew alongside again. I must have damaged something, she thought, when I hit that torched car. But I can't stop now. She twisted the throttle again, and the bike roared ahead. The fault seemed to have cured itself. She leaned into the first zigzag as the BMW fell behind.

But when she shifted her weight to go the other way a shadow crossed the road in front of her. *What the hell's that? A fox.* Instinctively, Sarah swerved to miss it, but she was already leaning over too far, she lost her balance and went into a skid. As her back wheel came round she felt herself turning sideways, and released the throttle, trying to wrench the bike upright, but it was too late. The bike hit the grass verge, ploughed into soft mud, and flung Sarah backwards into a hedge.

Afterwards, she tried to work out how long things had taken. In her memory it seemed like a dream sequence, lacking logic. The crash must have lasted milliseconds, yet the details of it - the jolt as she flew into the air, the shadow of the escaping fox - were printed on her mind in slow motion. That's because you didn't hit your head badly, the doctor said, you were lucky that hedge was so thick. She didn't feel so lucky when her broken arm was in plaster for a month, though, or when she lay in bed and felt the myriad cuts and grazes on her back, legs, head, and arms itching like fire. She remembered lying in the hedge, trying to work out where she was and why there were twigs in front of her face, and blood dripping over one eye. But part of her mind kept telling her that the twigs and blood, close as they were, weren't nearly so important as the man getting out of the car. In the dream that was really a memory she watched him take a large adjustable spanner out of the boot and limp slowly towards her down the road. Part of her mind told her this was important, she should get up and do something about this, but she couldn't think what or why. After all it was comfortable here in the hedge and the man looked strong, he was swinging a heavy spanner in his hand so probably he had stopped to help her. She knew something had gone wrong but she couldn't quite remember what it was.

Then the man came closer so Sarah could see his face and she screamed. She knew what was wrong now, this man meant to hurt her, she had to get away. Only something was wrong with her body, it didn't seem to work very well. She thrashed her limbs in the hedge, but she was trapped like a fly in a web. The man grinned like a spider, raising the spanner slowly above his head as she struggled.

Then a white van stopped with a screech of brakes. The man with the spanner hesitated and turned. Amazingly, the man who got out of the van was her son Simon. What was he doing here? Sarah couldn't understand it, but Simon had no doubts at all. He ran at the first man and threw him straight to the ground. There was a fight, a threshing of limbs in the grass and mud in front of the hedge. Sarah couldn't see it all, but there were groans and thumps and Simon seemed fiercer and angrier than he'd ever been in his life before, even when he was a teenager and fought Bob. Although she'd been afraid of the man with the spanner she felt sorry for him now, and when Simon stood up she could see he wasn't moving at all.

Then, very gently, her son helped her out of the hedge, a process which hurt and seemed to take for ever. For some of this time, strangely, she heard sirens approaching in the distance, though she couldn't think why. Then, as she stood up, as weak and wobbly as a rag doll with Simon's strong arm round her shoulder, a police car drew up and Terry Bateson got out. A short time later an ambulance arrived. She couldn't imagine why.

'I called them, Mum,' Simon explained gently. 'You told me a man had died.'

Then the floodgates of memory opened, and Sarah broke down in tears.

63. New Start

IT WAS a sunny day in early April. Sarah stood on the balcony of her new flat, enjoying the spectacular view across the city. The flat was on the fourth floor of a modern block built on the site of an old warehouse beside the river Ouse. Immediately below her she could see swans and pleasure boats on the water; beyond them, just across Skeldergate bridge, was the Crown Court and the castle, Clifford's Tower, its mound covered with daffodils.

Sarah drew a deep breath of the warm spring air, and leaned over to wave to her son, Simon, as he emerged with Lorraine onto the riverside walk below. Lorraine walked slowly, Simon's hand in hers, but she smiled as she looked up. She's less nervous of me now, Sarah thought. Perhaps that's because she's come to see me as more vulnerable. Sarah's right arm was still in plaster after the accident, and Lorraine had been surprisingly helpful in organising the flat warming party that was just ending. Not long now, and they'll be asking me to babysit, Sarah thought hopefully. If they trust me, that is.

She could hear the sound of Lucy Parsons washing up in the kitchen, chattering cheerfully to Terry Bateson's two young girls and her own daughter Emily. That was another thing that Sarah was pleased about. The mortgage on this flat was costing half her income, but it had three bedrooms, one of which Sarah had given to Emily, for her to decorate with her own posters and memorabilia. Emily was delighted - she could glimpse York Minster from her bedroom window, and threatened to bring all her student friends to stay.

'So I still have my family around me,' Sarah said, to the man beside her. 'That's the most important thing, really, isn't it?'

'I suppose it is,' said Terry Bateson, watching anxiously as his youngest daughter carried six cups piled on top of each other into the kitchen. 'Those are the people who really matter, after all.'

He studied Sarah critically, seeing the arm still in plaster, a half-healed scar on the side of her neck. She looked pale, he thought, thinner than he remembered, and there were lines on her face he hadn't noticed before. 'How are you coping, really?'

'Me?' She turned to face him, a wry smile playing on her lips. 'Not so bad, all things considered. I wake up screaming in the night now and then, but that's par for the course, so they tell me. I've got rid of the bike, at least - wrong image for a granny, Simon says. I hardly need it here, anyway.'

'I'm glad to hear it. But I really meant ...'

'How I'm coping with Michael's death? Yes, I know.' She looked away, at the young leaves on the trees on the riverside walk. 'It hurts, of course, and I sit here shaking sometimes, picturing the way he went. That's the worst, but ... I'm still here, with my family, and friends, and my career. He'd lost all of that, you know. So had Alison too. One crazy moment when they were kids had poisoned the rest of their lives. They never really recovered from it, either of them.' She turned back and smiled at him. 'I'm not like that, Terry. Never will be, I hope. Neither are you.'

'No.' Terry remembered how Sarah had nearly lost all hopes of a career when she'd become pregnant with Simon at the age of fifteen, and thought of his own trauma, too - the death of his wife. 'What doesn't kill you makes you stronger, so they say.'

'If you let it, it does. But Terry, since you're here, I wanted to ask - what's become of my client? Former client, that is.'

'Jason Barnes, you mean?'

'Yes. Since he tried to murder me, I'm excused from representing him further. It's a rule the Bar Council have introduced. Very humane of them.'

Terry smiled. She hadn't lost her sense of humour. 'He confessed, as you know. But he didn't give us the full details until last week, when he came out of hospital. Your son Simon wasn't exactly holding back.'

'Reasonable force, Terry. He was rescuing his mother.'

'Don't worry, he won't get prosecuted, we're not that stupid. After all, I wouldn't have been there to arrest Jason if he hadn't called in. But anyway, this confession was quite satisfying, in its way.'

'Why?'

'Because it explained where we went wrong.' Terry sighed. 'You know we arrested a young sex offender, Peter Barton - the one who'd been stalking women and pestering them all around the city? Well, he made a full detailed confession too. He didn't just claim to have killed Alison, he told us exactly how he'd done it, and almost everything he said matched the evidence. So we had to take him seriously. The one thing that threw us was a scrap of cloth on the barbed wire fence which we sent to be tested for DNA. When Peter confessed, we thought it must be his. But when FSS eventually found the cloth, which they'd lost, and tested it, it had Jason's DNA on it, not Peter's. If we'd known that before ...' He shook his head.

'You'd have arrested Jason before he did all this damage.'

'If we could have found him, yes. At least he would have been our main suspect.'

'So what actually happened that night, when Alison died?'

'Well, Jason stole a car in Leeds, drove it to Crockey Hill, crept across the fields, and broke into Alison's house. Then he murdered her almost exactly as Peter Barton described. He found her in her bath, dragged her downstairs, and hanged her. She probably confessed to him before he died; that's how he found out that Michael was involved in Brenda's death as well. So he stole her mobile phone and took a picture of her which he sent to Michael later. Then he drove to Leeds and torched the car, hoping her hanging would look like suicide. But what he didn't realise, of course, was that this sad little pervert Peter Barton was watching his every move through the windows. Which was why he broke into the house later, fantasising that he'd done it all himself.' Terry shook his head wearily. 'The older I get, the more I think there's no limit to the evil that people can get up to.'

'Not everyone, Terry,' Sarah said after a pause. 'Most people just get along. And some even try to do good.'

'Yes, well.' Terry looked behind him into the flat, where a sudden squabble had erupted between his daughters over the last slice of chocolate cake. He turned to go in, with an apologetic smile at Sarah. 'We can always try, can't we?'

Printed in Great Britain
by Amazon